Jumping

Back

Into Love

Book 1: Love as Big as Texas Series

Danette Fogarty

To my friends and family,

You give me strength.

Christina:

Thanks for giving me

Hailey.

Jason, Chris, Randy, & everyone at

Skydive Spaceland;

YOU GUYS ROCK!!!!!!

And, of course, Texas.

Chapter 1

Searching for the right parking lot was the first test. How did a hospital have different parking lots? What was the point of that? As she pulled into the Northwest parking lot of the Regional Medical Center, Raelynn Woodsen couldn't keep the nerves at bay. It had been a lot of years since she was here, she avoided the place at all costs since it was the place years ago she received the worst news of her life and the best thing in her life. There was no time for dwelling on the past. Raelynn looked at her watch and grimaced, they said be there at 12:15pm sharp and she would not be late.

She exited the vehicle and slowly trudged up to the entrance of the huge building. She tried to smile in greeting at the people coming out but the smile didn't reach her eyes. What was she doing here? The soft swoosh of the automatic doors opened and she had no choice but to enter.

Surprisingly, the lobby was decorated in muted tones of brown and green. There were fall decorations up which made it seem even more welcoming. As if a reception area of a hospital could be welcoming. People here were sick or dying. Giving herself a mental shake, Raelynn took a deep breath and walked over to the reception desk. She smiled shyly at the young woman she was supposed to check in with and noticed the woman barely heard her name and gestured her to sit in the waiting area nearby.

The seat was reasonably comfortable but that was about it. Tension filled Raelynn's every cell. Why did she come alone? She could have asked any of her friends to accompany her and they would have obliged her happily enough. She didn't because if she talked about it, it was a possibility.

Looking at her watch, she noticed fifteen minutes went by. They told her to be on time to check in so she could go to the appointment promptly and they weren't calling her name. She noted the others who came and went and had their names called. This was like being in school and not being picked for a sports team in gym class. What an absurd thought; where did that come from?

She was becoming more nervous by the moment, why didn't they call her name. Finally having enough with waiting, she went up to the desk once again.

"Did I check in at the right place?" She asked the receptionist.

The woman smiled warmly, "Yes, Ms. Woodsen, the clerks all seem busy right now so I'll check you in."

Ingrained manners kept Raelynn rooted to the spot with a smile pasted on her face, "Ok."

"Can I see your ID and insurance information please?" The receptionist asked.

Without saying anything, just keeping the ridiculously false smile up, she handed the woman the necessary documents. Why didn't they do this before?

After checking the information, the woman gave the cards back to Raelynn and smiled, "I need to put this wristband on you." She motioned for Raelynn to put her hand out.

Having the band put around her wrist was torture. It made her "feel" like a patient. She did what was asked though, not willing to give in to her fears completely.

After diligently replacing the cards in her purse, she took the paperwork the woman gave her and went down a hallway towards yet another reception area. Fantastic; more waiting! The hallway was lined with windows that let the natural light of the sunny afternoon into the area. How come she felt so dark then?

Raelynn handed the second receptionist her paperwork and was directed to sit once again. Luckily her wait this time was significantly shorter. A woman in pink scrubs came out and introduced herself as Belinda.

Raelynn couldn't help but smile at the technician, she was funny and pretty. Although older than Raelynn, Belinda was good and put her patient at ease quickly with a warm smile and thoughtful gestures. They walked through a set of doors and into a small room similar to one at a doctor's office. Raelynn sat in the one seat and Belinda walked up to a computer.

"So you're here for your first mammogram?" Belinda asked with a smile.

This lovely woman made it feel so much less scary.

"Yes," Raelynn replied, "I went in to have my yearly exam and a breast exam to prepare for this mammogram." She took a breath, "And then the doctor found a lump in my right breast so they were kind enough to get me in for the test quickly."

Belinda nodded, typed, and then pushed the computer screen aside. "Okay, so we're going to go in and take some pictures now."

She directed Raelynn to a changing area, grabbed a pink shopping bag and put it on a bench. "If you'll take off your clothes from the waist up and put them in the bag," she handed Raelynn a gown, "put this on, opening in the front, and then come on out. If I'm not right outside, there's a waiting room just two doors down, have a seat and I'll be right back."

As she removed her top and bra, Raelynn felt very exposed. Her emotions went into a tailspin the day before and she couldn't believe so much could happen in one day.

She was at the doctor's office, joking absently with him, something she did to ease the discomfort of getting her yearly exam. They were chatting when he stopped while doing an exam on her right breast.

"There's a lump there." He said nonchalantly.

That's all that Raelynn really remembered. Just a year ago her aunt underwent treatment for breast cancer and she knew of several women who had the disease. No way could it happen to her! But here she was with a lump in her breast feeling so lost. She called to schedule the mammogram as soon as she got home from the doctor's office. Luckily her daughter, Hailey, was gone at class. She didn't need to see her mother in panic mode.

The lady whom she spoke to about scheduling the appointment was very nice and competent. She had Raelynn scheduled for the next afternoon so she wouldn't have to wait.

6

Raelynn came back to the present with a jolt. She put her blouse and bra in the bag, held the gown to her with a death grip and picked up her purse. Belinda was not in the hall so she did; in fact, have to go to the waiting room. It was a closet with benches. The color on the walls was a soothing green but it did nothing to sooth Raelynn's nerves.

"Are we ready?" Belinda asked cheerfully a few minutes later.

Raelynn jumped a little, she hadn't heard the tech come to the doorway. "Yes, I guess so."

"Don't worry, I'll explain everything that we're doing," Belinda said.

Raelynn could only smile.

Belinda took her bag with the clothes and her purse and set them on a chair for her and gently guided Raelynn over to the machine.

It didn't look that imposing, not what Raelynn necessarily expected, but still....

"Ok," Belinda was opening up the gown. "We're going to do the right breast first; we'll take a couple of different x-rays so we can see from different angles."

"My friend said hers didn't hurt so I'm not worried," Raelynn said shakily.

She wasn't fooling herself or the technician but she felt the need to fill the void with small talk.

Nodding, Belinda gently guided Raelynn's breast onto the small platform, "She's right, it's not too bad for most people."

Raelynn appreciated the caring nature Belinda showed. She followed the instructions carefully, not wanting there to be any problems that would require her to redo the procedure.

After about four pictures of each breast, Belinda excused herself to take the images to the radiologist to make sure they were good.

Raelynn stood there looking around the sterile room. It was no different than any other x-ray room she'd seen before. There were the regular x-rays during her childhood and Hailey's because of child's play that ended roughly. A smile came to her face for a moment but was erased quickly by the reality of why she was in this particular room.

Belinda came in a few minutes later and said they needed some different views. There were two spots actually; one in the left and one in the right. Belinda assured her it was routine, "Sometimes people have very dense breast tissue so things don't show up clearly."

Even though she was nodding, Raelynn's stomach was dropping down into her feet. One lump was crazy enough but two? This was a joke right? She wanted to cry but it would do no good since she didn't really know what was going on.

"Ok," She decided to be proactive. They were her breasts after all. "So what does dense breast tissue mean?"

Belinda explained how as women age, the density of their breast tissue changes and when you're younger and it's denser; sometimes the image can be misleading. That helped Raelynn breath a tad bit easier.

These images were quite a bit more uncomfortable than the first set but it wasn't anything Raelynn wasn't willing to do in order to make sure it was all ok.

"That's it," Belinda announced. "I'll run these down to the radiologist again and we'll have you wait in the waiting room until I'm done." She motioned for Raelynn to follow her.

Once seated, Belinda peeked back around the corner of the room, "Oh, it is not uncommon for the radiologist to request an ultrasound." Sensing this would upset her patient, she quickly said, "but it doesn't mean anything, they just want a different view."

Left alone, Raelynn began crying. Again, why did she come alone? Wiping the tears away, she was ashamed that she'd let herself be this upset. It was all routine; everyone said so. So why was she so upset?

Belinda came back a few minutes later and smiled, "They do want an ultrasound so just wait here and another technician will come in for that." She extended her hand out to Raelynn's. "It was a pleasure meeting you."

Before Raelynn could even thank her, she was gone. On to the next patient Raelynn assumed. At least Belinda made the whole thing bearable.

Raelynn picked up her phone and started playing solitaire on it in order to calm her nerves. It helped a bit and did manage to take her mind off of being half naked and in a thin hospital wrap that only had one snap. What was that about? One snap?

She was jolted from her ridiculous musing by another technician who called out, "Woodsen?"

Raelynn got up and went toward the woman. Unlike Belinda, this woman was not warm and welcoming. She was all business and simply didn't care that her attitude affected that of the patient.

"You can place your things on the chair and lay down on the bed," Was spoken directly and without warmth.

Raelynn did as asked but now her nerves were back on edge.

She watched as the tech did things to the machine, checked Raelynn's bracelet, and pulled the gown aside.

"Show me where the lump is," She said to Raelynn.

Ok, Raelynn thought, why is she asking me, there are like ten pictures of her breasts in the next room showing where the stupid lump is. "I'm not sure," she said, "the doctor found it."

"Well, where do you think it is?" The tech asked shortly.

It took every ounce of inner control to keep Raelynn from screaming at the tech. She pointed wordlessly to the right side of her right breast.

The woman put some gel on the ultrasound wand and went back and forth over Raelynn's right breast. She would stop and take a "picture" and then move on. After about five minutes she put the wand in a holder. "I'm going to have the doctor look at these."

What the hell just happened? How could she have such a good experience with one tech and such a negative one with another? This was a nightmare come to life. She had breast cancer and her daughter would be all alone. She was thankful for the relative darkness in the room because her tears would not be easily noticed.

The tech returned and introduced the doctor. The tech ran the wand back over Raelynn's breast and was talking to the doctor in medical lingo so Raelynn felt like a complete outsider. It was almost humiliating.

Finally the doctor said, "It doesn't look like anything worrisome. We'll have you come back in three months for a follow up ultrasound and if it's changed in size or shape, we'll be aggressive."

With that, he smiled and left.

The tech put the wand away again and handed Raelynn a towel, "You can use that to wipe off the gel and go ahead and get dressed."

Dismissing her with a look, the tech got up and went into an adjoining room.

Sooooo, she didn't have breast cancer but had to come back in three months for a follow up. What just happened? She absently got up and re-dressed. She grabbed her purse, walked out of the hospital and got into her car. Then she proceeded to sob like crazy.

After almost a half hour of letting out every tear she possessed, she wiped her eyes, blew her nose, checked her face in the rear-view mirror, and backed up to leave the place she hated.

Dinner was going to be phenomenal, Raelynn was sure of it. Hailey was due home any minute and she was determined to have a lovely spaghetti dinner made. The garlic cheese toast was almost done and, although Raelynn tried to cut down on carbs she figured she deserved it after the trip to the hospital earlier.

There was music playing in the background, an eclectic mix of soft rock from the seventies through current with a bit of country thrown in. It reflected the myriad of emotions Raelynn felt.

After she returned home from the hospital, she went directly into the shower to wash away, even if only emotionally, the experience of the mammogram and the fear that went along with it. She was okay. That's what she had to keep telling herself. She was okay.

She may be okay physically but during the drive home and subsequent afternoon, she realized she was not okay emotionally. Why did one have to sit down and pick through what's missing in one's life? Why did people play it safe? What if she had been

diagnosed with breast cancer? What would she have done?
There were so many things she wanted to do. She preached to
Hailey about experiencing life and yet she herself was doing no
such thing.

After her shower she did her hair and makeup, lightly as
she did every day, and got dressed in her conservative clothes.
She went onto the patio of their condo and watered her plants
like she did every day. Then she sat down at her desk and tried to
figure out what she would miss if today turned out differently.

She got out a pad of paper and a pencil and started two
lists. The first was the things she was thankful for:

1. Hailey
2. Career
3. Family
4. Friends
5. Time with Anthony

The second was things she wanted to do:

1. Skydiving
2. Horseback riding
3. Learn to Tango
4. Skinny dipping
5. Travel to Europe
6. See Hailey graduate from college
7. Have Grandkids
8. Get a dog
9. Fall in Love

She scanned the list several times to see if there was something she wanted to add. All of the items were things she desperately wanted. Although the last thing on the list threw her for a loop; did she really want to fall in love again? She sat back in her chair and looked absently out the window. Her time with Anthony was so short but she knew she loved him. She wanted to feel that way again.

Now, two hours later, she was still thinking about it. Maybe it was time to start living again. A shame that it took something so scary to make her re-evaluate her life but it was what it was. She was just straining the pasta when she heard the commotion that was her daughter at the front door.

"Hello," Hailey yelled from the entryway.

Raelynn put the strainer in the sink and wiped her hands on a towel as she walked to where her daughter was busy putting her backpack in the closet. She never took it to her room which puzzled Raelynn but her daughter was not nearly as OCD as Raelynn was.

"How was your day?" Raelynn asked as she hugged her daughter tightly.

Hailey carefully pulled back from her mother's embrace, "Ok, what's wrong?"

She knew her mother and her mother never greeted her at the door unless there was something serious going on.

"Nothing," Raelynn tried to act naïve but she knew Hailey wouldn't buy it. The child was smarter than she should be.

Raelynn started back to the kitchen and started wiping down the counter; anything to keep her from looking at her much too observant daughter.

14

"Mom?" Hailey asked, her eyes narrowing.

Her mother was nothing if not predictable. It made growing up pleasant for her but probably not so for her mom.

Sighing, Raelynn took a bottle of wine she was chilling in the refrigerator out and poured herself a glass. She lifted the glass to her lips and tasted the sweetness of the cool liquid before meeting her daughter's gaze.

Setting the glass down, she went over to her desk and picked up the paper with the lists. Without saying anything, she handed the paper to Hailey. Her daughter took it and scanned the page, her brow furrowing. Raelynn's palms were sweaty, she was nervous about her daughter seeing some of those things. She shouldn't be; they were close and didn't keep secrets. But she always held her secret desires deep down. It was if by writing them or, Heaven forbid, saying them out loud made her vulnerable in some way.

Hailey was very confused. Her mother handed her a paper with lists on it; very un-mom like in her opinion. She read the lists and was shocked. Her mother wanted to do these things? HER mother? Not knowing what to say, Hailey went into the living room and sat down one the couch, the papers still in her hands.

Oh crap! Raelynn surprised her daughter. Now she was embarrassed and hoped Hailey didn't think there was something wrong. Well something was wrong. For two days something was very wrong and Raelynn only now recognized what it was. Her just existing in this current life was not enough anymore.

She sat down across from her daughter in an overstuffed chair, "I know you may think I've lost my mind...."

How did she explain? She didn't want to needlessly scare Hailey so she left out the breast cancer scare.

"I was driving home and reflecting on what's missing in my life." She felt like a louse, she didn't want Hailey to think she was unhappy. "Not that you aren't the absolute best thing that ever happened to me."

Hailey smiled, "I know what you meant Mom."

Raelynn let out a breath, "Good." She took Hailey's hand into her own. "Maybe it's a mid-life thing but I find a lot lacking in my life and it's time I get out and do something about it."

There! It was out. Hopefully her daughter didn't admit her into the closest insane asylum.

Hailey stood and threw the papers in the air.

"Whoo hoo!" She smiled at her mom, "It's about time!"

What? Did she miss something? Cocking her head, Raelynn stared at her daughter, "Hailey did you have something you wanted to say?"

Relief pummeled her, "Yes mom," she sat back down, "I've been meaning to talk to you about what I consider your 'existence,' it's just a shame." She patted her mom's hand. "I love you so much and you're still young. You need to go out and live a little."

Raelynn was floored for the second time today. How did her daughter see what was so painfully obvious and yet she was ignorant of it until a health scare brought it to the surface? Now she was ashamed.

"Are you disappointed in me?" She asked Hailey.

Shaking her head, Hailey tried not to cry, "No, no Mom." Now she was sad, "I just know that you've been in this sort of rut;

raising me, working on the business, and you never go out and just let loose."

Nodding, Raelynn thought the same exact thing. "I know."

Clapping, Hailey jumped back up, "Now, let's see, what should you do first?"

Fear crept into Raelynn's mind. "We don't have to do it all today you know."

Her daughter was a spectacular person. She was a spitfire; just like her father, who went out and didn't sit idly by watching life go on around him. Obviously Raelynn was not like Hailey or Anthony.

"Mom," Hailey looked at her mother pointedly, "you will do one thing on this list by the end of next week." She poked the paper, "Swear to me right now!"

Definitely a spitfire, Raelynn smiled, she wouldn't have it any other way. "Yes, I swear."

The next morning Raelynn was swearing alright. She was swearing off wine for the rest of her life. The hangover was a new thing. Raelynn was always the "safe" one. She was the designated driver if she and friends went out. She was the one who thought ahead of the consequences. Thinking back, she was surprised to find that she was most definitely not always like that. There was a time when she was carefree and eager to get out into life.

Gingerly making her way to the bathroom, Raelynn looked at herself closely in the mirror. The reflection was the same as it always was; a woman gracefully aging and doing all she needed to do to get through life. The word stuck in her mind; needed. She did what was needed, not what she *wanted*. The next logical question was simply….. what did she want?

She and Hailey drank wine and went over the lists in details the night before. It was great, the two of them just talking and reminiscing, and planning their adventures. She felt bad now for not realizing that Hailey needed to see this. She needed to see her mother trying to do something crazy for a change, not just what was expected. She would not disappoint Hailey by chickening out. She would do everything on that list; even if it scared her beyond belief.

Washing her face, she decided the first thing she was going to do was get her hair cut. She always wore her hair straight just below her shoulders. That was long enough to pull it back when she wanted it out of her face. She'd been told she had great hair. It was light brown with highlights of blond here and there. Looking closer, she could see the grays peeking out in places. She never wanted to color it, thinking that it was more natural and made her look less "made up." What a joke! She looked plain, that was a fact.

After completing her morning routine, she decided to go to the beauty parlor to get step one of her transformation into the land of the living completed. Not hearing Hailey up; it was still before noon after all, she left a quick note on the dining table and went off in search of a new look.

An hour later, she was panicking. She went to a nice salon located a few minutes from their condo. She went there periodically for a trim but never even thought about more. Now she was being done up in foils to put in the new color palette for her hair. She let the stylist talk her into a more dramatic blond emphasis with light red highlights here and there. "Subtle but sexy" is what the stylist said. Well, that certainly sounded different than Raelynn.

"How are you doing?" Renee her stylist asked.

Raelynn smiled shyly, "I'm good."

She thought about Hailey's reaction and it boosted her confidence about the change. It was only hair for goodness sake.

"Okay," Renee put the foils away and turned to Raelynn, "you mentioned a different makeup look."

Nodding, Raelynn steeled herself. She could do this, "Yes, I want something that makes a statement."

"Great," Renee answered, "we can certainly do that."

Two hours later, Raelynn's pocketbook was a bit lighter but her spirits were through the roof. Holy Cow, she didn't recognize herself.

Renee was a magician! The 'color palette' was fantastic; it brought out Raelynn's green eyes. Her hair was now cut to frame her face. Renee showed her how to blow it out so it looked full and sassy. They worked on her makeup and Raelynn now knew what colors she could use to show off her features. The look they went with for the day was cute. She couldn't help but look at herself in the mirror. Was it really the same woman who woke up this morning?

She walked into the house with a lighter spirit and went into the kitchen to look at the mail she picked up on the way in. Looking through the envelopes, a weird feeling worked its way up her spine. What was wrong? She looked up and into her daughter's eyes. They were large and her mouth was hanging open.

"Good morning," She smiled to Hailey.

Hailey didn't recognize her mother at first. What happened? They went to bed last night talking of change but Hailey wasn't completely convinced that her mom would go through with it. That was Raelynn, the most dependable person on earth! But now, looking at this "hot" woman standing in their kitchen, Hailey thought maybe her mother really was determined to change.

"Good morning," Hailey finally returned. She was trying to find the words, "What did you do?"

Suddenly unsure if she did the right thing, Raelynn nervously wiped her hands down her sides. "Do you hate it?"

She would be devastated if Hailey didn't like her makeover but she would deal with it.

"Hate it?" Hailey asked incredulously, "NO WAY MOM!" She got up from the dining room table and walked over to her mom. She motioned for Raelynn to turn, "You look gorgeous!"

Relief ran through Raelynn, "Oh good, you like it." She kissed Hailey on the cheek. "I love it!"

Just to see her mom beaming like she was at that exact moment made Hailey so happy. Her mom was the best person; she was kind and considerate. Even with getting a bum deal so young, Hailey could never remember her mom being selfish or self-serving. She deserved to find every single bit of happiness she could.

Hailey hugged her mom quickly, "I'm going to get ready; I'll be right back."

Watching her daughter bounce off in the direction of her room, Raelynn was so happy. She was going to do whatever she could to keep both her and Hailey happy. No matter what she had to do or overcome to do it.

They debated a few minutes on what they would do for the day since it was Saturday and neither of them had to work or go to class. That was unusual, to have a day together just the two of them.

The weather was perfect and Raelynn was with her favorite person, Hailey, so anything was possible.

Chapter 2

Raelynn smiled as she and Hailey walked out to her car. Looking at it, Raelynn wondered why she bought it. It was a fine, dependable, car. Just what she was doing; being fine and dependable? They got into the car and Raelynn looked at her daughter with a conspiratorial look.

Hailey loved her mother's mischievous side, although she rarely saw it. "What?" She asked knowing that her mother was up to something.

Giggling, Raelynn looked around to make sure no cars were coming and started backing out of the parking spot. "You'll see."

Twenty minutes later they were pulling into a car dealership near downtown Houston.

Hailey looked at her mother, her mouth hanging open. "Are you kidding me?"

She would love it if her mom bought a new car although it was weird seeing her mother making these drastic changes so quickly.

"Nope," Raelynn pulled into a spot and grabbed her purse.

Two hours later they were driving off the lot in her mother's new convertible. The wind was blowing their hair and Hailey thought this was the craziest, most impulsive thing her mother ever did. She loved it! The problem was, would her mother keep it up or would she revert to her very safe and practical life.

Thinking back, Hailey recalled her childhood as a happy one. Her mother was always there. She knew she was luckier than most kids, even with only having one parent. Raelynn never made her feel like she was missing something with her father being gone. Hailey's only regret was that she never met her dad. From what her mother told her, he was great. She was always told how much she was like him. She stole another glance at her mother while she was driving. Her hair blowing in the wind, sunglasses on, she was smiling. Hailey thought for the first time that maybe they were wrong; maybe she was actually more like her mother.

"Where to now?" Hailey asked her mom.

Raelynn looked at her daughter, a smile on her face, "Well, let's see." She thought for a moment. "Aha," She glanced at her daughter, "how about the beach?"

Nodding, Hailey smiled back, "I think that would be great!"

They sped down the highway, only doing two miles over the speed limit. There were some things Raelynn would not change. She kept chanting to herself, baby steps; baby steps. Her new car was fantastic and handled like a dream. She was so excited to have the freedom to feel the wind in her hair. Looking at Hailey, she could see the absolute joy in her daughter's face. What parent doesn't want that for their child?

As they drove, Raelynn thought that maybe she really was changing. Things were clearer, she had a purpose. Her thoughts were interrupted by Hailey.

"Mom," Hailey shouted to be heard over the wind, "this is so awesome!" She threw her hands up into the air, "Whoo hoo!"

Raelynn shook her head and smiled. Things would have to be different; she would have to change if she really wanted to live again.

They pulled onto the main street that abutted the beach in Galveston. It was pretty crowded, there were people already gathering for their day, so it took a while for them to find a spot to park. Once that was done, they locked the car and started out toward the beach.

The water was dark gray with short white caps forming as it neared the shore. The beach was a great place to reflect, as you felt so small and insignificant compared to the vastness of the water. Raelynn plopped down and watched Hailey meander through the shallows. It reminded her of when Hailey was little and she would bring her here for a day of fun.

Those days were filled with just taking care of Hailey. She loved her daughter dearly and was always proud of her. She was the best thing Raelynn ever did. Anthony would be so proud of her as well. Remembering him wasn't nearly as painful as it used to be. Now it was like looking at someone else's life.

They met at college in New York. Raelynn was studying finance and he was in the engineering program. Raelynn was dragged to a party by a friend when she should have been studying and didn't want to go. They were there, her friend off flirting, and she was just standing by the wall when she saw him across the room. He was full of life and exciting, everything she wasn't during her college years. She was the wallflower, the quiet one, the dependable one. He overwhelmed her with his mere presence and she fell hard.

Hailey struck up a conversation with a boy in the shallows and they both turned and waived at Raelynn. She waived back and watched her daughter, being pulled back into the memories.

Anthony was a year ahead of her and already had his life planned out. He received a job offer from a company in Texas and was going to move down there after graduation to be an engineer on oil platforms. The whole thing sounded extremely exciting to Raelynn as she listened to him for hours talking about all of his big plans. She was bowled over by his boisterousness and zest for life. Her plans after graduation included going back to the Midwest to live in her hometown and working for a local CPA firm. She remembered being in awe of his bravery at striking out on his own.

After a year of dating, and Anthony pulling her out of her shell as much as anyone could, she decided that she would take a leap of faith and follow him to Texas. She called her parents and thought they would die of shock. She was going to tell him the night before he graduated but he surprised her with an engagement ring. Thinking back, Raelynn was genuinely surprised by his proposal. They were so different and it always made her wonder what he found so appealing about her. She was just plain Raelynn. Of course Anthony never made her feel plain, he doted on her.

They were married at the courthouse the day after he graduated college and two weeks later he was off to start his career. Raelynn buckled down and finished her last year of college in one semester; she was so eager to be with Anthony.

They moved into a little apartment after she arrived, Anthony stayed with a co-worker to save money while she was still in school. It was ridiculously small but it was their first home together and they were happy. Anthony worked crazy hours and Raelynn found a job interning at a local CPA firm. Money was a little tight since they both had school loans but they were making it. She would call home and let her family know she was so happy every couple of days. They were good memories.

Raelynn wiped the tears away and smiled at Hailey playing tag with some kids. Her daughter was so much like her father.

She had just arrived home from work when she got the phone call. Anthony was on a rig inspecting something and there was an explosion. He was dead.

The next weeks were filled with craziness as there was a mistake in the design that caused the explosion so there were news people around and it was a big scandal. All she cared about was that her husband was dead and no one could bring him back.

A month after Anthony's funeral she still wasn't feeling good physically and, at the urging of her friend Melissa, went to the doctor. He smiled and announced that she was pregnant.

It was such a blow to Raelynn that she had to go home and lie down. She was pregnant with Anthony's child. She thanked God immediately that he blessed her with part of her husband. She vowed then and there that she would make their child a priority in her life. She followed through on her deal with God and Anthony and made Hailey the center of her world. She gave Hailey all the love, guidance, patience, understanding, and structure she could give.

But now Hailey was an adult and, although she still needed Raelynn on some levels, she was starting to make her own choices. Raelynn watched her daughter in wonder and hoped that Anthony was proud of her for the choices she'd made regarding their baby girl.

Hailey ran over to her mother after she was out of breath from running around with the kids. "Hey there, quit thinking!" She knew her mother far too well.

Raelynn smiled, "I will."

It was a standing joke between them over the years.

"No you won't," Hailey laughed and pulled her mother up by her hand.

Mother and daughter ran and played on the beach.

The rest of the day was spent playing on the beach and looking for shells. They walked up to the Pleasure Pier, which was like a miniature Coney Island. Raelynn heard it was built a few years back but never came before now. Seeing Hailey acting so carefree, she wondered what took her so long.

Once the two returned home, they both showered and went to bed almost immediately. It was a great day and Raelynn was so thankful they were spontaneous and did it. Her new car was a great gift to herself as well. She didn't intend on blowing all of her hard-earned money but she certainly didn't have any guilt in spending a little here and there if it made the time she and Hailey spent together that much more fun.

Raelynn turned onto her side and looked at Anthony's picture on her nightstand. It was taken at their apartment when she first moved down to Texas. He was so happy she was with him and she was so scared but as soon as they were together, she knew this was home. How sad that their time together was so short. A tear slid down Raelynn's cheek as she drifted off to sleep.

Sunday morning Raelynn woke to noise coming from somewhere in the condo. She sat up quickly, her protective mother instincts kicking in. She grabbed a robe and went to find out what the ruckus was.

As Raelynn entered the dining room, she was floored. Hailey was setting the table with dishes. Something was cooking on the stove that smelled great.

Hailey turned around from setting the table and saw her mother's shocked expression. She laughed, "Good morning."

27

Raelynn wanted to know what was going on. "Hailey," she slowly walked to the table, "what are you doing?"

Rolling her eyes, Hailey pulled out a chair and motioned for her mom to sit down. "I cooked breakfast."

"I realize that," Raelynn sat and touched the silverware absently, "I am just surprised that you're up at," she looked at the clock, "nine am."

"Yes," Hailey brought a steaming dish of eggs, potatoes, and sausage to the table. "I figured if you could make some changes then I could too."

It was very difficult for Raelynn to contain her emotions, her daughter was so special. She nodded and smiled.

They ate breakfast leisurely, with classical music playing in the background. The windows were partially open to allow a nice morning breeze in. There was talk of the new car and their beach excursion. These were wonderful memories they would each file away. Raelynn cleared the table and loaded the dishwasher. Hailey went to her room to change.

Raelynn wondered what they would do today. She walked over to her desk and picked up the list of what she wanted to do. She shook her head and smiled. Should she have shown Hailey? Certainly her daughter would make her do these things. But that was the point wasn't it? She had to make some changes and do something to help her live again. Not that she wasn't living exactly; she was just living so safely that she wasn't opening herself up to experiencing life.

Hailey came into the room and Raelynn put the list back down on her desk. She went to get changed. When she came out twenty minutes later, she noticed Hailey absorbed in something on the computer. She went over and looked over her daughter's shoulder and he stomach flipped.

"Don't freak out," Hailey blurted out quickly. "I'm just looking."

Taking a deep breath, Raelynn forced a smile. "I know, I'm just scared."

It was a website for a local skydiving location. It was called Skydive Spaceland and it looked great but it didn't quell the nerves running at high speed inside of Raelynn. She scanned the screen, everyone looked happy even though they were jumping out of perfectly good airplanes. It was the first thing on her list. She couldn't blame Hailey for looking at the website.

A few minutes of watching her mother watch the computer was all Hailey could take. "What do you think?"

Raelynn swallowed hard, "Well, I said I would do it, and I will."

"Today?" Hailey asked.

Raelynn walked away from the computer and started pacing the living room. She could do this right? She honestly didn't know. Looking over and seeing Hailey's hopeful face was all the incentive she needed.

Nodding, she grabbed her purse, "Yes."

Hailey stood up and ran over to her mom. "Oh My Gosh!" She hugged her mom, "You are sooooo cool!"

Somehow Raelynn didn't feel particularly cool, she felt nauseous. "Well, let's go."

Hailey looked at her mother to make sure the clothes she had on were the right ones according to the website. "You need to put on sneakers first and then we're ready."

Raelynn obediently went into her room and put on her tennis shoes. She put on a t-shirt and comfortable cotton pants earlier so those must be acceptable. After all, what did one wear to jump out of a plane?

They left the house and drove south on Hwy 288. The sky was a bright blue and dotted with the occasional cloud. A few minutes into the drive Raelynn realized she didn't write down the directions. She almost pulled over when Hailey lifted up a page with the map on it. Leave it to her daughter to cover all the bases. She chuckled and continued down the road, the butterflies in her stomach increasing.

They turned onto FM 1462 and were now in what could only be described as, country. There were farms and ranches divided by fencing and the occasional house dotting the landscape. It was very quiet, which was nice. Hailey was playing with the radio station and stopped on one playing, Sailing by Christopher Cross. She giggled when Raelynn shot her a look.

"Just to get you into the mood." Hailey snickered.

They turned once more onto FM 521 and there was a sign ahead denoting that this was, indeed, the place. The big hangar would have been a giveaway anyway but Hailey pointed.

They pulled into the gravel driveway that led to a parking area outside of the hangar. It was packed and they were forced to park pretty far from the main structure.

Raelynn's heart was beating so loud, she thought people around her could hear it. She grabbed her wallet and locked the doors.

They were walking toward the hangar and saw a lot of people in the main area.

Raelynn looked at Hailey, "I don't know if today was a good day to come down here."

"Mom," Hailey pushed her mother gently to get her to start walking again, "let's just go and look."

They entered the main area and it was organized chaos as far as Raelynn was concerned. She could see a seating area straight ahead; there were picnic tables on the right with hooks for jump suits and other equipment. The souvenir shop and office were marked with signs on the right. There were groups of people everywhere.

Hailey led the way to the office and opened the door for her mom. She was actually surprised that they came and her mother didn't chicken out before now.

Raelynn looked around the office and was very intimidated. It was packed with people. Some were sitting at a table filling out paperwork and some were at the counter. She didn't really know where to go. A nice young lady came over towards them with a big smile.

"Good morning," the woman said brightly, "how can we help you?"

Hailey didn't wait for her mom to answer, "Hi, my mom is here to jump."

Raelynn wanted to just fall into a hole in the floor. Leave it to Hailey to make it sound so blunt. The young woman didn't look the least bit phased by Hailey's announcement. She looked at a clip board she was holding.

"I'm really sorry," She said, "we're doing a group jump today and, as you can see, it's pretty big so we can't take any more jumpers today." She grabbed a flyer and gave it to Raelynn. "Here's some information and we can schedule you for a jump tomorrow for sure."

Relief flooded Raelynn's chest. "I can't, I work during the week."

She snuck a look at Hailey. Her daughter did not look happy.

"Well," The woman said, "then let's schedule you for next Saturday."

Hailey smiled smugly at her mother, "That's great!"

Raelynn was smiling but it was certainly forced and she was secretly yelling on the inside. The reprieve was a welcome one.

"I'm Dawn," The woman said and led them over to a counter. "I'm going to get some information and we'll set up your reservation for next Saturday." She smiled reassuringly, "You'll have a blast."

Raelynn wasn't going to argue but she wasn't sure that she would describe what she would have as a blast; perhaps a small coronary was a better way to phrase it. She looked at the other people there and, truth be told, they all looked so happy and excited. At Hailey's prompting, she handed over her driver's license and her credit card. All the while, looking around at the other jumpers and wondering why they were here.

After Dawn rang up her total, she signed the receipt and they went back out into the main part of the hangar. Instead of leaving, as she thought they would, she was dragged out the other way into a fenced in area just outside by Hailey.

"We're going to watch some of them land," Hailey knew her mother was nervous but she wasn't going to let that keep her from completing the list.

"Ah," Raelynn answered meekly as they went out and looked up into the sky.

The blue sky looked so big from where they were. It was beautiful and it occurred to Raelynn that she didn't appreciate the beauty of such things as much as she should. Not that she needed to stare at the sky for hours on end, but certainly taking a couple of minutes to admire it wouldn't hurt. A few minutes later, Hailey nudged her and pointed. She could faintly see black spots in the sky.

"There they are," Hailey shouted.

Raelynn was wondering what she was so excited about; it wasn't like they knew anyone who was jumping. Of course, her daughter's excitement was becoming contagious. She watched intently and felt excitement herself as the spots took shape and she could see the jumpers coming down slowly. They looked graceful and were spinning one way and then the other.

As the first skydiver came down, Raelynn held her breath. He landed on his butt, like he was sliding into home plate. The next one came down gently and landed in a standing position. The others were coming down quickly and it was obvious how thrilled they all were. A couple of them were high-fiving as they collected their gear and walked off the landing area. Hailey, Raelynn, and a few other by-standers were clapping.

The group started coming in their direction and Raelynn watched them intently. She wanted to know what they thought, they all looked so happy.

"It's pretty contagious," A voice said from behind her.

Raelynn turned around and looked into deep blue eyes. The blue eyes were attached to a handsome face so Raelynn smiled.

"It sure looks like it," was her reply. She wanted to roll her eyes; she couldn't have sounded more ridiculous.

"Are you jumping today?" The voice asked.

Raelynn cocked her head and put her hand up to provide some shade to her eyes. She wanted to see him better. "Uh, no." Again, slick.

"Do you know someone jumping?" The voice asked.

His voice was so melodic, Raelynn was entranced. He exuded a quiet strength and he only said a few things to her. She looked at him more closely. His features were almost chiseled; his jaw was strong and clean shaven. The sun reflected off of his light brown hair. It was only then that she noticed he was in a jump suit.

Feeling silly she smiled, "No, I was going to jump but there was no room."

It was then that she noticed her interaction with this stranger had her daughter's full attention. How could this get any worse? She didn't know what she was saying and this man was staring at her intently.

"I'm Seth," the voice said quietly as he held out his hand.

Coherent thought left Raelynn's brain. She stood there looking at his hand and knew she should use her manners but her brain couldn't make her move. When Hailey nudged her, she was kicked into action. She shook his hand. His palm felt rough but he took her hand gently.

Hailey couldn't believe her mother, here was a man introducing himself and she just stood there looking at him. Geez. She had to step in.

Hailey half stepped in front of her mother, "I'm Hailey and this is my mom, Raelynn." When the man turned his eyes to her, she thought they looked kind.

"Hi Hailey," he let go of Raelynn's hand and shook Hailey's. "Are you enjoying watching the sky divers?"

Was her mother going to interject at any time here? Hailey was mentally shaking her head, "Yes, mom is going to jump next Saturday. Are you an instructor?"

Seth looked from mother to daughter. There was a slight resemblance but that was about it. He thought it odd that the mother was jumping and not the daughter. It seemed that the roles would be reversed. This lovely woman looked a little too reserved to be skydiving.

"Yes, no." He smiled, "I'm trained as an instructor but here I do videography for the sky divers."

Hailey nodded, "That is so cool." She nudged her mom again, "Don't you think so mom?"

Raelynn took a deep breath, "Yes, very." She couldn't seem to say anything intelligent. He probably thought she was some sort of freak or something.

An announcement came over the PA, "Group 2 report to the tables."

Seth smiled, "That's me. I hope to see you next Saturday."

Raelynn just watched him walk away. Finally, she turned and looked at her daughter; Hailey looked upset.

"Mom, what is wrong with you?" Hailey was frustrated.

Raelynn made sure she had her wallet and keys and started making her way back through the hangar. "Nothing," she said tightly.

As they were walking out she noticed a group headed toward a plane. Seth was walking with the group wearing a black jump suit. He was tall, she hadn't noticed that before. She also noticed how his walk was more of a swagger, very confident and with purpose. Raelynn could admire that since she was neither in this particular instance.

They made their way to the car and got in without saying anything else. The drive home was spent in silence, she and Hailey each thinking about what happened and what lay ahead.

Hailey couldn't take it any longer when they pulled into the garage, "Mom, what happened?"

Raelynn didn't understand the question, "I don't know what you mean."

Shaking her head, Hailey entered the condo first and through the flyer on the table, "I'm talking about a man talking to you and you just stood there."

Frustration started building in Raelynn, "Hailey, he was just being kind, just let it be."

Hailey didn't believe her mother. Not that Raelynn talked with men, come to think of it, she never talked with men except those she worked with or her clients at the CPA firm. She didn't date. That was something Hailey worried about over the years, her mother's lack of male companionship. When she was little it was about her having a dad but now it was her worried about her mother being alone. The thought saddened her.

Raelynn was certainly not going to ruin the weekend by arguing with her daughter. The man, Seth, was just being nice; it was nothing more than that. Although she couldn't forget those intense blue eyes and how they made her speechless. She couldn't remember that kind of response to anyone except Anthony and that was almost twenty years ago. Putting her purse away, she took a deep breath and went to make amends with Hailey.

Monday morning held none of the excitement the weekend brought. Raelynn woke up at six fifteen exactly and did her usual morning routine. When she looked in the mirror after her shower she wondered how her life became so monotonous. She went into her closet and picked a black pencil skirt with a ruffled white blouse. It was a little dressier than she usually picked for work but she was making changes right? She chose a pair of heels a good inch higher than her usual sensible shoes. She did her hair and makeup the way the stylist showed her and when she looked again as she was finishing, she was happy.

She packed her lunch and packed Hailey's, so she would eat at least one healthy meal during the day, grabbed her briefcase and left the house. The morning was partly cloudy but mild in temperature with light breezes. She kept an umbrella in her car in the event of rain and made the daily trek to Lake Jackson.

The drive was over thirty minutes and a lot of people commented about why she would want to drive so far to work. Of course, it was sensible for Raelynn as Hailey chose a community college closer to Houston. She didn't want Hailey commuting so far so she bought the condo. It made sense to her and she would always do what was best for Hailey.

The sky was blue, dotted with clouds. It reminded her of the day before when they were watching the group skydiving. The man with the silky voice popped into her mind, making her blush. They spent maybe two minutes in a practically one-sided conversation. He was just being kind. Raelynn was coming into Lake Jackson so she put the handsome stranger out of her mind for the time being. She was going into work and learned how to focus on just that over the years.

The CPA firm she was part owner of was in downtown Lake Jackson in a brick building. Every day when Raelynn pulled up, she couldn't help but feel pride. She worked very hard to build the clientele and was finally reaping the benefits of being driven in her career goals.

She got out of her new car, smiling at the impulsiveness she had in buying it, and went inside.

The lobby was done tastefully with brown leather furniture and bright pictures on the walls. People didn't view going to their CPA as anything other than a necessary evil so she and her partner, Melissa, wanted to make them feel welcome. They were doing very well and it was reassuring to both of them that their business was booming.

Putting her lunch in the small refrigerator in the break room, Raelynn grabbed a water bottle and went into her office to start her day. The office was large, her and Melissa having the two largest ones. They each had an assistant and two other interns that worked with them part time. It was relaxing work for Raelynn as she always felt good with numbers. It was particularly demanding on some levels but most jobs were.

She was just digging into her pile of files when she heard Melissa come down the hall.

"Good morn…" Melissa stood in Raelynn's office doorway, her jaw slack.

Raelynn smiled, "Good morning."

Her friend looked fantastic! What happened between Friday and now and why didn't her best friend tell her? "Okay," She dropped her briefcase near the door and sat down across from Raelynn, "what happened and who is he?"

Her brow furrowed, Raelynn didn't understand. Oh yes, the hair, clothes, and makeup. "There is no HE, but I decided to get my hair done and learn some new makeup tips."

"Well, well," Melissa purred, "I have to stay, you look amazing."

Raelynn blushed, "Thanks Mel." She didn't know what else to say.

Melissa took a breath, "Does this mean you are going to start dating?"

"No," Raelynn needlessly straightened papers that were already perfectly straight. "I never stopped dating."

Smiling, Melissa nodded. "I'm sorry dear friend but yes you did."

She was not willing to get into an argument first thing on a Monday morning, even if she did not agree one bit with her friend's assessment of her love life. She heard it from Hailey yesterday and now from her best friend. It was not easy to take.

"I have a lot to get done; can we discuss my love life over lunch?" Raelynn wanted to be diplomatic.

Melissa nodded, "Sure."

She watched her friend leave the room and sighed. It was so easy for Melissa, she was stunning with long dark brown, almost black, hair and she was always dressed nicely with perfect makeup. It always seemed to be so easy for some women but Raelynn was not one of them. For her, it was a conscious effort to dress up, do her hair, and get makeup done right. She peeked at the compact she kept in her desk drawer and liked what she saw. Putting it back, she decided she better get to work because Melissa would grill her over lunch about the events of the weekend.

The rest of the week was busy for Raelynn. After Monday's craziness and Melissa gushing over her newfound commitment to changing her life, it settled down into the comfortable existence Raelynn became accustomed to.

Friday went by quickly and she and Melissa decided to make it half a day since there was nothing pressing for the afternoon. That was a perk of being co-owner. She was straightening her desk when Melissa popped her head through the door.

"Hey there," Melissa said excitedly.

Raelynn waived absently, trying to get her desk set to rights for the weekend.

Melissa stepped into the office and stood there with her arms crossed.   When Raelynn looked up she could see the resolve in her friend's face.

"Yes?" She asked innocently.

"Don't 'yes' me," Melissa peered at her friend, "are you going to do it or not?"

Raelynn was getting riled, "Yes, I said I would didn't I?" Did they all think she was going to chicken out of everything? She was resolved to change, this was a part of it.

Melissa nodded, "Okay," she smiled, "can I come?"

Taking a deep breath, Raelynn looked up and into her friend's eyes. They were mischievous and that's what she loved about Melissa.

"I suppose." She mumbled.

"Yes," Melissa did a little dance, "I will pick you and Hailey up tomorrow morning at eight."

Nodding, Raelynn grabbed her purse, "Fine, we'll be ready."

As she was walking out to her car, Raelynn was getting mad again. It was like no one believed she would actually do what she said. Hadn't she been the dependable one her whole life? Hadn't she been the one who raised a daughter, alone, when her husband died? Hadn't she been the one who built a business from nothing into something? Hadn't she been the one who did everything that was expected of her? And now she wanted something dammit! She wanted to feel excitement and pleasure and alive again.

By the time she pulled into the garage at the condo, she was more calm but still annoyed. She went inside and put on her workout clothes. A stint at the gym was called for to relieve some of her pent up energy and emotions.

After an hour on the elliptical, she felt better; sweaty but definitely better. She was dissecting her life again and that wasn't the point anymore. It was not to dwell on what she did or didn't do in the past; it was about what she was doing now.

She made dinner and drifted through the evening in a kind of fog. She was sure that tomorrow was going to be exciting but she was trying desperately to not dwell on it because that would only scare her. Hailey made the appropriate small talk but Raelynn was pretty sure her daughter knew what was going on in her mind. Only time would tell.

Chapter 3

Saturday proved to be as nice as the previous one, the weather was slightly cool but the sun shone bright and Raelynn woke up with her stomach in knots. Surprisingly, she slept well but the nerves were getting the better of her. She dressed in a comfortable t-shirt, some leggings, and tennis shoes. She reviewed the website for Skydive Spaceland the night before to make sure she was doing everything right.

She settled on a piece of lightly buttered toast so she didn't have a completely empty stomach. It was tough to get it down, she was shaking already and they hadn't left yet. She checked her email and was answering one from her brother up north when she heard Hailey moving around. Amazing, the girl was sure motivated to get up when her mother was going to do something crazy. A few minutes later, Hailey appeared, smiling.

Hailey kissed her mom on the cheek, "Good morning."

"Good morning," Raelynn responded, her voice tight.

Hailey poured some cereal into a bowl, "It's going to be so much fun mom!"

Raelynn turned her chair so she was facing her daughter, "Fine, then you can jump for me," she was only half kidding but it was the half of her that was terrified.

Cocking her head, Hailey looked at her mom, "Normally I would so take you up on that offer but this is for you mom."

Raelynn nodded and turned back to the computer.

She sat down across from Raelynn. "I am so proud of you."

Sighing, Raelynn smiled, "Thank you baby." She looked at her watch, "We'd better get finished up; Melissa will be here in twenty minutes."

"I'm on it," Hailey chimed and ate her breakfast.

They got ready and were ready when Melissa rang the bell. The drive was spent with Raelynn sitting in the passenger seat listening to Hailey and Melissa chat like magpies. She loved them both and was always amazed at how easily they spoke about things. She was just trying to keep from passing out, her heart beat was erratic.

Melissa pulled into the drive of Skydive Spaceland and nodded. "This looks so cool."

"It is," Hailey responded and squeezed Raelynn's shoulder.

Raelynn would not fail Hailey, no matter how petrified she was at doing this. Her pride was at stake as well. They walked into the hangar and went to the office. Raelynn went up to the counter and saw the same young lady she spoke with the weekend before.

"Good morning," Raelynn said hesitantly.

Dawn smiled, "Hello again," she remembered this nice lady from last weekend.

"I'm going to jump today," She sounded so strange to herself.

"Great," Dawn said, "let's get you pulled up in the computer and we'll have you fill out your paperwork."

She smiled at the trio and thought that the one skydiving looked like the one least likely out of the three to do it. Shaking her head, she smiled, everyone had their own reasons for doing it, as long as they had fun, it was great.

Raelynn filled out the forms and stepped on the scale as instructed by Dawn. It was kind of unnerving to be weighed but it was to pair up the novice with the right instructor. She was glad that they were so professional about it. She was ready to finish when Melissa stepped up to the counter.

"Hello," Melissa said sweetly. "I'd like to pay for her to have her jump videotaped."

"What?" Raelynn asked.

Hailey was on her other side, "Yes mom, we want it recorded." She winked at Melissa, "Plus we can laugh at your antics."

Melissa handed Dawn her credit card and Raelynn snarled at her. She wasn't even sure she was capable of snarling but her friend and daughter were making more out of this than she wanted. As if jumping wasn't scary enough, now they would have it documented so she could relive the fear over and over. Fantastic! She stepped away from the counter resigned to let her friend and daughter humiliate her a little more.

They left the office a couple of minutes later and went to the waiting area to be called. Raelynn had to attend a brief class before she could jump. Dawn told her that Hailey and Melissa could accompany her to the class so they could see what was going to happen. She wasn't talking to them now so it was fine.

She sat down on a chair in the hangar and sulked.

Her name was called and she got up and found the group she was supposed to be in. They went up some stairs and into a classroom on the second floor. It was bright, as the sun shone through some large windows. Another instructor was there and greeted everyone warmly as they sat in chairs. She explained the basics of what was expected during the jump. She was great, punctuating the speech with bits of humor to put everyone at ease. As Raelynn looked around she noticed that either people looked scared out of their minds or just excited. She was in the scared group.

The instructor left the room and a short movie started. It was a man who looked like one of the singers in ZZ Top, his beard was very long. He talked about the legal aspects involved and Raelynn wondered why she even put this little adventure on her list. Was she nuts?

The class ended and the instructor came back in and asked if anyone had any questions. She left with one parting comment, "If you're going to be sick, make it good, these instructors have seen it all." Everyone laughed and left the room to go down and meet their instructor.

The group was told to watch a large monitor and look for their name. They would then walk over to the appropriate table and meet their jump instructor. Raelynn was paying attention to everyone else when Hailey nudged her arm.

"Mom," Hailey smiled, "you are paired with Chris," she looked around, "I think that's him."

"How do you know?" Raelynn asked.

Hailey pointed behind them, "All the instructors' pictures are up on the wall so you see who you're with."

Raelynn felt stupid. How did she miss that? She saw a smiling man walking toward her and tried to paste a smile on her face.

"Hello, I'm Chris," the man said.

"Raelynn," She reached out to shake his hand and was embarrassed that she was so nervous.

"Come on over, we'll get you suited up." Chris smiled and went toward a row of jump suits hung up.

Raelynn followed him and stood there as he picked up a blue jumpsuit and handed it to her. She stepped into it awkwardly; her limbs didn't seem to want to work. She giggled nervously as he helped her zip it up.

Chris saw this every day, people were naturally scared of jumping. "It's okay, you'll do great." He reassured her.

Raelynn smiled genuinely, "Thanks," she looked at Hailey. "I thought it would be less intimidating."

"Most people say that," He pulled on a harness to hook around her shoulders and thighs. "We are safe and have a lot of experience."

Nodding, Raelynn looked at him, "Thank you."

Melissa was standing to the side thinking how scared Raelynn looked, "Are you sure she should be doing this?" She was sure her friend needed some excitement but this seemed somewhat dramatic.

"Yes," Hailey said sharply, "I requested Seth be her videographer." She looked around, "I think he'll be here shortly."

"Is that the guy you told me talked to her last weekend?" Melissa was trying to speak softly so Raelynn wouldn't hear them.

Hailey nodded, "He seemed to like her and she just stood there like a tree."

Melissa laughed, she could picture the scene. "Your poor mom, she never thought she was attractive, she always wondered what your dad saw in her." She smiled at Hailey, "He saw her for what she was, a sweet and loving person."

Hailey always liked hearing about her dad but now was a time for her mom to go out and find something or someone new.

They were conspiring, Raelynn was sure of it as she watched her friend and daughter talking. She felt a niggle at the back of her neck and was about to say something when she saw Seth walking up to her. He carried a small camera with him. The ground was falling beneath her feat as she watched him. The man was graceful in a completely masculine way.

"Hello again," Seth said smiling.

He wasn't sure he would see the stunning woman from last weekend. She said she was coming but he had the feeling she wouldn't follow through. She looked terrified and he was used to that. But there was something about her that made him want to talk to her. That was why he walked up to her the previous weekend. She was a thinker; he could see that right off. He watched her watching the landings and wondered what was going through that pretty head of hers. He was somewhat put off by the fact she wouldn't speak to him, had he been rude? The way her daughter jumped in led him to believe she was shy. But this morning when Dawn told him he'd been requested as a videographer, he was surprised.

Now that he saw her again, the surprise was pleasure. She was beautiful but in such a quiet way that you had to look closely. Her hair was pulled back and she was very nervous but that only added to her beauty.

"Hello," Raelynn managed to answer when he was a couple of feet away.

48

He was as handsome as she remembered. His blue eyes searched hers and she felt so exposed. There was nothing intimidating about him at first glance but once you looked, there was no mistaking the intensity he held inside. Raelynn wondered what it would be like to kiss him. Where did that come from? She shook herself and tried to focus on Chris.

"Ok," Chris said, "this is your altimeter," he strapped a gage onto her hand. "It tells us our altitude. We will be pulling the chute when we're at seven thousand feet."

"Seven thousand," Raelynn said quietly.

Chris laughed, "Don't worry, you'll remember."

Nodding, Raelynn felt foolish.

Seth stepped up, "I'd like to do a bit of an interview with you before we go up; can you step over here?"

She followed his instructions; she would do whatever he wanted if he kept talking to her like that.   She felt a rush of awareness that chased the nerves away for a moment.

"Ok," He was adjusting the camera, "I'm going to ask you a few questions, just answer honestly."

Raelynn waived Hailey and Melissa over; she wasn't going to be subjected to this alone.

The next five minutes were filled with Seth asking her about why she wanted to skydive and what Hailey and Melissa thought about it. She answered but sounded like a robot. It was just embarrassing in that she was so tongue-tied.

Chris came over and told her it was time. The group was gathering and getting ready to go to the plane.

They lined up, Raelynn was at the back of the line and since she had a videographer, she would be the first to go. Oh great, just what she wanted to hear.

Hailey and Melissa stood there smiling and waving. Raelynn wanted to slap them for looking so smug.

She climbed into the small plane and saw two bench seats going the length of the back. Everyone sat in a line on the seats. As soon as they were in, the door was rolled down and they started taxiing. Chris was behind her telling her how he was now strapping them together. He was tightening the straps which made Raelynn feel a bit more secure and more scared at the same time.

Seth could see she was scared but that made her even more enduring. He asked the same questions he asked every time he did videography and yet knew this was different. He studied her as Chris joked with her to put her at ease and that made Seth feel better. He turned on the camera and faced it out the window then focused on her.

"Ok Raelynn," He said loudly over the roar of the propellers, "what's going on now?"

Raelynn didn't want to answer questions, she was too busy looking at the distance between her and ground growing. A quick glance at her altimeter showed they were already five thousand feet up. Whoa, this was happening so fast. Her heart started pounding and her palms started sweating.

Chris yelled in her ear, "Hey I feel like I'm forgetting something."

Giving him a "mother" look over her shoulder, she retorted, "Well, it's on you."

He and Seth both laughed.

There was a single jumper sitting on the floor near the door who opened it about halfway. She assumed he was going to jump first.

"Okay," Chris said, "we're almost there. Are you okay?"

"Yes," Raelynn had every confidence in him, it was her she was worried about.

Chris sensed her hesitation, "As soon as we get the go ahead, you and I will move toward the door." He checked their harness and tightened it a little more. "When we're at the door you're going to lean your head back against me and we'll count to three. Then we're out of here."

"Okay," She sounded so confident in her own mind. She looked at Seth and his smile made her feel a whole different kind of excitement. Goodness, the man was hot!

That was the last thought Raelynn had because Chris tapped her shoulder and motioned toward the door. The lone jumper went out first; he was followed by Seth as he needed to jump to get the video of her jumping. They got to the door, counted to three, and jumped.

Raelynn had a preconceived notion of how it would feel and the reality was nothing like it. She felt free! They were plummeting toward the earth and all she could think of was how totally awesome it was. She was screaming but with excitement not fear.

Chris tapped her arm to get her to look at the altimeter. He explained that he would signal her when it was time to pull the chord and she would do it. Now it seemed like it was happening too fast. They were facing Seth who was taking video and she stuck out her tongue. It was completely unlike her but this was fantastic.

The signal given, Raelynn grabbed the chord and, with Chris' help, pulled it down. The chute deployed and they were yanked upward. Nothing too rough but a jolt nonetheless. Now they slowed and she could hear Chris explain how to control the chute. They turned a few times and he let her control the pulleys. They were drifting toward the ground and the whole thing was overwhelming.

Once they were close, Chris had her demonstrate how to lift her legs for landing. She did as instructed and they prepared to land. She thought they would land on their butts as she saw the others do the last weekend. But they landed softly and she held her legs up until Chris told her to put them down.

It happened too quickly, was all Raelynn could think when they landed. She waited for Chris to unstrap her harness then turned and hugged him. She was thankful she had him as her instructor because he was patient and fun. That made the experience all the better.

Seth walked up to them once they were down and asked Raelynn how she liked it. This was certainly not the same woman who went up. This woman was animated and looked almost wild. He was very aroused by it and was surprised because he'd been jumping for years and never experienced this with any of his jumps. With her, though, it was altered.

Raelynn waved at Hailey and Melissa who were in the viewing area yelling. She turned to Chris, thanked him again, and went over to Seth. She was riding on the high of jumping and instinctively reached up and kissed him on the lips. The impulse was very non-Raelynn-like. After she pulled away, she wondered if she made a grave error, he looked stunned.

"I'm sorry," She said quietly and walked toward her daughter.

"Did you see that?" Melissa asked Hailey out of the corner of her mouth.

Hailey looked at her mom's friend astonished, "Yep." She looked back at her mom with a big, dopey grin on her face.

As she neared, Melissa opened her arms for a hug, "Oh my Gosh, how was it?" She asked her friend.

Raelynn hugged her quick and stepped back, "It was amazing Mel!" She was smiling so big it hurt her cheeks.

She grabbed her friend and daughter in another embrace and wondered if this is what it was like to live fully.

The three walked back to the hangar so Raelynn could take off the jump suit. She went to the restroom to check her face and hair quick and returned back so she could talk with Chris.

He filled out her jump log and said she did great. It was thrilling to receive such praise. She thanked him again and they went to the office to wait for her video to be done. They were told before she jumped that they could leave a tip for anyone they wanted when they were done. Raelynn was so thankful for the help Chris and Seth gave that she was generous.

The three women left the office and sat down in the waiting area so they could see Raelynn's video come up on the screen.

Seth was in the editing room piecing together Raelynn's video. He was amazed that she seemed so shy one moment but planted a kiss on him the next. As if he wasn't already attracted to her; that upped the ante big time. He was so used to this that it didn't take much to edit the video. He was done in a matter of minutes and took the hard copy out to her.

Raelynn was chatting with Hailey and Melissa and occasionally commented on another skydiving video. She was still riding on the excitement the experience created inside her. It was like this intense energy was pouring out of her and it was kept in for way too long. She looked up and saw Seth coming towards her. The excitement was compounded. She stood as he neared.

"I wanted to give you your video and say how much fun it was," He handed her the cd.

Raelynn looked at him and then down to the cd. She was again at a loss for words, "Thank you."

"Mom," Hailey said behind her, "your video is up on the screen."

They all watched the monitor, Raelynn was initially embarrassed that she was on the screen but couldn't help but be mesmerized by the sound of Seth's voice.

She watched it and was surprised at how calm she looked because she sure didn't feel that way. She snuck a glance at Seth who was watching the video intently. He was a good eight inches taller than her, his shoulders were wide and he looked so strong. She had the impulse to kiss him before and it returned. What was wrong with her? He turned and looked at her. All time stopped. She could wrap herself up in his gaze; it held her to the spot.

"Raelynn," He whispered, and, without thinking, bent down to kiss her.

It was a quick kiss but that did nothing to quell the chaos it created inside of Raelynn. Holy cow, the man had fantastic lips. She wanted nothing more than to keep kissing but she remembered where they were. She pulled away, looking chagrined.

"I'm not sorry," Seth said quietly and then pulled himself away.

Raelynn had no response to what just happened. It was the sexiest thing she could remember ever happening to her and that opened up a whole other train of thought she was not prepared to deal with.

Hailey and Melissa looked at the pair, at each other, and back at the pair. Nobody said anything.

Raelynn absently ran her hands down her sides, "I suppose we should get going." She smiled shyly and turned to Hailey and Melissa. "Let's go girls."

The three of them started walking out of the hangar. Hailey turned back to look at Seth and saw him just standing there staring after her mom. There was something about the way he looked that made Hailey almost feel sorry for him. It was one thing for her mother to skydive, it was certainly another for her to start dating. But, Hailey remembered and started smiling because it was on her list. She wrote that she wanted to fall in love again. Without thinking, Hailey ran back to Seth and grabbed a pen off of a nearby table. She wrote her mom's cell number on a piece of paper lying there and handed it to him without a word. She high-tailed it back to her mom and Melissa who were now weaving their way through the parking lot.

Seth stood there and looked at the slip of paper he was handed. Well, well, Raelynn Woodsen would definitely be hearing from him, he smiled and went back into the office.

The women returned to Raelynn's condo so she could change. She ran into the bathroom to slip on some nicer clothes and glanced in the mirror. Her eyes were bright and her skin flushed. She moved a hand to her cheek and thought about the two kisses she shared with the amazing Seth. Now was not the time to dwell, they had plans.

They went to lunch and spent the rest of the day goofing around. A few stores were visited, they saw a movie, and had dinner out as well. By the time Raelynn's head hit the pillow that night, she was exhausted, but in such a good way.

Sunday morning proved to be rainy but Raelynn didn't even seem to notice. She got up and got ready quickly. There were some chores she needed to do at the condo and then she planned to do some grocery shopping for the week. It was easier to shop on the weekends because she couldn't rely on getting home on time during the week. She didn't hear Hailey, not surprising; so went about doing her chores.

She was finishing up cleaning when her phone went off. Probably Melissa seeing if she was still excited about her adventure yesterday. She picked up the phone and smiled.

"Yes I'm still excited about yesterday, are you happy?" She asked sarcastically.

"Um," Seth said, not expecting that particular greeting, "Hello?"

Raelynn flushed, she didn't look at her caller I.D. and rolled her eyes, she didn't recognize the number. Trying to regain her composure she cleared her throat. "Hello?"

Seth smiled; she realized he wasn't who she thought. "Raelynn?" He asked.

She knew that voice, it made her skin tingle. "Seth?"

"Yes," He said, not sure what to say. "How are you?"

Raelynn wanted to die, she was being foolish. "I'm fine, thank you." She sat down on the sofa, trying to relax. "Why are you calling?"

His suspicions were confirmed, her daughter gave him her number without letting her know. This may not go as well as he hoped. "I was hoping to ask you out to dinner."

She was surprised that he got straight to the point. It was easier to deal with. "Uh," She was trying to decide what she should say when he interrupted her thoughts.

"I know you were surprised by the kisses yesterday, I was too. I am not expecting anything, just hoping we can get to know each other a little more over a meal." This was not his smoothest invitation by far. He was surprised at how nervous he was.

Raelynn smiled, "I'd love to." She answered before she thought about it.

"Great," He rushed, "I would like to pick you up Friday about six thirty if that's okay."

Raelynn went over to her desk and checked her calendar, "That would be great." She meant it and excitement built up in her belly creating a warm sensation.

She gave him her address and confirmed the time for Friday. After writing it down on her calendar, she sat down at her desk and thought about what she would do. She hadn't been out on a date in way too long. She was still sitting there when Hailey wandered into the room.

"Morning," Hailey mumbled.

"Good morning," Raelynn smiled at her daughter.

As Hailey ate breakfast, Raelynn finished her cleaning and made her grocery list. Hailey declined the invitation to join her so she went out and did the shopping. She returned to a pacing Hailey in the dining room.

"Is something wrong," Raelynn asked as she put the grocery bags on the counter.

Hailey stomped over, her hands on her hips, "Were you going to tell me about your date?"

Raelynn calmly put the milk in the refrigerator, "Yes," she was trying not to laugh at her daughter's reaction.

"When?" Hailey demanded.

"Hailey," Raelynn said sternly, "I'm an adult and, although I would most certainly tell you, I'm not required to inform you instantly." She sighed and hugged her daughter. "I'd just hung up with Seth when you came into the room, you were half asleep."

Hailey knew she was acting crazy but this was big news. She could never remember her mother going out on a date the whole time she was growing up.

"I'm sorry," Hailey said softly. "This is big news."

Raelynn kissed her daughter on the forehead, "Yes, I suppose it is but it's not until Friday."

For the life of her, Hailey could not understand how her mother could be so calm about this; she was thinking it was a huge deal. She called Melissa as soon as she saw the calendar and her mom's friend was just as surprised as she was.

They finished putting the groceries away and Raelynn sat down to take care of some bills while Hailey worked on her homework due that week. The rain continued to stream steadily down the windows, making them both content to be in the house. Dinner was quiet and they spent the evening catching up on the shows taped on the DVR.

Outside, Raelynn was content to be with her daughter. But inside, she was going through everything in her mind. What would she wear? How would she do her hair and makeup? Where were they going? Excitement hummed through her steadily. She hoped he would kiss her again, only this time, a real kiss. If the short ones they shared the day before were any kind of meter, then a real kiss from Seth would blow her socks off. Did she dare ask him? Did she just take it upon herself and kiss him?

She looked at Hailey, embarrassed that she even considered asking her daughter for dating advice. That was not what they did. She would save her questions and drill Melissa at work about what she should do.

Monday was chaos from the start. Raelynn overslept, something she NEVER did. After getting to work thirty minutes late, she was overrun by messages from clients and questions from the interns. Lunch was spent at her desk trying to fix an error on a tax form and get that to the appropriate places.

By the time she got home, Raelynn was exhausted. She needed a hot shower and some form of food. Scowling at the stove, she was in no mood to cook; she ordered a pizza and plopped down on the overstuffed chair in the living room. Hailey had classes and wouldn't be home until late. She was about to pour herself a glass of wine when her phone went off saying she had a text. Great, more interruptions.

She picked up the phone and was about to be mad at whoever disturbed her when she read the text. *Good evening, I hope your day went well. I was thinking of you.* It was sent by Seth and her insides turned to mush instantly. How sweet was he?

She smiled and sat back down, cradling the phone. What did she say? The truth worked best. *Good evening to you, it was awful but your text brightened it considerably. Thank you.*

Her insides tingled waiting for his response. Was she too forward? She wasn't very experienced at this flirting thing but it just came easily with him. She was pleasantly surprised when he responded quickly. *I aim to please you ma'am.* ☺

Oh goodness, the man could make texting sound sexy! She was aroused and felt kind of guilty sitting here thinking what she was thinking. Well, two could play this game. *Well, you say that now but can you deliver?*

She sat there staring at the phone after she pushed send. Did she push it too far? Was she being too forward? She was shaking when the response came back. *I most certainly can. I look forward to proving it to you on Friday.*

Well then, that settled that. The man was quickly becoming a most fascinating subject. She would need to take a cold shower if this kept up. Her thoughts were so crazy that she didn't even feel like they were hers. *I look forward to making you prove it.*

Seth sat back in his office chair and was astounded. The woman may be shy in person but in texting, she was amazing. He was turned on and didn't know if he could wait until Friday to see her. He texted her on a whim because he was, in fact, thinking about her. She'd occupied his thoughts since Saturday and was driving him to distraction. He didn't know what to say to that. *Yes, ma'am, my pleasure. And hopefully yours too.* ☺

The doorbell rang, making Raelynn jump. She was so absorbed in her phone that she forgot she was waiting for the pizza. Well now, how did she prepare for Friday after this? What did he expect? What did she expect? She paid the pizza delivery guy, giving him a generous tip, and set the pizza on the counter. She got down a plate, a napkin, and grabbed a slice. The wine poured, she sat back down and ate quietly looking at her phone every few minutes and wondering if he was going to text her again. After dinner was done and she had no further texts, she decided to change into her pajamas and watch tv.

Hailey came home later that night and knew something was up. Her mom was sitting in the living room and watching television but she wasn't watching the tv at all, her mind was far away. Hailey had that same look from time to time when she met someone special. Was it actually possible for her mom to be into this guy Seth? She sure hoped so for her mom's sake.

The week flew by and it was Thursday night when Raelynn was able to come up for air. They tried to keep Fridays light so they could leave early and so Thursday nights became a bit of a cram session to keep up. She and Melissa ordered Chinese take-out and sat in the conference room working on a particularly detailed profit and loss statement submitted by one of their largest clients. It was no different than any other Thursday night until Raelynn's phone went off.

She glanced at Melissa, who was absorbed in whatever she was reading, and looked at the phone. It was a text from Seth. Her heart sped up as she opened the message. *How are you tonight? I'm very excited for our dinner tomorrow night. I hope you bring your appetite······*

Raelynn's cheek reddened as she read the text. Oh Lord, he was creating havoc with her insides. If the man was standing in front of her, she'd probably jump him right then and there. That particular thought made her breathing labored.

Melissa looked up and noticed her friend was different, "Are you okay?"

Raelynn put the phone down quickly, "Yes, I'm just going to get a water, do you want one?" She didn't wait for an answer before getting up and grabbing her phone. She didn't want to respond while someone else was around.

Once she was in the break room she started texting her reply. *I'll bring it but the question is can you satisfy it?*

She grabbed the waters, put hers up to her forehead in an effort to calm herself, and walked back into the conference room. Melissa took hers and mumbled a "thank you" and they both got back to work.

After twenty minutes Melissa couldn't take it anymore. Raelynn was fidgety and couldn't focus since her phone went off. "Okay, give it up, what's going on?"

Raelynn pretended she didn't know what her friend was asking. "I'm fine."

"Don't lie to me baby," Melissa glared at her friend, "who were you texting?"

There was no use in lying; Melissa would weedle it out of her in no time. "Seth." Maybe if she played it off, then they could drop it.

"Oh Seth," Was drawn out. Melissa knew it! Raelynn was the sensible one but now she was acting very unlike herself. "Is everything okay?"

Raelynn wanted to say no and ask her friend a hundred questions. She knew how things worked between men and women; she had a daughter for crying out loud. The problem was that she really hadn't wanted anyone since Anthony and that was far too long ago. She couldn't do it though so she just smiled, "Yes, we're going out for dinner tomorrow night."

That seemed to placate Melissa and they finished their work pretty quickly after that. She was actually relieved when they parted ways and she was able to have some time alone. She re-read the texts Seth sent and was aroused in seconds. She decided one last text before tomorrow wouldn't hurt. She got into her car and typed quickly. *I have every confidence you can, don't be late or there will be consequences.*

Seth read the text and was glad he was alone. These little teasers were quickly turning into an addiction. He read them all week, going over what they meant. He knew what he meant but maybe it wasn't what she meant. He was acting like a teenager and the thought made him smile. Maybe it was about time he let someone in. With shaky fingers, he typed the reply. *I wouldn't dream of disappointing you. We'll see who is satisfied more.*

Raelynn read the text and put her head down on the steering wheel in an effort to control her raging thoughts. Her body was ready and she didn't know what to do with the sexual energy running through her. She was at war on the inside between what she so desperately wanted to do and what her upbringing and lifestyle trained her to do. It would be interesting to see which would win out.

Chapter 4

Friday proved to be more stressful than Raelynn planned. She got to work and had to sit through two meetings for last minute changes with clients. After that she was hard pressed to catch up with the work she was planning on doing first thing. It all seemed to go down hill after that. The afternoon was spent clearing up what she could and the next time she looked at her watch, she saw it was after four. Crap, she needed to leave or she would not be ready when Seth came to pick her up for dinner.

Seth, the thought of him brought an immediate response. She only had to think of him and her heart started racing and her breathing grew shallow. What would happen if he kissed her again? She would probably melt into a puddle on the floor, that's what. Thinking about him was not getting her home to get ready so she quickly put her desk to rights and left work.

On the way home she was forced to slow down for a traffic accident. Any other day it would not have mattered but tonight was important. She got home at five thirty, sure she would be late. She still had to decide what to wear, all the outfits she tried on during the week were too plain or too big or she just didn't like them. She wanted something, anything, that made her feel like she felt when she talked to him or texted him. She wanted to feel sexy.

She threw her purse on the counter and marched into her bedroom stripping off work clothes as she went. They went into the laundry hamper and she turned to go shower when she saw the box on her bed.

Crossing to it, Raelynn slowly picked up the cover. Inside was a red silk dress that felt decadent when her fingers touched it. A note was in the box as well, Raelynn picked up the paper with shaking hands and read it.

Mom:

Melissa and I thought you needed something amazing for tonight. Have fun, I won't wait up.

Hailey

Tears were streaming down her cheeks as she admired the dress. It was perfect for what she wanted to portray. She whispered thank you and went to get ready.

At six twenty-two Raelynn walked out of her bedroom feeling ready for her first date in ages. The dress felt heavenly as it caressed her skin. It was form-fitting but not tight and showed off her shape in the best possible way. She turned every which way in the bathroom to see if there was some imperfection in her body and any that she thought she had were perfectly camouflaged by the material. Makeup and blowing out her hair made her feel pretty and sensual.

Raelynn diligently transferred her necessary purse items to the clutch she was taking for the evening. She just finished dabbing on perfume when the doorbell rang. She tried to quell the butterflies running rampant in her belly as she walked to the door.

The only thing she could remember was opening the door and feeling a rush of heat. Seth was standing on her threshold with a bouquet of flowers looking dashing in a gray suit. She couldn't even speak; her reaction to seeing him was so strong.

Finally, once the embarrassment was too much, she managed a weak, "Hello."

Seth watched her open the door and he was stunned. This seemingly quiet woman was sexy as Hell and smiling at him. He was thinking about kissing her when she said something. It was only polite to respond but he didn't know what she said.

"Come in, please," Raelynn backed up a step to allow Seth entry.

Seth smiled and handed her the bouquet, "Thank you."

She watched him walk through her entryway into the living room. She couldn't remember ever having a man in the condo so she wondered what he thought about it. It was only a dinner date; she should just focus on her manners.

Seth entered the living room and thought it reflected his impression of Raelynn. It was nice and welcoming. He couldn't, however, focus on anything specifically because her perfume surrounded him and did something wonderful to his senses. He turned around and looked at her fully.

"You look stunning," He walked up to Raelynn slowly and ran his hands down her arms until her hands were locked into his. "I know this is fast but if I don't kiss you right now, I'm going to explode."

Any hesitation Raelynn had about whether he thought the same way she thought about those texts disappeared. She smiled sweetly, "Well, I would hate to be responsible for you exploding so if it helps you out, okay."

He growled and pulled her to him. His hands moved up to her neck and held her in place as he lowered his mouth to hers. It was an easy exploration as she was welcoming. As soon as she opened her lips though, he plundered. All he could taste was her and she was amazing! Her lips were soft and she responded so openly to him, it drove him further into the depths of passion.

Oh my Lord, she was saying in her head. Did kisses feel like this? If so, why has it been so long since I've had one. Her head was spinning and her hands travelled up and down his back. He was telling her with his lips all her body wanted to hear. Her tongue had a mind of its own and dove deeply into his mouth. He tasted minty and smelled so male; she only wanted to get closer.

The kiss finally took everything out of both of them and they parted almost as fast as they joined. Raelynn's cheeks were flushed because she realized she dropped the flowers somewhere along the line. She bent to pick them up and shakily walked to the kitchen to put them in a vase.

Neither of them were talking and Seth was somewhat relieved. He needed a minute to get his libido under control and keep himself from grabbing her and taking her right there. She must be feeling something similar as she was awfully quiet while putting the flowers in a vase. Guilt wound its way into his mind.

"Raelynn," He walked to the bar that separated the kitchen and living room. He needed something between them to keep his hands off of her, "I hope I didn't scare you."

"No," Raelynn looked into his beautiful blue eyes, "not at all, I just haven't done this in a long time and you make me want to do things I've not thought about in a while."

Well that statement did nothing to calm his raging hormones. She was exciting because she said what she meant, he appreciated that. He was tired of the games men and women thought they had to play.

"Really? How long?" He asked playfully but noticed he embarrassed her when she looked up at him. "I'm sorry," He walked around the bar and stood in front of her.

Raelynn was mortified, maybe she wasn't good at kissing and he felt sorry for her.

"Hey," Seth smiled, "I didn't mean to insinuate anything; I cannot remember a kiss I've enjoyed more." He went on when she smiled, "Those texts about had me in knots for days."

Relief poured over Raelynn, "Good, I thought it was just me."

Now he was in trouble, the woman just admitted how turned on she was, he didn't want to rush it between them so he tried the noble route, "Okay, well let's have some dinner and we can talk about it."

She nodded, put the flowers, on the table, and followed him through the living room. She grabbed her clutch off the table and they left, Raelynn locking the door behind her. The ride to the restaurant was quiet but nice. Neither of them seemed to feel like they had to talk and Raelynn suspected they each needed to think about the chemistry between them.

The restaurant was in south Houston, a steak place, and Raelynn heard it mentioned but never ate there. They were greeted by the hostess and seated quickly. She looked around once they were seated to get more of a feel. It was lovely and upscale; Seth had good taste.

"I hope you like steak," Seth stated once they were handed the menus.

Raelynn smiled, "I love meat." The comment was meant to be sassy and she thought she hit her mark if his sharp intake of breath was any indication.

Seth was riding a very fine line of torture. He was aroused and loving every second of it. She was a minx with her shyness and then this other side of her that was so open. "If you keep talking like that, we won't get past the salads."

"Well if you keep looking at me like that, I won't have time to order a salad, I'll demand you take me back to my place and show me what we've been texting about." There, she put him in his place, and made her insides explode with awareness at the same time.

Never in his life could Seth remember a woman being so direct about her physical needs. There wasn't even a category in his mind he could place her in. Just when he thought his libido couldn't take any more, she said something that turned it up a notch. He pretended to concentrate on his menu in a last-ditch effort to not embarrass himself in public.

Raelynn mentally shook herself. What was wrong with her that she felt the need to say such things to him? She was no sexual pro but something about him made her want to try to be just that.

The server came over and took their orders. Raelynn ordered a glass of wine with her dinner and was glad Seth chose to stick to sweet tea since he was driving. It was sweet of him to consider her feelings.

"Are you okay with me having wine?" She didn't want him to feel uncomfortable.

Seth smiled, she was so sweet and shy when she spoke, "Yes, I'm just hoping to get you relaxed."

She couldn't help it, she giggled, "Dare I ask, relaxed for what?"

Now he was feeling a little shy, he leaned forward and took her hand into his, rubbing his thumb across the back of it. "For whatever you want."

Raelynn swallowed hard. Oh Lord, she wanted to be naked with him right now.

Just touching her hand made him hard, thank goodness there were tablecloths so the other patrons couldn't see his condition. If they were anywhere even remotely private, she would be underneath him and he would fill her with everything he had to give.

Raelynn stared into his eyes and said nothing. She didn't need to. He knew exactly what she wanted and she knew what he wanted. So why were they at a restaurant pretending they actually wanted to eat? Because he was a gentleman and she should be some semblance of a lady. Although that was the last thing on her mind, she did slowly pull her hand from his and sat back to give them some distance.

She took a deep breath, "What is it about you that makes me feel this way?"

Seth was surprised at the question. He wondered the same thing, "I have no idea, but I'm pretty sure I feel the same way."

His candor was appreciated even if it didn't do anything to suppress her wants. There had to be some explanation. A woman, especially her, didn't just change how she was in a matter of days. "I play it safe Seth." She took a breath, "I don't do this."

"I don't either Raelynn," He sucked in a breath trying to say the right thing. "I consider myself a pretty decent guy but you make me want to be anything but that."

This was not the time to stoke the fires inside of them. "Maybe we should talk about other things, like our lives." She had to get this under control in some way.

Seth nodded, "Yes, well I skydive. But you know that. I also own a small ranch and have horses and cattle."

This interested Raelynn, "Really?" She was curious, "So which is your job?"

"Neither," Seth said quickly, "I do what I love to do so I don't consider it work."

How fascinating, "I am impressed. I own half of a CPA firm in Lake Jackson and I enjoy what I do but I still call it work." She chuckled.

"I should have known." He said quietly.

Her shackles came up fast, "What does that mean?" She said tightly.

"I apologize," Seth leaned forward and took her hand again. "I only meant that you seem pretty proper." Oh, this wasn't coming out right. Crap!

Raelynn could see he was squandering to recover and she had the choice to rescue him or make him suffer. Although suffering held some appeal, she decided to help him out. "I know what you meant." She squeezed his hand, "I epitomize a regimented lifestyle. I think I gave Hailey a scare when I handed her my list."

Seth cocked his head, "What list?"

Shoot, Raelynn didn't mean to mention the list. Talking about it now seemed so stupid. But it wasn't stupid; she so desperately wanted to do what was on the list and live again. "I made a list a while ago, two actually, one of the things I am thankful for and one of the things I want to do."

"I like that," Seth said softly, "You aren't afraid to say what you want. That is very sexy Raelynn."

His voice hummed along her skin making her shiver. They would be so good together in bed, she knew it. "Why thank you," She was shy again.

"Hey," Seth said, "don't be embarrassed."

The server brought their salads and placed the plates in front of them with a flourish. When they were left alone again, Raelynn giggled.

"What?" Seth asked.

She shook her head, "I was just thinking that at least we made it to the salads."

Seth threw his head back and laughed, "And so we did."

They ate their salads slowly, glancing at one another and enjoying the time together. The rest of the dinner was done and before either realized it, they received the check.

Raelynn was thinking of what would happen next, "So Mr.," she wound her arm through his as he pulled her chair out for them to leave, "what's next?"

"Well," Seth leaned in and whispered in her ear, her hair moving with his breath, "we can walk along the river or I can take you home, it's your decision."

As far as Raelynn was concerned, there was no decision, "Take me home please," came out in a rushed breath.

He growled, "I was praying you would say that," he placed his hand on her lower back to guide her and it took every ounce of restraint he had to not grab her in the middle of the restaurant.

They walked to where his car was parked and he tucked her in before going to the driver's side. Raelynn was touched by his manners. Some men didn't really see the point to the gestures but she really appreciated them. Anthony had impeccable manners. The mere thought of her husband brought a sharp stab of pain and an avalanche of guilt. She tensed and looked out the passenger window in an attempt to clear her mind.

Seth knew something happened. She was different as soon as they got in the car. He didn't think either of them said anything so she was thinking of something, or someone. He was guilty of that from time to time so he understood. He would give her some time and hopefully it would pass. She was amazing, he wanted her and yet he knew it would be okay if they didn't make love.

They reached her condo and Raelynn was no better emotionally. Thinking of Anthony was like a wet blanket on her fiery impulses. It wasn't fair to Seth and she knew that she should say something. But what did you say when you teased someone and then backed off? It was not a game to her but maybe he would take it that way. Once the car stopped in the parking space she turned to him.

"I am sorry," She started. As soon as she looked into his eyes, her breath hitched, he was looking at her, really looking at her and it was driving her crazy. "I was okay until I thought of someone and now I'm unsure."

Seth touched her cheek with his hand, softly caressing it, "Why don't we go in and talk about it." His hand moved down her cheek to touch her neck, he could feel her pulse wildly beat just as his own was, "I don't expect anything Raelynn."

Relief flooded her mind, "Thank you."

She reached up and put her hand over his on her neck. He felt so good; she knew she would kiss him in the car if she didn't move soon. She let her hand fall and turned to open the door.

Seth followed suit and got out of the car. He met her on her side and walked her to her door. She didn't tell him goodnight when she opened the door so he followed her inside.

Raelynn flipped on a light, she was usually so good at making sure lights were on so Hailey wouldn't come home to the dark and she forgot tonight. She shook her head and smiled.

"What?" Seth asked softly.

She turned and looked at him; his eyes sparkled in the dimly lit room, "I was just thinking that you make me forget myself."

Seth walked up to her and held her hands in his, "Is that a bad thing?"

Smiling, Raelynn led him to the sofa and sat down, pulling him down next to her. It was so easy to touch him, "No, but it's definitely not me."

He didn't understand, "What's wrong with that?" He was usually a person to go with the flow.

"I am so not the woman you think I am," She looked down, embarrassed and afraid he would leave her once he found out she was plain old Raelynn.

"I think," He brought her palm to his lips and kissed it slowly, "you are exactly the woman I think you are."

All coherent thought was leaving her brain, she watched him kiss her palm with breathless wonder. He did such delicious things to her body. Instinctively, she licked her lips.

She may think she's not exciting but she didn't see herself though Seth's eyes. He watched her react to him and it was like a drug to his senses. He couldn't keep himself from touching her, even if it didn't lead to anything tonight.

How did he know what words would settle her? She was perplexed by it all, "I was married to Hailey's father." She blurted out quickly.

Ah, Seth thought, this was who she was thinking of. "Okay." He said, he would not press her; it was her decision what to say.

"His name was Anthony." Tears automatically filled her eyes, "He was my first love." She put her hands in her lap, nerves filling her heart. "He died before he knew I was having Hailey."

So much information in so few sentences, Seth thought. He didn't know her well enough to understand what it all meant but he could see she was struggling. What should he ask? "Has there been anyone since?" He went out on a limb because he thought maybe that was the problem.

Raelynn looked away for a moment, "There was someone about ten years ago. We met at a conference in Dallas." She was wondering what he thought.

Seth nodded in understanding, "Can I ask what happened?"

She shook her head slightly and finally looked at him, "I couldn't choose him over Hailey."

He was confused, "Did he ask you too?"

"No," Raelynn was fumbling this all up. "I just couldn't choose the relationship with him because I thought it would take away from my commitment to Hailey."

Still not sure what she was getting to, he looked at her. "So you don't want to go any further with us?"

His directness was a Godsend as far as Raelynn was concerned, "Oh yes I do."

Now he was confused, "I'm sorry, I don't think I'm getting the point here."

"I know," She smiled, "I'm not good at this, I just was thinking of Anthony and I felt guilt and it's all just churning inside of me." She through her hands up in frustration.

Seth nodded again, "Do you mind if I get some water?"

Raelynn was surprised by the question, "I'm sorry, I didn't offer you any." She made a move to get up and Seth gently put his hand out to stop her.

"I'll get it." He got up and went into the kitchen.

He found a glass and poured water from the tap into it. He came back into the living room and placed the glass on a coaster. He sat back down and took her hands into his again. She turned to face him fully and he looked into her eyes.

"Now," He said softly, "I just wanted to give us each a moment to breathe." She was so beautiful and this was not something he even thought they would do tonight. "I cannot

76

deny how much I want you." Saying the words had a definite effect on his body.

Realynn smiled brightly.

"However, I will do whatever you need here," He reached up and ran his thumb across her cheek and wiped the tear that she shed. "If you need to evaluate where we stand then that's what you need to do."

Just having him say those words to her made Raelynn realize how she was completely over thinking the situation. She wanted him, he wanted her, they were consenting adults, heck, Hailey was an adult.

He watched her thoughts race through that beautiful head and wondered what she was thinking.

"You are a sweet man and you make it so easy." She leaned close and looked at his lips, "I am going to kiss you now."

That's all he heard and his brain went fuzzy. Her lips met his and fire spread throughout his body.

Raelynn remembered saying she was going to kiss him and putting her lips to his. That was it, after that it was all touch. Her hands grabbed his shoulders and shoved him against the back of the sofa. She moved closer and was pulled onto his lap. He lifted her like she was nothing and that made the kiss even better. She wound her arms around his neck and played with his hair as he made love to her mouth with his. Sensations coursed through her body making her feel bold.

Seth was pretty sure this was the most kissing he ever did with a woman. It didn't matter because he could just kiss her forever. Her lips were soft and pliant and evoked want out of him in spades. She was soft, leaning against his chest, and creating delicious friction against his pants. His hand found her leg and ran up and down her thigh; finally, he reached under the skirt of her dress and ran it up until his hand met with lace. Jolts of hot need shot into his gut.

Raelynn was throbbing, the need to touch overwhelmed her and she moved. She stared at him for the moment as their lips parted. She stood up and, not looking anywhere but at him, she took his hand and pulled him over to the center of the couch. She pulled up her dress so she could straddle him and lowered her body onto his lap.

No way was he going to survive the onslaught of desire he felt for Raelynn. She couldn't understand the chemistry that moved between them and neither could he. Of course, he didn't want to understand it, he only wanted her.

"You are incredible," He whispered when their lips broke apart for a moment.

Raelynn laughed, "No, but I thank you for thinking so."

She didn't want to talk, she wanted to kiss him and feel his hands on her. She took them and placed them on her sides so his thumbs could brush the bottom of her breasts. She didn't have the guts to place them directly on her breasts although she wanted him to touch them in the worst way.

When Raelynn deliberately placed his hands on her, he thought he might die of sweet agony. Her body felt so good, she was soft and tight all at the same time. It perplexed him how a woman's body could feel so different but so right all at once. His hands had a mind of their own though; he moved them up and filled them with her breasts. He could feel her nipples harden and rubbed them through the silk dress.

Oh, this was heaven, Raelynn thought. She could feel her nipples pulse under his thumbs and she was grinding her pelvis against his. The hardness in his pants hit the right spot and she was thrust into a release she didn't even know she could have.

"Ahhh," She yelled as she threw her head back. Her fingers dug into Seth's shoulders. The shudders took her over waves of pleasure, her stomach tightening.

Seth was so close to release and then she went over the edge. He was shocked in a completely good way, he watched her as she came and wondered how she could possibly think of herself as safe or controlled. Everything they did together was exactly the opposite.

Raelynn was mortified, she just climaxed while sitting on a man's lap in her living room. He must think she was awful. She dropped her head and tried to think of something to say when the tears came. As if it couldn't get worse, now she was crying.

"Hey," Seth pulled her head up gently. "Are you okay?" He was worried and in awe of her all at the same time. He still wanted her but it was seeing her release that brought him joy.

Raelynn looked at him through her tears, "Yes, just mortified."

He brought her hands up to his mouth and kissed each one, "Why would you say that? That was the most erotic experience of my life."

She moved her hands to his cheeks and leaned in to kiss him softly on the lips. "You are a kind man."

Seth laughed. "I am not; you just got me on an off day."

He was teasing her, she loved it, "I'm sorry that you didn't finish." There was the embarrassment again.

"Raelynn," He moved her off of his lap, her rubbing against him was too much when they needed to talk. He turned so they were facing each other, "I could have a number of times; it was far more arousing to watch you."

She never spoke of sex so openly, it was weird but it felt so right with him, "Really?"

"Yes," He kissed her on the nose, "definitely."

Just then the front door opened and Hailey came in, "Mom?"

Raelynn wanted to die now; her daughter would take one look at them and know what they were doing, she knew it. "In here," She said and mouthed 'I'm sorry' to Seth.

Hailey walked into the living room to see her mother on the couch with Seth, she could tell by the state of their clothes and faces what was going on. "Oh, hi Seth," She said as nonchalantly as she could.

"Hi Hailey," Seth returned. What else could he say?

Trying not to smile, she turned, "I'm going to bed, goodnight mom and Seth."

Raelynn shook her head, "Oh gosh, that was awkward."

Seth nodded but laughed, "She knows what's what."

"That's what scares me," Raelynn said quietly. She was pretty sure that her daughter knew more about sex than she did at this point. Although the last couple of hours were very educational for her.

Seth wanted to stay but it was not the right time, "I'm going to get going."

Raelynn's smile fell away, "Really?"

He would not lie to her, "There is nothing I want more than to stay with you tonight but I think it's better if I go." He got up and straightened his shirt. He could only imagine what he looked like.

"Okay," Raelynn said, she wanted him to stay too but it was good that he had the presence of mind to be reasonable. "When will I see you again?" Oh, the question sounded so desperate and she was feeling guilty again.

Seth led her to the door and turned to kiss her quick before he left, it was a fast but no less potent than their earlier kisses, "I was wondering if you would like to come to the ranch tomorrow?"

"I'd love to," Her smile returned, "I want to be with you as much as possible."

He was already wrapped up in the spell that was Raelynn, "I have to do some jumps in the morning but should be done early afternoon, I'll call you."

"Okay," Raelynn said, she would be so excited to see him again, "Goodnight."

He kissed her one last time, "Good night."

He left and Raelynn locked the door behind him. She leaned against it and took a shuddering breath.

Gathering her strength, she walked through her bedroom and into her bathroom to do her nightly routine. Once she looked in the mirror, she stopped and studied her reflection. She looked thoroughly made love too that was for sure. Nothing she could remember even came close to the erotic experience she just shared with Seth. He was absolutely amazing!

Shaking her head and taking a cleansing breath, she started washing her face. Ten minutes later, having washed up and brushed her teeth, she came into the living room and found her daughter sitting on the chair and staring at her with a funny smile on her face.

"Hailey?" She asked, "are you okay?" Her mom senses kicked in right away.

"I'm fine," Hailey responded, "how are you?" She wanted to know.

Oh Lord, Raelynn smiled shyly, she and Hailey didn't really talk about sex so it was uncomfortable. "I'm fine."

Hailey laughed and sat back, "Really?"

Now who was the mother here? "Yes," Raelynn said.

"Mom" Hailey leaned forward again, "I am happy to see you look happy."

How did she respond to that? "Thank you."

"I'm going to bed for real now, I just wanted to make sure you were okay," Hailey got up and kissed her mother on the forehead.

"Okay," Raelynn said, "sweet dreams."

Hailey laughed as she went down the hall to her room, "You too."

Raelynn laughed. Her daughter was wonderful. A lot of the reservations she held inside regarding Hailey started to dissipate. Her daughter was supportive and she was very thankful for that. On a whim, she went over to her phone and picked it up.

Her fingers shook, remembering what she did earlier with Seth, *I hope you made it home safely. I miss you already and can't wait until tomorrow.* She hit send.

She sat down on the couch, which she would never look at the same way again, and was channel surfing the tv when her phone pinged a response. She gasped with excitement as she read Seth's response.

I had to take the coldest shower in history and couldn't stop thinking of you. Thank you for a very exciting evening, I miss you too and will be happy when we see each other tomorrow. P.S. I can still smell your perfume on my shirt so I'm going to sleep with it next to me and dream of your sweet lips.

Did the man not know what kind of gem he was? He was texting her things she only dreamed of hearing a man say. Holy cow, she was going to jump his bones the first chance she got. She put her phone down and shut off the lights. She was still floating on after-glow as she drifted off to a peaceful sleep.

Saturday morning was bright and Raelynn woke up early. She thought it was probably from the excitement caused by a certain man. She made breakfast, not expecting to see Hailey for several hours yet. She was reading the paper when her phone rang. She was surprised because it wasn't even nine o'clock yet.

She looked at the caller ID and saw it was Melissa, "Hello," she said.

"Don't hello me young lady," Melissa demanded, "I want details."

Raelynn laughed, she was sure her sneaky little daughter notified her friend of what she walked into the evening before. "I'm afraid I don't kiss and tell."

Melissa pursed her lips, "You cannot keep me in the dark here, I know what Hailey said and it sounds like you had an amazing evening."

"I did thank you," She would throw her friend a bone, "it was very exciting, but I won't divulge any other details."

"You suck!" Melissa said it but didn't mean it, she was just so excited for her friend.

"That is not what I was told last evening," Raelynn blurted out, she knew it would get Melissa's goat. "I was told I was incredible."

"You were not!" Melissa yelled, no way, this was better than what she imagined.

Raelynn laughed again, "Yes."

"Are you seeing him today?" Melissa didn't care if she was being nosey.

Raelynn carried her plate to the sink and rinsed it with the phone tucked in her neck, "He is jumping this morning and will call me when he's done. He invited me to his place." She was getting nervous just thinking about it.

"Really?" Melissa purred, "don't forget to give Hailey the address, he seems nice but he could be a serial killer you know."

She loved Melissa, it was her penchant for the dramatic that made them mesh as friends in the first place, "Yes, mom." She replied sarcastically.

They hung up a few minutes later after Raelynn assured her that she would be safe and have a good time. Melissa did have a valid point though; she moved into her bedroom to make the bed and straighten up, they didn't know much about Seth. Even though they went out last night, neither really revealed much about their lives. A wiggle of doubt hung in Raelynn's mind as she showered and dressed for the day.

When she came out Hailey was hunched over a bowl of cereal at the kitchen table. Raelynn could not understand why her daughter was not a morning person; she and Anthony always got up early to face the day.

"Good morning daughter," She kissed the back of Hailey's head as she went by.

Hailey nodded and mumbled, "Morning," before returning to her bowl of cereal.

Raelynn folded the paper she read earlier and placed it in the recycle bin, "What's on your agenda for today?" They usually laid out plans first thing and then went about their day.

Hailey shrugged, "I think I'm going to go job hunting today with a couple of friends."

The comment surprised Raelynn, "Really?" They discussed Hailey working during college but she was under the impression she would support her daughter until she had her degree.

"Yes," Hailey turned to look at her mom, "I want to make some fun money and get out of the house."

The reasons seemed valid so why was Raelynn questioning her daughter's decision. "Are you sure?"

Hailey smiled, "Yes, I'm sure, I can't mooch off of you mom."

Raelynn was surprised, that comment was not what she expected from her daughter, "I haven't made you feel that way have I?"

Sighing, Hailey rinsed her cereal bowl and placed it in the dishwasher, "No mom, I'm sorry if I upset you, I just feel like I need to do some stuff on my own."

That, she could understand, Raelynn was much the same way in high school and that's what prompted her to go away to college in New York. "Okay sweetie."

Hailey went into her room and Raelynn stood in the kitchen and wondered if their relationship just took a turn.

Chapter 5

Raelynn watched Hailey go off on the job hunt with her friends and sat down on the sofa to read a book. She would read a couple of lines and then be distracted by either thoughts of her steamy love session with Seth the night before or worrying about what her daughter thought about all of this. She was sure, given Hailey's ecstatic reaction to the lists, that she was all for her mother getting into a relationship. But reality could be a big letdown and she was wondering if that's what Hailey felt.

She wanted Seth, that was apparent, but she wasn't sure that want was enough to upset the balance of her life with Hailey. It was just the two of them, had been for Hailey's whole life. She always thought it was the best thing she could do for Hailey but now she really questioned if it was the right thing. Hailey was so loved but she never had the love of a father. Raelynn knew, in her heart, that Anthony knew her and protected her but Hailey only knew her father through stories. She and her own father struggled for years to find closeness but she knew he loved her unconditionally. Would a relationship with Seth bring up unresolved issues for Hailey? Was it worth the risk to find out?

Raelynn sat on the sofa staring out the window and thinking about the upheaval she was feeling emotionally. The new sexual experiences were off the charts. According to what Seth said, they were pretty intense for him as well. But was sex enough? She was over thinking it, she knew that rationally but it didn't shut her brain off.

Her musings were interrupted by a text on her phone. She jumped up and checked it, thinking it was Seth but it was from Hailey. *Mom, we are going to lunch just wanted to let you know. Love you.*

She smiled at her phone, thankful that her daughter was so incredible. She was respectful and showed her love openly to Raelynn. She knew, from talking with other parents, that Hailey was not the norm within her generation. Raelynn was proud of herself and Hailey but now things were changing.

Another text showed up on her phone. This one was from Seth, *I'm on my way home. I'll call you when I'm cleaned up and give you directions. I can't wait to see you.*

The text was enough to get her blood pulsing. She so wanted to see him too and she was torn too between being with him and trying to see what was up with Hailey. Maybe now was the time to just sit back and see what happens. She responded to Seth first, *I will be waiting.*

She took a breath then responded to Hailey's text. *Ok sweetie. I've been invited to Seth's house this afternoon and will leave his address on the counter. Call my cell if you need me. I love you too and I'm proud of you.*

She smiled when Hailey's text came back, *Sounds good, have fun. Be good.*

Again, Raelynn wondered who the parent was and went to change clothes.

The drive to Seth's ranch was nice. Since it was clear, Raelynn put down the top and enjoyed the wind and sun on her face. She pulled her hair back with a clip to keep it out of her face and just enjoyed the scenery. She knew that this part of Texas was crisscrossed with country roads but she never took the time to explore them.

She followed Seth's directions and was surprised by how close he lived to her place, it only took twenty minutes and she laughed outright at when she turned into his driveway. It was a traditional ranch gate, complete with a huge SS on the top of it. He was really a cowboy. She drove through the gate and down the long gravel drive. There were fences on either side and she could see cattle and horses in the distance. How big was his ranch? She pulled up to a beautiful log cabin home, shut off the engine, and just stared.

Seth saw Raelynn come down the drive, he was watching out the living room window, excitement pulsing through his veins. He spent the day counting the minutes until they were together. A few of his co-workers at Spaceland gave him looks earlier, he was quieter than usual. Well, now she was here and that was all that mattered.

Raelynn smiled as Seth came out the front door and crossed the large porch on his way to meet her. He was in jeans that hugged his thighs, a tight gray t-shirt, cowboy boots, and was the sexiest thing Raelynn ever looked at.

"Hey," Seth said as he descended the front stairs and made his way to her car. He opened the door and helped her out, then he pulled her into his arms and kissed her senseless.

Raelynn was swept off her feet, "Wow, a girl can get used to that kind of greeting."

"I sure hope so," He said and grabbed her hand to lead her into the house.

She followed him inside and noticed that the house was much larger than she originally thought. It was gorgeous and rustic with modern touches. They went through a large entryway flooded with light from the glass door and into a great room. There was a large fireplace at the far end of the room; the furniture was large and overstuffed with splashes of color. It was cozy and Raelynn felt welcomed immediately. He led her to one of two of the couches in the room and sat down.

"How was your day?" He asked. He wanted to know everything about her.

Raelynn smiled, he was so sweet. "Quiet." She answered.

Something didn't seem right when Seth looked into her eyes, "Something happen?"

How could he read her so easily? "Well, I think that Hailey is reacting to our," she didn't have the word to describe what they were.

"Date?" Seth supplied, he didn't really know what to call what they had, it was too new.

Smiling again, she squeezed his hand, "Okay, date."

"Was she mad?" He didn't know how Hailey's reaction to him would play in all of this. From what little he knew of Raelynn, she was a devoted mother so if Hailey disapproved, they wouldn't stand a chance.

"No," She looked around the room, trying to form a rational thought. Being near Seth made that very difficult, "She said something about mooching off of me today, which is completely ridiculous."

He wasn't catching on to what was going on yet, "What do you think?"

Raelynn stood and paced in front of him, "I don't know what to think. She has been my whole world Seth for eighteen years and now you come along and I'm overwhelmed." She was being dramatic; she knew it but couldn't stop herself.

"Hey," Seth said, he pulled her back down to face him. "I'm probably talking out of turn here but I think you may be borrowing trouble where Hailey is concerned," he could see he stepped on her toes but they needed to clear this up, "I see her as this bright young lady who loves you and wants to see you happy."

Inside, Raelynn knew he was right. She was putting up barriers and there was no reason to do so. They only had one date, two if today counted. It was just so new and different and she was excited and.........and nothing, he was right. She nodded.

"You're right; I'll let her tell me if anything is wrong." She scooted closer and kissed him.

The kiss turned them both from cinders into a raging fire as soon as their lips met. She moved closer until she was leaning against him, she didn't want to sit on his lap after what happened last night. It was still embarrassing to admit she came just by kissing him. She wanted much more of him, in every sense.

They ended the kiss when they were both breathless, "Dear Lord woman, you are wearing me out." He said.

Chuckling, Raelynn rubbed his cheek with the back of her hand; the roughness of his stubble was soothing against her hand. "Ditto kind sir."

He stood up and pulled her up with him, "Well, I have a treat for you."

She loved treats, especially the sexual ones he was so keen on giving her. "Really?"

Her tone set his libido on edge, "Not that kind, not yet anyway. Come with me."

This was mysterious but Raelynn relished in his attention. She blindly followed him through the house; they passed the dining room and walked through a spaciously modern kitchen. She wanted to look around but it was clear Seth had a particular destination in mind.

They walked out the back of the house and headed toward the barn. It was a massive structure with two large doors that stood open. Raelynn could smell hay and leather; she assumed they were a normal part of ranch life. As they entered the barn, she could see the stalls along both sides. She was interested in stopping to peek at the horses but Seth was on a mission.

"Here we are," Seth said as they exited the back side of the barn.

Raelynn came out and stopped. There, in front of them, were two horses, saddled. They were beautiful, one spotted and the other a deep brown. Their coats glistened in the sunlight. She looked at Seth questioningly.

Seth brought her hand to his lips, "They are our transportation for the afternoon."

How could he have known that horseback riding was on her list? She looked from him to the horses and back again. "This was on my list."

Smiling, Seth was glad he chose the ride, "I'm glad I could do that for you then." He never asked her if she liked to ride and some people were very afraid of horses.

"They're gorgeous," Raelynn took a step forward then stopped, "which one is for me?"

Seth led her over to the brown horse, "This is Lucy and she's a very calm mare." He lifted Raelynn's hand and rubbed it over the mare's nuzzle.

Raelynn loved the slick feel of the mare's coat and she must have liked Raelynn's attention because she made a noise and moved her nose into Raelynn's shoulder. "Oh she's so sweet."

"I knew you two would get along," He gave Raelynn a quick squeeze. "Have you ridden before?"

She shook her head, "Yes, but it's been years."

"That's okay, once you're on, it will all come back to you." He gestured with his hands to boost her up into the saddle.

Once Raelynn was up and seated, Seth went around the horse making sure her stirrups were adjusted correctly and showed her where to hold the reigns. She was a little nervous but he made it sound so easy, she knew he would never give her something she couldn't handle.

Seth situated Raelynn then jumped up into his saddle. He explained his mount, Lex, was a painted horse who liked to get a little unruly from time to time. As soon as they were both seated and he was sure Raelynn was okay, they set out on a leisurely walk.

The sun shone brightly in the late afternoon, in the summer it would be oppressive but right now it was comfortable. He gave her a cowboy hat to wear so she wouldn't have to squint or get sunburn on her face. It was weird adjusting to the saddle but, once she got over her initial nervousness, she enjoyed the ride. Seth was knowledgeable and pointed out things that he thought she might like. Although, she just wanted to be with him so anything else was just a bonus.

The horses seemed to know where they were going so Raelynn and Seth were really just along for the ride. They talked about different experiences they had as kids and discussed Texas. Raelynn told him about her upbringing in the Midwest and he thought she adjusted well for being a yankee.

A couple of hours into their ride, Raelynn looked up to notice clouds moving in quickly overhead. "Should we be worried?" She asked Seth.

"I should've noticed before," He was mad at himself for not. They were at least several miles from the house and he was pretty sure they wouldn't beat the rain. "I know where we can go for some shelter." He clicked and guided the horse in a different direction. "Do you think you would be okay with a cantor?" He didn't want to put her in any danger.

Raelynn thought she could handle it, "Yes, I think I'm okay with that." She was a little worried that he seemed worried about the clouds; she could see rain in the distance.

Seth pointed ahead to a tree line, "Through there is a cabin we have on the property we use, we can put the horses in a shed nearby so they'll be out of the weather."

She nodded, "Whatever you say."

"Okay, here we go," He nudged his mount and gestured her to do the same.

The horses knew the drill and Lucy was great at following Lex. Raelynn held on how he instructed her to and didn't fear that she would fall off but knew her butt would be sore after they were done. She could see the cabin he mentioned and just then the rain started coming down.

They rode straight to the shed; Seth jumped off and motioned for her to get into the cabin while he got the horses settled. She ran for the door and was glad it opened easily. The cabin was small but seemed sound. She was wet and wrung out the bottom of her shirt. She looked at her new surroundings. There was a bunk in one corner, a fireplace in another and a table with a couple of chairs. Not the Ritz but it was quaint in a very rustic way. She turned around and found Seth standing in the doorway.

"I'm really sorry," He said as he stepped inside.

He was soaked clean through and thought she must really think he was an idiot for getting them caught in the rain. The truth was, he was just so content being with her that he lost track of time and didn't notice the change in weather.

Raelynn smiled, "You planned this didn't you?" She wanted to tease him.

He shook his head, "Yes, you got me, I thought, I'll get her out onto the property, then make it rain, so I can corner her in the worst cabin ever."

She laughed, he was so cute, "I thought so."

They were both laughing as he shut the door.

He went to the fireplace and found some paper to start it. "It will get cold with our clothes being wet so I'll start a fire."

"We could always just take them off," Raelynn offered and then realized what she said. Oh.....

Seth turned to face her, he couldn't say anything. He just looked at her, her hair matted to her head, her wet shirt clinging to her; he could see her nipples jut against the fabric. He finally found the courage to walk towards her.

He swallowed hard, "Is that what you want?"

Oh yes, Raelynn's body was yelling, but her brain was unsure. Once he touched her though, she was a goner and nodded slowly.

He stepped closer and cupped her face in his palms, looking at her eyes until their lips met. Her mouth was so hot! He moved his hands down her shoulders and arms and around her until they were cupping her bottom. He squeezed gently, pulling her to him.

Oh sweet Lord, he was so good. Raelynn didn't feel her wet clothes, she didn't care that they were in the middle of a storm because the one inside her was out of control and took over all of her senses.

He pulled her shirt up and over her head, once it was gone, he started tasting her shoulder. Her skin was slick from the rain and she tasted sweet. One hand moved up to wrap her waist and hold her to him while his mouth ravaged her. She was shaking and he couldn't tell if it was because of his loving or if she was cold.

He pulled his head up, "Are you okay?"

She was floating in a haze of want so it was difficult to get her lips to function, "Yes, please make love to me Seth."

How could any sane man resist such a beautiful request? He wasn't sane right now but he would never deny them what they both wanted. He moved his fingers up and gently pushed her hair back from her face. Her skin was soft and flushed from his erotic attentions. Her eyes were dark with want and he smiled.

Leading her by the hand, he went to the bunk, it was a small bed, meant for one but neither of them seemed to care as he grabbed a blanket from a shelf on the wall nearby and laid it over the mattress. Then he turned to her and pulled off her camisole. The only sound in the room was their ragged breathing. He tossed the wet clothing aside and looked at her, she was standing there in jeans, tennis shoes, and a bra and she was the sexiest thing he ever saw. He watched her chest rise and fall causing the lace top of her bra to move in an exquisite dance against her skin. He reached behind her and unhooked her bra, letting it fall to the floor so he could see her breasts.

Raelynn could barely breathe, he was slowly removing her clothes and she could only stand there and watch him do it. As soon as her breasts were free she raised her arms and gently guided his head toward them. She wanted him to taste her. As he suckled first one nipple, then the other, she thought she would go up in flames for wanting him.

"I know baby," He murmured against her nipple, "I want it too."

His soft breath made her hum with pleasure, she looked into his eyes, "We need to get your clothes off too."

Far be it for Seth to disregard the lady's request, "Help yourself."

He wanted her to undress him. Raelynn felt a rush of heat stream through her belly as she pulled his shirt up and over his shoulders. His chest was muscled and dusted with hair that ached for her to touch it. She did what she wanted, she ran her hands all over him, and lightly rubbed her fingers in circles around his nipples until the urge to taste was too strong. She returned the favor he gave her and felt him tense when her tongue flicked his nipple.

She ran her fingers around the waistline of his jeans until they found the fly and she popped the buttons with her fingers quickly. She could feel him strain against the fabric and felt herself pulse with the knowledge that she made him so hard. Once the back of her fingers brushed against his hardness, he jumped. She couldn't help but giggle.

"Are you okay?" She asked innocently.

Seth thought she was adorable, she was flush with want and yet she could find humor in his condition. "Was this," he kissed her lips, "by chance," another kiss, "the appetite you were texting about on the phone?"

He was so wonderful, "No," Raelynn laughed and pushed his jeans down his hips, "this is just the appetizer." She laughed outright at his shocked expression. "I'll let you know when we get to the main course." Her tongue snaked out and flicked his bottom lip.

That was the last straw for Seth; he turned her so she was facing away from him. Her bottom was tucked against his hard arousal and he caressed her breasts while kissing her neck and shoulders. Once she was panting, he knew she was ready and reached down to undo her pants. They fell down to the floor in a wet pile and she stepped out of them. They each took a second to get off their shoes and socks and grabbed for one another, falling onto the bunk.

They were both laughing trying to touch and kiss everywhere. Limbs were tangled and slid easily with the rain water still clinging to them. Breath caught and they explored each other thoroughly. Finally Raelynn couldn't take it any longer.

She sat up and looked at Seth, "I need you inside of me, now."

He could not deny her this either, "My pleasure."

He stood up so she could have room to lie out on the bunk. Her body was ready for him and her eyes summoned him. She was gorgeous, her hair framing her head and her lips swollen from his kisses. He gently pulled her legs apart so he could watch her when he first touched her. His fingers were soft as they travelled up her thighs. He watched her as she watched him. The dance lovers danced was never so erotic to him and he knew she felt the same, their souls were one as he sat beside her and moved his fingers up to the apex of her thighs. His fingers deftly parted the curls covering her sex and his first touch of her almost drove him insane. She was so wet and ready for him. She moaned and he could not resist, he climbed over her and rested his hard sex against her intense heat.

Raelynn arched up trying to give her body release, he was right there and he didn't enter her. What was wrong? Her eyes flew open and she panicked.

"I want to watch you baby," He whispered and exhaled softly as he finally entered her.

Her mouth formed an oh, she could not speak as the absolutely breathtaking sensations took over her. She spread her legs wider so he could settle into her. Once he started moving, she was lost and her body took over, it knew exactly what to do.

Seth pumped into her so hard and fast that he thought his heart would beat right out of his chest. He was so close to release but didn't want to go over without her.

Raelynn could feel it build, the intense pressure inside her was trying to get out, she threw her head back when it finally was too much, "Seth, please." She yelled.

"I know baby, I want us to come together," He murmured to her and they both crested the wave together.

Oh Lord, it was amazing! Raelynn smiled and fell back sprawled out on the bunk. Seth was over her but shifted so she wasn't bearing all his weight. When strength returned to her limbs, she ran her fingers up and down his back. He was slick from their lovemaking. She was smug with satisfaction that she did that to him.

A while later, when their breathing was normal again, Seth shifted to his side and tucked her in front of him so he could hold her more fully. "How are you doing?" He mumbled into her hair.

Raelynn looked over her shoulder and smiled, "Is it possible to die from pleasure?"

He was relieved she found release, he was so afraid she wouldn't be able to. "I don't think so but you never know."

Raelynn turned over so they were face to face and body to body. Her hands leisurely explored his hips and side up to his ribs and tugged playfully on his chest hair. "I have never been so thoroughly made love to Seth, thank you." She was embarrassed because tears came to her eyes.

He wanted to reassure her, "You are most definitely welcome." Brushing her hair from her face he didn't want to be anywhere else but here with her. "I think we have a problem here."

Raelynn's eyes darted around, what was wrong? "What's that?"

"I don't think I can keep my hands off of you and I want to make love to you again," He wasn't going to lie to her about what he wanted.

She laughed, "I think we can arrange something."

She wrapped her arms around him and pulled him on top of her. They were kissing and moving to get more comfortable. This time was quicker than the first; they knew what they wanted and didn't waste time melding their bodies. He pulled her legs up so her bottom was off the bed; enabling him to drive into her harder and faster. She could feel the muscles of his thighs as they pounded against hers, the thought driving her over the edge fast. She yelled outright as her climax pummeled her insides. He was right behind her and growled as his own orgasm came.

The lay in a heap on the bunk; and enjoyed their newly found intimacy. Seth finally noticed that the rain stopped and suggested they get back to the ranch.

It was not on Raelynn's list of priorities but the real world was bound to intrude some time. She got up and laughed as they each searched for their clothes. There was a small mirror on a wall near the kitchen area of the cabin. She glanced in the mirror and grimaced at her appearance. Her hair looked like it was ravaged by a pack of wild dogs. Her lips were swollen. She looked, thoroughly loved. She smiled and went outside to see what Seth was up to. The rain left and in its wake was humidity. The temperature was mild but she felt sticky. Oh well. She noticed Seth leading the horses out and realized she needed to use the bathroom. This was embarrassing. What's so embarrassing, the man saw every part of you, just let him know.

Seth led the horses out and saw Raelynn looking uncomfortable. He hoped she didn't regret their lovemaking because he most certainly did not. "Are you okay?" He asked as he neared her.

"Um," Raelynn looked around, "is there a bathroom?"

Seth smiled, "Behind the cabin there's an outhouse."

She nodded, "Thank you."

Raelynn took care of her bodily functions and would be thankful for indoor plumbing from now on. She came back around the cabin to find Seth waiting patiently with their horses. She walked up to him and gave him a kiss, "Thank you."

He didn't care what she was thanking him for, he loved her kisses. "As I said before, my pleasure."

"Dear God, I hope so," She said as she got on her horse.

Goodness she was going to drive him to distraction with her cuteness. He got up on his horse and they started back home.

It was getting dark by the time they reached the barn, Raelynn was surprised that they were gone so long. Surprisingly, her butt didn't hurt but a few other parts were sore. That, she could handle.

They dismounted and a ranch hand appeared seemingly out of nowhere to take the horses away and rub them down from their adventure. Seth took her hand and they walked slowly back through the barn and back to the house. She was starting to pout for fear that their time together would end.

Seth felt her start to tense as they neared the house. He watched her and noticed her facial expression change. He opened the door and let her enter first. Once they were in the kitchen he steered her to one of the chairs at the table and guided her to sit.

"Okay, what's up?" He asked as he sat across from her.

Raelynn looked at him, her head cocked, "Why do you ask?"

Seth took her hand, "I'm no expert at the puzzle that is Raelynn yet, but I can feel the change in you."

Was it possible for him to read her so well after only two days? Had they only been "dating" for two days? This was a lot to take in for her. She didn't know what to say.

"I guess," She smiled shyly, "I am reluctant to let you go."

He stood and kissed her on the lips, "Why do you have to?"

It was a question Raelynn chewed on while he got up from the table. She was still contemplating it when she saw him set a glass and plate in front of her. He was so sweet.

"What's this?" She asked and looked up into his beautiful blue eyes.

Seth took his plate and glass to the seat next to hers and set it down, "My sorry excuse for a dinner I suppose."

They dug into the sandwiches, the afternoon's activities drained them and they needed some source of energy. After the food and drink were consumed they took their dishes to the sink and washed them quickly. Then, they went into the great room and snuggled on the couch while a movie played quietly in the background.

Raelynn woke feeling warm and cozy; once she opened her eyes and didn't immediately recognize her surroundings so she shot upright. Oh yes, she was at Seth's house.

"Are you okay?" Seth asked, he felt her move and woke up.

Raelynn was looking around for her purse and phone, "What time is it?"

Stretching, Seth looked over at the clock on the wall, "I think about midnight."

"Crap, really?" She asked feeling around in the semi-darkness for her things.

"Raelynn, what's wrong?" Seth asked her, she looked like a deer caught in head lights.

Panic set in, "I never called Hailey to check in, she's probably worried sick." Finally she found her phone and dropped her head when she saw missed calls from Hailey. She quickly hit dial and let it ring. Hailey picked up on the second ring.

"Hey baby, it's mom," Raelynn said softly, "did I wake you?"

Hailey smiled at the clock, her mom was so busted, "Nope, whacha doin?"

"I'm sorry, we fell asleep. I'm still at Seth's place." She looked around for her shoes and started slipping them on.

"Mom," Hailey was touched that her mom was worried, "stay there, I'm fine. I only called earlier to let you know the girls and I went to dinner and then when I got home."

"Are you sure?" Raelynn was feeling decidedly uncomfortable now. She snuck a peek at Seth who was lounging on the couch she just vacated. He looked calm.

Hailey giggled, "Yes, I'm sure. Let's just remember this little incident when I call to say I'm staying at my boyfriend's place okay?"

Her daughter was a gem, "Yes, next one is on me." She smiled for the first time, "Good night."

"Good night mom," She took a breath then yelled, "GOOD NIGHT SETH!"

Raelynn watched Seth laugh and felt relief, "He heard you, I'll call in the morning."

She hung up the phone and dropped it back into her purse. She slowly got up and walked over to him. He was just looking up at her like he didn't have a care in the world. When she was next to the couch, he opened his arms and she crawled into the cradle of his body.

He wrapped his arms around her and breathed in her scent, "Crisis averted?"

"Yes," She sighed and settled in the comfort of his body immediately. They were both asleep in minutes.

The morning sun in her eyes, Raelynn woke in increments. Her limbs felt so heavy. She tried to move them but they wouldn't budge. When her mind was more alert, she realized Seth was wrapped around her. If it weren't for the insistence of her bladder, she would be most happy to stay there. He was warm and made her feel so safe. She opened her eyes and looked up into blue eyes staring at her.

Seth woke early, a hazard of living on a ranch, and laid there watching Raelynn sleep. Her breathing was deep and even so he knew she was out cold and didn't want to disturb her. She was beautiful, even with having been riding horses, caught in the rain, making crazy love, and sleeping on a couch. What was the deal with them and couches? He was lost in his musings until he felt her move and look up at him.

He smiled, "Good morning beautiful."

Raelynn was fairly certain that she looked anything but beautiful. "Hi," she muffled her mouth against his shoulder because she hadn't brushed her teeth yet.

He released her and they both got up slowly. "There is a bathroom off of my room, go upstairs and it's at the end of the hall."

How did he know? Seth just knew. "Thank you," She started up the stairs slowly. Boy was she sore this morning.

Seth used the guest bath downstairs, splashed water on his face, and finger combed his hair. Looking in the mirror he thought he looked pretty smug. Fantastic sex could certainly do wonders for a man. He walked out and, not hearing Raelynn come down, went into the kitchen to make them breakfast.

Raelynn walked through Seth's bedroom and felt like a voyeur. The room was large, the master she assumed, with a huge bed dominating the space. There were several dressers and an overstuffed leather chair in the corner with a small reading lamp next to it. A magazine was folded open over the arm of the chair. It was neat and the bed was made but it smelled like Seth which drove her nerve endings crazy.

She entered the master bathroom and gasped. It was huge! There was a large Jacuzzi tub big enough for two people, an equally impressive shower with glass walls and two shower heads. She went to the sink farther in the room; the first one looked like the one he used. She opened the drawers and located a washcloth, a hand towel, and even a new toothbrush. After taking care of her personal hygiene needs she neatly folded the washcloth and towel and went back downstairs to find him.

Chapter 6

Raelynn found him in the kitchen. He was running from the table with dishes to checking the pans on the stove. She stood in the door way and quietly observed him. His movements were confident so she supposed he was comfortable in the kitchen. Whatever he was cooking smelled great so she entered the room.

"Can I help?" She asked with more confidence than she felt. How did she act when she spent the night with someone? She certainly had no real experience.

Seth smiled, "Yes, thanks." He pointed to the refrigerator, "Would you mind getting the juice out?" He stirred the scrambled eggs. "There is orange, apple, and grapefruit in there, help yourself to whatever you prefer."

Raelynn grabbed the orange juice, put it on the table, then walked up behind him and slid her hands up his back to rub his shoulders.

She whispered in his ear, "What do you prefer?"

How did the woman make a simple question sound so sexy? He turned around and pulled her to him, "I prefer you." He kissed her hard.

Raelynn was in the clouds, his lips were better than any breakfast she could eat.

Slowly, Seth pulled his lips away; he didn't want to burn their breakfast.

She watched him and smiled, knowing she made him as riled as she was. They sat down, Seth spooning eggs, sausage, potatoes onto their plates.

"My goodness," Raelynn said her eyes large. "I don't know if I can possibly eat all of this."

Seth chuckled, "I'm used to large helpings for myself and the ranch hands, sorry. You eat what you can."

Raelynn cocked her head and studied him, "You know, you are a very nice man."

"Ahhh," Seth put down his fork, "Raelynn, men don't want to be called nice, it makes them think that they are about to be dumped." He shook his head solemnly, "Men want to be called dangerous, sexy, bad boys."

She couldn't help it, she had to laugh. "Are you serious?"

"No," Seth said, his smile peaking through, "I'm just messing with you."

Raelynn tried to glare but it was virtually impossible when she knew he was joking, "Would it help if I told you that you were sexy," she leaned over and ran a finger up his arm, "and told you that you make my body tremble when you touch me."

The air went from comfortable to charged in a millisecond. Holy crap, she was so hot! "Um," he swallowed, "yes."

She laughed, "You are cute." She leaned over and gave him a peck on the cheek and sat back down to concentrate on her food.

They ate in comfortable silence, each commenting on little things. Raelynn asked about the house and he asked her about her business. She felt content, way too content, for only having known the man for a week or so. It was like the more they knew, the better it felt, but the more she grew worried. Not having had a relationship in years, she wasn't sure what to expect.

They took a walk around the property after breakfast. He smiled when Raelynn insisted she clean up breakfast since he cooked. Now they walked and talked about the ranch, she was curious as to what a working ranch did. He was patient with her questions, asking a few of his own here and there. They were leaning against the fence of a training corral when she looked at him with serious eyes.

"What do you want?" She asked pointedly. The nerves were back again.

He looked at her smiling, "You."

Well that was direct, and sexy as Hell. How was she supposed to have a serious conversation with him when he made her insides curl up in a tight ball of need?

She smiled and looked across the corral to see a ranch hand bring a young horse in. She watched him coax the animal into the ring and watched as he put the horse through some paces.

"Thank you," She finally answered, "but that's not exactly what I meant."

Seth stood, one boot hooked on the bottom rail, his senses on full alert. He could joke but he knew when a woman wanted to have a serious conversation. This was it and he was afraid she would not want to be with him because he didn't have an answer. They only started dating, he hoped to take it slow and see what happened.

He looked at her, his eyes serious, "I know what you meant, I was buying some time because it's not an easy question to answer."

It was interesting how he knew what she meant. Over the years, she heard a lot of her friends, Melissa included, express how men were oblivious to women's wants. She appreciated that he at least made an effort.

"No it's not," She was as confused as she suspected she was. "I want to be with you as much as possible."

Searching Raelynn's eyes, he knew she was conflicted. He knew enough about her to know that she would be uncomfortable with how to navigate through a relationship. It wasn't exactly familiar territory for him either.

"I want to be with you, but I understand that this is new and we'll go as slow as you want." He leaned in, tipped his hat up a bit, and kissed her softly.

Her nerves sung when his lips met hers. It was difficult to not beg him to take her inside and beg him to make love to her again.

The horse in the ring made a noise, which made Raelynn jump. She turned her head and could see the hand was struggling to get the animal to calm down. Without a word, Seth climbed over the fence and approached the animal slowly. He spoke softly and, within a few minutes, had the horse allowing him near. It was sweet to watch him rub the horse's nuzzle. She observed him for a while, just watching the way he moved. It was obvious the men who worked on the ranch respected him and he them. You could tell a lot about someone by how they interacted with their co-workers. Raelynn could respect the way he handled himself.

After a while, she decided to head back to the house and get her things. It was time to go. He was still working in the corral and she didn't want to interrupt him. She needed some time to think through their intimacy and how she wanted to proceed.

She was getting her phone and putting it in her purse when she heard Seth come in.

"Raelynn?" Seth asked as he came into the kitchen.

She answered, "In here," she grabbed her jacket.

He found her near the front door, "Are you leaving?"

Raelynn nodded, "Yes, I need to do my weekend errands and talk to Hailey and get ready for the week at work." She was babbling, she knew it.

"Is everything okay?" He could see she was thinking about something.

She smiled and touched his cheek with her hand, loving the way the stubble tickled her palm, "Yes, very okay."

He wasn't sure but he would let her go. "Okay, call me later?"

Nothing would keep her from that, "Of course."

Seth walked her out to her car, tucked her in, and waived as she turned down the driveway. He couldn't shake the feeling that he'd missed something.

The drive home was quick and Raelynn sighed when she entered the condo. She could hear Hailey somewhere doing something. The child was not quiet at all.

"Hello," she yelled out.

Hailey came out of her room and met her mother in the living room. "Hello, how does it feel to have a walk of shame?"

She was now officially embarrassed, "Thank you for your sensitivity." She kissed her daughter on the forehead.

Hailey turned to go back to her room, "Anytime," she was laughing.

Raelynn shook her head, the child was incorrigible. She threw her purse on the counter and went to shower and change.

The rest of the day was nice and quiet. She did her chores, made out her plan for the week, and had a quiet dinner with Hailey. She would think of Seth a lot but tried to put him out of her mind and focus on her time at home.

That evening, as she and Hailey sat in the living room watching a home remodeling show they were fond of, Hailey turned to her and looked serious. Raelynn muted the television and turned her attention to her daughter.

"Is there something you need to say Hailey," It was a statement, not a question.

Hailey smiled, "How does he make you feel mom?"

Wow, that was not what she was expecting Hailey to say. She looked down at her hands for a moment and looked back at Hailey. It was not something she could easily describe.

"Well," She cleared her throat, "he makes me feel special and protected." The words were tough to find.

Hailey nodded, "That's good, you need that mom."

She wondered what prompted the question. "Are you okay with me seeing him?"

"Oh yes," Hailey answered quickly, "I only ask because I've not really dated too much and wanted to know what I should look for."

How sweet was that? "Hailey, I think you should be with someone who makes you happy to be you, someone who never makes you feel bad for it, who supports your wants and dreams."

Hailey's eyebrows shot up, she was surprised by the comment, "Then how come you've not found someone before now?"

Funny that Raelynn always thought they were so close. This was something they never talked about and that saddened her.

She didn't know how to answer, but the answer was simple, "I never thought anyone was worth it before now."

She smiled as Hailey nodded. They were now finally two adults talking, not mother and daughter. The shift was apparent and Raelynn knew it would happen but didn't want to admit her little girl was all grown up.

Hailey got up to make some popcorn which was her way of saying the conversation was over. Raelynn could respect that, there were a lot of changes going on but she was confident they would make their way through it.

Sunday nights usually ended with them both going to bed a bit earlier and Raelynn got ready as she always did. Once in bed, though, she couldn't sleep. She missed Seth which was ridiculous since they only spent one night together, on a couch no less. She punched her pillow and finally resigned herself that she had to let him know.

She picked up her phone and started typing, *I hope you aren't in bed already, but if you are, I wish I was with you.*

The phone was silent for less than a minute before his response pinged, *I am not in bed because you would be all I was thinking about if I was. I missed you after you left.*

How did he know what she was thinking? Her fingers flew over the keys, *I am in bed, all alone, and aching for you.*

Seth sat at the desk in his home office. The day was spent doing the mundane paperwork necessary for ranch operations but he wished he was with Raelynn instead. He became almost giddy when her text came through. She was so exciting when she texted, she made him hard and needy. He loved it.

If you want to come over, I can help you solve that problem. Slowly, of course, we would probably need all night to figure out exactly what is the best way to solve your "aching." This banter was making him physically uncomfortable but there was nothing he would rather be doing.

Raelynn gasped at his response, it made her tremble, thinking of him helping her with her "ache." She would certainly like to figure that out. *Not sure you could keep up, I ache a lot you know.*

He laughed, she was a flirt, *I would give it my very best effort. We could take it slow or fast, I would even help you decide you wanted to be on top of the situation.*

These texts were definitely taking a more intense turn. She had to think of exactly the right response. *I believe you would "try" but I need some guarantees here sir. My aches are serious business, requiring personal attention and full cooperation.*

Seth laughed, *Would you like references? I am sure I can find someone to vouch for my abilities. As a matter of fact, I enjoyed the company of a very delectable woman just yesterday. I think if you spoke to her she would put in a good word.*

Raelynn's smile faded as she started reading but returned when she understood what he meant. She was embarrassed by her candor in their texts but he was so intriguing. She felt sexy and wanton around him. *If she's a lady, she would never kiss and tell. However, I myself enjoyed the company of a very intensely sexy gentleman yesterday if you'd care to speak with him. I am pretty sure he'll give me a good recommendation.*

Whoa, the woman was intriguing; *A true gentleman does not kiss and tell either so we'll have to just go with our gut on this one. If you care to, you can come over and I'll show you what I mean, I believe a demonstration is in order.*

Oh how she wanted to go, but it wasn't in her to do so. She was always the rational one, and this one time she didn't want to be rational, she wanted to throw everything into the wind and feel and touch and taste everything he offered. The throbbing spread through her belly, winding its way to her sex and she was almost panting as she thought about their lovemaking in the little cabin.

Seth was worried, she didn't answer. Did he say something wrong? *Are you okay? Did I say something to offend you? I didn't mean to if I did.*

The phone pinging brought Raelynn out of her fantasy, she was beet red, *No Seth, you didn't. I was actually replaying our little escapade yesterday in my mind and am now in a very needy physical state.*

He read her text and was puzzled, *Then why aren't you on your way over here so we can make love all night long?*

Because, Raelynn sighed as she typed her response, *as much as I want to, I have obligations.*

Seth nodded and typed, *I understand what you are saying, I just want you to know that the two aren't mutually exclusive. I promise I won't intentionally interrupt your life, I just want you and I'll take whatever time you can give.*

Where did this man come from? Now a different ache was filling her chest. She only felt like this one other time and she wasn't willing to open that door yet. Fighting her feelings was what she was accustomed to doing. *Thank you for that. I will call you this week if that's okay. Good night.*

He read the text and couldn't help but think he did something wrong. Sometimes navigating the waters of a new relationship was rough and he was a patient man so he would deal, *Good night Raelynn, please snuggle into your pillows and feel me holding you close.*

The next morning, when Raelynn woke, she felt tears on her cheeks. She didn't remember what she dreamt so it was weird that she was crying. She got up and showered, all the time replaying her text conversation with Seth. Applying shampoo and rubbing it into lather; she recalled their first meeting at Skydive Spaceland. She shut him down pretty quickly. Why was that? He was handsome. His hair was light brown with just a hint of wave. She thought about how his cowboy hat left a ring through it when he took it off at the cabin. That train of thought took her through the rest of her shower, her hair, and her makeup.

As she slipped on her skirt and shirt, she wondered what he thought of her. She finished getting ready, made lunches, and was out the door. The drive to work was spent listening to soft rock music. The day was bright, the sky blue, the breezes light, it was perfect.

Once in her office, Raelynn put all thoughts of Seth out of her mind and focused on work. Melissa was a little late, having met with a client over breakfast at a local diner. She thought that was why they were so successful; Melissa's personality really drew in business.

When Raelynn looked up again, it was lunch time. She went into the little kitchen they had for employees and sat at the table eating her tuna salad sandwich and yogurt.

"There you are," Melissa plopped down across from her with a salad and dug in. "How was your morning?"

"It was fine," Raelynn sipped her water, "yours?"

Melissa stood and walked to the refrigerator to get a water, "Good, I think we'll get that account," she took a drink of water from the bottle, "I heard you stayed at Seth's house Saturday night."

The hairs on Raelynn's neck stood up, she was embarrassed from head to toe. It was one thing for Hailey to know but her friends? She wasn't sure about that just yet. There was, however, no use in lying to Melissa, the woman could give CIA interrogators a run for their money, "Yes," she said quietly.

Melissa sat down and leaned closer, "I want to know everything."

"You will not know anything, it's personal." Raelynn certainly didn't feel comfortable revealing details of her and Seth's lovemaking without his permission.

Shaking her head, Melissa patted Raelynn's hand, "I knew you'd be tight-lipped, perhaps I should call Seth?"

Oh no, "You wouldn't do that would you?" Her palms were sweaty.

Melissa sat back, her eyes large, "Of course not!" She looked at Raelynn, "Are you afraid?"
This was so crazy, "No, I would just be mortified if you called him."

Interesting, Melissa thought, "Did you have fun at least? I'm sure it's okay for you to divulge that."

"Oh yes!" Raelynn blurted out breathlessly, the red crept into her cheeks again, "it was amazing."

Okay, this is the best part, "REEEAAALLLYYY?" Melissa never saw this side of Raelynn. When they met, she was newly married to Anthony and within weeks he was gone. This change in her friend was amazing.

"Yes really," Raelynn said quietly. "That's all I'm saying, eat your lunch."

"Yes ma'am," Melissa said dutifully and dug into her salad. She couldn't keep from smiling though.

The afternoon flew by and Raelynn organized her desk just as she always did. There was great comfort in the day to day routine she developed over the years. As she got into her new car to go home, she considered how maybe comfort wasn't at the top of her list of needs anymore.

Driving home, she hummed along to the radio, undid the top button of her blouse and just daydreamed. She shocked herself when she impulsively turned off the highway onto FM 1462. There was only one reason she would go this route. Without delving into her psyche, she just went with her gut. Isn't that what Seth recommended anyway just last night?

She pulled into the parking lot and was surprised by the number of cars there on a Monday afternoon. Not everyone works nine to five Monday through Friday Raelynn, she said to herself as she got out of the car.

Nearing the hangar, her pulse sped up. There was only one reason she was here and that was to see Seth. Of course, she paused at the hangar doorway; they never discussed what either of their schedules was for the week. Maybe he wasn't even here? She took a breath and continued inside.

She walked up to the board that listed the instructors and videographers and their assignments. She didn't see his name so thought maybe he wasn't working today. On impulse, she walked out to the observation area. There was a group just starting their landing approach and she watched as they gently came down.

It was so freeing, she thought as she recalled her own jump just a little over a week ago. It was still fresh, the feeling of being alive and experiencing something so profound. She wondered if these people felt the same way.

"Do you know someone jumping?" A quiet voice asked.

A feeling of de ja vu snuck up her spine, she didn't turn around, "No, I'm just watching and wondering if these jumpers feel the same way that I felt." She turned around slowly, "You see, I did my first skydive recently and it was amazing."

Seth stared at her; she was a sight to behold, her frame backlit by the late afternoon sun. He was putting his gear away for the day when he thought he saw her walk outside to the observation area. At first, he thought his mind was playing tricks since she was never far from his mind. When he walked out and saw her there in her business clothes, hair up, and her conservative heels, the punch to his gut threw him. He watched her for maybe two minutes but he couldn't keep away.

"And how was it? Your first jump I mean?" He drawled.

She stepped closer, being sure not to touch him, "It was amazing, sensual. I thought it took my breath away."

Just her words set his body on fire, "Are you ready to do it again?"

Raelynn was pretty sure they weren't talking about skydiving anymore.

"I'm pretty sure I'm up for it, are you?" She whispered in his ear, still not touching him.

She didn't wait for him to answer, just walked past him, through the hangar and out to where her car was parked. It was very uncharacteristic for her to do, but she did that when she was around Seth. She clicked the unlock button on her keys and was about to get into the car when she heard footsteps.

She was leaving? Seth couldn't believe it. They were flirting and he was on fire and she was just walking away. He ran out to the parking lot and caught up to her when she was at her car. He was on the opposite side.

"Are you leaving?" He asked.

Raelynn smiled, "I guess so."

This was not how he thought this conversation would go, "Why?"

It was simple to her, "Because you've not asked me not to stay."

How could one statement from her make him burn uncontrollably? "Stay," he whispered.

Raelynn didn't understand herself much less him right now. Why was she acting this way? Why was she so drawn to him and so afraid at the same time? She gathered her strength and started to walk around the car to where he stood. She didn't say anything, just stared into his eyes until she was right in front of him. She took his face into her hands and brought his mouth down to hers. Their lips met and explosions of need went off throughout her body. She boldly explored his lips and mouth with her own.

He watched her come around the car and kiss him. There was no rational thought after that. He didn't touch her except where their lips met and melded. All of his senses were firing and he was overcome with need but it was her call.

The kiss ended once Raelynn pulled back, her breathing was ragged and she was flushed with want. She opened her eyes slowly and looked into Seth's. What was he thinking? She was thinking that if she didn't get away from him soon, she'd ask him to make love to her right there.

He just watched her, a myriad of emotions flickered across her face, her eyes told the whole story though, she was confused. He wasn't all that clear right now either so he could empathize.

"Wow," He said.

Raelynn smiled slowly, she felt the same way, "Yes."

"Come home with me," He looked back at the hangar, realizing he was still at work. "I have to get my stuff and we'll go to my place."

It would be so easy, she thought, to do that. But it wasn't right. At least not for her.

"I can't." She said softly.

Seth didn't want to pressure her but he wanted her like a man wanted water after days in the desert.

He put his forehead against hers, his breathing still unsteady, "I understand."

She was surprised, "Do you?"

Seth smiled, she was so beautiful, "Do I understand why you won't go home with me and let me make love to you until we're both exhausted and can't physically move? No, but I understand that you may feel overwhelmed because I do."

Raelynn couldn't help herself, she laughed. "You are crazy but it's adorable." She pulled away so she could look at him fully, "I am overwhelmed Seth, thank you for understanding."

He watched her walk back to the driver's side of the car, "Can I call you?"

She smiled, "I'd be very upset if you didn't."

Raelynn got into the car and buckled her seatbelt, she saw him come to the driver's side so she put down her window. "Yes sir?"

Seth impulsively reached in and caressed her cheek with the back of his fingers; her skin was soft and made him ache. He didn't know what he wanted to say exactly, he just didn't want her to go.

She looked up into those blue eyes and felt like she was swimming in a fog of sensations; there was no way a woman could think when a man looked at her this way. Why was she leaving? She covered his fingers with her own, squeezing slightly.

"I have to go," She said unconvincingly.

He smiled, she was as lost as he was, "I know."

Her phone pinged and she looked down at it, it was a text from Hailey. *Hey Mom a friend of mine thinks she knows Seth, what's his last name*

Raelynn read the text and alarm swept through her. She didn't know.

Seth noticed the change in her, "Is everything okay?" He asked.

She looked at Seth, "Hailey wants to know your last name." She was mortified. Her daughter asked a perfectly legitimate question and she didn't know the answer. She slept with this man, stayed at his house, and didn't know his last name. What kind of person was she? What kind of example was she setting for Hailey?

"No," Raelynn was trying not to cry, "I just realized I don't know your last name," She wanted to be anywhere but here right now.

Seth didn't understand, "It's Rhodes."

Raelynn picked up her phone and typed the response to Hailey, *It's Rhodes.*

She put the phone down in the cup holder and started her car. She needed to leave. "I have to go."

Seth knew that their conversation was over, "Okay," he said and pulled his hand out of the window.

He watched her pull out of the driveway and knew something more involved was going on here besides his name. Once her vehicle was out of sight, he slowly went back inside to collect his stuff.

Raelynn drove home safely despite feeling like she was going to throw up everywhere. She was embarrassed by her irresponsible behavior. Had she not been with Seth when Hailey texted, what would she have said? He probably thought she was a lunatic or something but that couldn't be helped. She was a mother first, that meant that she was the adult and had to set a good example of behavior for Hailey.

Hailey was her whole life from the moment she was born until now. She wanted her daughter to be proud of her and this was not the way to do it. Hailey needed her to be what she had been all along, the rock that held them together. No man could just come in and take that away! Not even a man that made her head spin and her pulse race and made her body come alive.

She fixed dinner, picked at her food, and went to bed early. She heard Hailey come in the door and pretended to be asleep when she heard her enter the bedroom. She couldn't face her just yet. It was cowardice but she needed to figure it out.

Tuesday was cloudy which mirrored Raelynn's mood. She got up and did what she did every day but it was done without thinking. Her thoughts were muddled as she drove into work. When she got there, she immediately asked the interns not to disturb her. That was cowardice too but she needed to be alone for a while.

She managed to speak very little during the work day which suited her just fine. She was relieved that Melissa was out with client meetings so she wouldn't be subjected to her friend's questions.

Once home, she changed into her workout clothes and did a solid hour at the complex's gym. It was a big reason she chose the condo, the amenities were great. After her workout, she spent twenty minutes in the sauna, hoping that her mood would be lifted along with the steam. No such luck.

She and Hailey had a nice dinner, her daughter talking about her classes and some of her friends. Raelynn was glad for the distraction; it took her mind off her own issues. Once in bed though, Seth invaded her mind and body. Even with not being physically near her, she could feel him. She dreamed about his touch, his kisses, how he felt as he moved inside of her. She would wake up trembling from need. Even though her mind was in flux, her body knew exactly what it wanted, Seth.

The week passed with Raelynn doing everything she was used to doing. That, with going to the gym every day helped her keep her sanity, but just barely. There was no way she was going to keep this pace up, it just wasn't healthy. Melissa asked her several times but she brushed off the questions and changed the subject, letting her friend know it wasn't a topic she wished to discuss.

Friday evening came and she was just cleaning her desk when she heard someone in the hall. Melissa must have forgotten something.

She called out, "What did you forget?"

She looked up; the smile on her face fading when she noticed it wasn't Melissa standing in her doorway. It was Seth. And he looked pissed off.

"I didn't forget anything, what did you forget?" He asked very calmly.

Chapter 7

Raelynn didn't know what to say. He was staring at her and she could sense anger emanating from him and the only thing she wanted to do was go up and kiss him.

Seth slowly entered the room and closed the door behind him. He ran into Melissa as she was leaving and asked her to let him in so he could speak to Raelynn. She looked a bit unsure at first but she let him in, for which he was thankful. He'd been calling Raelynn all week and she hadn't answered. He was pissed now and he wanted answers. Going to her condo held some appeal but he didn't know if Hailey would be there and he didn't feel comfortable having this discussion in front of her anyway. He wanted answers and he was going to get them.

This was not a good situation, Raelynn knew it. She knew he called and texted and she just didn't reply. She didn't read the texts, wanting to figure it all out before they talked. He wanted to talk or he wouldn't be here. She put her papers away and sat down. She was trembling too much to stand and carry on a conversation.

"I'm sorry I haven't answered your calls or texts, I've been busy." She said with a shaky voice.

Seth clamped his mouth, his jaw pulsing, she was lying, he was sure of it. "Really? That's going to be your excuse?"

Okay, this was awkward, "It's not an excuse, and it's the truth." Her voice was no better and she knew he knew she was lying.

"Do you think I'm stupid Raelynn?" He asked.

His hand was gripping the door to her office so tightly, his knuckles were white.

A niggle of fear started in her neck, "I'm sorry." She whispered.

His temper was the least of his worries; his physical response to her was so intense he was physically shaking. He didn't believe her so his thoughts and body were warring with one another to see who would win out. His body won the battle.

He let go of the door and walked slowly and deliberately to where she stood. His eyes were glued to hers, daring her to look away. He could see she was scared and he was too. This wasn't how he wanted to talk to her but being around her, he couldn't control himself.

She sat in her chair and stared into Seth's eyes as he approached her. He towered over her; his hands were clenched as if he was trying to control his temper. She was scared but exhilarated all at once. It made her breathing shallow and her heart pound. What did she do?

Once he saw the fear in her eyes, all of his anger left. He would never hurt her, never! He knelt down in front of her, taking her hands into his. They were like ice so he rubbed them as he stared into her eyes. They were as confused as his were.

"I won't hurt you baby," He whispered, "I've just missed you and want to know why you won't talk to me."

Raelynn couldn't help it, a tear slipped down her cheek. He was hurt and she did that. Another blanket of guilt was thrown onto her shoulders. She was tired, tired of lugging around her emotions, tired of trying to figure it out, but she couldn't explain it.

Her tear undid him, he gathered her into his arms, kissing her head. She was scared, that he knew, but why shut him out?

They had something more going on, he was sure of it. He couldn't name it just yet but there was something there.

She pulled away from his embrace, even though it was exactly the last thing she wanted to do.

"I can't do this." She said, and pushed back her chair so she could stand.

She walked around her desk and paced, wringing her hands in frustration. She looked over to see him stand up and watch her. His eyes followed her movements and caused her body to tingle with their intensity.

"I can't," She stopped and her hands straight to her sides "sleep with a man and not know his last name." She was mad now, "I can't be stupid here Seth, not when I have Hailey to think about."

That's what this was about, she was embarrassed about what they did, "Do you think you're stupid?" He asked.

Raelynn looked out the window, the sun sitting low in the sky, "When it comes to you, yes."

That said a lot. "Do you think I'm stupid?" He needed to know.

"What?" She didn't understand why he was asking.

Seth started toward her slowly. "Do you think I'm stupid?"

Raelynn looked away and back to him, "I don't understand."

"Well, you're saying you're stupid so you must think I'm stupid because I didn't find out everything about you before we made love." He was a step away from her and fought every impulse he had to touch her.

"It's not the same thing at all," She was mad now.

Seth wondered how she would look when she was riled, if he wasn't so worried, he would find it cute. "Isn't it?" He took her hand but she didn't let him hold it but a moment before she took it back.

Raelynn wanted to run away, but she was an adult and had to face the music, "First of all, you don't have a child that you've raised for eighteen years alone and have been the only consistent thing in her life." It all came out in a flood. "Or do you?"

She realized she didn't know that either, did he have children, did he have a wife, she never asked. Oh my Lord, she really was stupid.

"No," Seth said softly, "I don't have children."

Her shackles were up in full force, "Well then you have no idea what I feel, or what I think."

He nodded and stepped back to give her space. Crowding her now would only make her feel more cornered and they wouldn't resolve her issues.

"No," Seth said, "I don't. But I know you're using Hailey as an excuse to shut me out."

Anger, so acute traveled up her body and she did something she had never did in her entire life, she slapped him across the face.

Seth saw it coming and didn't back away; she needed to face the truth. His cheek stung and he was hurt emotionally but if it helped her, then he would let it go just this once.

Raelynn regretted her actions as soon as she realized she struck him, "Oh my God, Seth."

She backed away from him and dropped down in a chair before she fell.

Seth knew this was not going to be resolved. They were both too compromised. He was a gentleman so he wouldn't make her feel bad but this wasn't going to work if she wanted to hide from what they felt.

He looked at her, her head was bowed, her shoulders slumped, he needed to go and let her figure it out, "I need to go." He said softly.

Raelynn's head shot up, her hand covering her mouth and tears streaming down her cheeks, "I understand and I'm so sorry I hit you."

"I know," He knew she meant it, it wasn't something she did. If he didn't know anything else about her, he knew she was a lady.

She watched Seth leave her office, waited until she heard the front door close, and sat in the chair of her office and cried.

Hailey knew something was up. Her mother was always up before her. So when she woke up late Saturday morning and saw she was still in bed, she called Melissa. They spoke for five minutes, Melissa assuring her that she was on her way to their place. Hailey got ready and started making breakfast when she heard the knock at the door.

Melissa swept into the condo and gave Hailey a quick hug in the entryway, "Is she up yet?"

Hailey shook her head no. "I started breakfast," she walked into the living room and nodded toward her mom's bedroom, "you get her up and I'll set the table."

Melissa opened up her friend's bedroom door; she knew the condo well and even helped Raelynn pick it out. The room was very dark; she could barely make out the shape that was Raelynn on the bed. Slowly, she sat on the edge of the bed.

Raelynn heard her friend, she wasn't particularly surprised that Hailey called Melissa; she just couldn't make her body get up and go this morning. She woke up hours earlier, just didn't want to do anything.

"I'm up," Raelynn said.

Melissa smiled, "I figured."

Raelynn turned slowly, her whole body aching from sobbing in the office chair after Seth left her last night. She couldn't remember ever crying that much, not even when Anthony died. That fact just made her cry harder.

"Can I help?" Melissa asked, gently rubbing her friend's leg.

It was not an easy question for Raelynn to answer. "I don't know."

Melissa stood and walked to the window, she threw open the curtains, letting light pour in. Once she turned back, she saw Raelynn's swollen eyes. "You've been doing a bit of crying I see."

Raelynn snorted, "Yes I have."

"Well," Melissa grabbed her hands, "let's get you in the shower and ready before Hailey calls the paramedics."

The panic of her daughter's worry pulled Raelynn out of her fog, "I'm sorry."

Melissa walked into the bathroom and started the shower. She grabbed a towel and placed it on the table next to the bathtub, "I know," She said softly and left Raelynn to get ready.

The shower was hot and Raelynn let the water help loosen up her achy muscles. She leaned against the wall and tried to gather her wits. She felt so lost and alone and it didn't help that guilt over slapping Seth in the face hung over her like a dark, gray cloud.

Getting ready took all of her energy and when she came out she saw a concerned looking Hailey and Melissa sitting at the dining table. She sat down and looked at the two women she loved most in the world; and didn't know what to say.

Hailey looked at her mother and couldn't contain her emotions, "Mom, what is going on?" The tears were at the corners of her eyes and she tried valiantly to keep them from falling.

Raelynn's heart broke, knowing that she hurt Hailey and Seth troubled her to her core. She took Hailey's hand and gave it a reassuring squeeze. Looking at Melissa's encouraging smile helped so she started the story of the last couple of days; her visiting Seth at work, the kiss, the revelation that she didn't even know the basic things about him like his last name, the avoiding part, how he confronted her, and finally, how she slapped him. When the last word was out she looked from one to the other, waiting for the repercussions.

"Mom, are you okay?" Hailey asked. She was still trying to process the events her mother explained.

Raelynn nodded but wasn't sure that was the truth.

Melissa sat back and looked at Raelynn, "Why do you feel guilty about not knowing him as well as maybe you think you should?"

The question was relevant and Raelynn considered it carefully before she answered, "I guess it's the fact that I've raised Hailey all alone and expect a lot out of myself as her parent. I should be setting a good example, not bed-hopping with the first handsome man who happens to come along."

Hailey chuckled, "I'm sorry," she said at her mother's look. "I wasn't laughing at you mom, just surprised by the fact that you think you somehow have a lack of judgment where Seth is concerned."

"I don't know what you mean," she could feel her shackles rising again.

Hailey took a breath, "Ok, you didn't know his last name right?"

Raelynn nodded.

"Okay, so you found out as soon as it came up," She looked at her mother through a different lens, "did not knowing his last name make you feel bad or did it make you feel like you didn't have control?"

Her daughter was much too smart for her own good, "I guess both," she smiled, "I think I just let go and then got caught unprepared."

Melissa snorted, "Nothing wrong with letting go honey, you've had this iron grip on your life and we respect you for doing everything you could for both you and Hailey," she slid a plate in front of Raelynn, "now you can make some mistakes, if that's what you think you've done."

Raelynn stared at the plate of food as if held the secrets of the world.

"Now," Melissa grabbed a carafe of juice and poured herself a glass, "I don't think you've made a mistake, it doesn't appear to me that Hailey thinks you made a mistake, and, from what you've said, Seth doesn't think you're somehow less for feeling like you do."

The blanket of guilt was wrapped around her once again, Seth, she thought, he would never forgive her for her behavior.

Hailey could see her mom was losing the battle with the guilt, "Why did you slap him?"

Tears formed in Raelynn's eyes, she was ashamed, "Because he said I was using you as an excuse to push him away," she sniffled and wiped absently at the tears on her cheeks, "I think he used the term 'shut out' but I'm not sure."

It didn't surprise her, "I can see that, you did that with what's his name from Dallas."

Raelynn's head shot up, her eyes large, "You knew about him?"

Hailey smiled, "Yes mom, I did." She winked at Melissa, "I figured it out and didn't want to pester you about it because it was over pretty quickly. You did the same thing then didn't you?"

Another layer of the guilt blanket just fell over her shoulders. "Yes but I didn't think I was doing that now." She would rationalize as much as she could.

"Well," Melissa took a quick bite of eggs, "the question is what do you want to do now?" She could see the wheels turning in Raelynn's head, "Before you answer, ask yourself, what do you WANT to do, not what do you think you have to do."

That was the question of the year as far as Raelynn was concerned. "I don't know."

"I don't believe you," Hailey said quickly, "I think you do but you're scared."

Tears streaming down her face, Raelynn nodded, "I think you're right baby girl."

Hailey loved the endearment her mother used for her over the years. She wished there was something she could do to help. She watched her mom and thought maybe she could.

The three of them sat at the table and quietly ate their breakfast. No one talked, there was no reason to. All of them knew it was up to Raelynn on how she would continue and whether Seth would be a part of that decision.

Melissa stayed through the afternoon but went home to get ready for a date. She offered to stay and cancel her date but Raelynn told her not to. One of them should have a good time at least. Hailey made plans with friends the day before so Raelynn shooed her out of the house to get away from the craziness for a while. She sat on the chair in the living room and stared out the window. The trees surrounding their patio swayed with the breezes. She didn't know how long she sat there but didn't move until the sun was dipping low in the horizon. Her stomach growled so she got up to make a sandwich when her phone went off.

She didn't want to talk to anyone but it could be Hailey so she walked over and looked at the screen. It was a text from Hailey that said, *Don't be mad mom I love you.*

Raelynn stared at her phone wondering what Hailey meant and was about to text her that when the doorbell chimed. Oh great, she looked awful and someone was at the door. She walked over and looked out the peep hole; she could only see a bush.

What the heck? She opened the door slowly to see it wasn't a bush but a huge bouquet of flowers. Lord they were massive; she thought Melissa or Hailey was trying to cheer her up. It was a beautiful arrangement, all sorts of wildflowers.

Before Raelynn could speak to the delivery person, the flowers lowered and she saw Seth standing there. Her eyes were wide and full of questions.

He was pretty sure the only reason she opened the door was because she didn't think he was the one outside. After the previous night's confrontation, he wasn't sure she would ever speak to him again. He wasn't sure he wanted to speak to her either for that matter; she hurt him, not physically, although his cheek was smarting when he woke up, but his feelings definitely took a hit.

"What are you doing here?" Raelynn finally managed to ask.

He smiled, "I'm bringing you flowers," he thought that was apparent since he was standing there with a big bouquet in his hands.

Raelynn shook her head, "I can see that, I'm just wondering why you came here after what I said and did last night," the tears started again and she didn't even try to stop them.

Seth put the arrangement on a table nearby and gathered Raelynn into his arms. They were standing in the doorway of her condo but he didn't care, she needed him and, damn it, he needed her.

As soon as Seth's arms came around her, she crumbled emotionally. She grabbed onto him tightly and just felt wave after wave of relief that he was here mixed with apprehension that he would push her away.

He couldn't stand it any longer, he wanted them inside where the neighbors wouldn't see and he could hold her better. He released her, grabbed the flowers, "Why don't we put these in a vase?"

Raelynn nodded and stepped inside to allow him in. She shut the door behind him and walked into the kitchen. He was looking in the overhead cupboards, for a vase she assumed. She watched his graceful movements, the way his shoulders flexed as he reached up, the way his jeans stretched tightly across his thighs, just watching him made her tremble with desire.

He found one and went about transferring the flowers into it, oblivious to her blatant ogling. There were so many that he had difficulty getting them into the wide-mouthed vase so she helped him. They worked silently until the flowers were settled and placed on her dining table.

They really were spectacular, Raelynn thought as she stared at them. Wild and so colorful, like how she pictured Seth she supposed. "They are gorgeous, thank you," She turned to see him looking at her intensely.

"Are you ready to talk about last night?" He asked without preamble.

She appreciated the honesty, "I don't think so but we need to."

Seth nodded and walked over to sit on the sofa. He waited for her to settle beside him before he spoke, "Hailey called me today."

Raelynn was surprised, "Why?"

"Because," he took her hand and rubbed his thumb across the back of it, loving the softness of her skin, "she was afraid you wouldn't."

Shame filled her, "She is right, I don't know if I would have."

Well at least she was honest, "That doesn't make me feel better Raelynn."

"What do you want me to say Seth? You were right; I've been putting Hailey up as an invisible barrier." She let go of his hand and stood. "After Anthony died, I was so alone and then I had Hailey, she was mine and mine alone."

Seth nodded, he could understand that but not why she would push him away.

"If I let someone in like I let Anthony, what if they left or worse?" She didn't dare say the words, "It wasn't just me who would be hurt Seth, it would be both of us." She shook her head, "I wasn't willing to take that chance."

He couldn't help it, his voice increased in volume, "And now," he stood toe to toe with her. She would have to face it now, "Are you willing to take the chance now?"

She stood there, tears streaming down her face, her shoulders slumped, and looked at this beautiful man, "I want to." She squeaked.

Seth sighed and pulled her to him in a hug, "That's enough for now baby," he whispered against the top of her head.

Raelynn didn't even have the strength to lift her arms; she just leaned into him and let him hold her. It was if his arms surrounding her created a balm that made the hurt a little easier to bear.

They stood in her living room like that for a while, each trying to figure out what this meant.

Seth let go of her long enough to bend down and pick her up into his arms. He smiled at her gasp of surprise. He wasn't going to stand there when they could be more comfortable, "Bedroom?" he asked.

Raelynn pointed and let him carry her to her bedroom. The door was slightly ajar so her feet pushed it open the rest of the way. She flipped on the light with her free hand as they entered, the small bedside lamp casting a soft glow in the room.

Seth looked around the room that Raelynn slept in. It was a comfortable room with feminine touches, the bed was in the center of one wall and flanked by two petite nightstands. There was a media chest with a small tv in the corner and a larger dresser on another wall. The bedspread was a pale green and looked soft. He could feel that it was just that as he gently placed Raelynn on the bed. He assumed it was the side she slept on because the clock and a book were on the table at that side.

She watched him as he went around to the other side of the bed and kicked off his shoes. He crawled onto the bed and pushed up the decorative pillows so he could lean against them. Once that was done, he pulled her so she could rest against him. Her hair tickled his chin and he could smell the shampoo she used.

Neither of them spoke, they just cuddled up and held one another.

A while later, Raelynn shifted so she could look into his eyes. She was going to fall asleep if she didn't move; the beating of his heart under her cheek was soothing. He looked down at her, his eyes intense.

"Thank you," She tried to keep her emotions tamped down.

Seth looked into her eyes; they looked lost, "For what baby?"

She was embarrassed, "For not giving up on me when I behaved so badly and I slapped you," She hiccupped trying to hold the tears back.

"Oh baby," He felt her pain, "I know you are sorry." He smiled as she rubbed his cheek with her palm.

"I really am Seth." Tears again, darn it, "I am so sorry."

Okay, he was going to cry if she didn't stop, "Well, let's not worry about it anymore."

She nodded and smiled, "Are you hungry?"

The question surprised him and he chuckled, "I could eat," he said.

"I'll be right back," She scooted off the bed and went into the other room, "the remote is on the dresser if you want to turn the tv on."

He found the remote and surfed through channels while she was in the kitchen. The thought of them being in her bed was very distracting and he was cursing himself for being insensitive when she came back in. She was carrying a large bowl of popcorn and he smiled.

"I know," She said sheepishly as she handed him the bowl, "it's not much."

He kissed her head when she settled in beside him, "It's perfect."

They lay on her bed and watched movies for the next couple of hours; both of them munching on popcorn. Raelynn went into the kitchen and poured them each a glass of wine at some point so they were drinking that. It was a quiet, relaxing evening and Seth was glad he came over.

The second movie they picked was just starting when Raelynn heard the front door open, she sat up quickly. "Hailey's here."

Seth knew she was uncomfortable about Hailey seeing him in her room but they were adults and so was Hailey. The kid knew more than her mother wanted to admit. He didn't move.

Hailey entered the living room and heard the tv on in her mom's room. The door was open so she went over to peek in. A smile formed when she saw Seth sitting next to her mom on the bed. He looked very relaxed but her mom looked stressed.

"Hi," Hailey smiled, "I see you two are talking again."

Yep, Seth thought, the kid was sharp. "Yes, thank you," he said, winking at his co-conspirator.

Raelynn watched her daughter closely, looking for any sign of the previous stress she exhibited. Seeing none, she got up and gave Hailey a hug, "Yes, thank you."

Hailey hugged her mom, "You're welcome." She gave Seth a thumbs up behind her mother's back. "I'm off to bed; Aly roped me into going to the gym tomorrow and going for a bike ride."

Raelynn laughed, Hailey was strictly anti-exercise. It didn't help that she was naturally small and didn't need to. "You poor girl."

"Hey Seth, are you staying over?" She was curious to see what he would say and what her mother would do. Seeing her mother pale wasn't a good sign, but someone had to speak up.

"I don't think we've discussed that," Raelynn said quietly.

Seth watched Hailey watch Raelynn. It didn't take a brain surgeon to figure out that Hailey was trying to force her mother to face her hang ups. The question was, would Raelynn fight her or try. It didn't appear that Raelynn was going to make any commitment on the matter.

"I'll see if she snores before I make my decision," He said flatly.

Hailey laughed outright, she wasn't sure which was funnier, his joke or her mom's reaction to it. He was good for her, Hailey was sure of it. "Ok cool," she said, nodded, and left the room.

"I can't believe you said that," Raelynn hissed when her daughter left the room.

He looked at her innocently, "What?" He scooted over so she could sit next to him, "It's a deal breaker for me you know."

It was difficult to be mad at him when she was trying not to laugh. She settled for tossing a pillow at him. She went back to snuggling next to him.

The movie was good, predictable, but good. As the credits rolled, Raelynn looked up to see Seth sleeping. She just studied his features as he slept. He was a very handsome man, his hair curling slightly around his ears, his square jaw slightly rough from a day's growth of beard, his eyes looked peaceful.

She slowly picked up the remnants of their meal, such as it was, and cleaned up. When she went back into the bedroom he was sitting there looking at her. She stood in the doorway and stared back.

"You were sleeping," She said softly.

He stretched his arms, finding a more comfortable position, "I got cold when you left."

She stepped into the room and turned to the dresser. She opened a drawer and grabbed a lighter out. Without saying anything, she started lighting the candles that were placed around the room. Each of them shed a soft glow, their flickering light creating fascinating pictures on the walls. When she lit the last one, she returned the lighter to the drawer and shut off the bedside lamp with the switch. She closed the door and leaned against it, her hands behind her back.

Seth watched her as she moved, entranced by her movements. She was curvy and soft and he knew what those curves felt like beneath his hands and with his lips. He was getting hard as he watched her. When she was done and against the door, he wondered what she was thinking. He didn't dare move.

"I was thinking," She said softly as she pushed away from the door.

Seth swallowed hard, his mouth felt dry, "Yes?"

She climbed onto the end of the bed, looking into his eyes as she moved, "I was wondering if you'd like to test your theory."

"What theory?" He asked, his hands itched to touch her but she had to make the first move.

She crawled up the bed her knees straddling his legs, "The theory you had about being able to make love all night until we were too weak to move."

Oh God, she was beautiful. "Is that what I said?" He didn't even know how he could form the question; she filled his mind with wants and needs.

Her hands ran up his legs, she could feel his thighs flex as her fingers moved over them, his reaction making her bolder. "I'm not quoting mind you but I think that was the gist of it."

That was it, he was gone. "Come here," He said slowly.

There was no mistaking how much he wanted her which made Raelynn burn from the inside out. She wanted him so much. When she was cleaning up in the kitchen she was thinking how nice it was to be with him. How he made her feel so safe, how everything felt right when she was in his arms. That had to mean something; even her crazy, regimented brain could see that. Not to mention that her body quivered thinking about them naked in her bed. When she finished up, she just wanted to see him in candlelight.

She inched up the bed, over his legs with slow determination. There was no need to rush, she wanted to feel everything. Her hands led the way up his torso, pulling his shirt up as she made the ascent. His skin was hot to the touch. She skimmed her nails softly up his sides and smiled when he squirmed.

"Are you ticklish Seth?" She purred in his ear.

He sucked in a breath, "I didn't think I was but maybe." Her hands felt so good on him.

He didn't dare touch her yet, he knew once he did, they would go a hundred miles an hour and he wanted her to enjoy it.

She was straddled across his lap and used her hands to push his shirt up and over his head. She concentrated on his

145

chest; rubbing her fingertips in small circles. Then she would take her fingers and rub them through the dusting of chest hair he had. She never thought she would be so enthralled by a man's chest. She could see, and feel, his chest moving as his breathing became more ragged.

She looked up into the blue eyes that were now dark gray, "Do you like how I touch you?"

How did one question make him want to groan? "Oh yes," he said breathlessly.

She took his hands from his sides and brought them both to her mouth so she could kiss, first the palms, then she slowly kissed the tip of each finger. When that was done, she took his index finger and put it in her mouth, twirling her tongue around the tip of it, along with sucking it slowly and nipping the tip with her teeth.

Seth's nerve endings were stretched to their limit. He wrapped the hand she didn't have around the back of her head and gently guided it toward his. He had to taste her lips.

Their lips met and little explosions went off inside of Raelynn. The physical ones were spectacular but what made her tremble was the one going off inside her chest. She could only describe it as her heart opening up to him. This scared her and exhilarated her at the same time, making the experience all the more intense.

Seth felt the shift in her and responded in kind. He moved fast and turned them over so he was over her, looking into her green eyes as she lay beneath him. Her heart was beating hard; he could feel it under his own.

He rested his weight onto his elbows; his hands free to finger-comb her soft hair. Although his body was screaming for release, he wanted to take a moment to look at this complicated creature he was lucky enough to be with. She had him, he knew it but was pretty sure she didn't have a clue.

Raelynn stared up at Seth and watched him watch her. What did he see? Did he see that she was so afraid and so aroused? Did he see her insecurities? Lord knew she had enough of those. And yet, as she looked at him, she could only see warmth.

Not being able to take the intensity of his gaze, she shifted. "Seth, is everything okay?"

Her question pulled him from his thoughts, "Oh yes baby; everything is just fine."

She squirmed, creating a friction between them, "Then make love to me." It sounded like whining to her ears but she didn't care, she needed him.

"Of course baby," He whispered and lowered his lips to hers.

Now the kisses were pure heat, all semblance of sanity out the window. Lips fused, tongues collided, and made delicious licks of pleasure stream through Raelynn's body. She arched up, trying to get closer to him.

He pulled his head up far enough so he could help her pull off her top, her lace bra underneath drove him crazy and he was most thankful that the closure was in front, he could easily unclip it and pull the lacy fabric away. Her breasts were beautiful, the nipples hard, begging for his attention, which he happily provided. His tongue swirled and nipped; he could feel her pleasure from her soft sighs and her legs wrapping around his.

This was crazy, she wanted him, "Seth please?" She begged between pants of pleasure.

The sound of her voice almost drove him over the edge; he undid his pants with one hand as the other softly massaged one of her breasts, his tongue manipulating the other nipple into a rock hard nub.

How did she still have so many clothes on? She wanted him inside her, now! She pushed her pants down; thankful she didn't have shoes on. She started giggling as Seth was fighting with his own jeans. Her insides melted as he smiled mischievously.

"You think this is funny?" He asked.

Raelynn nodded, "Yes," she was teasing him.

He flipped himself over bringing her on top of him. She was splayed over his chest, their legs tangled. "I'll show you funny."

She sure hoped so. They finally got off the remainder of the clothes and lay there panting.

Seth pushed her up so she was straddling his abdomen. His hands slowly moved up her thighs, softly kneading her skin as he moved them up her sides. Slowly, she closed her eyes from the sensations, her soft skin glistening in the candlelight. He moved his hands across her shoulders and down the sides of her neck, bringing them down so they could fill with her breasts.

Raelynn never let a man freely touch her like this and wondered why since it felt so heavenly. She let her hands fall to her sides, wanting to concentrate on Seth's ministrations. Her head fell back as his hands massaged her breasts, then they moved down her stomach and he splayed them, palms wide, across her lower abdomen, his thumbs moving lower to massage her sex.

Oh, she was wet! So wet! And hot! He could feel the heat of her against his belly and when his thumbs parted her, the heat intensified. The nub of pleasure he could feel grew bigger as he pushed her up and up. Her thighs were trembling and she was panting, he knew she would reach the peak soon and he wanted to watch her crash with pleasure.

No, no, she didn't want to come this way but she was helpless to stop it. His thumbs were massaging her so amazingly, the waves of pleasure just built and built and then. Oh, she swept over the edge of reason, smashing into a million pieces of sharp pleasure.

Seth was mesmerized by her orgasm, she looked so absolutely gorgeous. Her body tensed as she rode the waves, finally falling onto the bed beside him. He smiled slyly as he watched her recover.

Her body was on fire, she felt hot and cold at the same time. Finally her breathing evened out and she opened her eyes to see Seth looking at her. She tried to disguise her embarrassment but wasn't quite successful.

"What?" he asked softly.

She lifted her palm to his cheek, pleasured by him turning his head enough to kiss it softly, "I'm just embarrassed that I climaxed without you."

Seth winked, "Oh I'm just giving you enough time to recuperate and then we'll come together, I promise.

The words started a stirring low in her belly, "Ok then, let's get to it." She smiled and kissed him.

Seth took her words as a challenge; one he was easily up to. He pulled her to him so they were touching from chest to toes. His fingers cupped her bottom, pushing her close so she could feel how much he wanted her.

She could feel his hardness and her body reacted of its own accord. She didn't even know where these wants came from. She reached between them and wrapped her hand around him, feeling him pulse in her hand. She couldn't help it, she groaned. Just feeling him made her want more.

He moved so she could slide beneath him. His eyes were on hers as he slid into her slickness, he sighed in pleasure. "Oh baby, you feel so good." He whispered.

She was so close to the edge again, his words driving her body to heights she never experienced. "Harder," She panted.

Seth moved, filling her as deeply as he could, his body wanted this, wanted it every time he was around her. He drove into her, over and over again until he felt the climax coming over him. "Raelynn," He said through clenched teeth.

"Yes," she whispered, her own orgasm coming fast. "Yes, Seth, harder," She was swept up into chaos, her body convulsing with shots of heat going everywhere. She could feel him follow her, his breathing ragged, his body shaking with release.

They fell into a tangled heap. Neither moved, just enjoyed the afterglow of their lovemaking.

Raelynn ran her fingertips up and down his arm lightly, not wanting the connection between them to be broken. The man was a genius in bed!

Chapter 8

She managed to open her eyes when the licks of desire were dying down. He was looking at her again with those eyes. They were the color of the ocean, deep blue, and so profound she felt as though she could dive into their depths. For someone who didn't say a lot about himself, his eyes revealed a sensitive soul. They fascinated and puzzled her at the same time.

Seth wondered what she was thinking, "Are you better now?" He asked as he ran his fingertips over her hip. He loved the feel of her skin.

"Oh yes," Raelynn said and stretched like a satisfied cat waking from a long nap.

He smiled, "Good," he leaned in and kissed her on the tip of her nose.

Raelynn giggled, he was so cute. "Why do you do that to me?"

"What?" He asked; his brow furrowed.

She sighed, "You make me want to just feel everything, I don't think, I just want."

It was amazing to him that she could explain his feelings so clearly, "I feel the same way when I'm with you."

Raelynn looked down, her cheeks turning pink at his response.

"Hey," Seth tilted her chin up with his finger, "I find you extremely sexy and amazing."

What woman didn't want to hear a man say that? She didn't know which was more heady, his lovemaking, or his words.

She ran her fingers up his arm to his shoulders and made a path down his chest. When he sucked in a breath from the sensations her fingers made, she smiled knowingly. She did that to him and knowing how it felt made it that much better.

"Are you hungry?" She asked, her eyes following her fingertips as they touched his skin.

Seth growled, oh the woman made him crazy in a completely good way, "Yes, wait is that code?"

She couldn't help it, she laughed, "No, I was actually asking if you were hungry as in would you like food?"

He laughed, "Yes, I am."

"Okay then," Raelynn jumped up from the bed and rummaged in her dresser for some sweat pants and a long-sleeved t-shirt, "let's go."

Intrigued, he got up, dressed and followed her into the kitchen.

"I am going to make you an omelet," She started pulling out ingredients from the refrigerator and motioned for him to sit at the bar. "Do you like omelets?"

Seth smiled, "Yes, there isn't much I don't eat."

"Good," Raelynn nodded and grabbed a bowl to mix the eggs in.

He watched her; she looked very comfortable making their late night snack. He propped his chin into the palm of his hand and just enjoyed the view of her. He was curious about her life.

"Do you like cooking?" He asked.

She nodded, "Oh yes," she poured the first egg concoction into the pan. "It took a while for me to get good; Anthony ate a lot of burnt food when we were first married."

As soon as the words were out, she stopped and looked at Seth. Was he mad that she mentioned Anthony? Over the years, she was very open with talking about him for Hailey's sake and she didn't have to consider another man's feelings before now.

Seth sensed her change and spoke up, "It's okay to talk about him Raelynn; you were married and have a child together."

Sighing, Raelynn walked over to him and kissed him. "Thank you."

"As long as I get kisses, no problem," He grabbed for her as she went back to the stove, just missing her and making her laugh at his antics.

Hailey stood in the hallway listening to her mother and Seth as they talked and joked; a smile plastered on her face. She was glad that she called Seth earlier and asked him to come over. It amazed her how her mother didn't understand how much she needed him in her life when it was very plain for Hailey to see. She went back to her room; she planned to text Melissa and let her know that the current crisis was averted.

Raelynn finished cooking up their omelets, slid them onto plates and set them on the bar. She took the seat next to Seth and dug in, surprised by how hungry she actually was.

Her cooking was great, Seth ate every last bit and sat back, his stomach sated. "Thank you, that was delicious."

"You are welcome," Raelynn smiled as she took their plates to the sink. "I enjoy cooking and miss cooking for a man."

There was that confession stuff again, why did she keep saying these things? It was confusing when all of the feelings she experienced for Anthony found their way to the surface. It complicated things and made her mind fuzzy. Plus she was paranoid about upsetting Seth. Even though he said it was okay, was that just for now or would he tire of her dead husband's ghost hanging around?

She was becoming slightly easier to read, once Seth started watching her. He could see when she was lost in thought and doubting herself, her brows pressed together. It was adorable but still he worried that they were only putting a band aid on the issues with their lovemaking. It was something they each would need to work on.

He came up behind her as she was washing the dishes and put his arms around her waist. She smiled and leaned back into his chest, she could feel his heat permeate her clothes. He rested his chin on her shoulder so she could feel his breath whisper along her cheek and it made her warm all over. He didn't speak so she didn't either.

Driven by instinct, he moved his hands from her waist and moved them down her arms and into the soapy water so they covered hers. His fingers moved with hers as they swept across the plates with the dishcloth, creating a wondrous friction against her skin. She felt her pulse speed up as she watched his fingers with hers in the water and the sluicing sound the sudsy water made during their chore. How did the man turn her on with helping her wash a couple of plates? She somehow, managed to get through it without turning around and making love to him on the kitchen floor, but just barely.

The dishes finally done, she took his hand and led him back to her room. She may have kept her wits around her in the kitchen but in here, she could let go. This was where she didn't have to pretend to be sweet, responsible, Raelynn and she very much did not want to be that person with Seth.

She yanked his hand so he cleared the doorway of her bedroom, closed the door and pushed him back against it so she could assault his lips with her own. It was too long since their lips met and she couldn't wait one second longer. Her tongue darted out and begged for entrance into his mouth. Once granted, she moved closer, as if that was possible.

The woman could kiss, was the only thought Seth could register. She did the most inconceivable things to his body with that mouth, just kissing him. He lifted her so they were connected from mouths to hips and walked the few steps to the bed. Without breaking his hold on her, he got on the bed and pulled her with him.

Her lungs were on fire from lack of oxygen and Raelynn did not even care. His lips were so pliable and so arousing, would she ever tire of kissing him? She doubted it was possible. Finally she had to take a breath so she could get some oxygen. Her pulse was beating so loud she was sure he could hear it. She stared at him.

"Goodness you can kiss," She said breathlessly.

He laughed, "I was just thinking the exact same thing." He stared at her, making small circles with his palms along her back.

She shook her head, "I think it's all you here."

He smiled at her shyness, "Raelynn, you have got to be the most arousing woman I have ever met."

It was tough to not shrug off his compliment because it made her uncomfortable. She never considered herself "arousing" and to have someone say that about her felt weird. It was him and what he did to her that made this happen, she was sure of it.

Seth sighed; he could see she didn't believe him. She didn't believe she was capable of all she was actually capable of. It was time to show her all the possibilities. "Hey," He sat up and pulled her up so she could face him, "can I ask you something?"

This was frustrating as her body hummed with need but she shook herself mentally, "Yes," her hands were aching to grab him and rip off his clothes.

Her eyes were full of need and that made it more difficult for him because his mirrored hers, he was sure. "Can I see your list?"

What? She was confused, "I'm sorry?" She asked.

"Your list, the one you made," He said and moved to get off the bed.

Raelynn nodded, "Oh yes, hold on, I'll get it."

She scooted off the bed and went out of the room to get the paper. Why did he want to see the list now? She was thoroughly confused. Grabbing the list, she was walking across the living room when she heard Hailey moving around. Crap! How could she have forgotten her daughter was in the house? Here she was attacking a man in her room. Doubts crept up her spine and she walked into her room and quietly handed the list to Seth.

Uh oh, Seth thought, he noticed the tight set of her shoulders when she came back into the room. She was gorgeous, her hair mussed from their lovemaking, her lips swollen from his kisses. His body responded to her nearness, making it difficult to think of anything except burying himself inside her and never stopping.

Raelynn watched as he read the list. What did he think of it? It was silly wasn't it? What was she thinking, telling him about it anyway? She felt foolish.

He read the list and was amazed at what she put down. There was the Raelynn he knew was trying to come out to experience all life has to offer and there was the conservative, safe, Raelynn who manicured her feelings over the years. He could see how important Hailey was to her as she put down something that would benefit her daughter. His heart swelled at the admission.

"It's stupid isn't it?" She reached out to grab the paper and frowned when Seth moved it out of her reach.

"Raelynn, stop," He said it more sternly than he meant to but she was being silly.

She was embarrassed and didn't know what to do so she plopped on the end of the bed and folded her arms across her front in a gesture of self-protection.

Seth thought she was adorable when she pouted, "I'm not trying to make you feel bad, I was just thinking of how I might help you with the list."

It was touching, what he said, but she didn't need him to help her. She looked into his eyes, "Thank you Seth, I appreciate your understanding but I want to do it myself."

He wouldn't force the issue because she wasn't feeling great about it, but he would think about it and conspire with Hailey if necessary. The kid was a good plotter. "Okay sweetheart, come here so I can hold you."

She couldn't resist him when he spoke to her like that; the words and his tone were like soft caresses across her skin. She got up and shut off the light. Silently, she made her way back to him and they lay in the bedroom, the candlelight the only illumination, and let the night comfort them.

It was early when Raelynn woke up, she was alone and that made her feel sad. She looked across the bed and sighed. He didn't stay. What did that mean? Did it mean he changed his mind? She got up and went to the bathroom. When she came out, she saw the note left on the nightstand; she picked it up and read it.

Raelynn,

I wanted to stay but I have an early appointment with a horse trainer and I have to get to Spaceland before noon. Thank you for the incredible night. I watched you sleep for a bit and wanted nothing more than feel you next to me. Sleep well and know I'll call when I'm done for the day. I'd like to see you.   Seth

Well, it was something, she thought as she crawled back into bed. She drifted back to sleep, his note in her hands and his touch on her mind.

The day went as most Sundays did; the girls got up, had breakfast and prepared for the week ahead. Raelynn went about her routine, wondering if she was this boring all the time. She used to have fun right? She was the quiet one in college and truly believed she found Anthony on a fluke. With Hailey, she was just like her dad, but what about Seth? Would he find her too mundane? The man lived on a ranch and jumped out of airplanes on a regular basis. But when they were together, the sparks between them made her alive. Would that transfer to her daily life as well? She shook her head, too many questions to answer on a Sunday morning.

Seth walked into the house at dusk, tired and cranky. He was hungry, he missed his lunch. That was how it went, you got going and met your clients and focused on the jumps. It was exhilarating and fulfilling but really made him forget about the basic stuff, like food. He went to the frig and pulled out the makings for a sandwich.

As he sat down to eat his dinner, he gazed around his kitchen. It was spacious and clean but was it something Raelynn would like? Where did that come from? Why did it matter what Raelynn thought of his house? Simple, because he could see her here. He could see her making dinner or watching television with him in the great room or organizing a party for friends, basically just about anything. Whoa fella! He was thinking way too much about way too much and it was time to get some perspective. He tossed his plate in the trash and went out the back door to the barn. A bit of time with the horses would help right about now.

It was after eight and Seth still hadn't called. Raelynn looked at the television but didn't watch anything on it. She was worried. Hailey was finishing up a paper she was writing for a class so was scarce most of the day. Being alone with her thoughts didn't help Raelynn and she was going to call Seth when she heard the familiar sound of a text on her phone.

Sorry it's late, got home and did some work with the horses so I'm beat. Can I get a raincheck?

At least he was okay, Raelynn thought. She herself got wrapped up in work so understood how it happened. She smiled, remembering the previous night and how wonderful it was to have him in her bed.

I will accept your raincheck but you better make it up to me, I was lonely when I woke up this morning in my bed all alone. She pushed send, a tingle up her spine.

Seth smiled; he worked for hours to get her out of his mind, only to end up more frustrated because he wanted to be with her. He typed his response, *I'll be happy to make it UP to you in every way I can think of. Let's start with dinner at my place, you pick the day.*

Hmm, Raelynn thought as she read, what was her schedule like this week? She walked over and looked at her desk calendar, the script neat and clear. She was free Tuesday evening. Mondays could be iffy so she didn't want to risk canceling because of something at work.

She thought of what she should say before clicking the keys, *How about Tuesday? You make the dinner and I'll bring dessert. Pick either whip cream, caramel sauce, or hot fudge····..*

Seth's pants were tight just reading her text, he could imagine them doing all sorts of things with those ingredients. Did he have a new tarp they could throw on his bed so they could experiment? His thoughts were running crazy with wanting her. He could taste the sweetness of the hot fudge as he drizzled it down her thighs. Oh God, the woman drove him crazy! He typed with shaky fingers, *Screw it! Bring all 3 woman! I want to see if they taste as sweet as you do.*

She laughed, looking up to make sure Hailey hadn't come into the living room, *You are a naughty boy, I was thinking about dessert and here you are, making assumptions about my use of toppings in the bedroom. I guarantee you anything I make will be eaten in the dining room so I hope your table is sturdy.*

Okay now he was in actual pain. The woman could make his thoughts swim with a friggin text! He never even contemplated the dining room table for anything other than serving dinner on. He walked into the room and actually looked at the table, pressing down on one side to test its sturdiness.

Raelynn didn't get a response so she was pouting again. She set the phone down and went to the bathroom to start her nightly routine. Minutes later, she came back out and noticed she missed a text from Seth. *The table has been tested, looks good. I only buy high quality furniture so we're good to go.*

She couldn't help it, she laughed hard. He was adorable. And a flirt. Somehow she thought she could live with that. She looked at the time and noticed she would need to get to bed soon but she wanted to text him some more. *I am glad to see my safety is a concern to you, I'd hate to be in a compromising position and have the furniture fail us. Now I know that we can experiment a little, is your dining room table the only place we should try???? I was hoping we could see how many rooms we can "test out." It's good to know if you've had good taste with everything.*

He shook his head and took a deep breath; a cold shower was in his immediate future for sure. *I'm going to throw myself into a tub of ice cubes now, sleep well, I'll talk to you soon.*

That was it? He didn't say when he would call her or whether she should call him. Maybe he was just giving her space to think things through. She was like a yo-yo the last couple of days. Thinking about it, she was surprised she could keep up with herself. She put the phone down and went to bed wondering what she would do about Seth.

Monday was like every Monday, crazy. Raelynn hit the ground running only stopping for a lunch meeting she and Melissa set up the week before. It was with a new client. He was the owner of a new business in the area that dealt with construction. She wasn't clear on all of the particulars, having just set up the meeting. She and Melissa arrived at the restaurant a few minutes early to secure the table and be prepared.

"So how was the rest of your weekend?" Melissa asked as she got out her notebook.

Raelynn blushed, "It was good." She handed Melissa a pen and took one out of her briefcase for herself. "He stayed most of the night on Saturday and we weren't able to meet up yesterday since he was working."

"Most of the night?" Melissa asked. She was about to pry out more information when a man approached the table.

"Hello ladies," He said and extended his hand to Raelynn first, "I'm Mark Wesley." He looked between the two women. "I believe we have a meeting scheduled."

Raelynn went into work mode immediately. She gestured for Mr. Wesley to sit and began her spiel about their company and what they offer to their clients. He listened intently and only responded when he needed clarification on something.

Melissa's portion of the presentation came and Raelynn happily turned it over to her. She took a sip of her water, the cool liquid soothing her parched throat. She watched their new prospective client as his attention was directed to her partner. He was a tall man, well built; a little slick was all she could think. His suit was tailored and he was certainly polished but there was an underlying current of danger she couldn't quite shrug. The thought was an unusual one for her so she pushed it to the back of her mind and kept her attention to what Melissa was saying.

Once the two of them were done, they asked Mr. Wesley if he had any questions.

"I have a couple," He said, taking out his own notepad. "What kind of contract are you expecting me to sign?"

The question threw Raelynn as they usually didn't require a contract from their clients, "I'm sorry."

"Well," Mark leaned a little closer, "I deal with a lot of confidential information and would require you both to sign non-disclosure agreements." He handed them each a stapled pack of papers. "I also require all of my dealings be done at my convenience."

Melissa spoke up first, "Mr. Wesley, we make every attempt to make ourselves available for our clients."

"Good," Mark answered smoothly, "I'll expect you both to review these, sign them, and get them to my assistant so we can begin work immediately."

Raelynn was surprised, was their meeting over? They didn't even order lunch. She looked at Melissa as their newest "client" got up without preamble.

He shook their hands, "Ladies, it was very pleasurable; I hope to meet with you soon."

Raelynn looked after the man as he left the restaurant and looked over at Melissa. What just happened? Melissa was looking at her, clearly as confused as Raelynn was herself. They ordered their lunch and contemplated the man who just blew them away.

The rest of the day was smooth enough, Raelynn only needing to deal with minor issues. Both she and Melissa were very satisfied with the performance of their interns. Too bad they would leave after six months and two new ones would replace them.

She was grabbing her bag when her phone rang. The temptation to let it go to voicemail was strong but the sensible Raelynn popped up and said, 'answer it.'

"Hello," She said distractedly, trying to make sure her desk was in order.

Seth smiled, "I was wondering if you would still be there." He got home a few minutes earlier from working with the horses all day and only wanted to hear her voice.

"I am, you almost missed me," She sat back down at her desk, wrapping the phone cord around her finger absently.

"Well, it's a good thing I caught you," He sat down on his sofa, a beer in his hand and thoughts of her filling his mind.

She smiled. "Oh yeah, why is that?" She asked softly, she couldn't help but bait him.

"Because," He leaned back, "I'd hate to think of you driving when I explain what I miss doing with you."

Her nerve endings came alive; she felt the delicious pull between her legs, "Really?" She purred, "And what would that be?"

His pants were tight, again. "I was thinking we'd start out with me kissing the back of your neck and working my way down your arm to your hand, where I could kiss your palm and put your sexy fingers in my mouth so I could suck on them softly." He fondly remembered her doing to him the other night.

Oh goodness, Raelynn's breathing was getting shallow, "Well, then I would have to use my other hand to slowly unbutton my blouse so you could see my breasts strain against my bra."

This was getting interesting; he wanted to see how far they could go. "Then I would need to use one of my hands to tease your nipples through your bra. Is it one of those lacy ones, I really like those."

She could actually feel herself getting wet from his words. She looked around, making sure she couldn't hear anyone else in the office. She didn't want anyone to hear what she was saying. "It is," She said softly.

"Why don't you undo your blouse now?" He could picture it clearly in his mind.

Raelynn was torn, oh she wanted to do what he asked, the excitement of it filling her with need. But what if someone came in? Don't think Raelynn, just do, she was saying to herself. "Okay," She said, "I'm unbuttoning my blouse; the fabric is soft to the touch and falls away easily. My bra is light blue and trimmed with black lace on the top."

He wanted to touch the bulge in his pants but wanted to see to her needs first. "Good baby, can you undo it and let those breasts fill your hands like they fill mine?"

Her chest was heaving as she did what he asked. The closure was in the back but she easily undid it, her breasts felt heavy, the nipples hard little nubs that ached for his touch. She pulled the lace out and let it fall to the floor, her free hand taking one of her breasts into it, rubbing softly. The ache was only momentarily eased. "It feels good," she moaned.

"Yes baby," He whispered into the phone, "rub the nipple like I do, make it feel better."

She was a hot ball of need, ready to explode, "I don't know if I can." She said.

He tried to rub the front of his jeans just to alleviate some of his own discomfort. "You can baby, just move your fingertip over it, put your finger in your mouth and get it wet first, that will make it feel better."

Just the act of putting her finger in her mouth to wet it, gave her a jolt of pleasure. This was way above and beyond what she was used to doing. It was exciting to see what he would ask her to do, she couldn't stop. "Ok," Her breath raspy, "oh Seth it does feel good." She was surprised at the sensation.

Now they were getting to a point of no return quickly, at least for him, "I wish I was there tasting them. I would be kneeling in front of you and spreading those sexy legs so I could feel you under that skirt I know you're wearing."

The ache was too much, "Seth, we need to stop." She was saying the words her body definitely did not want to hear.

He agreed but it was difficult, "I know," he sighed, "but you are wonderful."

She blushed, still trying to juggle her phone as she picked up her blouse and bra. "I don't think so."

"You have no idea how erotic you are," He sat forward and took a long drink of his beer. "Are we still on for dinner tomorrow night?"

She smiled and adjusted her clothing, "Oh yes sir we are."

How did one comment get him so riled up again? "Don't say it like that. We'll never get off the phone."

Raelynn laughed, "I know, and I'm making a meat loaf for dinner so I need to get home."

She made the everyday things sound so nice, he smiled into the phone, "Did you want me to come over?"

She picked up her briefcase, "I'd love it but we just took on a new client and I'm reviewing some papers," She didn't discuss the details of her work, it was bad business to do so, "I think you would only distract me."

It was amazing how well she had him pegged, "You are exactly right about that, I guess I'll just sit here, all alone," he sighed dramatically, "no one to make me feel better."

Raelynn snorted, "I think you'll live." She grabbed her suit jacket, "Good night sir, I'll call you tomorrow when I'm leaving work."

"You better," He growled, "good night Raelynn." He said and hung up. Yet another cold shower was his companion for this evening.

Raelynn threw her bag in the car and decided it was nice enough to drive home with the top down. Spring was in full bloom and the weather was pleasant. She put the top down, put on her sunglasses, and pulled out of her parking spot; a big smile on her face.

Driving home was lovely. She turned up the radio so she could hear it over the wind and enjoyed the feeling of freedom. Country music blared, making her think of a certain cowboy and riding horses and making love in cabins. By the time she arrived home, she was fighting a very insistent urge to get back in the car and go over to Seth's house. But she looked at her briefcase and the paperwork and knew the right thing would be to focus on work.

She was finishing dinner when Hailey walked in the door, the commotion of a bag dropping and shoes being flung off, made Raelynn smile.

"Hello Hailey," She said as her daughter walked into the living room.

Hailey smiled in return, "Yum, meat loaf," she said, "hello mom."

Her daughter was nothing if not predictable in certain areas of her life. She came into a room full of energy. She headed for either food or drink and then threw herself onto the couch or hopped up on a bar stool and watched her mother.

Hailey came into the kitchen and grabbed a soda out of the refrigerator, popped the top and took a long drink, then jumped up on a bar stool and watched her mother finish making dinner.

"How was class?" She asked Hailey as she did her test of dinner.

Hailey sighed, "Good, I'm getting my butt kicked by my biology teacher but otherwise they were good."

College wasn't easy, as Raelynn remembered her experience in much the same way. Although it was a little tougher for her since she decided to go to college far from home. She was glad Hailey decided to stay home because Raelynn wasn't ready to part with her little girl just yet.

They chatted through dinner and cleaned up together. Hailey was off to her room to finish some homework while the lecture was still fresh in her mind so Raelynn opened up her briefcase and took out the packet Mr. Wesley gave her at their lunch meeting. She scanned the whole document, seeing that it was indeed a non-disclosure agreement. The thing that bothered her was that it seemed odd as compared to their usual dealings.

She called Melissa, discussed what they each thought and decided to take the contracts to their lawyer the next day. She put the papers back in her case and noticed a little slip of blue paper in the same pocket she had the papers in. She pulled it out, seeing that it was a blue sticky note that must have been attached to the papers. She read the short note and frowned, it said *Dinner?*

It must have gotten mixed up with her packet at Mr. Wesley's office. She tossed the paper out and put it out of her mind for the evening. She'd rather concentrate on catching up with her favorite show on tv. That and figuring out what she would wear to Seth's the next evening. She already let Hailey know she wouldn't be home for dinner.

The next morning, Raelynn was getting ready for work when her phone rang. She didn't recognize the number but she and Melissa both gave their cell numbers to their clients.

"Hello," She said absently.

A man's voice came on, "Ms. Woodsen?"

She couldn't place the voice, "Yes?"

"This is Mark Wesley," He said clearly, "I was wondering if you and your partner were able to go over the agreement I gave you yesterday."

She thought this was an odd conversation for so early in the morning, "Yes Mr. Wesley we have and we'll get back with you later today on that." She was trying to get her bags together so she could get off to work.

"And the other paper?" He asked.

She was confused, "The other paper?"

He cleared his throat, "The blue piece of paper asking you to dinner? Did you get that as well?"

So that wasn't a mistake, she was surprised by his directness, "Honestly Mr. Wesley, I thought it was a mistake, if you'll call the office later, we'd be happy to set up a business dinner with you."

Mark Wesley stood on the deck of his house, looking out into the dense woodlands surrounding it. Privacy was very important to him, almost an obsession on some levels. He was impatient as well and didn't like his advances ignored.

"Raelynn," He said in a low voice, "I was hoping it would be a private dinner that included just you and I."

She was shocked, what did she say? "Mr. Wesley," She hoped that relayed that she wasn't comfortable with him using her first name, "I'm afraid I don't know you well enough to agree to that, not to mention if you're a client, I wouldn't feel very comfortable with seeing you on a social level."

She was trying to be diplomatic. It wasn't as if she hadn't turned down dinner proposals before, they just weren't from powerful businessmen whom she suspected weren't turned down very often if ever.

"I see," He answered coolly, "I guess we'll discuss it further then at a later time." He hung up the phone and went back into his house. This didn't sit well. Not at all.

Raelynn hung up her phone with a sneaking suspicion that this wasn't the last she would hear about it. If she let it, she would worry to distraction and she didn't have the time to do that. Leaving a quick note for Hailey, she ran out of the house.

Upon arriving at work, the office was up and going. Raelynn jumped in and fielded the normal tax calls along with requests for appointments. She was finally able to meet with Melissa after lunch and told her about the strange phone call she got from Mr. Wesley in the morning.

"Okay," Melissa said, "that was uncomfortable and I wasn't even involved."

Raelynn nodded, "You're telling me. Somehow though," she took a quick sip of water, "I don't think he's the type of man to let a little thing like my professional morals get in his way."

Nodding, Melissa sighed, "Well, I dropped the agreement off at Scott's office this morning. He left me a voicemail saying it was above board so it's up to you whether we proceed."

It was a tough decision, they needed high-profile clients like Mr. Wesley in order to expand their business, "I say let's go ahead, at least it will give me an excuse to not see him socially."

Melissa smiled, "I agree. Speaking of social how is Seth?"

She couldn't help it, she blushed, "Melissa, Seth is fine, thank you for asking."

"A little birdie told me you were going to dinner at his place tonight, are you staying over?" Melissa leaned in, eager to hear the scoop.

Raelynn mock slapped at her hand, "I don't think so, it's a weeknight."

Melissa tsked, "You have got to get out and get crazy."

Thank goodness her friend wasn't in the office the night before, Raelynn thought, she would have seen firsthand how crazy Raelynn managed to get.

"Why are you blushing?" Melissa asked though slatted eyes.

Looking down at her very interesting water bottle, Raelynn smiled, "I don't know what you're talking about."

There was an interrogation coming, Melissa knew it, but before she could start in, their intern, Patrice poked her head in the break room door, "Ms. Melissa" she said in a southern drawl, and "your two o'clock appointment is here."

Melissa scowled, "We'll have a talk later."

Raelynn saluted her friend, "Sure." Although she had no intentions of letting herself get into that conversation. She pushed away from the table and went to finish up her work.

The next time Raelynn looked up, it was past five. Where did the afternoon go? It was wrapped up in figuring out a long-time client's particularly odd spending habits that he insisted were tax write offs. People were complex creatures, especially with their money. She cleaned off her desk, locked up the office, and went to her car.

After checking her phone to make sure she didn't miss a call from Seth, she drove over to the local grocery store. Her list was short, whipped crème, caramel sauce, and hot fudge topping. She stood in line fidgeting and thinking everyone knew why she was buying just these items. The cashier smiled benignly and

Raelynn blushed. What was wrong with her? She finished checking out and walked briskly out to her car. She put the bags in and grabbed her phone. She pushed call on Seth's contact listing.

He was just finishing up his shower when he heard his phone go off. The towel half hanging off him, he reached for the darn contraption and swore when it slipped out of his still-wet hand. Finally, he picked it up and hit answer.

"Hello," He said tightly.

Raelynn could hear something in his voice, "Are you okay?"

Chastising himself, he smiled, "I'm sorry, the phone slipped out of my hand and I was afraid I'd miss your call."

Aww, she thought, he was sweet, "I probably would have just tried to call you back in a few minutes."

He chuckled at himself, he was acting like a school boy, "I know. I just wanted to talk to you now and tell you to get yourself over here."

Now how could she resist when the tone of his voice felt like silk over her skin? "I'm on my way."

"Good," He said, "drive safely but fast."

She smiled, "Okay, that's a bit of a contradiction but I'll do my best." She looked at her watch, "I should be there in about twenty minutes."

Seth nodded, "Okay."

Chapter 9

Seth took ten minutes to get ready and spent the rest of the time looking out the front window for Raelynn's car. He was nervous and didn't know why. The woman was beautiful and made him crazy with wanting but there was something more there. He couldn't put his finger on it but he would eventually. His pulse sped up when he saw her car come down the drive.

She parked next to the house and smiled when she saw Seth coming towards her car. The man was gorgeous in jeans and a t-shirt. His shoulders were hugged by the cotton fabric and she could see them move and ripple when he reached for her car door.

Wrapping her arms around him as she got out of the car, she gave him a kiss. It was filled with missing him and she hoped he felt it as much as she did. "Hello," She whispered when she could manage to pull her lips from his.

"Well hello ma'am," he responded. "I surely do like the way you say hello." He squeezed her to him once more and reluctantly let her go enough so she could walk up to the house.

She turned around, "Oh I almost forgot dessert," she squealed and went back to the car. She pulled out the bag with the items she purchased and a container.

They walked up to the house and ascended the front steps. Impulsively, Raelynn turned around, "Seth the view from here is spectacular," She watched the sun hanging low in the sky and spreading a fountain of color over the pastures in front of the house. It was amazing.

"I've always thought so," He loved his house, even though it was a lot different than he originally intended it to be. Those thoughts would need to be tamped down for now.

They went inside and straight to the kitchen. Raelynn was puzzled because there was nothing on the stove and the oven didn't seem to be on, at least she couldn't smell anything cooking.

"Seth," She said in her best mom voice, "you promised me dinner, I will not settle for pizza or something ordered."

He put up his hands in defense, "No ma'am, I'm grilling out on the patio." He motioned outside.

Raelynn put her dessert and the bag from the grocery store in the refrigerator and followed him out the back door. They made a left away from the barn and walked around the house. There was a lovely little patio set up on this side of the house. It was stone and decorated with some wrought iron bistro tables along with a pretty complex grill set up. It was impressive and completely out of step with the way the house was set up. Inside it was pretty masculine but this looked like it was designed by a woman. Her curiosity was piqued but she didn't want to ask too many questions. It was wonderful just being with him.

"This is lovely," She said and sat at the table he set for them.

He winked at her and went over to the grill, "Thank you." He was turning the chicken and steak over; he wasn't sure what she preferred so he made both.

There was a salad tossed and chilling in his little mini frig so he pulled it out, tossed it a little and put it on the table. The meat was done so he pulled it off the grill and carried it to the table.

How many people were eating? She looked at him, "Is it just the two of us?"

He looked chagrined, "Yes, I didn't know what you would like so I just made a lot. Is that okay?"

This man was surprising; he seemed almost shy now, "Yes, that's perfect Seth. You are sweet to think of that."

Relief flooded his chest, it was important that they have a great dinner. He was unsettled with her but still wanted everything to be perfect.

They sat and ate, each asking about the other's day. Raelynn liked hearing about his ranch. She had a pretty good idea about what he did at Skydive Spaceland but asked some questions about how he started.

Seth told her how his dad was a skydiving enthusiast along with his brother and they took their kids out as soon as they were old enough. It was like a bug, you just caught it. He never had any close calls so he was comfortable with jumping. He knew friends who ran into complications from time to time but explained how, if you were smart and trusted your gear; you were safer than in most cars.

Raelynn listened to his stories and was absorbed in them. He led such an interesting life compared to hers. He lived ten times what she did and yet he was interested in her. It boggled her mind just like it did when Anthony told her he loved her so many years ago.

He knew the moment she thought of her late husband. There was a cloud that came over her eyes. He doubted that she would ever completely lose that and wanted to be the one who helped her with it. He reached across the table and took her hand between his fingers.

"Tell me about Hailey's father." He said it softly; he wanted to know but didn't want to seem pushy.

She was so surprised by the request; she didn't know what to say. "Um," The words wouldn't come which frustrated her.

Seth wanted her to be okay with discussing her late husband. Seth didn't view the man as a threat but saw how she might interpret his questions. "Where did you meet?"

Remembering was always a bit painful, "Well, a friend dragged me to a frat party that I did not want to go to but felt like I should." She took a sip of her wine, "I was a bit of a wallflower," she nodded at his surprised expression and thought was being kind to her.

"I was," She smiled, "and Anthony, oh he was larger than life." She took a breath, "He filled up a room; Hailey is like him in that respect."

He nodded and smiled in return.

It was tough for her to hold Seth's hand and talk about Anthony. She wasn't used to the conflicting feelings, "He drew me in and I was lost. We were married within six months and he was dead less than a year after that."

The pain was still there for her, Seth could see that for sure. "How did it happen?" He wasn't sure he was completely comfortable with knowing but he was pretty sure Anthony would need to be resolved if they could have a relationship.

Raelynn was speechless by the question, this part was hard, she nodded and started, "He was doing an inspection of an oil platform and someone mis-labeled a natural gas line. The explosion took out the whole platform and he was one of nine men killed." She had to look away to compose herself.

It was hard for Seth to comprehend her type of loss. His, thank goodness, experience in loss was limited. There was one thing he could compare but it seemed far less important than her being left so young and then finding out she was pregnant. "I'm sorry."

She knew Seth meant it, as much as he could understand. "I used to be but not now."

Her confession surprised him, his eyebrows rising.

"That sounds crazy right?" She asked and looked at him, his blue eyes sparkling in the fading light. "I used to think, why did I have so little time with him? And then I finally just resigned myself to thinking that he lived what he was meant to and had to move on." She swiped at the tears, "Some of us are put here to live a lot in a short period of time. It's how it is."

He appreciated her take on it but wasn't all together sure it was reconciled as much in her heart as it was in her mind. He could take a lesson from her for sure.

Now Raelynn was embarrassed, this was supposed to be an erotic evening for the two of them and she was talking about her late husband and crying. "I'm sorry if I've ruined the evening for you."

He lifted his hand and caressed her cheek, "Sweetheart, I asked." He smiled, her eyes were so beautiful, "I needed to know if Anthony was going to be something between us."

His statement threw her a little, "Really?"

"Yes," Seth felt funny saying it out loud, "it's clear that you loved him and if you aren't ready for something with someone else, I would understand. I wouldn't like it one whit but I would understand."

"You are adorable," She stood and came around the table so she could sit on his lap, "I am so lucky you are a sensitive man."

Her sitting on his lap was making parts of him very sensitive. "Well I won't be if you keep sitting on my lap like this." He kissed her neck. "I think we should clean up our mess and head inside."

There were insinuations in his voice that made her skin blush. She dutifully grabbed what she could and followed him inside.

They cleaned up the remnants of their dinner, Seth washing dishes and Raelynn putting the leftovers in containers and putting them in the refrigerator. She finished first, so she leisurely leaned against the counter and watched him. She remembered the other night when he "helped" her with the dishes and her stomach tightened in anticipation. She would never be able to do dishes again without blushing.

"What is going on inside that head?" Seth asked. He glanced over and noticed that she looked intense.

She smiled and leaned in to kiss him on the neck, "I was just thinking that I will never do dishes again without thinking of your hands on mine in soapy water."

His body sprang to life with her words, "Woman you are going to have to stop talking like that if you want me to finish."

Raelynn smiled against his neck, her breathing labored, "Oh I think we'll get you to finish."

He pulled his hands out of the water and grabbed her to pull her close; the water from his hands dripping down her shirt and skirt. He laughed at her shocked expression. "Sorry about getting your clothes wet, we'll have to get them off you now." He didn't wait for her to answer before sweeping her up into his arms and carrying her to the living room.

How could she not be swept up, literally and figuratively with him? He made it so easy to just let everything go and just feel. Oh and he made everything feel so good!

Seth sat down on the couch, pulling Raelynn onto his lap and holding her to him while he concentrated on her mouth. This woman made his blood steam through his veins; his whole thought process revolved around her and what he could help her experience. Her lips welcomed his, making him moan.

Running her fingers through Seth's hair, Raelynn thought this is what heaven must be like. All sensation, reality being pushed away. Their mouths melded so she had no idea where she ended and he began. Tongues danced and swirled, creating a phenomenal friction that shot sparks all the way to her toes. If only she could get closer, she wanted to be with him in every way.

Reluctantly, she pulled her head back just far enough so she could see Seth's eyes. "You are a wonderful kisser sir."

Seth smiled, "Thank you ma'am, I certainly do try to please."

His words only added fuel to the fire inside of her, "Well I hope so, please take me up to your room and show me how you'll please me."

"Yes ma'am," he said enthusiastically. He picked her up and proceeded to take her upstairs.

"Seth put me down," she laughed, "I am too heavy for you to carry upstairs."

His eyes shot to hers, "What?" He shook his head, "Raelynn you weigh nothing, I like carrying you."

Her limbs were melting with desire, "Really?"

Seth stopped and looked at her intently, "You really don't see what I see do you?"

Raelynn didn't understand the question and just stared at him.

He put her down carefully and made her face him, his hands cupping her face so he could look into her eyes. "You are gorgeous and sexy and you are amazing."

It was difficult for her to keep looking at him when he said those words. She certainly didn't see herself that way so she couldn't comprehend how he did. There wasn't anything she could think of to say, she just wanted him with her.

When Raelynn didn't respond to his words, he was momentarily concerned that she didn't want to make love. They stood at the base of the staircase and stared at one another, their chests heaving, their hearts racing; it was erotic just staring into her beautiful green eyes.

Raelynn slowly smiled. Without saying anything, she covered his hands with her own and pulled them away from her face. Holding his hands, she turned and started up the stairs. He was following her, their hands entwined.

As they walked down the hall to his room, Raelynn wanted to show him how much she wanted him and how much she wanted to be the woman he described.

She walked into the room. His bed was how she remembered it; big and masculine. It fit him and how she viewed him. In her eyes, he was a phenomenal person, he made her feel safe and he certainly made her feel like a woman. She came to the foot of the bed and turned to face him. She pulled his hands up to cup her face again.

They were standing next to his bed, staring at one another; neither speaking.

Raelynn moved her hands from his, still staring into his eyes, she started unbuttoning her blouse. When Seth moved his eyes off of hers, she brought her hands up to his face and held it, silently telling him to not move. His eyes were dark and hungry; they described everything she was feeling. She continued to remove her clothes, keeping her eyes on his.

Seth was sure he was going to explode; the heat in the room was about one hundred and fifty degrees. Raelynn was taking off her clothes but only wanted him to look into her eyes. Instinctively, his body responded to her, he was so hard he was on the verge of pain. Finally, she was done and turned her attentions to his clothes, again, silently telling him to look only into her eyes.

She moved her hands up his arms and to his shoulders, she could feel the muscles bunch with tension as her fingertips skimmed his skin and t-shirt. The only time she allowed him to move his hands was when she lifted his shirt over his head. When his eyes moved over her, she blushed and tilted his chin up with her hand so he was looking into her eyes only.

She took her palm and ran it down his chest, feeling the tickling sensation his chest hair created. His abdomen was chiseled, probably from working on the ranch, the muscles constricted as her fingertips passed over them. The feeling caused her to burn with need low in her belly.

The act of exploring his body was making her quiver, she wanted him so badly. Her fingers fumbled with the fly of his jeans. She looked back up and saw him smiling slyly at her difficulty. She would not be dissuaded; she wanted to see him naked. The buttons finally gave way and she pushed the denim down his thighs. Of course as she knelt to push down his jeans, his hands left her face and rested on her shoulders.

Raelynn stared at his naked form, knowing he wore nothing under his jeans, caused a whole new sensation to stream up her spine. She openly stared at his nakedness, knowing she made him that hard made her want him even more; as if that were somehow possible. Her thoughts took over and she wanted to taste him. This was never a consideration before so she was nervous. Running her hands back up his thighs, she rested them on his hips and slowly kissed the tip of his sex.

Need shot up his body, oh Lord, Seth tried to resist the urge to grab her and throw her on the bed. He tilted his head down and looked into her eyes; they were looking up at him and seemed unsure.

"Are you okay?" He asked.

Raelynn was embarrassed, "I want to taste you but I've never done this before and I don't want to mess it up."

Seth growled, "Baby, there is no way you could mess it up and you do what you want, I just want to be with you."

His words gave her the surge of confidence she needed. She leaned in and kissed the shaft gently trailing kisses up the length of him. She could feel his body tremble so she was emboldened and took the tip of him into her mouth.

He was going to die of sweet agony. How did the woman doubt her abilities to make him burn? Her tentativeness actually made the experience sweeter, although if she didn't stop, he was going to embarrass them both.

"Baby," He rumbled, "you need to stop or this is going to end way too soon."

Raelynn stopped making love to his manhood long enough to look up into his eyes, "But I was just starting to get the hang of it."

Her words were going to tip him over the edge, "Yes you are," he pulled her up so they were face to face, "and never worry that you don't know what you're doing."

She could see that he was sincere, which helped her not feel like she was floundering. She kissed him, tasting his lips and knowing he wanted her as much as she wanted him.

They crawled onto the bed together, kissing and touching as they made their way up. The comforter on the bed felt soft on their skin and made them even more eager.

Finally, they were at the top of the bed, laying face to face, the only light was the bedside lamp. It cast a soft glow that didn't quite reach the edges of the massive room. The shadows surrounding them made a cocoon so they were alone in their own world. They were two lovers trying to find their way through the haze of want and need.

Seth softly touched Raelynn's cheek with the back of his fingers, "You make me want you more than I ever thought possible."

"I know, I feel the same way," She replied, a smile playing with the corners of her mouth.

He pushed her hair back and leaned over to kiss her shoulder, it tasted so delectable and he couldn't stop. His kisses left a moist trail over her neck, shoulder, and down so he could suckle her nipple in his mouth. He remembered the phone conversation they shared the night before.

Raelynn could feel his maleness against her thigh and wanted him inside her, NOW. Without thought, she followed her body's wants and pushed him over onto his back. He groaned at being pulled away from her breast but did as she commanded with her body. She straddled him and rubbed her wetness against him, making them both moan.

It amazed her how her body just instinctively knew what it wanted with Seth. Her nails dragged down his arms as her hips moved against his. When they reached his hands, she wrapped her fingers around his and held tight.

Seth was going to die a very sweet death, he was sure of it. He could feel them both move against one another and his body cried for release. He clenched his jaw, trying to stave off the sensations; he wanted her to go over first.

She let go of one hand and reached between him, she licked her lips when her hand found him and wrapped her fingers around the length of him. His hips bucked up in response and she smiled knowingly. In the next instant, she was guiding his length into her, enjoying the slow torture of crazed excitement it created inside her.

Raelynn grabbed his hands and pushed them over his head, resting them on the pillows, she held him there, her hands on his forearms as she rode him. Over and over, her body taking his into it, her moans of pleasure filling the room.

He could feel his release and was adamant about them going together, "Baby, I need you to come with me," he said through clenched teeth.

"Yes," Raelynn was saying loudly, "I'm almost there Seth," her rhythmic moves increasing until she was riding him fast. "Yes, Yes," she yelled.

185

They both cried out with release, Seth filling her with his heart and soul and Raelynn dropping against his chest out of exhaustion.

He held her, running his hands up and down her back, filling her body tremble with the aftershocks of her climax.

When she could finally form a coherent thought, she slowly pushed herself up enough so she could see his face. There were tears streaming down her cheeks.

Seth was immediately worried, "Are you okay, did I hurt you?"

She shook her head no, "I think my orgasm was just so overwhelming, I started crying."

Her admission stirred his insides, physically and emotionally. He should be sated after their lovemaking and only a few minutes later, he was thinking of what he could do to love her again.

"I think," He pushed her hair behind her ears in a reassuring gesture, "that's a good thing."

Raelynn nodded, "I think so too. God, Seth, it was incredible!"

Her words mirrored his thoughts, "I would have to agree." He leaned up and kissed her softly on the lips.

They lay in the bed, naked, just trying to absorb the overwhelming senses their lovemaking created. After a bit, Seth got up and went into the bathroom. Raelynn felt cold without his heat next to her. She turned over so she was facing the bathroom door; she wanted to give him privacy if he needed it. She could hear him moving around and heard water running. Her smile returned when he walked out of the bathroom. He walked over to where she was and held out his hand. When she took it, he pulled her up and guided her to the bathroom.

She walked into the room and was amazed at the transformation. The room was lit with candles strategically set. The tub she admired the day she was here was filling with steamy water and bubbles. She looked at Seth with a smile.

"I thought you might like a bath," He grabbed a towel out of the linen closet and walked to the tub. "Your bath my dear."

The man was a gem, "I thank you sir," she stepped in and sighed with pleasure. The water was just hot enough, her muscles loosened as she emerged her body in it.

Seth watched her get into the tub and thought it was about the sexiest thing he'd ever seen up to this point. Now he knew her body and knew what it did to his own. The thoughts roused his libido, making him turn away quickly before Raelynn noticed it. He walked back to a small cabinet and pulled out a bath sponge.

The water sloshed over her body, creating a tingling sensation along her skin. She couldn't remember it being this sensitive before. It was Seth, she thought as she sunk to her chin in the bubbles. He made her feel everything. She started, her eyes flying open, when she felt something brush against her leg. He was moving a sponge along her foot.

"Well, I thought you might join me," She whispered.

Seth smiled, "I would like nothing more but I need to leave you alone for a few minutes."

She didn't understand, "Is everything okay?"

He laughed, "Raelynn, I want you again and don't want to attack you."

That made her smile, "Seth, you can attack me anytime you want." She meant it, if he could make her feel all of this; she was crazy to make him stop.

"I may take you up on that young lady," He winked at her.

His tone made her nerves jump with excitement. She reveled in his touch as he ran the sponge up and down her legs. The bubbles acted like a blanket that popped and hissed with the movement of the water. She never even realized how bubbles made noises or how water massaged her skin. Sensations pummeled her as he gently washed her body. She leaned forward so he could run the sponge up her back. The water running down her skin made it heat up. She sighed as he soaped her shoulders.

Raelynn opened her eyes when she didn't feel Seth behind her; she turned to see him walking back over to the sink and reached below. He was still naked and just watching him crouch down made her tremble. His body was lean, his muscles bunched and flexed with his movements. He was simply beautiful. Her eyes met his as he stood and smiled at her.

He walked back to the tub, the shampoo and conditioner in his hands. His eyes stayed on hers as he knelt down next to the tub. There was a cup on the side and he dipped it down into the water. Her gently tipped her head back and slowly poured the water down the back of her head coating her hair with its wet warmth.

There was something very vulnerable about her tilting her head back and letting him pour water over her hair. He guided her around so her head was near the faucet, leaning her back and turning the water on slowly. He poured the shampoo into his palm and started massaging it into her hair. The tingles graduated into little explosions of sensation on her scalp as he worked her hair into a rich lather.

Seth watched her face, her eyes closed, her head tipped back and feeling his fingers in her hair. The ecstasy he saw on her face was palpable. His fingers wound their way through her hair and made circles on her scalp. He never considered that washing a woman's hair could be so erotic. His body was revving up from the inside out.

He used the cup to rinse the shampoo from her hair slowly. The water would move and lap at her skin, making her shudder. There were so many sensations pulsing through her, she was in awe of them.

Seth made sure the shampoo was out and poured the conditioner into his palm. Women didn't just wash their hair; they needed to make it soft. He loved Raelynn's hair; its slickness caressed his palms as they ran the length of it. He finally finished rinsing the conditioner out of it and grabbed a big, fluffy towel he had next to the tub.

She heard Seth release the plug on the tub the water swirling it and draining, leaving a trail down her skin as it emptied out of the bath. She opened her eyes and saw him standing with a towel opened for her to step into.

Raelynn stood and let him wrap the cotton towel around her; she drowned in its warmth. She looked at him, "Thank you."

"You are," he kissed the tip of her nose, "most welcome."

He smiled at her and lifted her up into his arms; the towel creating a soft friction on his skin. He stopped to grab another towel and left the bathroom, carrying her to the bed. He lowered her softly and crawled behind her so he could use the second towel to dry her hair.

Was the man a genius? He knew exactly what to do to make her feel pampered. No one ever gave her body the attention he did. His legs were surrounding hers and she put her hands on them, slowly rubbing up and down their length as he dried her hair. It was ecstasy and comfort intertwined.

Seth made sure her hair was as dry as he could get it with the towel. It wasn't extremely long but fell below her shoulders to the top of her shoulder blades. He reached for the brush he grabbed with the towel and started brushing its length. The repetitious movement lulled him into a web of desire he knew only Raelynn could help him sate. Her head fell back when the brush reached the base of her scalp, making her hair fall farther down her back. He was envious of the silkiness that touched her skin. He wanted to touch her as her hair did. Once he was assured her hair was brushed, he gently gathered it into his hands and moved it over her shoulder. That exposed the other shoulder so he could kiss it.

When Seth's lips touched her skin, she was sure she would die of want. All the feelings she was experiencing were flowing around her and making her head spin.

"Ah," She sighed on the edge of a breath when his tongue tasted her skin.

He smiled against her skin, "Yes baby, I know."

"Seth," She turned her head to look at him but he started kissing her neck, "are you going to make love to me again?"

Goodness, he wanted to, "Is that what you want baby?" If she said no, he would somehow stop, although he had absolutely no clue how he would do it.

She smiled, "Yes please."

Her tone made him pulse with an indescribable need. "Well, I'm here to please you."

Raelynn pulled the towel from around her and stood so she could pull it away. She dropped it to the floor and watched him as he watched her. His jaw was clenched; his hands lay on the bed, the brush still in one of them. She reached down and pulled it from his grip, laying it on the night stand. She turned back to him and pushed her hair back over her shoulder, causing her breasts to jut out towards him, the hard pebbles of her nipples begging for his attention.

She was like a goddess, standing in front of him naked and wanting. He reached up to run his hands up her sides, memorizing the curves of her body, committing them to memory.

Her hands found his hands and followed them up to his shoulders. She leaned into him, loving the feel of his hands roaming her body. When they reached around her and grabbed her bottom, she was alive with need.

Seth could not wait a moment longer; he pulled her toward him on the bed, moving her beneath him so quickly she gasped in surprise. His eyes focused on hers, gold flecks sparkling in the semi-light. He used his knee to gently part her thighs and slowly found her wetness with his rock hard manhood. The slowness in which he entered her was a sweet torture he would never forget. She was all heat and his body pulsed with desire in every pore of his being. He moved slowly at first, wanting to draw out the pleasure for both of them.

It was slow and sweet and the best feeling Raelynn could remember feeling. She wrapped her legs around Seth's waist, enjoying his intake of breath when he went deeper into her. She didn't know where she ended and he began and she didn't want to know. Their dance of desire sped up and she was panting.

"Seth please, harder, faster," she all but screamed.

His tempo increased and he thought his heart would beat out of his chest, "Yes," he gasped for air, "baby."

Her body clenched as it tipped over the edge of madness; she called out his name, not even caring how she sounded. She smiled as he tightened with his own release.

His body was too weak to stay above her, he lowered himself to his side, pulling her tight against him. He wanted to feel her softness as he came to earth from the heights of his climax. She was as breathless as he was, their chests heaving together.

Raelynn was exhausted, emotionally and physically. How was this even possible? How did her body run away like a roller coaster when he was around her? After an eternity, she could finally breathe normally and lay there in Seth's arms thanking the powers that be that she had this time with him.

Seth roused, it was late, and he focused on the bedside clock and noticed it was after midnight. He looked around and didn't see Raelynn, panic filled his chest. He sat up, trying to adjust to the darkness, "Raelynn?" He called out.

She came out of the bathroom, in her clothes, and smiled, "I'm sorry, I was trying not to wake you."

It was impossible for her to look at him, tousled and sleepy, and not want to crawl back into his bed. "I have to get home." She sat on the edge of the bed and rubbed his fingers with hers.

"Why?" Seth asked. He assumed that she would stay over.

Raelynn smiled, "I have work tomorrow and didn't bring a change of clothes."

He looked around for his jeans, "Well, let me walk you out at least."

She watched him as he got up and put on his jeans, the man could be a model any day. Her eyes were studying his movements, pleasure nipped at her heels. She had to stop ogling him or they would end up back in bed.

He dressed quickly and walked her downstairs and out to her car. She unlocked the door and got in, putting down the window. He crouched down and kissed her through the window, "You could stay you know." His need for her outweighed his general rule of no overnight guests.

Oh how she wanted to, but alas, the sensible Raelynn woke her up and made her dress and hounded her brain to go home to Hailey. "I know but I have to go." She started the car then looked at him, his features partially shaded by the darkness of the yard. "We never did have dessert you know."

He groaned, the woman was going to kill him and he would love ever second of it. "Come inside and we'll have some."

Raelynn shook her head, "I doubt we'd even make it to the kitchen Seth." She kissed the hand he rested on the bottom of the window opening of her car. "I'll come over in a couple of days and feed you dessert."

The tone she used skipped over his skin and he smiled, "That's a promise." He stood so she could back up, "Text me when you get home so I know you made it safely."

There was that sweetness again, he threw it in there and it made her tremble with warmth. "Okay I will." She blew him a kiss and pulled out onto the driveway.

He watched her go and hated it. His body wanted her here with him. After her tail lights crested the rise in the driveway, he walked slowly into the house. His shoulders sagged like a little boy. If he was pouting then so be it.

Raelynn pulled into her garage twenty minutes later. She shut off her car, pulled out her phone and sent Seth a text. *I'm home safe, I had a great time tonight thank you.*

She laughed at her text, she did not have any idea what to say to someone you just made love with for hours and who made you feel like a dry piece of timber that would combust with the slightest spark. She sighed and opened her car door. After grabbing her brief case and locking up the garage she quietly entered the house. No noises from Hailey so she tiptoed into the living room and jumped when she saw her daughter sitting on the chair and looking at her like her mother might have after she broke curfew.

"Hailey," She grabbed her chest in an effort to control her shock. "I didn't know you were still up."

Oh, Hailey thought, she was so busted. "How was your date mom?" Her tone dry, she loved that her mom looked like a deer caught in headlights.

"It was fine," Raelynn answered quickly and put her purse and briefcase on the bar in an effort to hide her embarrassment, "how was your night?"

Hailey smiled slowly, "It was fine, uneventful; however I can see yours wasn't." She got up from the chair and walked over to her mom. She leaned up and kissed her mom on the cheek and walked toward her room, "Good night mom." She threw over her shoulder.

Raelynn was trying not to laugh, she imagined the roles reversed so Hailey must really be getting a charge out of busting her, she shook her head and heard her phone ping; it was Seth. *You are welcome but you should have stayed.*

She wanted to stay with him but it was better that she came home. She walked into the bathroom and gasped at her reflection. Her clothes were wrinkled from being tossed on the floor, there were stains on her shirt and skirt where the soapy water from Seth's hands grabbed her. Mortification wrapped around her but gave way to laughter at the absurdity of it all. She got ready for bed, thinking that she owed Hailey a lot since her daughter didn't pick on her too badly. But there was always tomorrow.

Chapter 10

The alarm was going off and Raelynn wanted to ignore it. The stupid thing would not shut off though and she finally got up and punched the button. Well, she was up now and might as well get going.

Fixing breakfast always put Raelynn in a good mood, she loved preparing food for Hailey. Maybe it was the feeling that she was doing something with her daughter. It was always fine when it was just the two of them but now she found herself thinking how nice it would be if Seth was there with them.

She stirred the eggs and got out some bacon, Seth drifting around in her mind. The man invaded her thoughts a lot more than she was comfortable with. He was in her mind when she woke up, when she went to bed, when she was driving, when she was sitting, she was probably never going to be able to take a bath again for thinking of how he "bathed" her. Just thinking about that caused her face to blush. It was very hot in the kitchen so she opened the patio door to let the morning breezes in.

Hailey wandered into the living room and plopped down on the chair. Raelynn smiled at her daughter, not a morning person but beautiful nonetheless.

"Good morning, breakfast will be ready in about two minutes." Raelynn called to the room.

Hailey grumbled, "Morning," and got up. She stretched and made her way to the dining table.

They ate in relative silence, Raelynn lost in her thoughts of the skydiving cowboy she was falling for. She watched Hailey start to wake up and smiled. "How did you sleep?"

"Okay," Hailey replied between bites of scrambled eggs. "You?"

Raelynn sighed, "Okay, not as long as I would've liked but I forgot to turn off the alarm last night."

"I'll bet," Hailey snickered.

Mom behavior took over, "Is there something you would like to say?" She was looking at her daughter intently.

Hailey looked appropriately chagrined, "Not really although it was fun to see you come in so late and look like you were busted by your parents."

Embarrassment was not something Raelynn liked to feel under any circumstances but especially not when it was due to something she did that was somewhat irresponsible. "I apologize for that."

Shaking her head, Hailey frowned, "Why?" She pushed her empty plate away, "You didn't do anything wrong Mom, I'm sorry if I made you feel that way."

"Oh you didn't sweetie," Raelynn patted Hailey's hand, "I just don't want to set a bad example."

Hailey got up quickly and put her plate in the sink, "Mom, you have never set a bad example, if anything it's kind of nice to know that you can have fun. I almost gave up hope."

It was shocking to hear her daughter say such things to her. "You know, I haven't just sat around for eighteen years twiddling my thumbs." The anger was unexpected but she couldn't help it.

"Haven't you?" Hailey asked quietly.

Well this was not going well and she was getting very mad. "No," She pushed away from the table, "I have not."

Raelynn started washing dishes and didn't say anything further to Hailey; she was really ticked off and couldn't put her finger on the exact reason why. She had a good life, maybe she didn't act CRAZY, but she had fun. After getting the dishes done, she finished getting ready for work. She managed to say goodbye to Hailey before leaving but it was tense. She did not like having anything disrupt their environment but it was just irritating how both Hailey and Melissa accused her of just waiting around.

As she drove down the highway, she wrestled with her thoughts. The problem was that they were right but Raelynn did not want to admit it. After Anthony died, she did hide behind Hailey. It was easier than putting herself out there again. That was why she made the list wasn't it? Because she realized she wasn't living. Even it was true though, she most definitely did not want to acknowledge it to anyone. And where did Seth fall into all of this?

She slowed to allow a truck pass her and contemplated the situation. Seth saw her when she was doing things out of character like skydiving. The lovemaking couldn't even be measured on any scale she could find but what happened when the newness wore off? Would someone like Seth be interested in plain old Raelynn?

The questions went unanswered as she pulled into the parking lot of the office. Work would help, she was sure of it.

As she walked into the office, Raelynn heard someone, "Hello?" She hollered.

"Hey," Melissa yelled out. "In my office."

This was odd; Raelynn dropped her stuff into her own office and went into Melissa's. She sat down in front of the desk, "You're here early."

Melissa smiled a smile that said, 'I know.' She shuffled papers, "Our newest client, Wesley decided to have a courier drop off some of the documents he wants us to go over and called me very early this morning."

Oh him, Raelynn thought. "Okay, how can I help?"

Melissa gladly divided up some documents, they went over what was needed and each of them went to work. It took a couple of hours but everything was audited and calculated per Mr. Wesley's specifications. They put the documents into a pouch and went about working on some of their other clients' tax documents.

Lunch flew by and Raelynn ate at her desk. She didn't do it as a general rule but sometimes there just weren't enough hours in the day. The afternoon slid by quickly and she was surprised it was almost six o'clock when she surfaced. Her phone held a couple of messages so she played the voicemails while straightening up her desk.

The first one was from Hailey, "Mom, I'm going to stay at school late to study with some friends. I'm sorry if I upset you this morning. I love you and I'll grab dinner here so don't worry."

Raelynn smiled, she was glad they never managed to stay mad at one another for very long.

The second voicemail was from Seth, "Hello beautiful lady who left my bed way too early last night." She sat down and listened, his voice soothing her, "Call me when you can."

She erased the messages and sat staring at nothing in her office. He made her feel so many things that it was difficult to sort it all out. Then again, she was just acting different right now because it was new, the fear she felt this morning came back and she put her phone away.

The drive home was long and by the time she got into the condo, she was in a sour mood. She dropped her purse and case on the sofa and went into the bathroom to shower. The water ran over her skin. She hoped it would wash away her fears and doubts but knew it wouldn't.

She spent the evening watching television and making an effort to not call Seth. What did she say to him? She was no closer to any resolution when Hailey came home. Raelynn tried to put on a brave face for her daughter, managing small talk until Hailey decided to turn in. When she was left alone again, her mind rambled at the speed of light. Her inner voices were so loud; she went to bed just to quiet them.

The rest of the week was much the same, Raelynn over-thinking her not-quite relationship with Seth, working like a dog, and trying to keep her time with Hailey happy. By Friday, she was frazzled and even Melissa was giving her funny looks. Luckily Seth hadn't called again so she didn't feel so bad; he was probably as busy as she was. She was just chickening out and she knew it.

After lunch her phone rang, she didn't know the number and answered it, "This is Raelynn Woodsen."

"Raelynn," Mr. Wesley said, "how nice to speak to you again. I was wondering if you were able to go over those documents I sent a few days ago."

She was puzzled, "Yes sir, I was under the impression that those were being returned to you by messenger." She would talk to Melissa as soon as she hung up.

Mark Wesley sat in his office, absently looking out the window and enjoying the sound of a certain lady's voice in his ear. She sounded so proper which was very appealing to him. "I didn't send a messenger; I was hoping you might drop them off this evening."

The uncomfortable feeling she was beginning to feel did not sit well. Catering to their clients was something she and Melissa boasted about so she couldn't very well say no. "I'm sure I could. What time?"

"How about five?" Mark checked his watch.

This was not a good idea, Raelynn's inner voice was saying. "Yes sir, I'll drop them off then."

Mark smiled, "Great, I'll see you then."

"Goodbye," Raelynn said as politely as she could. As soon as the call was disconnected she headed for Melissa's office to see what her friend had to say about it.

They talked about all the possibilities and came to the conclusion that precaution was best when dealing with their new client. Raelynn would drop off the papers and would call Melissa when she arrived and when she left. Melissa didn't want her to go alone but Raelynn assured her it was probably just her own over-active imagination at work.

Raelynn left work early in order to make her meeting with Mr. Wesley. She pulled up in front of the building that housed his offices and was impressed. It was only two stories but sleek and new. It said, "I'm successful." She could admire that but still he seemed a little too full of himself for her taste.

She entered the main office and greeted his receptionist. The woman was all business and barely smiled. Raelynn sat in a chair waiting for a few minutes and looked around. Everything was nice but stark. It wasn't as welcoming as their office was. Well everyone was different.

"Ms. Woodsen," The receptionist said, "he'll see you now."

She smiled as she passed the other woman, "Thank you."

His office was big, she thought as she entered. It was the size of hers, Melissa's, and their waiting area combined. She decided to be all business now and extended her hand as she neared his desk, "Mr. Wesley."

"Please," Mr. Wesley motioned to the seat across from him, "call me Mark."

She nodded and gave him the pouch with the documents, "I think you'll be satisfied with our audit."

"I'm sure I will be," He said smoothly. "How about a drink?" He got up and crossed to the small bar he kept stocked.

She shook her head, "No thank you, I'm driving." That voice in her head was starting to say things again.

He smiled and poured himself a drink, "I can have someone drive you home."

She just bet he would. "No thank you, I just stopped to drop these off, I have plans with my daughter this evening that I cannot be late for." She hoped Hailey forgave her for using her as an excuse.

Daughter? He didn't know that particular detail. "Really? How old is your daughter?"

It wasn't top secret information so Raelynn answered, "She's eighteen, a freshman in college."

"Ah," Mark nodded, he was glad that child was really an adult. He didn't want anything in the way of dating Ms. Woodsen.

Raelynn stood, his look made her very uncomfortable, "Please call the office if you have any questions; Melissa or I can answer anything."

He nodded and walked her to his office door, "Well how about dinner to discuss things?"

"I'm sure we can set something up, I'll have to check with Melissa though," She had her hand on the door when he put his hand on her arm. The touch made her shiver, and not in a good way.

He smiled, "I was thinking it would be just you and I." He ran his hand over her arm, "Maybe dinner at my home?"

She had to tread carefully. It was obvious that Mr. Wesley did not normally have anyone turn him down. "I don't think that would be wise, since it would be more social than work related. I'm sorry." She didn't want him to touch her anymore so she smiled, and turned the knob to open the door.

Mark watched her go with a smile pasted on his face but underneath he was seething. She was polite enough but it was still a rebuff and he certainly wouldn't accept it. He was very interested in Raelynn Woodsen and when he was interested, he pursued, and when he pursued, he won.

Raelynn got into her car and drove around the block before stopping to call Melissa. She relayed the meeting, such as it was, and was relieved to be out of there. Melissa wasn't sure they should keep him as a client but Raelynn was confident that her statement was taken seriously. She drove home and put Mark Wesley out of her mind.

"Hailey?" She called as she entered the condo.

The door was unlocked and she heard voices so she went into the living room to see who Hailey was talking to but as soon as she entered the living room she stopped. Hailey was in the kitchen along with Seth and they were cooking. They didn't hear her come in since there was music playing and they were talking loudly. She just stood there and watched them.

Hailey was leaning against the counter and listening as Seth explained something about whatever it was he was cooking. It smelled heavenly and Raelynn felt hunger pangs in her stomach. She put her purse down and moved closer to the kitchen.

"Hello," She said when she was close enough for them to hear her.

Hailey turned and smiled, "Mom, hey. We're making you dinner," She gave her mom a hug, "actually Seth is cooking and I'm watching."

Raelynn turned her attention from her daughter to Seth; he stood at the stove, a spoon in his hand and watched her. He didn't say anything, only smiled. He looked like an oasis in the desert of her life and she walked over to him and hugged him tight.

"Hi," He whispered into her ear.

A tear slipped down her cheek, "Hi back." She said and pulled away quickly. She turned and went into her bedroom, hoping neither of them noticed her tears.

After cleaning up and getting her emotions under control, she changed into jeans and a t-shirt and went back out into the kitchen. They were setting the plates on the table.

Raelynn taught Hailey how to set a table at an early age and was glad her daughter used her manners with Seth. They seemed very at ease with one another and it made Raelynn want him more. What was she going to do?

"Mom come on," Hailey said and sat down.

Raelynn joined them, "Seth this looks great." She was not surprised he could cook since he made dinner for her the other night.

Seth smiled, "Thank you."

The curiosity got the best of Raelynn, "How was all of this planned?"

Hailey smiled and spoke first, "I texted Seth and asked if he was free tonight, you've been so busy and stressed this week, I thought it would be nice. I promise I offered to order dinner but he insisted."

She looked from her daughter, to Seth, and back again. "I see."

Seth watched her closely; he knew something was bothering her. She hugged him when she came home and that made him feel good but it wasn't like the other night. He never would have thought a hug would feel like a life line but, with her, it was. The week was dragging on without her so when Hailey invited him over, he jumped at the chance to be with Raelynn. Plus he thought spending time with Hailey would be good for all of them. He had nieces and nephews so kids were not a foreign concept but he wasn't their father, he was the cool uncle who brought them cool gifts and let them get away with stuff their parents wouldn't. It was fine before but now he started thinking that he wanted something more.

They ate the meal, Hailey and Seth doing the majority of the talking. Raelynn nodded and commented when it was necessary but mostly watched the two of them. She liked how Hailey acted around Seth, she hoped he would see her daughter how she did, a very boisterous and head-strong woman but also a great person.

After dinner, Raelynn offered to clean up since they cooked. She put the dishes in the dishwasher as they sat in the living room. She was just about done when Hailey jumped up, her phone in her hand, "Mom, I'm going out okay?"

Nodding, Raelynn smiled, "Yes, go."

Hailey left in a flurry of energy and Seth chuckled. The kid was pretty cool; he understood why Raelynn loved her so much. He walked into the kitchen and leaned against the counter so he faced Raelynn as she finished washing dishes.

"She's a great kid Raelynn," He said.

She nodded, "Thank you, I think so."

He didn't want to do it but he had to know, "Are we going to talk about it?"

"About what?" Raelynn asked.

He shook his head and pushed away from the counter, "Are we going to do this again?"

Raelynn hated to admit it, but he was right. She dried off her hands and went into the living room. He followed her and sat beside her on the couch. "I've had a rough week."

Seth considered what she said, it was simple and explained her distance but he wasn't sure it was the whole story. "I'm sorry."

"Why?" She started to fidget from her nerves. He smelled so wonderful, male and dark and mysterious. Just being close to him put her on edge and now she was fighting that and her doubts.

He didn't understand, "Why am I sorry?" He put his hand on hers, "I don't want you to have a rough week."

She huffed, "You never have a rough week?" She was getting upset and didn't know why……again.

"You know, it's hard to get upset about something when you're jumping out of an airplane, you just think about the experience, not what your checkbook says or what bill you didn't pay, or any of that menial stuff." He loved his life and what he did and he would not apologize for that.

She stood and paced, "It must be nice, I don't have that luxury Seth." She snapped, she couldn't help it.

"Oh don't get me wrong," He stood and faced her, "I get pissed off like I am right now because I'm pretty sure you're picking a fight with me."

Damn it! He was right. This flux of emotions inside of her was too much to bear right now. "I'm sorry." She sighed, "You're right."

"Come and sit down," Seth coaxed her back to the sofa. "Talk to me." He wanted to help.

She looked at him and just shook her head, "I don't know what's wrong, I only feel so out of sorts, so twisted up, so unsettled." She looked away then back to him, his eyes searching hers, she hoped she could give him the answers, "I just feel like this has been a vacation of sorts and it will end and I'll go back to my life and you to yours."

"Okay," He said quietly, "do you want me to go?"

Now she hurt him, "I don't want you to go; I just want to have some semblance of control over the chaos in my head and in my heart."

He cupped her chin and tilted her face up, "Baby, that won't happen." He smiled, "You can't control something like that."

"No!" She shouted, shocking them both. She stood and walked to the window, "I have to, you don't understand, I have to keep everything going here for Hailey and I."

It was starting to get clearer, the mystery that was Raelynn. "I don't think I can convince you of it Raelynn, you have to figure it out on your own." He came up behind her and kissed her shoulder through her t-shirt and rubbed her shoulders with his hands.

His touch felt so good, she let her head fall back so it was resting against his shoulder.

Her move exposed her neck and he couldn't resist kissing it. The skin was soft and smelled faintly of her perfume. It was like smelling a meadow. She responded to his touch as easily as he responded to her mere presence.

Raelynn wanted to clear her head of him but it was impossible, he was embedded in her mind and her body wanted more. She turned and wrapped her arms around his waist. She laid her head against his shoulder.

Seth wrapped his arms around her, just relishing having her so close. He wouldn't try to hide his physical condition, couldn't if he wanted to anyway, but she needed to know what she did to him. They didn't have to make love but he wasn't going to just go away and not try to make her see how great they were together.

"Come on," Seth whispered against her hair, "let's go for a ride."

Raelynn was surprised by the comment. She didn't want to be without him so she nodded. They left the condo in his truck. A few minutes later they were headed down the highway toward his house.

She kept her window down, allowing the evening air to play with her hair. It was starting to get humid so the breeze felt good. She didn't even care where they went as long as they were together.

Seth pulled down a back road that abutted his property on the west side. It was slow going since the road was basically a gravel drive but he knew it like the back of his hand.

The bumps made her grab onto the truck door and wonder where they were going. She didn't want to ask, she assumed Seth had a plan in mind.

He got to a tee in the road and stopped, he put the truck in park and cranked up the radio, a slow country song started playing.

Raelynn smiled, "I love this song."

"Really, come on then." He grabbed her hand and helped her out his door. They walked around to the front of the truck so they were illuminated by the headlights. Seth took her into his arms and started dancing with her to the song.

This was a dream, was all Raelynn could think; it was so crazy and romantic. He held her closely, but not tightly, and that made her feel very safe. Although her heart was beating like a racehorse; which made her feel very un-safe, she couldn't stop. The contradiction added to her awareness and as she looked up, she saw him looking at her.

They swayed to the music on the deserted road, only lit by the headlights of the truck, and stared at one another.

She couldn't stand it, "Kiss me Seth."

"Yes," He lowered his head and his lips met hers.

Heat exploded between them. Seth's hands roamed her back, wanting to feel every part of her, it was like they never made love before; he wanted everything and he wanted it with her.

Raelynn felt his tongue slide into her mouth and wanted to weep from the sweet agony his kiss created in her chest. His lips roused hers, which made her push closer to him.

Her hands were in his hair, grabbing it, holding him still so she could assault his lips with her own. Heat bloomed low in her belly making her push her hips into his. The denim of her jeans was wreaking havoc against her thighs as they rubbed against Seth's. The familiar heat she experienced with him found its home deep inside of her. It was like a drug, his lovemaking, only meant for her and only this potent between the two of them.

Seth was lost, he couldn't even come up through the fog of desire she created around him. He ran his fingers under her t-shirt, lightly caressing her ribcage, swiping his thumbs against the bottom of her breasts. He groaned when the nipples hardened and he could feel them against his chest. They caused little darts of pleasure to shoot through his gut. Before he could think, he pulled her shirt up and over her head.

Yes, Raelynn thought, this is what she wanted, him with her and making her feel the frenzied need only he could arouse in her. She didn't care that her shirt was off and her bra was then removed, it was sensual knowing they were outside. She could feel the breeze on her skin, loving how it kissed her back and wound her hair around their faces. She instinctively pushed her breasts closer to him; she wanted no barriers between them.

She pushed Seth's shirt up and off, replacing it with her lips as she kissed his shoulders and chest. His skin was hot, making her body burn. His muscles moved and pulsed underneath her fingertips as they explored.

"Baby," Seth ground out, "I need you."

All Raelynn could do was nod, there was no way she could speak. Her want was deep and primal. Instead, she undid his jeans and pushed them down.

This was crazy, they were stripping in the middle of a road at night and were lit up by his truck lights. It was also the sexiest thing he ever wanted to do with anyone.

She couldn't kiss him enough, her lips found his again and they clawed at one another, trying to remove clothes in their hasty need to join themselves in every way possible.

"Please," Raelynn groaned when they were naked.

Seth still held her and somehow managed to keep them swaying to the music of the song coming from the truck.

Seth was panting, "Yes."

It was too much; she jumped up and wrapped her legs around Seth's waist in one quick move. His hardness was pushed up against her wetness and she gasped from the pleasure. It wasn't enough though; he needed to be in her.

Raelynn was kissing him, her legs wrapped around him like a vice. He was moving and she was frustrated because he wasn't closer. When she finally pulled her head up, she noticed him trying to carry her toward the back of the truck. She couldn't help it, she started to giggle.

"I am not," He stopped to kiss her, his teeth nipping her top lip, "going to make love to you on the hood of my truck, we'll at least be lying down in the bed."

He was so wonderful, "Personally I wouldn't have minded you throwing me on the hood; the vibration from the engine might have been interesting."

Seth stopped and looked at her, she was naked and he was holding her and walking, it was difficult to see in the dark once they left the light of the headlights but he was pretty sure she was teasing him. "Do you want me to go back?" He started to turn around.

"No," Raelynn said quickly, "I want to make love with you Seth."

There was nothing he could do to deny her this. He silently got to the back of the truck and set her down so he could make it more comfortable. If anyone drove up, they would see two people naked walking around a truck. The thought produced another wave of awareness to course through him. He kissed her quickly and walked to the cab to grab a blanket he kept in case of emergencies. After getting it spread out, he climbed up on the lowered tailgate to help her up.

She knew he was going to gently lay her down in the bed of the truck but she didn't want slow and sweet, she wanted hard and fast. "Seth sit on the tailgate with your legs hanging down."

It was tough to decipher her words through his blood pulsing but he did as she asked; maybe she wanted to stop and talk. He would do it but it would be painful.

Raelynn watched him as he positioned his body the way she asked. His body was a work of art, muscled and heated from their lovemaking. Watching him show with his body how he wanted her gave her a rush of self-confidence. Without thinking, she hopped up on the tailgate and straddled him, her legs wrapping around him and guiding him into her as she settled.

Seth sighed with pleasure, she was amazing. She was hot and wet and almost drove him over the edge when she guided him into her sweet warmth.

She threw her head back in delight and started rocking her hips on his, making her body sing with sensations. Her arms held onto his shoulders, the fingernails digging into the skin. It was erotic and wild and she didn't ever want to stop.

"Seth, YES," She yelled in ecstasy as she increased the tempo.

He watched her wild abandonment in wonder, trying to hold off his own release so he could build it for her.

The fireworks of her orgasm spread over her quickly and she saw spots as she squeezed her eyes shut with the shower of sensations. A primal sound made its way out of her throat and she opened her eyes in time to see Seth go over his edge. A smile formed on her lips as he yelled out her name before slumping back against his hands in surrender.

Where did this woman come from? How did she know exactly what he needed to be sated both mind and body? He didn't think there was any way he would ever tire of being with her.

Seth pulled her up onto the bed of the truck and laid down, tucking her in beside him. They could hear the radio belt out a tune and felt the truck idle beneath them and he thought it was so crazy how they played off of one another with their chemistry.

Raelynn was embarrassed by her behavior. She honestly didn't know where it came from. A flush shown in her cheeks and she hoped Seth would think it was an effect of their intense lovemaking.

He rubbed her shoulder with his fingertips. It took a while for his breathing to get under control and a lot longer for his thoughts to organize because she tied him up in knots.

She looked up at him and smiled. "Hi," she whispered.

"Hi yourself," Seth returned. "Are you okay?"

Raelynn chuckled, "I am pretty sure I'm very okay. Thank you."

This lady was adorable, laying naked in his arms, in the back of his truck, "You are," he kissed her lips softly, "welcome."

Feeling shy, Raelynn sat up and looked for her clothes, darn it, they were at the front of the truck. There was absolutely no way to get out of the back of the truck in a ladylike fashion. She thought maybe speed was the best route so she crawled down quickly and hopped down.

Seth was wondering what happened, they were content one second and then she was gone. He followed her as soon as she rounded the end of the truck. It was like she was in a hurry now. Did he say something wrong?

"Raelynn," he said as he came around the front of the truck. He noticed she already had her underwear and bra on, "are you sure you're okay?"

He stood there naked and Raelynn almost buckled. She wished she could be so free and not care but then her conscience piped up and made her wake up from the dream she created with Seth.

"Yep," She grabbed her shirt and quickly pulled it on. "I'm just feeling embarrassed about making love outside," she pulled her jeans up, "and on the back of your truck." Aha, she located both shoes, "And I'm pretty sure this was a dream and I'm going to wake up."

Her words were rushed and Seth couldn't understand why she was so upset. He smiled and walked toward her. "It was not a dream," He pulled her to him, "and it was fantastic." He watched her bow her head, "I thought it was really hot."

Raelynn pushed him away, "You're making fun of me now." It was tough enough to admit but he didn't have to tease her.

"Not really," He snaked his arm around her waist and pulled her to him, "but just a little bit."

She smiled despite her worries, "Okay, get dressed."

Raelynn jumped into the cab of the truck as he got his clothes on. She watched him carefully and wanted to make love to him again. What was wrong with her? She was ready to jump the man eighty times a day. By the time he got into the truck, she managed to work herself into a major stress bomb.

Seth wasn't sure what to do. He wanted to take her to his place but was afraid she would say no. Of course not talking about it was not the right thing to do. He put the truck in gear and backed up a bit so he could turn it around on the narrow road.

She stole glances at Seth as he drove; her stomach in knots. Why was it so intense with him? She never felt this way. Even with Anthony, all she could remember was it was comfortable. It was exciting for sure, but not this crazy, out-of-control desire. She needed space but then she ached to be near him. There was no easy way to figure this out. 'Do you really want to?' Her inner voice asked.

It was clear she was chewing on things in her mind. Her announcement about control explained a little bit but he was having difficulty understanding the problem. They nearly combusted in bed, and anywhere else it seemed, so why was she fighting it?

By the time Seth pulled into the parking lot of her condo, Raelynn was downright scared. She twisted her hands together hoping the action would bring her some clarity. No such luck, as Seth put the truck in park and turned to look at her.

"I know," She said, "I'm being ridiculous."

He smiled, "I don't know if I would use that description but it's clear you're upset."

She nodded, "Yes I am, I don't want you to go. I want you to stay with me tonight."

Wow, Seth thought. She said it so quick; he thought he heard her wrong. "I want to stay with you Raelynn. I want to hold you next to me and feel you sleep, your skin against mine." He pulled her hand to his lips and kissed the back of it, "I want to make love with you and feel you pulse around me, I want to taste you, all of you."

It was so hot in the truck, she couldn't breathe. She sat there staring into his eyes, wanting him. "Okay," she whispered.

She didn't need to tell him twice, Seth jumped out of the truck and walked around to her side. He opened the door and pulled her to him, sealing the deal with a kiss to knock her off her feet. His tongue dancing with hers, giving his silent promises of the pleasure he wanted to give her.

They walked into the condo, hand in hand. They didn't turn on lights, just went to bed.

Chapter 11

The morning sunlight peaked through the curtains, into Raelynn's eyes. It was bright, reflecting the lightness she felt inside. Seth slept next to her and she cherished the sound of his deep breathing next to her.

Morning brought the light along with a couple of new revelations. First, she loved sleeping next to him. He was warmth and comfort, along with excitement and affirmation. She moved her head slowly, not wanting to wake him, and watched him as he slept. Their lovemaking was crazy and romantic and basically indescribable.

They showered when they arrived home and he carried her to the bed, laid her down, and made love to her slowly. He drew out the experience so she was begging him for his love before he gave her satisfaction. They slept for a while but then she woke up with wanting and took him. She smiled like a Cheshire cat, knowing she surprised him by waking him up to her touch. His release prompted her own to come quickly. It shocked her that watching him tumble would bring her along so easily.

Seth stirred and opened his eyes, to see Raelynn staring at him. His body responded to hers quickly. "Good morning baby." He whispered.

She loved that endearment. It made her feel wanted and loved. WHOA!!!!!

"Good morning," She said and looked away to hide her feeling of pure terror. Loved? No one said anything about love here.

She hid her fear by getting up and going into the bathroom. She washed her face and brushed her teeth, trying to figure out how to get the word out of her head. It was like a pebble in her shoe that she couldn't find and refused to be dumped out. When she came out in her robe, he was sitting up in bed; the covers draped low on his body, giving her a wonderful view of his chest.

"I had to brush my teeth and wash my face," She said slowly, "I'm not used to sleeping with anyone." She just stood there looking at him looking at her.

Seth refused to be embarrassed, he couldn't remember a more memorable evening. "I'm not exactly a pro either," he pulled the covers off and slid off the bed. He walked around the bed smiling, "Do you, by chance, have an extra toothbrush in there," he pointed to the bathroom, "I didn't bring mine along.

She laughed, "Yes, in the second drawer," she smacked his bottom playfully as he passed.

It took all of her restraint to not push him back on the bed and ask him to make her feel like he did last night. Once she heard the water running, she decided it was safe to get dressed. She threw on jeans and a short sleeved top, wanting to be casual. They didn't speak of today last night; they only focused on the moment. So what now?

Seth came out of the bathroom and smiled. She was thinking again. The woman was always turning things over in her mind. How she wasn't completely exhausted from all that thinking, he didn't know. He went up behind her and gently sat on the mattress. He rubbed her shoulders with his hands, feeling her relax.

"Thank you for last night," He whispered in her ear.

Her skin tingled from the feel of his breath, "You're welcome. Thank you."

He wanted to see her so he turned her around to face him. "Why are you so worried?"

It bothered her a little that he knew her so well already when she couldn't figure anything out. "I don't know."

"Do you have doubts about us spending time together?" He couldn't understand if she didn't want it as much as he did.

Raelynn looked down at her hands and then looked up at him, "I enjoy spending time with you Seth."

He smiled, "Then what's wrong, you seem awfully serious for so early in the day."

Lord, he could make her feel so silly with her over-thinking and fears. She knew he didn't do it intentionally, he just didn't understand what this was for her.

She sighed, "When was your last relationship?"

He certainly wasn't expecting that question. "About a year ago."

Something was different, she felt him tense at her question.

"My fiancé broke up with me." He said flatly.

"I'm sorry," She cupped his cheek with her palm. "Are you okay?"

He was sure there was more to that question, "If you're asking if I'm over it, I am. We weren't meant to be."

Raelynn nodded, "Okay."

Seth watched her get up and leave the room. He expected an inquisition about his failed engagement. Raelynn was nothing if not a thinker and that would have been a lot to digest for her. He followed her into the kitchen.

She got down her griddle and some plates from the cupboard. After pulling out the fixings for her blueberry pancakes, she turned to find Seth standing at the bar looking at her.

"I hope you like blueberry pancakes," She threw over her shoulder as she got a bowl out to mix the batter in.

He leaned against the bar, "I do." This was opening a can of worms but he couldn't help it, "Raelynn, why didn't you ask me about my relationship with my ex-fiancé?"

Crap, she knew she could never play the 'I'm not interested type' so she shouldn't even try. "I was giving you space."

Space? "Okay, that doesn't sound like something you would say." He said matter-of-factly.

"Then what would I say Seth?" She stopped her stirring and looked at him.

He sighed, "Well, first you ask questions, and then you gnaw on it for a while."

Anger was building, "Am I a dog?" She put the spoon down on the counter because she was pretty sure she would hit him with it if she kept it in her hand.

"No," He said loudly, "what?" Now he was really confused.

She stomped the feet steps to the bar where he stood, "Let me get this straight," she sighed, "I don't pry and ask a million questions about your ex-fiancé, who, I might add, I didn't hear about before today, and then I'm not GNAWING on it like a dog with a bone so there must be something wrong!" Why was she so prone to violence with him, "So tell me all about her Seth?"

The realization that he stepped into a big steaming pile of crap hit him like a brick. "I am sorry." He really was. "It was wrong of me to assume you would or would not do or say something."

"Too late now buster," Raelynn was sneering, "we're going to sit here so you can tell me about the woman who booted you out." The words felt like spears leaving her mouth. Her tone and meaning were horrible and she was immediately ashamed of them.

Seth would have preferred a slap; the words injured his feelings much more. "I'm going to go."

Raelynn stood there and watched him silently pick up his jacket and leave. The front door made a quiet click as it shut behind him. She sank to the chair in the living room and cried.

Hailey stood in the hallway in front of her room and frowned. What was wrong with them? She quietly went back into her room to call Melissa.

The rest of the weekend was spent doing what she always did every weekend. For eighteen years she prided herself on giving Hailey the stability of their life and the predictability was reassuring during those years. Now, it seemed so boring and stale. Seth brought something she so desperately missed; living......experiencing.......loving.

She refused to call him; he was the one who left. She was rude though and that she couldn't understand. It was so much NOT like the person she considered herself to be. By Sunday afternoon she was driving herself crazy with her thinking.

222

Sometimes you just couldn't think your way through it. She was at her desk and trying to get her bills paid when she saw the slip of paper with the list on it.

Picking it up, she became even madder. This darn paper started it all! No, she yelled at herself, she started it herself with dreaming that things could be better, would be better. They aren't all that great at the moment and she better figure out how to fix it. Groaning, she put the list down and got up to get her keys.

The day was bright and clear, a direct contradiction to the storm brewing inside of Raelynn. She drove with purpose, not caring if it turned out horribly, it was what she needed. She turned into the drive for Seth's ranch, dread creeping up her spine. Her breathing was shallow and her palms started sweating because she had no clue what she was going to say to Seth when she did see him.

Once she parked, she looked around and didn't see his truck. He could be anywhere. She got out and headed toward the barn. One of the ranch hands came out, she thought his name was John, and walked up to her.

"Ma'am," He said and tipped his hat in greeting.

She smiled, "Hello, I was hoping Seth was home."

John grinned, this was the filly who had Seth tied up in knots, he'd bet his last dollar on it. "He's off skydiving today ma'am." He checked his watch, "I think he'll be back in an hour or so if you want to go in and wait."

What did she do? It didn't seem right to stay but she didn't want to leave either. "Um," She said not really knowing what to say.

"We're about to go out and check some fences," He was going to ask her to go in and wait but she interrupted him.

"John, I'd love to tag along if that's okay," She said, rubbing her hands down her jeans.

Oh no, he wasn't having a woman along with him for this. "I'm sorry ma'am but it's hard and dirty work."

Raelynn didn't want to be rude but she was pretty sure men were pigeon-holing her way too much these days, "I can assure you, I can hold my own."

John looked at her and sighed. Seth was going to have his hide but he was used to women laying down the law, they usually got their way or made you pay when they didn't and John wasn't in the mood to take that on today. "Well ma'am, I'll saddle up a horse for you then."

An hour later, Raelynn was shocked at how much fun she was having checking and fixing fences. John was patient with her and allowed her to help him. It was, as he said, dirty work for sure and physically demanding but it made her focus on what she was doing and not worrying about Seth and her own issues. They were putting up the wiring on a fence; she was holding the post and gripping the end of the wire with pliers while John was ratcheting it tighter.

Sweat was pouring down her back and she was pretty sure she was filthy everywhere but she was having a ball. John didn't speak much but he did answer her questions about what they were doing and the workings on the ranch. She studied him as he worked. He seemed a bit older than she was, very lean, bow-legged, and a good man if their time working was any indication.

After they completed the re-wiring on that section, they mounted the horses and walked along the fence line. Raelynn was about to ask a question when she heard the distinctive sound of a horse. She turned around to see a horse and rider bounding for them. Once they were close enough, she saw it was Seth.

Lucy was nickering in response to the approaching stallion Seth was riding and Raelynn thought she understood exactly how the animal felt. Seeing Seth atop a horse and riding for them in a hurry, her body sped up inside like a freight train.

Seth pulled up on his mount when he was close and jumped off. He was pissed and wanted to know what the hell was going on, "John what is she doing out here?" He yelled to his foreman.

John tipped his hat back and looked calmly at Seth, "She's helping me mend some fences."

Raelynn sat on her horse and watched the interplay between the two men. For the life of her, she couldn't understand why Seth was angry.

"She shouldn't be out here and you know it," Seth yelled as he walked up in front of John's mount.

John smiled, "She's doing fine Seth." Yep, this was the one who had him tied up alright. If he didn't think Seth would yank him off his horse and beat the tar out of him, he might laugh. He was too old and smart for that these days so he let Seth have his tirade.

Seth yanked off his hat and hit his thigh with it, "Dammit John, what if she got hurt?"

Neither of them was acknowledging her and that made Raelynn very angry. They were talking about her like she wasn't even there. He didn't even say hello to her. Well that was BS and she wasn't about to take it. She gently guided Lucy away from them and when she was clear, she prodded the horse into a gallop.

John stared at a seething Seth and wondered what the woman did to him, "I can see that you're upset Seth but maybe you should be taking care of her."

"What the Hell does that mean?" Seth shouted.

"It means she's taken off on a horse and you're going to have a hard time catching up to her," John pointed to Raelynn's shrinking form in the distance.

Seth closed his eyes, "Dammit," he jumped back on Lex and took off after her.

If she wasn't so mad, she would have enjoyed the ride more. Lucy may be a sweetheart but she had the heart of a racehorse. Once given her rein, she took off. Raelynn could feel the excitement vibrate through the horse and absolutely loved the feel of the wind whipping past her. The powerful animal just ran and it was freeing to be along for the ride. If only her insides weren't in turmoil over Seth's behavior and her own.

She came up to the corral area and slowed Lucy to a walk. The horse's breathing matched her own, but they both needed to let go a bit. She jumped off once they got to the barn and she guided Lucy into a small penned area. She remembered that you needed to cool the horse down after a hard ride so she made sure to remove the saddle and brush down Lucy before turning her into the corral. She watched as the horse went over to the water bin and took a long drink.

A few minutes later, she heard Seth bounding towards them on his stallion. The man may drive her crazy but he was amazing to look at. He came skidding to a halt about twenty feet away and jumped off the horse. Without speaking, he did what she did for Lucy and turned the animal loose so he could cool down. He watched Raelynn watching him and both anger and arousal warred in his blood.

"What was that about?" He demanded when he finished getting his horse taken care of.

Raelynn watched him, he was sweaty and mad and sexy as anything she'd ever seen. "I don't know what you mean." She really was at a loss.

"Dammit Raelynn, you don't go out and do fence work!" He yelled.

She frowned, "What do I do then Seth?" Her tone was quiet.

He looked away then back at her, "You stay here and do your CPA work. You could get hurt out there."

Okay now he was just being an ass and a sexist ass no less. "I appreciate your concern but John and I were doing fine. I enjoyed it."

"No you didn't, you're just saying that." He pulled his hat off, "All women say that when they just want you to take care of them."

The comment hit her full force and she was speechless. Never, in a million years, would she have even considered Seth would say something so absolutely horrible to her or any woman, for that matter. She was so shocked, she couldn't respond right away. Finally she found her voice and stomped up to him.

"I don't know what prompted that statement," She said slowly and quietly, trying to keep herself from spewing out horrible epithets, "but I am not a liar." Dawning came slowly, "That's what she did to you isn't it?"

Now Raelynn was the one who understood him a little too well. He was tired, he didn't want to fight with her but it was clear they each had their issues. He nodded and walked around her and toward the house.

She stood there looking out into the vast pastures, trying to figure out what just happened. Was he mad? Was he worried? Was he just as confused as she was? Probably all three. So was this how it was going to be between them? Moments of ecstasy surrounded by emotional pitfalls neither of them was ready for? She loved him, wasn't that enough?

There was that word again! She was feeling light-headed, so she sat down on a bench nearby. She loved Seth. Lord, she never thought she would say that about a man again after Anthony. Now, here she was and didn't have a clue how to cope.

John found her like that, sitting on a bench outside the barn, her face in her hands. He felt sorry for her and he was riled up at Seth for hurting her. He walked over and gently touched her shoulder. She jumped and he felt bad for startling her.

"John," Raelynn gasped, "I'm sorry. I didn't hear you come up."

He smiled and sat down beside her, "I'm sure you didn't ma'am."

She smiled at the man, he was so sweet, "You know you don't have to call me ma'am."

"I'll call you Lynn then," He said as he looked directly into her eyes.

Raelynn hated that nickname; she was called that all through school, people couldn't figure out that Raelynn was her name. But when he said it, it sounded sweet. "That's fine."

He slapped his hand on his thigh, "Had a teacher named Lynn once, pretty thing." He got up and walked over to the hose to wash his hands.

She sat there looking at this man who was so simple but very understanding, "What did Seth's fiancé do to him."

A look of disgust came over his face, "Oh that one. She wanted money alright; thought Seth was the means to that end. Once she figured out he wasn't going to spend it all on her, she high-tailed it outta here."

Raelynn wanted to cry, she was feeling awful over what she said to him.

John, shut off the hose and put it neatly back on the rack, "He built that house for her, or what she wanted it to be." He shook his head, "Left a week before the wedding, hooked up with some businessman out of Houston."

She felt bad for asking John to tell her this; it should have been Seth who told her. That little fact upset her. He was willing to ask about Anthony but not discuss his own heartbreak with her. Why was that?

John strode over to the corral and hooked his boot on the bottom part of the fence; he waited for her to join him before continuing. Oh Seth would be hot under the collar about him revealing his ghosts to her but Lynn was good stock, she could take it and she was good for Seth. The boy just couldn't see it yet.

"Seth's always been a hard worker, got that from his daddy." He looked at Raelynn and smiled, "Our daddies worked this land together and now we do."

A lot of information in one sentence. Raelynn realized how much John loved Seth and he was giving her a warning about hurting his friend. She respected that. It was time she and Seth figured out a few things, she leaned over and kissed John's cheek, "Thank you, you are a good friend."

He tipped his hat, smiling, "Thank you ma'am."

Raelynn walked through the barn and up to the back of the house. She didn't knock because she was afraid that if she did, he wouldn't let her in. Thankfully, the kitchen door was unlocked so she went inside. She didn't hear him so she went through the kitchen, past the dining room, and into the great room. Still no Seth. She heard a noise upstairs so went up quietly. When she reached the top of the stairs, she could hear his boots pacing on the hard wood floor in his bedroom. She crept down the hall.

Seth was mad as Hell. The woman knew how to hit him good, he should have been prepared for that. But it was Raelynn, she had nothing in common with Nicole so why was he treating her this way? He never accused someone and he told her she was just like his ex-fiancé. That wasn't fair.

He came home yesterday, wounded, and worked hard on the ranch. John commented that he was acting like the devil was biting at his boots and he was right in some respects. This morning he was scheduled at Skydive Spaceland so he went. It was nice to be focused on the jumps so he retreated into the solace he found there. New jumpers were always fun and their concerns allowed him to release his, for a while anyway.

Then he came home and was actually ecstatic that Raelynn's car was parked out front. He ran through the house looking for her. When he didn't find her, he went out to the barn where one of the boys said she was out fixing fences with John. He couldn't pinpoint the exact feeling that knowledge brought about, maybe a mixture of jealousy about her being with John and worry that she would realize ranch life was dirty and hard and she wouldn't want him anymore once she found that out. He changed, got on his horse, and tore out after her. When he first saw her out there, his heart skipped a beat. She looked so natural on the horse and helping John. But the fear won out and he said some stupid things.

"Now who's the one thinking?" Raelynn asked from the doorway of his bedroom.

Startled, he looked up, "I was going over our conversation in my head."

She nodded, "And?"

"I'm an ass," he said flatly.

Raelynn nodded, "Well, you're in good company there."

The woman surprised him, he expected her to say something like it was all his fault but she didn't, she was a good person. So why was he acting like she wouldn't be?

He tentatively moved a step closer to her, "I don't want to fight with you."

"I don't either Seth, I'm very sorry for being a bitch to you yesterday, I was lashing out." She wrung her hands, not knowing what else to do.

He took another step, "It appears that we've both been doing that."

She pushed off the doorframe and came into the room, "I'm sorry." A tear snuck out and caught her off guard. She didn't want to cry but she couldn't help it.

"Baby," he murmured and closed the space between them quickly. He took her into his arms, relieved with the fact that she was holding him tight in return, "I know."

They stood in his room, holding one another for a while. There wasn't anything either of them needed to do except that. Raelynn finally gave in to her feelings and pulled away far enough so she could look at him. He looked exhausted, his eyes probably mirroring her own. She led him to the bed and sat down on the edge. She pulled off her shoes and crawled up to the head of the bed, motioning for him to join her. He pulled off his boots, situated himself next to her, and pulled her into his side where they both fell asleep.

Her phone was ringing and she needed to get it. But she was so tired; she didn't want to open up her eyes. She felt it vibrate in her pocket and it was silenced. Good, she wanted to sleep some more. Seth's low voice brought her the rest of the way awake. He was talking to someone. She opened her eyes and looked over her shoulder to see him talking on her phone.

Seth woke up when Raelynn's phone rang and got it out of her pocket. She was sleeping so peacefully that he didn't want to wake her up yet. "Hello," He said softly.

"Seth?" Hailey asked, "Is that you?"

He smiled, "Yep, are you okay?"

Hailey was relieved; she hoped her mom and Seth figured out what they were doing. She was exhausted watching their slow progress, and she wasn't even in the relationship. He was a good man and treated her mom well. In Hailey's eyes, that's what counted. She wasn't as worried about her mom when Seth was around.

She remembered she was on the phone and came back to the present, "I'm fine, I was just letting mom know I was going to be home about eight."

Seth peeked over and saw Raelynn was awake and looking at him. He hoped she wasn't mad that he answered her phone. She looked beautiful, sleep still clinging to her eyes. He rubbed her leg with his hand, "I'll let her know if that's okay." He said to Hailey.

"Thanks, have fun," Hailey said smiling. She hung up and went back to where her friends were waiting.

Raelynn sat up, "Was that Hailey?"

Seth nodded, "Yes, she'll be home around eight." He hoped she wouldn't leave, they needed to talk.

"Okay," She said and rubbed her eyes. She felt better, rested, and hungry. "Do you want me to make us some dinner?"

The offer took him by surprise, "No, we can order something though."

She cocked her head, trying not to take the comment the wrong way, "I don't mind."

"And that," He leaned closer and kissed the tip of her nose, "is what I adore about you."

That one word was enough for her; she tilted her head and kissed him on the lips. It was intended to be reassuring but morphed into heat in an instant. She ran her hands up his shoulder and neck and let her fingers roam though his hair, all the while, pulling him down so they could lie on the bed.

Oh she felt so good, Seth thought. But they needed to talk about what happened yesterday and today. If she kept kissing him, he would forget and make love to her as much as she would let him. Reluctantly, he pulled his head away and looked at her. Flushed from their kiss, she was so sexy.

"Baby," He whispered, "let's order dinner and then we can talk."

A bucket of cold water on her body would have been more effective but she settled for knowing he was right. Why was he the reasonable one? She smiled and pulled her hands out of his hair.

"You're right," She said, trying to right her clothes.

They went downstairs, Seth went into his office to order some dinner, and she went into the great room to curl up on the couch. She looked at the room differently since she learned it was built with another woman in mind. Was Seth the one who decorated it or was it the mysterious ex-fiancé? That line of thought would not do her any good. She put the woman out of her mind and turned on the television. He came in a few minutes later and handed her a glass of wine.

"Dinner will be here in about thirty minutes," He said as he sat down beside her on the couch. She looked sexy as Hell sitting in the room, curled up; he wanted to love her right there.

Raelynn could see his eyes as they said the same things hers were, 'I want you,' but they had to figure out what to do. She mumbled, "Thanks," and settled in next to him.

He ran the fingers of his free hand down her arm, making circles on her soft skin. It was enough contact to keep him from stripping her down naked but just barely.

The doorbell rang and Seth got up to answer it. Raelynn took a few deep breaths to get her body under control. It was like they never made love before. She smiled shyly, hoping he didn't guess her thoughts, when he came back in.

"Chinese," He announced, then stopped, "You like Chinese right?"

She laughed, "Yes, so you're lucky."

He was lucky, lucky to have her here with him. That was what mattered at the moment.

She watched him put the bag down on the coffee table and walk down the hall toward the kitchen. He came back a couple of minutes later with plates, forks, and the bottle of wine they started to drink earlier. He also had a smile that melted her bones. He neatly set up their table, grabbed some pillows off the furniture so they could sit on them, then pulled her up and guided her down onto the pillows. She felt so pampered.

"Thank you," She said when she settled onto the floor. He sat down beside her and lifted his glass to hers. "What shall we drink to?" She asked.

Seth thought about it for a second, "Well, why not, figuring out what we both want."

It was the truth, so she smiled, "I'll drink to that." She tapped her glass to his and took a drink. The wine was sweet and felt good on her tongue.

He watched her drink her wine and was turned on. The fact that something so simple made him want her never seemed to amaze him. He turned to his food, knowing food was important.

They watched television and ate Chinese food. Seth cleaned up the cartons while Raelynn picked out a movie from his collection on the built-ins. She scanned the titles slowly, wondering if his pick of movies reflected him. There were the usual "guy movies" full of action and cars but, surprisingly, there were quite a few dramas and even a few romantic ones. She was fascinated by the variety in titles as it did nothing to solve the mystery that was Seth. It was difficult not to think of what John divulged earlier about the woman who was stupid enough to leave him. She wanted to ask but was afraid. She didn't realize she was staring into space until Seth was behind her and made a noise.

"Sorry," She said, "I was zoning."

Seth smiled and handed her a refilled glass of wine, "You don't normally zone as far as I can see Raelynn."

He was right, darn it, "I was thinking of how I could ask about the woman you broke up with last year." She worried that he would become angry but was surprised when he nodded and walked over to sit on the couch.

This was it, Seth said to himself, time to fess up. "Go ahead, ask away."

"What was her name?" She asked quickly. As if knowing the woman's name would make it easier.....

He cleared his throat, "Her name was Nicole; she was a teacher at a private school in Pearland."

Raelynn nodded, "John mentioned that she was not nice." She wanted to put it kindly.

"John what?" He asked, he was not expecting John to blurt out his history to Raelynn.

She realized she was wrong to say that, "I'm sorry, I asked him when we were cooling down the horses." She rubbed Seth's arm, trying to reassure him, "He only mentioned that she was materialistic and left when she found someone else."

Well, at least he didn't have to go through the whole story, she knew the important parts, "That about sums it up."

"He also said you built this house for her," She wanted it all out.

Seth nodded, "We had the blueprints drawn up by a friend of mine, it was the two of us who designed it but it was what she wanted," he looked around the room as if looking at it for the first time, "she wanted a 'statement' from the house we lived in."

How awful; was this woman stupid? "She was just the wrong one Seth. She wasn't good enough to realize how wonderful you are." She brought his hand to her lips and kissed the knuckles softly.

He watched her and felt warmth fill in the areas Nicole left cold. It was like her presence healed the hurts. "Thank you Raelynn."

"You are welcome you kind man," She said between kisses.

The wine relaxed her and she felt awareness every time her lips met his skin. His hands were worn from the work he did on the ranch but created such pleasure when they touched her. Just thinking about the contradiction was arousing.

"I think you better stop doing that," Seth said, he didn't want her to stop but it was the wisest thing to do.

Raelynn listened to him but that didn't make her stop, "Oh, I think I shouldn't stop." She said, and took his finger into her mouth. She sucked lightly on the tip of it, swirling her tongue over it. The friction made her shiver with excitement.

Seth sucked in a breath; oh the woman took him there in a fraction of a second. "Baby," He whispered.

She looked up from her attention to his finger but didn't stop sucking on the tip of it. She was not interested in talking just now; she was far more interested in watching what her touch did to him. She took her free hand and rubbed it up his thigh. His jaw tightened and he swallowed. The motion of his reaction melted her inside.

He couldn't move, all he could do was watch her kiss and tongue his finger. It was mesmerizing and made him hard. When her other hand moved up his thigh and kneaded it rhythmically, he wanted to forget his thoughts on giving her time.

She took his finger out of her mouth, "Well, what we have here is a dilemma, I want you to make love with me and you are determined to not make love to me."

He sighed, "Uh, I wouldn't say determined," his fingers shook as they covered the hand she had on his thigh; he moved it up so she was cupping his fly.

"Oh," Raelynn smiled, "I suppose determined is too harsh of a word."

Seth groaned, "Raelynn we are quickly getting to the point where I'm not going to let you go."

Raelynn stopped her ministrations and cocked her head, "Where on earth did you get the notion I wanted you to let me go?" She kissed his knuckle once more and then brought his hand up to her neck. The feel of his fingers on her skin made it tickle.

He was being driven insane in the most erotic way, "I meant," he swallowed hard; "I wanted to give us some time to figure out our doubts here." It was so difficult to think clearly when she looked at him like that.

"I'm pretty sure," She inched closer to him, "that I know what I want right now." She was now close enough to kiss him, "I want," she nipped at his lower lip, "you to show me what you're thinking."

That was it, he was lost. He grabbed her around the waist and pulled her onto his lap. At least there she could ease some of the ache in his pants. He kissed her madly, holding her head still so he could taste every inch of her lips. Their hips meshed, grinding against one another and both of them were moaning and aching in no time.

He was not close enough, Raelynn thought. She pulled off her top and bra and threw them into the recesses of the room. His shirt followed so at least her breasts could feel his chest, the hair tickling the nipples into hardened peaks of desire.

Man, the woman could kiss! He was cupping her bottom and holding her against him, the gyrating of her hips gave him ripples of pleasure. He pushed her up onto her knees so he could ravish her breasts with his mouth. All the while his hands were undoing her jeans and pushing them down so he could touch her.

Oh, she was in Heaven, his fingers and tongue knew exactly what to do to get her body to respond. She had no control over it; she was just acting out of instinct and loving every second of it. She was on her knees, her breasts in his face while he suckled each one in with great tenderness. His hands pushed down her jeans and panties and he rubbed her bottom roughly making her want him more. She held his head with one of her hands and used the other one to guide his hand to her sex.

Yes, Seth thought, he would feel her heat. When his fingers parted the folds of her, he thought he would die of frenzied excitement. She was so hot and wet and she was rubbing against his hand with wild abandonment.

"Seth," She whispered with a ragged breath, her thighs trembling with a release she wanted to hold back. "I don't want to come yet."

"Yes Baby," Seth urged, "come." He looked up to see her eyes dark with desire, her body was reaching for the release, "I want to feel you come in my hands, reach for it, let go baby."

His words were all she needed, she exploded, inside and out, in a grand show of release. It took all of her strength, she slumped against him.

Seth gathered her into his arms. He was hard with want but knew she needed to recover from her release first. The wait would be worth it, he knew it without a doubt.

A while later Raelynn opened her eyes and tried to focus. She was tucked against Seth and instinctively snuggled closer to his chest. She could hear his heartbeat in her ear and it soothed her. "Was I sleeping?" She asked.

"I think you were, but only for a little bit," He pulled back so he could see her face. Her cheeks still held the flush from their lovemaking, her hair was mussed, and she entranced him.

She didn't know what to say, "Thank you."

"Oh baby, it was my pleasure," He said before kissing her.

That's all it took to awaken Raelynn's body again. One kiss and she was on immediate alert, her body searching for his. It knew that his would give her what she wanted. She smiled slyly and looked at him, "Now it's your turn."

He would not forget the way she looked at that moment, like a wanton woman. He was all hers, she only had to ask and he would do her bidding.

Raelynn stood and pushed her pants down, once rid of all of her clothes; she pushed on his chest until he was leaning against the back of the couch. She pulled his jeans off and threw them aside.

She stood and tapped her finger against her chin, "We may have to sit and think about what you want."

Whatever she wanted, he would do. He was erect and waited for her heat, panting with need. His eyes went wide when she turned around, straddled his lap and guided him into her. She leaned back against his chest, bringing his hands to cup her breasts as she rocked on him. Her back rubbing against his chest made incredible sensations scatter throughout his body; he felt her softness cover him and moaned from being so deep inside her.

Raelynn never considered the positions she made love to Seth in. It just felt so right in the moment. She moved her hips, leaning back against him, and held his thighs in place. His hands cupped each breast, periodically running a finger over the nipples to increase her pleasure. She could feel him getting close to his climax, his breathing was more ragged. She smiled, knowing she was making him feel this way.

"Yes Seth, it's your turn now," She brought his hand to her mouth and sucked on the finger; relishing the tremor she felt in his hand.

Seth poured into her, a moan from deep in his chest filling the room. He never, NEVER, thought he would have the sexual experiences he had with Raelynn. It was beyond his wildest dreams.

They sat there for a few minutes, allowing their bodies to recover from the intense lovemaking. Raelynn stretched and got up. She felt cold without Seth close to her. She turned around and saw him slouched on the sofa, a smile on his face.

She smiled, "You look like a sated man."

"Are you kidding me?" He looked up at her beautifully naked body, "woman you are going to kill me with desire and it will be a pleasure to die that way."

A small tinge of sadness darted through her, his mention of death always brought Anthony to her mind. Although, this time, it was more of a fond sadness than the grief she was so used to feeling. The feeling made her happy and sad at the same time. She grabbed Seth's hand and yanked him up off of the couch, "Let's go clean up." She led him upstairs to the shower; she would worry about her feelings later.

They showered together; taking an extra-long time to make sure each of them was clean from top to bottom. They laughed and played in the shower, throwing washcloths and kissing until they both thought they would combust. They did not make love again though; they just kissed like teenagers until late in the evening.

Raelynn couldn't remember a more fun time than the evenings she spent with Seth. Her body ached from their frequent lovemaking but she didn't care. She wanted to be close to him. They talked about the week's plans, making a note of each other's schedule so they could find time to spend together. He walked her out to her car when she said she had to go home. He didn't want her to leave but understood the demands of her business. He kissed her senseless and tucked her into her car. He stood there in the driveway until he couldn't see the tail lights any longer.

He was going to go in but noticed a light on in the barn. He walked over to find John doing something with a saddle. He leaned against the doorframe, "Hello there." He said.

"Did the lady get off okay?" John asked.

Seth wanted to chuckle at the play on words but decided against it. John was an old school cowboy and would not appreciate Seth's thoughts. "Yes, she just left." He answered. He wanted to clear the air before turning in, "She said you told her about Nicole."

John looked up from the saddle he was working on, "She asked, I told her the basics. That one," he pointed in the direction Raelynn's car went, "she's good for you. The other one wasn't."

And there it was; John's straightforward opinion. Over the years Seth learned to appreciate the candor his friend gave him. "Thanks," He said and went back to the house and his empty bed.

Raelynn arrived home and texted Seth, *I'm home, I miss you.*

She walked into the house and grabbed her phone when she heard the ping of his reply, *Not as much as I miss you. Sweet dreams, I'll have them because I'll be dreaming of you.*

Even texting, the man did crazy things to her insides. After checking to make sure Hailey didn't need anything, she walked dazedly into her room and got ready for bed. She slept very soundly and was relieved that, for the moment, she and Seth managed to put aside their respective issues.

Chapter 12

The week was crazy but good. Raelynn went about her daily routine as best she could but called Seth every night. They decided the early part of the week would be too busy for them to meet so they made plans for Thursday night.

She went into work on Tuesday and headed for Melissa's office. Her friend was quiet the day before, Raelynn was pretty sure she knew what was going on, as Hailey kept her updated. So it was odd for Melissa not to interrogate her. She noticed Melissa was on the phone so she sat down quietly in the chair in front of the desk.

Melissa turned around and mouthed 'one minute' to Raelynn. She rolled her eyes and finally managed to get off the phone with a particularly frugal client who wanted all the work done by their firm for a reduced rate.

She hung up and sighed, "Hello there." She looked at Raelynn and smiled, her friend looked happy, really happy. It was a wonderful thing to see.

"Hi," Raelynn said, she didn't normally ask Melissa to do things for her, and especially not during their busy time at work. "I was wondering," She trailed off.

Melissa smiled and took a drink of her water, "Yes?"

Raelynn shifted in her seat, "I was wondering if you minded if I took off Friday?"

She couldn't help it, Melissa laughed. "Raelynn, you are the co-owner of this establishment, if you want a day off, take it." Her friend was a gem for asking though.

"I just know it's our busy time," Raelynn started.

Melissa interrupted her, "Stop." She came around the desk and sat in the chair beside the one Raelynn was occupying, "you take time to be with him, you both deserve it."

She was pretty sure she had the best friend and business partner in the whole world, "Thank you." She hugged Melissa and almost floated out of the office.

They didn't have much time to talk after that. They received another courier package from the ever curious Mr. Wesley. He wanted some financial documents of a local company reviewed since he was considering acquiring it. Raelynn worked on that while Melissa fielded their other clients' requests. They ended up staying late and ate dinner in the conference room.

Raelynn didn't get home until almost ten o'clock. She went into the kitchen and found Hailey at the dining table eating a bowl of cereal. The child amazed her with her eating habits. "Did you want me to make you something?" She asked as she sat across from her daughter.

"No," Hailey said, "this is fine."

They discussed their day, Hailey asking about Seth, which Raelynn thought was sweet. They didn't talk about the argument they both knew Hailey heard on Saturday morning. Raelynn considered that maybe her daughter didn't really want to know about her mother's love life.

Her phone pinged as she was turning down her bed, it was Seth, *How was your day? I hope it's not too late, I just got home.*

She smiled and typed, *I got home not long ago, long day. Mine was busy but good, yours?*

We have some mares getting ready to foal so it's a little crazy around here, I miss you. His response was quick, leading Raelynn to think he was just as happy to text her as she was him.

She typed fast, *I miss you too. It wasn't as much fun to look at my bed and know you wouldn't share it with me.*

Seth smiled, the woman tied him up in knots, *Say the word and I'll be there.*

She knew he meant it but they agreed on Thursday. She needed to get her work done so she could take Friday off. *Good night sweet man. Call me tomorrow if you have time.*

He couldn't help it, her saying no hurt, he understood but it still hurt, *Good night.*

Raelynn got into bed and wondered why she told him no. It took her a good, long while to get to sleep that night because Seth was dancing around the edges of her subconscious and making her body yearn.

Wednesday turned out to be rougher than the previous two days, and that was saying a lot. They had three new clients come in; the paperwork for Mr. Wesley was returned to him, so he sent some more of his own paperwork for review. Raelynn wondered if he was torturing them because she turned down his offer of dinner. She mentally hushed herself, he wouldn't do that. Not to mention, it didn't matter, she wouldn't date a client. As if that wasn't enough, she knew Seth occupied enough of her heart and she wasn't interested in any other man.

She got home late and found Hailey studying in her room for her finals. They were almost a month away but some of the classes were a challenge for her daughter. It made her happy to see Hailey so determined to do well in college.

Dinner was baked chicken and rice; one of Hailey's favorites. They sat down to eat and discussed their day. They were finishing up when Hailey looked at her mother very seriously.

"Mom," Hailey said quietly, "do you love Seth?"

Oh no, Raelynn thought. It was one thing for her to think her own thoughts but something altogether different to voice them aloud, much less to Hailey. "Um," She stalled.

Hailey was wondering why her mom wouldn't answer, "You look like it." She said.

That made Raelynn wonder, "How do you mean?" She asked.

"Well," She put her fork down and looked at her mother, "you seem so happy when you're with him and you seem pretty miserable when you argue."

How was it that she didn't teach Hailey about this sooner? Shame filled her; she should have discussed loving someone with her baby girl years ago. Instead, she built up Anthony into this ghost she would never know and skip the best part about him, how much he loved her.

"Hailey, I think I do love him," She admitted it and felt elation and dread at the same time. "But, I've not told him that. I don't want to scare him if he's not ready for the words."

She considered what her mother said, "Who cares if he's not ready mom, the point is you love him. You should tell him." She smiled, "If there's one thing not knowing dad has done for me, it's knowing that you shouldn't waste time."

247

Her daughter, she was sure, was a genius. She got up from the table and hugged Hailey tight, "You are so wise beyond your years." She whispered.

Hailey loved hugging her mom and squeezed her tight in return. She thought she would be jealous of Seth and her mom's relationship but, the truth was she thought it was cool and hoped to be in love herself at some point.

They cleaned up from dinner and settled in for the evening. Hailey finished a paper for her psychology class while Raelynn did some on-line bill paying and a few chores around the house. It was still early when Hailey turned in so Raelynn turned the television on for company while she worked a crossword puzzle. They were her guilty pleasure. She smiled when her phone went off beside her. She smiled brighter when she saw it was Seth calling.

"Hello there," She said.

Her voice was a Godsend, "Hello there yourself, how was your day?" He nestled the phone against his shoulder, while he got some food out of the refrigerator for dinner.

What did she say? "It was good, a little busier than anticipated but good. I missed you."

Seth smiled, "I missed you too baby."

His words whispered across her skin and made her feel so warm. She liked his texts but hearing his voice was so much better. It also made her miss him more.

"Are we still on for tomorrow night?" He asked slowly.

She looked up to make sure Hailey wasn't nearby, "Oh yes, I can't wait to be with you." Her words were breathless.

"You can't talk like that Raelynn, it drives me crazy," He groaned.

She had a wicked gleam in her eyes, "Really?"

He shook his head, "Yes really."

The man obviously didn't know about her mischievous streak, "Well, I'm sorry, I'm just so lonely, sitting here all alone, just my panties and bra on."

Ohhhh, "You are not just sitting there in your panties and bra on are you?"

She chuckled, "No, but I would be if you were here."

Goodness, "Stop it or I will be over there. I'm hanging up now before I get in my truck and drive over. You sleep well; I'll see you tomorrow at seven."

"Seven it is," She responded. "Sleep well."

She hung up and held the phone to her chest. The man turned her into some concubine and she couldn't, for the life of her, understand how or why. Sometimes it was best not to question, just to be. Like Hailey said, life's too short to waste.

Thursday morning was great, work was smooth and Raelynn completed the list she wrote to clear her schedule so she could take Friday off. Even though Melissa reassured her, she still felt obligated to do her share at the office. She and Melissa ate lunch in the break room and went over the plans for the next week. Just as they were finishing, Melissa's phone went off.

"Hello," Melissa said.

Raelynn watched while Melissa spoke on the phone and could tell she wasn't happy. There was a lot of eye rolling and patronizing. She held her breath as her friend hung up.

"Bad news?" Raelynn asked, knowing the answer.

Melissa sighed, "We've been summoned." She closed her folder hard,

This didn't sound good, "And?" Raelynn dreaded the answer.

"Mr. Wesley would like us to meet him at his office at four thirty this afternoon to go over his preliminary tax documents." She was ticked off.

Raelynn groaned inwardly. If experience was any indication, companies spent a lot of time doing tax preparation and CPA's spent a lot more than that trying to decipher that information.

"Well then," Raelynn grabbed her papers, "let's get going."

She and Melissa worked quickly to clear the rest of their pending work so they could be ready for their meeting with the intense Mr. Wesley. They arrived at his office promptly with everything they thought they would need for the meeting.

Once his assistant showed them into the office, they set up their calculators, notebooks, and enough pencils to write a good sized novel by hand. Surprisingly, Mr. Wesley came in and was all business. They went over all the information he was submitting for the taxes and then he asked them to look over some other financial information on yet another company he was looking at adding to his repertoire. The man was nothing if not driven.

"So that's it ladies," Mr. Wesley announced at the conclusion of the meeting.

Raelynn was relieved and noticed Melissa smile. "We will get right on this sir," Raelynn said and offered her hand for him to shake. He took it and smiled. Unfortunately, he held her hand in both of his and held it for far too long. She was getting uncomfortable and was, thankfully, saved by Melissa's interruption.

"Raelynn, let's get going so we can start on this," She announced while packing her supplies into her briefcase.

Mr. Wesley let go of her hand and Raelynn wanted nothing more than to run from the room. She wasn't afraid exactly, just intimidated by the intensity of his eyes on her.

They left and got into Melissa's car to go back to the office. Both were torn between wanting the business for their company and the need to keep away from a man who basically freaked them out.

"I'm sorry Raelynn," Melissa said as she pulled out of the parking lot, "I didn't realize how fixated he was on you."

She smiled, "He's harmless, he is just used to winning and I'm the current game."

Melissa pulled onto Oyster Creek Drive, "You sure summed that situation up."

Raelynn grunted, "I just know that when someone wants you, they usually want you more because someone else does. If I weren't seeing Seth, I'm sure our lovely Mr. Wesley wouldn't be giving me a second thought."

"If you say so," Melissa replied but she wasn't so sure she agreed with Raelynn's assessment. Only time would tell.

Raelynn looked at her watch, "Oh crap, I have a date with Seth at seven and I look awful," she was trying to fix her hair in the little mirror on the visor.

Laughing, Melissa pulled into their office parking lot, "Are you kidding me?" She parked the car and gave Raelynn a sassy look, "You look great, just go and have fun with your great boyfriend."

It was tough not to laugh at Melissa's dry sense of humor, "I will thank you." They got out of the car and started toward the office, "How's your love life by the way?"

Melissa gave her friend a frustrated look, "I don't want to discuss the number of not-quite-great men who've decided that I am on their list of things to do."

She was so funny, "I'm sorry friend. We'll have to get together soon and drink."

Melissa looked at Raelynn, her eyes wide, "Sure but that's not like you."

"It's not is it?" Raelynn asked, "I guess I'm changing a bit."

It's about time, Melissa thought. Her friend spent way too long burying her head in the sand after Anthony died. They were a great couple for the short time Melissa knew them. She was thankful she was there for Raelynn when he passed away and then when Hailey was born. A lot of the time she felt like a parent to Hailey. They were a family, the three of them. Now things were changing again. Seth was a part of the group and, although Melissa was happy for her friend, she was a little down about where they would all end up.

Each of them went to their respective offices to clean up for the day. Raelynn kept checking her watch, worried that she would be late for their date. Once she had her desk in order, she grabbed the bag she packed this morning and went into the bathroom to change. This was a big step as she wasn't used to dressing up. The one time Seth saw her in a dress was when they went to dinner. Other than that, he only saw her in work clothes or jeans. Now she wanted to blow his socks off. She changed quickly and came out. Melissa startled her with a whistle.

"Whoa," Melissa walked around her friend, "you look hot."

Raelynn flushed, "Thank you, I wanted to do something different."

Nodding, Melissa said, "Well this is different."

Her outfit consisted of a tight black leather skirt, a form fitting blouse in silky rose material, her hair was pulled up in a messy pony tail, and she refreshed her makeup to make it more dramatic. It was uncomfortable for her to see Melissa's perusal but she would need to get used to it.

"He's going to drool," Melissa smiled.

It was just something she felt like doing, "I hope so," Raelynn replied and grabbed her bags.

They walked together to the door, locked it behind them, hugged, and parted ways. Melissa called out, "See you Monday," before she got into her car.

Raelynn put the top down on her convertible and got in. The evening sun was low and the heat of the day was still there so the breeze felt great as she drove. The radio was playing soft rock and she was humming along. Traffic wasn't heavy but there were a lot of cars on their way north. She was glad when she reached the exit she needed to get to Seth's place. A few minutes later she was pulling into the driveway. She noticed the large double SS on the sign and made a mental note to ask Seth about it.

She drove slowly down the drive, not wanting to kick up too much dust. The land he worked had an odd effect on her. She looked around, seeing vast pastures, and felt a sense of calm come over her. It was very liberating; that feeling of freedom. Once she saw Seth out in the parking area talking to one of the ranch hands, her sereneness left her body. It was replaced with acute awareness.

Raelynn parked her car in the usual spot and got out slowly. He waived to her but turned back to finish the conversation with the other gentleman. It gave her time to get her bag from the back. When she closed the door, she leaned against the car, her ankles crossed, and waited for him to finish. She welcomed the chance to watch him. He was wearing his cowboy uniform of boots, jeans, t-shirt, and cowboy hat. The man should do clothing ads. She blushed when her eyes made it up to his face and he was looking back at her. Busted! She smiled shyly and waited.

Seth finished talking to one of the guys and turned around to go to Raelynn. She was leaning against her car leisurely. What was she wearing? His blood boiled in his veins. He watched her as she looked him over. When her eyes met his, she looked "caught." He decided to walk over and give her a proper welcome.

"Well, what have we here?" He asked slowly as he walked up to her.

She smiled, "I thought I'd dress up for you."

He reached her and took her hands in his, lifted them out so he could look at the outfit, "Baby, you did not have to but I sure appreciate the sight you make."

She reached up and kissed him, "Thank you."

They started to walk up to the house and saw half a dozen of the men standing outside the barn and "appreciating" Raelynn's outfit. Seth gave them a reproaching look and guided her inside.

Raelynn couldn't help it, she laughed. "They were just being kind Seth."

"Yeah, that's what we'll call it," He smiled because he was relieved that she dressed that way for him and him alone.

She turned around once they were inside and kissed him properly. Her hands dove into his hair, her senses taking him in. She had to groan when his hands went to her bottom and cupped it through the skirt. The feel of the leather against her skin felt erotic. Not that she needed any help in that department when it came to Seth.

They parted and Seth laid his forehead against hers, "I am not going to make love to you, we're on a date."

Raelynn stood there and twitched her lips in a sign of contemplation, "Well, I'm not sure I like your version of a date then."

Little imp, he thought, she would have him in knots in no time. "Well, I want you to know I'm a gentleman."

"Why do you think I want you so much, silly man." She said slyly.

Ugh. "You'll have to stop saying that young lady." He stepped away and walked into the room, pulling her behind him by the hand. "I will not be able to retain the gentleman status I previously spoke of."

Oh, he was so cute. "Maybe I don't want a gentleman this evening. Did that ever occur to you?"

"No," He swallowed hard, "I didn't. What would you like this evening?"

She rubbed her legs against his, "I think I'd like something a little more reckless."

The thoughts running through his brain were muddled with her, the possibilities were endless. He had to think and the mere fact that she was next to him, made him not think. He stared at her for a moment then inspiration hit and he smiled. Without saying anything, he led her out to his truck.

Raelynn was happy to follow but she was curious, "Seth, where are we going?"

He just kept smiling as he got into the truck but didn't answer her question.

They pulled out of the yard and went down a back road on the edge of the property. It was a little bumpy and Raelynn laughed as they were jostled around in the cab. He was smiling and looking at her then back to the road. She knew he was up to something.

A while later Seth pulled off the road. Since he knew the land like the back of his hand, it was easy for him to find the turn-off. Anyone else would've missed it. That was the point of having this spot.

"Where are we?" Raelynn asked.

Seth stopped the truck and all she could see was a large hill and rock formations in front of them. It was pretty in the dimming light of day, the last rays of the sun splashing off the rock and coloring it. She wondered if they were going to hike because she certainly wasn't dressed for that. Looking at Seth's smile, she knew it wasn't that simple.

He got out of the truck and walked around. He opened the door for Raelynn then took her hand. Once she was out, he grabbed his boots and pulled them off with his socks. "Take off your shoes." He said.

Hmmm, she thought, "Okay." They were pumps so she slipped them off easily.

Seth placed their shoes in the truck, grabbed her hand, and started walking.

The grass was cool and soft, Raelynn couldn't remember the last time she walked on grass in her bare feet. They were heading toward the rock formation and, as they got closer, she could see a gap between the rocks that wasn't visible from the road.

Seth led her through the hole in the rocks and watched her face as they came out the other side. He smiled at her gasp.

"What do you think?" He asked quietly.

She didn't know what to say, "Oh my, Seth, this is fantastic."

In front of them was a pond. It must have formed ages ago from water wearing the rock or something. It was fantastic, the rocks formed a bank on one side, a grassy field on the other.

"You wanted a little reckless so I thought we'd go for a dip." He removed his shirt as he spoke. The look of shock on her face was priceless.

She glanced around, "What are you doing?"

Seth smiled, "I thought it was obvious, I'm taking off my clothes so I can swim." He pulled her closer to him, "You need to get rid of your clothes so you can join me."

"This is on the list," She whispered and fought back the tears that wanted to spill down her cheeks. She said reckless and he thought of this, the man was wonderful. No wonder loving him was so darn easy.

He worried that she would back out but then they could find something else to do. "Come on," He was stripped down and walked to the edge and dove in.

Raelynn watched his naked body dive into the water and thought he was absolutely beautiful. His body was muscular and lean in all the right spots. She slipped off her top and bra and was working on her skirt when he surfaced.

"Whoo," He yelled, "the water feels so good but it's a little cool when you first get in."

She sighed and slipped off her panties. Without too much thought, she walked over and dove in. The cool water slid over her skin; the sensation making her feel free. She surfaced and smiled, looking for him.

"Oh my gosh Seth," She swam over to him, "it feels so good. Are you sure no one will show up?"

He shook his head no, "The only two who know about this place are John and I. We used to play here as kids. It was our secret hideout."

She treaded water and smiled, hearing about his life made her feel warm inside, "Really, did you bring girls here?"

Again, he shook his head, "Absolutely not, this was guys only."

"I feel privileged then," She splashed him with water and took off.

He swam after her, catching her easily. Their laughter echoed off the stone walls. The sun dipped below the horizon but the moon's light illuminated the water so they could still see. They swam and played like children until they were both exhausted. He pulled her out of the water and they sat on the rock near the edge of the water. It was smooth and high enough that only their feet could skim the top of the water.

She laughed, "This was so much fun, thank you."

Seth looked at her, his smile fading with awareness. He noticed everything about her as she sat there naked, her smooth legs swinging absently. Her toes created little ripples in the water. Her hair was slick against her head, its tips touching the top of her back. She was like a water nymph described in poetry. He couldn't remember a time when he was so in tune with another person. His eyes raised and found hers looking at him. He probably should be embarrassed but he wasn't.

He lifted his fingers to her cheek and softly stroked her skin, cool from the water, "You are so beautiful." He said.

She was shy, it was not something she was used to hearing, "Stop." She wanted to play it off.

"No," He moved closer and took her face into his hands, "I mean it Raelynn; you are the most beautiful person I've ever seen."

The tears she was able to hold back earlier spilled over and down her cheeks. His words did to her heart what his body did to hers, sated it in such a way that no one would ever be able to compare to it. The feeling of love bloomed throughout her body, filled every pore. It was overwhelming and scared her. She couldn't think, her breathing was labored.

"Thank you." She said, her eyes staring into his.

He lowered his lips to capture hers. Their coolness created a tingling in his. He inched closer so they were able to intertwine their bodies. Skin touched skin and heated instantly.

Raelynn ran her hands over his shoulders, rejoicing in the strength she felt, his muscles flexed as his arms moved over her body. Oh the sensations he brought about in her. Every inch of her yearned to be touched. Only he could fill her with the love she craved. They stretched out along the stone; it still held a hint of the warmth the sun brought to it during the day. It created a bed of smooth warmth for them to make love on.

Seth slowly lowered Raelynn so he could be over her. His legs between hers, he softly caressed her cheek again, as he did earlier. Usually it was all heat but this time he wanted to go slowly and show her how much she meant to him. As he entered her, he sighed as if coming home from being away for far too long.

She could feel the shift in their lovemaking. This was not a rush to reach climax, this was two people understanding the connection between them consisted of more than a physical joining.

He made love to her so leisurely. He knew his release would come but wanted to make sure she experienced everything he could make her feel, physically and emotionally. His skin melded with hers as they moved together in the act of love as old as time.

One moment she was watching Seth move over her, feeling his move inside her smoothly, and the next she was being swept over the crest of feelings. She cried out, not realizing how powerful the orgasm was until she was in the midst of it. Her tears fell, the love she felt for Seth burst out of every part of her. He followed her quickly, saying her name over and over.

They lay on smooth rock and held one another. Raelynn's tears falling silently between them. Neither spoke, they just came back down to earth together.

Seth felt her tears, they ran over his shoulder. He was afraid to speak but more afraid that he hurt her somehow, "Are you okay baby?" He asked softly.

"Yes," Raelynn whispered in return, "I'm just overwhelmed," She looked up at him in the moonlight and smiled, "I love you Seth."

The statement took him by surprise. He understood that she was feeling something for him, he knew it because he knew how he felt about her. He smiled, and kissed her. "Good, because I love you too."

Raelynn's heart soared, "Really?" She moved her head so she could see him better, "Hailey told me that I should just tell you, time is too precious, but I was afraid."

The knowledge that Hailey knew how her mother felt made his heart fill even fuller.

"Why were you afraid baby?" He asked.

The tears snuck out again, "It's been a long time since I've felt this way Seth. I am scared, scared it will all go away again."

He pulled her to him, "Don't be afraid baby, I'm here."

She hoped more than anything that what he said was true. They lay there in the moonlight until they grew cold. Slowly, they dressed and went to Seth's truck to go home.

Chapter 13

The weekend flew by and Raelynn was astounded that it was time to prepare for the upcoming week already. After they made love by the pond on their date Thursday night, Raelynn came home riding high on the feeling of love. Having it said between them changed things, whether they were ready to admit it or not. But, as luck would have it, the fates were not in their favor. She didn't let Seth know she was able to stay and was let down when he mentioned he had an early jump time at Skydive Spaceland. She ended up coming home on Thursday evening, being pulled in every direction. Melissa was shocked to see her on Friday but understood when she explained about Seth having to work.

Now it was Sunday and they still weren't able to mesh their schedules. He worked all weekend because they were doing a group jump. He loved it so she wouldn't ask him to cancel for her. She understood responsibility but it didn't stop her from being unhappy from not seeing him. He called her twice since Thursday and their conversations were sweet, the ones newly discovered lovers shared.

She was washing up some dishes when Hailey came in on Sunday evening. She was out shopping with girlfriends since late morning. Raelynn smiled at the noise level one person could create but that was Hailey.

"Hey mom," Hailey yelled from the entryway.

She laughed, "Hey Hailey," She responded.

Her daughter came in the room and stood looking at Raelynn.

When Raelynn looked up, she gasped. Hailey cut off her beautiful hair; it was short. "What on earth!"

"Do you hate it?" Hailey asked while absently touching her newly shortened locks.

Raelynn walked over to her daughter and made a circle around her. "No, I'm just shocked."

"My friend Courtney wanted to donate her hair to Locks of Love, so I decided to do it too. Our hair goes to help make wigs for people with cancer." She rushed because she was afraid her mom's reaction to her impulsiveness meant it wasn't a good one.

Raelynn started crying, "I know what it is and I'm so proud of you sweetie." She hugged Hailey close to her. It was reassuring to her as a parent when her daughter did something as thoughtful as this.

Hailey was relieved, not that she thought her mom would be angry with her but sometimes her decisions weren't thought through. She loved her mom but wanted to find her own way on some things and if it started with cutting her hair, then that was okay.

They spent the rest of the evening together talking about everything. Music was playing low in the background and Raelynn poured herself a glass of wine while Hailey stuck to soda. It was fun and comforting for both of them to have this time together. Topics turned from school to work and finally wound its way around to Seth.

Knowing her mother moved in slow motion on things, Hailey didn't expect an answer but asked anyway, "So did you tell Seth you loved him?"

"Actually," Raelynn took a sip of her wine, "I did and he responded in kind."

Hailey's eyebrows shot up, "Really?" She inched closer to her mom, "How did it go?"

There were some things Hailey didn't need to know so she skipped to the part where she was comfortable, "We went skinny dipping and when we were sitting on the bank, I just sort of said it."

"Skinny dipping?" Hailey laughed, "You go mom!" When her mother's face contorted, she stopped, "I'm just saying, you crossed something else off your list."

Raelynn nodded, "Yes I did." She put her glass down and tucked her feet under her, "It was so lovely to have him say it back." She sighed, "But I was scared too."

Hailey nodded, "I think that's to be expected mom, given what you went through with dad."

On some levels, Raelynn agreed with Hailey but on others, she wasn't so sure. "Your dad just swept in and I had no choice but to love him." She looked into the air, her eyes spanning the distance of twenty years, "But with Seth, it's different."

"Mom," Hailey took her mom's hand, "you've always told me that you love different people in different ways, why should this surprise you?"

Her daughter was good, "Thanks for tossing the words I used back at me." She winked.

"Anytime," Hailey said dryly.

Raelynn went to bed that evening and wondered how things changed over the last month or so. Was that all the time that passed since she went to the hospital? It seemed like yesterday on one hand, and years on the other. And how did she and Seth go on from here? How did it work? With Anthony they got married within a year and started their life. What did Seth expect out of her? As she drifted off, she thought of them together. That's what mattered.

The next Wednesday, Raelynn came home in a huff. Work was even busier with the April tax deadline looming in a few weeks. It was like the closer they got to the cutoff, the less prepared people were to do their taxes. Frustrating didn't even begin to cover the day, then, on the way home, she had a near miss with a truck full of kids. By the time she walked in the door, she was worked up pretty good. After checking her phone, and not seeing a call from Seth, she decided to go and work out to relieve some of the stress.

In the gym, she plugged into her mp3 player and took out her frustration on the elliptical cycle. After an hour, she was physically exhausted and got off the machine on wobbly legs. But her frustration was worked out and she was ready to be rational again.

She walked back to the condo from the gym and called out for Hailey. When there was no answer she decided to shower and get the sweat off of her body.

Standing under the hot spray of the water, Raelynn started crying. She wasn't usually this emotional but now everything was all churned up. She wondered if her admission of love to Seth was wise. They had yet to see one another again after that night. Oh that night, the heat from the shower mirrored the heat inside her when thinking about Seth making love to here on the stone ledge next to the pond.

They actually skinny dipped! She blushed with the memory. At first she was afraid that someone might see them but when Seth jumped in, she just went along. Maybe she was just brave enough when he was around? She moved the cloth over her skin with soap, making it slick with lather. If she closed her eyes, she could feel his hands on her, not the washcloth.

She allowed the water to rinse the soap away and followed it with her hands. Normally she didn't feel her body this way, at least not consciously. The need for intimacy was tucked away in a closet somewhere inside of her when Anthony died. Now the closet door was flung open and all of her pent up desire was spilling out. She liked the feel of her curves, apparently Seth did too if his responses to her were any indication. It was like they were both dry timber and once the spark of desire was set off, they went up in flames.

Lathering her hair, she recalled how Seth washed it for her that day at his house. How he bathed her and carried her to the bed where he made sweet love to her. A shiver flitted up her spine. She needed to quit thinking about it because now she wanted him. The big question was did he want her now that she said the words?

Those words played on her mind as she got out of the shower and dried off. They haunted her mind while she blow-dried her hair. As she dressed, she was cursing those words because she wanted to take them back. Once spoken, you couldn't take them back, she told herself, and she didn't really want to; she wanted the fact that they were spoken to not change what she and Seth found.

As she came out of her room, she heard Hailey playing music in her room. If Hailey was holed up, then she wanted privacy. Raelynn wasn't feeling overly sociable either so it was just as well. She went into the kitchen to find something to make for dinner. She pulled out a pan to make some rice in and slammed it down on the stove top, surprising even herself. Apparently all of her frustration was not depleted during her work out. Darn it, why didn't he call her? She thought that thinking of them being together was enough but now it wasn't.

Seth got out of his truck and roamed into the house. He was sweaty and dirty from working with horses all day. He just wanted to clean up and go to bed for some much needed sleep. The last couple of days were long and he was just ready for a rest. Looking at his watch, he wanted to call Raelynn but she was in the middle of a crazy work week herself.

He trudged upstairs and stripped his clothes of once he got to his room. He stepped into the shower and sighed. The grime and dirt washed away from his skin but the heaviness in his heart remained. It was because of the other night. She told him she loved him. She loved him, the thought made him smile. But, and with Raelynn there was a big but, saying it for her and going into a more serious relationship were two different things.

Seth stepped out of the shower and dried off quickly. He found a pair of sweats and threw them on. After finger-combing his hair, he went downstairs to his office, planning on doing some work. But after sitting at his desk and staring at nothing for fifteen minutes, he got up. It was no use, he was just going to think about her and what they were doing, what they could be doing, what they should be doing. Damn it! He screamed inside.

He picked up his phone and texted her, *I just got home, I've been thinking of you and I'm coming over.*

He didn't even wait for her reply, he went back up and changed into jeans and a button-down shirt. As an afterthought, he threw on a little cologne. He was going over and he was going to be with the woman he loved.

Raelynn heard her phone and walked over to where it sat on the bar. She read the text and smiled.

Hailey came out of her room, "Hey mom."

Raelynn looked up from her phone, "Seth is coming over, is that okay?"

"Sure," Hailey replied, "what's for dinner?"

The girl was a walking stomach, Raelynn thought, "Beef tips and rice," she looked back down at her phone and typed her response, *I'm making dinner, come and eat with us. We never did get dessert at your place, I'll see what we can do here.*

He read her text as he got into the truck. His jeans were already uncomfortable from her text. That would have to be tamped down, Hailey was there. He smiled and tore down the driveway.

When the doorbell rang, Raelynn rushed to the door. He was standing there and looked to her like water after spending days in the desert. She let him in and shut the door. When she turned around, he was right behind her. She started a bit because she thought he went into the living room. She tilted her head in question because the look in his eyes were so intense.

"Is everything alright?" She asked.

He took her into his arms, "It is now. I've missed you." He said into her hair.

Relief flooded Raelynn. She was afraid things would be strained between them and now he was holding her like he did the other day. She loved him, she was just so unsure when they were apart.

He held her there in the entryway of her condo, not wanting to move. The smell of something good permeated his brain once his fill of her was met. His stomach growled.

Raelynn looked up at him, his face embarrassed, "Let's get some food in you." She took his hand and led him into the dining room.

Hailey stood as her mom and Seth came in, she impulsively gave Seth a quick hug. He hugged her back which made her feel good. He seemed like a nice man.

She had to turn away and look at the dinner she was making or else she would cry. She didn't expect Hailey to hug Seth, by his expression, neither did he, but he hugged her back. The sight of them made her feel a myriad of emotions. She missed Anthony and grieved for what he and Hailey missed out on all these years, not being together. She was also more in love with Seth for accepting her daughter.

Raelynn served up dinner and they all sat down. The meal was casual, the conversation drifting over a lot of different topics. Hailey wanted to hear about the mares and the foaling at Seth's ranch. The topic was not appropriate dinner conversation as far as Raelynn was concerned, but she indulged Hailey this once. It also gave her another opportunity to watch Seth. He spoke about the ranch the same way he spoke about his position at Skydive Spaceland; with pure joy and a great amount of respect. She thought that spoke volumes about the type of man he was.

"Mom," Hailey said, "can we?"

She felt foolish for drifting off with her thoughts, "I'm sorry?" She asked Hailey.

Hailey rolled her eyes, "Seth said we can come over this weekend if any of the mares foal so we can watch."

270

The animation in Hailey's eyes was contagious, "Of course."

Her eyes met Seth's. He winked and squeezed her hand in his. It was like he sensed her consideration where Hailey was concerned and that endeared him to her.

They finished eating and Seth suggested he and Hailey clean up since Raelynn cooked. As they joked in the kitchen over who would wash and who would dry the dishes, Raelynn went into her room to compose herself. Having him here was domestic and something she could get used to. How did she express those thoughts to Seth?

She sat on the edge of her bed and picked up the picture she had of Anthony. He was smiling at something and looked so carefree. It was how she always remembered him. How would he feel about Seth?

Seth stood in the doorway to Raelynn's room and watched her look at the picture of Anthony. He never felt threatened by him as the man had been gone for a long time. But there were moments when he wondered if Raelynn could truly open up to him. She spoke of wanting control and being so reasonable but love wasn't that way. At least for him it wasn't. He saw them together, how did she see them? He turned around and left her in her room.

When Raelynn came out of her room, she found Seth sitting on the sofa, the television droning in the background. His eyes were closed and she wondered if he fell asleep while waiting for her. She walked over and sat down, smiling when his eyes snapped open.

"Hey," He said softly and moved over so she could snuggle up against his side.

271

She held his hand in hers on his leg, their fingers entwined, "You're exhausted."

He shook his head no, but they both knew he was lying. "I'm fine."

"No, you need sleep sir." She stood up, faced him, and offered her hand.

He sat there and looked up into her eyes, "Is this an invitation to your bed?"

She cocked her head to one side, "It's an invitation for you to come into my bed and sleep."

"Do you," He stood up and kissed her on the nose, "honestly think we'll go to bed and just sleep?"

The odds were not in their favor if memory served as an example but they were both tired, "At least for a little bit, we will."

He allowed her to lead him into her room. She turned and closed the door behind them. She removed his shirt, pushing it off of his shoulders. After that was off, she pushed him to sit on the bed and helped him remove his boots. He watched her work at pulling them off and thought she was cute. After they were off, she undid his jeans. Arousal traveled through him, it was impossible to not feel that when she was around him. He didn't try to hide it, he couldn't if he wanted to.

The man's body was exciting and electrifying! She undressed him and felt the muscles flex and release as her fingers moved over them. When he was only in his underwear, she pointed to the bed, issuing the silent order for him to lie down. She went into the bathroom and did her nightly routine. The only deviation was the pajamas she chose tonight were a matching negligée and panty set rather than her usual choice of t-shirt and shorts.

Seth was drowsy but that didn't stop him from wanting Raelynn. He could hear her in the bathroom, the water running, and wondered what she thought she had to do. When she came out and he looked up, sleep was no longer a priority for him. She looked gorgeous, backlit by the light coming from the bathroom, the sheer edges of the nighty she wore formed a halo around her form.

The room was dark except for a small lamp in the corner. She was wondering if this was a wise idea, Seth was tired and she shouldn't bother him. She was exhausted herself but having him here made her want to stay up and love him. She walked to the bed and stood beside it, looking down at him.

"I should let you sleep, you look beat," She whispered while trailing her fingertips over his hand.

His eyes moved up her body slowly, "I don't think I'm really thinking about sleep right now," he replied.

Raelynn chuckled, "Really? What are you thinking about then?"

He brought her fingers to his mouth, "I'm thinking of all the ways I want to make love to you."

The words just skipped over her skin, making it tingle with awareness. "I was hoping you were thinking that since it's what I was thinking."

"Really?" He looked up and into her eyes. "In what ways would you like to make love to me?"

The question triggered her mind to race, she didn't answer, only knelt on the bed, while still holding his hand. Her eyes looked into his, wanting to find out all the answers to her heart's questions in them. She saw want and tenderness and the love he professed only days earlier. Only time would tell if they were real.

He watched her, kneeling beside him, her eyes aflame with desire. His hands had their own intentions and moved over her arms to her shoulders. He kneaded them tenderly until he could see her relaxing. Once he knew she was pliable under his fingertips, he pulled her down so she was nestled on his lap. The silk and lace of her negligee tickled his thighs. One hand reached around her slim hips to hold her to him and the other reached around her neck to cradle her in his arms. He wanted to protect her.

Raelynn looked up into Seth's eyes when he held her and was content in the affection he gave her so easily. He touched her with a confidence she herself lacked. Oh she loved the feel of him but was unsure most of the time.

"I'm going to make love to you so slowly," he whispered before dipping his head low to capture her lips.

The kiss was slow; he took his time to discover her all over again. As if he didn't know how she would respond when his tongue met hers; as if he didn't know how to touch her to help her find release. He wanted that for her.

She looked at him, the soft light of the lamp, creating little flecks of gold in the blue of his eyes. "Yes," She whispered back, "please love me."

Her words tore at his heart, it was like she was asking for more than his physical love. He had no problem giving her whatever she asked, he loved her so much.

Seth shifted her so she was lying beside him on the bed. He was on his side, his head propped up on his hand, and trailed his fingertips over her from thigh to neck. He watched as his fingers traveled up and down the length of her, creating goose bumps on her skin. She was ticklish on her sides which made him smile. Every discovery he made about her was like a precious gift. He gently put her hand down when she tried to touch him in return. He would find his own climax soon enough, this was for her.

Raelynn watched Seth as he watched her body. His intense gaze made her burn inside, she wanted to feel him in every way. The slowness of his touch made her shiver and when he refused to let her touch him, she was frustrated.

He knew she was getting to a point where she would not simply lay there and let him touch her but he wanted to see how much she would take.

"Seth," Raelynn pleaded, "please."

He loved to hear her ask him; it turned his insides into a raging inferno of need. He moved so he was kneeling on the bed near her feet; his knees on either side of her legs.

She didn't understand what he was doing, she wanted him inside of her. She moaned when he started rubbing her thighs with the palms of his hands, massaging the muscles that were tense from sexual need. It was a contradiction of relaxing and anticipation.

He could see she was ready, "Baby, I want to taste you."

Raelynn was worried, she never allowed anyone to do that. Not even Anthony could convince her of its sexual pleasure.

Seth saw her apprehension, "Just let me taste you, if you don't like it, I'll stop." He skimmed his fingers up her legs and pulled her panties down slowly. "I promise."

There was no way she could resist him, "Yes," she was breathless.

He removed her panties the rest of the way off and put them aside. His eyes were on hers as he lay down between her thighs. His hands gently coaxing her to spread them for him to see. He watched her until his eyes were low and he could focus on her body. He could see the moisture and his mouth watered for wanting her taste on his lips.

He gently moved his fingers up her inner thighs until they brushed the soft folds of her sex. Once he touched her, she jumped a little. She didn't ask him to stop so he continued to caress her softness until he felt her rock into his hand. He knew then that she was relaxed enough and focused more on the sensations than her own self-conscious feelings. He parted her sensitive skin with his fingertips and found the nub of her desire with his tongue. Her taste and smell were intoxicating, they made him forget himself and focus on her wants.

Oh that felt so good, Raelynn thought to herself. Her hands were on his shoulders, prepared to pull him away if she felt uncomfortable. But she didn't, his tongue flicking her clitoris made her want to thrust her hips into him. Her hands roamed into his soft hair, holding his head still so she could move her hips against him.

Seth ran his tongue down the length of her and up again. She tasted so sweet and he was getting to a point where he was going to come if he didn't stop. Her center was swelling, and he knew she was close and he wanted to see her when she flew over the crest.

When Seth stopped his exploration of her center, she thought she would erupt in agony. But he moved up and positioned himself above her. His eyes were focused on hers as his hardness entered her. The feeling of fulfillment moved over her like a wave and when he began moving, she was lifted into the sweet oblivion of unrestrained desire.

He was so close, his body reaching for the summit, but he wanted her to let go. "Yes baby," He whispered.

Raelynn's eyes squeezed shut and then flew open as her climax engulfed her body. Her mouth fell open, her breathing erratic as she was carried over the edge, her body breaking into a million pieces.

Seth soared over the pinnacle of desire and fell along with Raelynn into the afterglow of their lovemaking. He could hear her breathing since it was as labored as his own. He was convinced that he would never get enough of her.

Raelynn stirred some time later and turned onto her side so she could face him. A self-satisfied smile played on her lips and she wove her fingers with his between them.

"Well, that was lovely," She murmured.

Seth's eyebrow arched. "I'm not sure 'lovely' would be an adequate description of that."

She pushed up so she could kiss him, her head slightly higher than his. Their lips met and enjoyed the sparks flitting through them with the contact. When she opened her eyes, the first thing she saw over Seth's cheek was the picture of Anthony on her bedside table.

Seth saw the expression on Raelynn's face change when he opened his eyes. He was going to tell her he loved her but her eyes looked distracted. He turned his head to see what she was looking at and saw the picture of her husband there. He imagined that a wide range of emotions was pulsing through her.

Raelynn was embarrassed by her reaction, it wasn't fair to Seth. "I'm sorry."

"Why are you sorry?" He asked, sitting up and pulling her up gently so she was nestled against his side.

She did not want to cry. "I just saw his face and it was like a splash of cold water."

He squeezed her reassuringly, "Have you grieved Raelynn?"

She pushed away from him slightly and gave him a confused look, "Of course."

Her tone was defensive so he knew he had to tread carefully, "I am sure you have on some levels but have you let go?"

"What's there to let go of Seth?" She moved over to the edge of the bed, "He's gone and he's never coming back." Her voice was raising and she was helpless to stop the emotion from entering her tone.

He knew she was lost to him for now, she was ticked and she would take it out on him. If that's what he could do for her, then so be it. "Baby, I was just trying to support you."

Raelynn hung her head down, she was ashamed of her response. "I know you are," She moved so she was next to him again. "I'm sorry, I have some sort of residual guilt thing going on and it's not fair to you."

It amazed him that she could accept what was, even if it wasn't very flattering to her. He never knew a woman who could surprise him like she did. "I love you," He tipped up her chin with his finger. "I'll do whatever you need."

Warmth filled her, his words soothing the hurt she felt. "I love you too."

She wrapped her arms around him and together they snuggled in bed and fell asleep.

The next morning she woke to the alarm and cursed it for going off. Why did life have to intrude on the cocoon of intimacy she and Seth created? It was funny that they really hadn't slept together as much as they made love in between naps. The thought made her smile.

"Now that's what a man likes to see first thing in the morning, a beautiful, smiling woman." He rubbed his chin against the top of her head, her hair tickling his skin.

She sighed, "Not for long, I'm afraid. Duty calls."

He nodded, "Yes ma'am."

As Raelynn showered and dressed for work, Seth made them a breakfast of eggs and bacon. He poured coffee into two mugs and placed it on the table when she came into the living room.

She was in Heaven, the man cooked and made coffee. "Oh thank you dear man, I need something to wake me up."

He came around and kissed her, "I can think of a few things."

"Oh, I would like that but," She looked at her watch, "if I don't get going, I'm going to be late for work. It doesn't set a good example if the boss is late."

Seth nodded, "Ok, let's eat and get you on the road."

They ate in comfortable silence. She asked Seth about his schedule and they agreed to try to meet up that evening. Hailey was going out with friends so it was easier for Raelynn to meet him at his place. They got their stuff and both headed out together. Seth walked her to her car and opened the door. The gesture made her smile her thanks. He was so sweet.

She got in and rolled down the window, "What would you like for dinner tonight?" Maybe she could pick something up on the way over.

"Just you," He said and leaned down to kiss her.

The kiss said more than, 'have a good day,' it said something like, 'I'm going to ravage you later.' When she pulled away, his eyes were dark and she almost said to heck with it all and took him back inside. Almost being the operative word. She watched him in her rearview mirror as she pulled out of the parking lot.

The drive to work passed by quickly, she was making mental notes of what she needed to get done. She would take care of calling some clients first thing so she could focus on the paperwork in the afternoon.

As she got out of her car at work, her phone went off. *Why do we have to work, it's much more fun to stay in bed.* Seth's text said.

Smiling, she opened the door to the office, she typed her reply as she walked back to her office, *Yes it is, but then we wouldn't be able to move.   We'd probably disable one another ;)*

"Is that from a certain skydiving cowboy?" Melissa asked as she entered Raelynn's office.

Nodding, Raelynn put her things away and pulled out the paperwork she took home but neglected to do. He was not that good for her work ethic but the man was magic with her heart and body.

Melissa plopped down in the chair, "I've already been on the phone with our newest favorite client."

They shared a standing joke that every one of their clients was their favorite. However, newest being the inflected word, she figured that Melissa was referring to Mr. Wesley. "And how is he this morning?"

She played with Raelynn's name plate, "He's summoned us again, he found, what he refers to as an error on one of the tax forms we did." She was frustrated, "Let's just dump him and be done with this."

Oh how Raelynn wanted to. But the fact was, the man provided them with a large amount of work and revenue and could be quite instrumental in referring them to larger clients. It wasn't in their nature to back down from a particularly demanding client and she didn't want to start now.

Raelynn sat down at her desk, "I know but it's a good boost for us." She pulled out her notebook, "Tell me what he said and we'll review it before we meet with him."

The work day started and it was all business from then on. Time flew by and, even though they were productive, there never seemed to be quite enough time to get it all done. It was after six in the evening when Raelynn came up for air. Melissa was wrapping up and made a noise which meant, 'let's go.' It took another fifteen minutes for them to get everything settled and lock up the office. They managed to get the meeting with Mr. Wesley moved to Monday because he was going to be out of town for the weekend. They were both relieved for the delay.

"Do you want to go out for a drink?" Melissa asked.

Raelynn felt torn, she and Melissa weren't able to spend much time together these days. She didn't want her friend to think she was neglectful. "Well," She said, pulling out her phone to text Seth asking him to wait for her.

Melissa gently pulled Raelynn's phone from her hand, "Don't you dare call and beg off with Seth; you two have plans, enjoy them."

It wasn't that simple, Raelynn thought, you didn't throw over your friends, "It's fine."

"No it's not," Melissa gave Raelynn her phone back, "GO!"

They hugged and parted ways. As she pulled onto 288 North, Raelynn was feeling guilty. There were plenty of times over the years that Melissa had dates but this felt so different. Maybe because it was her now, not Melissa.

The thought of Seth brought up a plethora of emotions. She was excited, aroused, and mostly scared. They didn't really discuss their plans, but they shouldn't really have to. They were two adults who just wanted to spend time together. The fact that her friend and Hailey liked him; well that was a bonus.

When she pulled up in front of his house, she was more settled inside. Of course that changed when she saw him come out of the house and down the steps toward her car. Would that ever change? That intoxicating feeling he made her feel with his presence. It was sure an addicting feeling. She smiled as he neared the car.

"Fancy meeting you here," She said as she got out.

She was adorable, her proper business clothes a direct contradiction to the fire he saw in her eyes when she looked at him. The woman could melt glaciers with that look.

He kissed her and squeezed her tight, "Hi there, how was your day?"

Raelynn grabbed her purse and started to follow him toward the house, "Busy but fine. Yours?"

He opened the front door and stepped back to allow her to enter first, "Same here, the mares still aren't foaling so we're taking shifts checking on them."

She felt bad keeping him at her place the night before when he should have been here. Was he changing to suit her needs? She didn't want that at all. Worry worked its way into her stomach.

"Is tonight bad?" She turned to look at him, "I can go home and we can meet up another time." She didn't want to be responsible for him missing anything.

"What?" He asked, shocked, "No, John has it with one of the hands tonight so I'm fine." Did she not want to be here? "Is it bad for you?"

Raelynn shook her head, they were a pair, "No Seth, it's where I want to be."

"Good," He started unbuttoning her white blouse, the feel of the fabric was soft against his fingertips, "I want you to be here."

He kissed her and all of her doubts and fears were put on a shelf very high up. She wanted to forget everything except his lips on hers. She pulled his shirt up and over his head, smiling, at his look of surprise. She wanted to get down to the heart of it, them together and naked.

They were kissing and taking clothes off, leaving a trail of fabric on their way to the kitchen. When they made it to the table, Seth only had his jeans on and Raelynn was down to her bra and panties. The kissing was much more intense, their breathing erratic, their need for one another all-consuming.

She pushed him down onto one of the kitchen chairs and knelt down in front of him. She slowly unbuttoned his fly, like she did the night she was first here. After his attention to her the night before, she felt more assured of her own abilities. As his jeans parted, she could feel him pulsing beneath her hands.

"Oh," He moaned, "baby you should not be doing that."

Raelynn smiled, then licked her lips, "Why not?"

Oh he knew what was on her mind, "Well, I want it to be good for you too."

"Seth," She freed him from his jeans, running her hand up the length of him, shivering with excitement at the hardness she initiated, "it will be very good for me."

He moaned as she took the tip of his member into her mouth. It was mind-altering to watch her make love to him with her mouth. If this was how she felt, he would gladly return the favor any time. His hands dove into her hair feeling the softness of it cover his fingers.

If she had any idea how powerful this simple act made her feel, she would have done it sooner. She didn't want to stop but Seth pulled her head up with his hands. The wild look in his eyes said what he wanted.

She stood and straddled him on the chair. As soon as they were joined, she started riding him fast. The need for release took her over and made her wanton. She threw her head back, allowing Seth to move her hips with his hands. They both crashed into their wall of abandonment together, Raelynn crying out first.

Seth held her against him, waiting for both of them to catch their breath. Finally, they were calm, she was so still he thought maybe she fell asleep. As gently as he could, he moved so he could stand and lifted her into his arms.

Raelynn lay her head on his shoulder, "I love it when you carry me."

He smiled and started toward the stairs, "I love carrying you baby."

She let him take her upstairs and put her on the bed. His bed was cozy and made her feel safe, just like Seth. Exhaustion took over and she couldn't even open her eyes. She could hear him moving around and settled when she felt him get into bed beside her. Sleep claimed her immediately.

The next thing Raelynn realized was she was alone in bed, she reached out for Seth and couldn't find him. Groggy, she sat up and looked around the semi-dark room. She didn't see Seth but smelled something wonderful. Her stomach growled in agreement so she found a t-shirt and slid it on before heading downstairs.

Padding through the house, she grinned at the sight of their clothes laying on the floor. She finally found him in the kitchen, cooking up something. It was interesting to watch him. He seemed pretty comfortable in here. Another interesting fact about Seth, she supposed.

"You're going to spoil me by cooking you know," She entered the room and walked over to him, wrapping her arms around his waist.

Seth scooped up the mixture of beef, potatoes, and vegetables. It was an easy, one pan meal John taught him how to make years ago. 'A man can't starve, he needs energy to keep workin.' John said at the time.

He placed the plates on the table and pulled out a chair for Raelynn, "Sit and eat, I need you strong so I can ravage you."

That statement made her tingle, "Well, we'll see about that." She responded.

They ate their meal and talked of John and what he and Seth used to do when they were younger. Raelynn laughed at the shenanigans Seth described. It was easy to forget the rest of the world when they were alone. She liked the sound of his voice, its deepness, his inflection when he spoke of something he really loved. It was hypnotic and she was lost in a whole new way.

After dinner, they rinsed the dishes and put them in the dishwasher. Raelynn remembered that she brought the "desert" items with her the week before and ran to the refrigerator to get them out. Seth leaned against the front of the sink, his legs crossed at the ankles, and watched her. He would never look at one of his t-shirts the same way now that he saw how it looked on Raelynn's body. She was giggling as she grabbed bottles out of the frig, a rather naughty gleam in her eye.

"It's time for dessert," She announced as she held the items behind her back.

He pushed away from the counter and started toward her, "What are you up to?" He asked.

She winked, "Nothing," and ran away from him, laughing as she dodged his hands.

They ran around the table and he caught her around the waist as she was heading for the back door. When he picked her up, he lost his balance and they fell into a heap on the floor.

"Are you okay?" He asked, checking her over.

She smiled, "Oh yes," she sat up and pushed her hair out of her face. "Close your eyes and I'll help you with your dessert."

He was somewhat reluctant to close his eyes, he'd seen 9 ½ weeks when he was a teenager. But he trusted Raelynn and complied.

Raelynn had a container of chocolate mousse in her hand, she opened the top and used her index finger to scoop out the creamy concoction onto her finger. "Open your mouth please." She asked in a husky voice, arousal creeping into it.

When she asked that way, he could not deny her. He dutifully opened his mouth and was rewarded with a sweet surprise. Although he wasn't sure if the chocolate or her finger gave him the most pleasure. His lips closed around her finger and sucked as the last remnants disappeared.

Raelynn repeated the movement several times, and each time his tongue skipped over her skin, she shivered in anticipation. He opened his eyes and looked at her.

"My turn," He said softly.

She expected him to put his finger into her mouth and parted her lips in anticipation. But he took his finger and made a line of the mousse down the inside of her forearm. The coolness of the whipped dessert gave her goose bumps. She watched as Seth brought her arm up to his mouth licking every inch of the chocolate creation off of her skin. How did he know what it did to her?

Raelynn wanted more of him, "Would you like to take this upstairs?"

"Yes," Seth responded, got up, pulled her up to him and took her upstairs to finish feeding off of her in every way he could think of.

Outside of the house, a figure stood near a tree, binoculars in hand, watching the two lovebirds and their little experiment in the kitchen. This would be interesting news for his client. A little too much for him, but he was being paid to watch. The pictures would tell the whole story. When the light went on upstairs, the figure left quietly, the same way he came.

Chapter 14

Raelynn stayed the night with Seth. When they woke up the next morning, she looked forward to spending the day in his life. Luckily she had the presence of mind to leave a change of clothes in her car so she didn't feel uncomfortable.

Hailey called mid-morning and asked if she could come over to see the horses. Seth agreed immediately and seemed enthusiastic which made Raelynn happy. It meant a lot to her that he was okay with spending time with Hailey. It was something she just wasn't used to thinking about but welcomed the feeling it gave her.

They cleaned out the horse stalls, making more of a game of it than anything else. Raelynn asked questions about the horses when they were giving them feed and water. Some horses received different amounts of certain food. The pregnant mares were being fed more to help them prepare for their foals. When Raelynn got to Lucy's stall, she entered slowly and pet the beautiful animal on her nose. Lucy whinnied in response which made Raelynn laugh.

Seth stood at the door to the stall, "She likes you."

Raelynn kissed the horse, "The feeling is mutual." She got the feed bucket and diligently put in the amount Seth instructed her to. She found that taking care of the animals was very relaxing.

They turned when they heard a car coming down the driveway, Raelynn exited the barn first and waived to Hailey as she got out of her car. Her shorter hair was pulled back into a little pony tail and she was dressed in jeans, a tank top, and tennis shoes. In her hand, she held a ball cap.

When Hailey reached her mom, she noticed that her mother looked very relaxed and very beautiful. It was kind of funny to say that since she always thought her mother was beautiful but being with Seth brought something out in her. Something Hailey was pretty sure was missing since her father died so long ago.

"Hey Hailey," Seth said as he came out to meet them. He impulsively gave her a hug.

She put her ball cap on her head, "I'm here so where are the horses."

They laughed and Seth motioned for the girls to follow him. He gave Hailey a tour of the barn and showed her the training corral and introduced her to John. He wanted to laugh at the way Hailey looked at John, like she was in awe of him. He was a real-life cowboy and had that effect on people.

The four of them spent the afternoon checking on the mares, Hailey asking a million questions and excited to see if one of the horses would go into labor while she was there. They had dinner together on the patio, the mild evening providing a cool breeze. Raelynn prompted John to tell her stories of their childhood similar to the ones Seth related the night before. John took great pleasure in exaggerating Seth's part in more than one plot. They were laughing and telling jokes when John suddenly stopped.

"What is it?" Seth asked. John didn't look serious unless he was.

John slowly got up and walked around the corner of the house, "I'll be right back." He said.

Raelynn watched the men and wondered what happened. She looked at Hailey who shrugged.

When John didn't return in ten minutes, the threesome cleaned up the dinner dishes and went inside. Raelynn wanted to ask Seth what was going on, he seemed tense, but didn't want to blow up the situation if it was nothing. After they went in, Seth excused himself and went outside.

Hailey was confused, "What happened?" She asked her mother.

"I honestly don't know." Raelynn responded.

She wanted to keep Hailey and herself calm so they did the dishes and she gave Hailey a quick tour of the house. Even she wasn't sure what all the rooms were, having only really been in Seth's room, his office, the kitchen, and great room.

The figure stood beside a tree with a telescopic lens, trying to get pictures of the woman. He didn't worry about the younger one, or the two men because they weren't the ones his client requested pictures of. He wasn't sure what all the fuss was about, this group was boring. At least the night before there was an interesting show with the two fooling around. He was frustrated when the older guy went somewhere and the other three cleaned up and went inside. He was adjusting his lens when he heard a noise behind him. Turning around, he was face to face with a shot gun.

"Friend," John said calmly, "you must be in the wrong place because you're trespassing."

Seth found John a few minutes later, his shotgun in some man's face. The guy looked scared out of his mind, his hands and palms up in front of him. If Seth wasn't so pissed that someone was on his land, he might take pity on the poor soul. He sped up his steps and reached the two.

"Who the hell are you?" Seth demanded. The guy looked odd, dressed all in black.

He sure didn't sign up for this, "I'm going to slowly reach in my pocket and pull out I.D." He pulled out a billfold and handed it to John, "I'm a private investigator."

Seth didn't care who the hell this guy was, he wanted him off his land, now. "Go!" He yelled.

The man didn't need to be told twice, he left quickly, practically running to his car. The trail of dust behind his vehicle was impressive.

John looked at Seth, clearly ticked off, "What the hell was that about?"

When Seth faced his friend, he was at a loss, "I wanted him gone."

"Seth," John placed his shotgun on his shoulder and started toward the house, "we didn't find out why he was here."

John was right and Seth was pissed, "I know, I just don't want Raelynn in the middle of anything."

Even an old cowhand could tell when someone was handing him a line of bull, "What aren't you telling me Seth?" John stopped and placed his hand on his friend's shoulder.

Seth looked at the house then back to John, "Nothing," he looked back to the house, where Raelynn and Hailey were. Knowing they were there did something funny to his insides and he liked it, he didn't want to lose that. "I'm just tired."

They walked back to the house, Seth heading for the back door and John going to the barn to secure his gun.

Raelynn heard the door and was relieved when Seth entered, "Hey, is everything okay?"

Seth walked over and hugged her, "Yes, just a coyote John saw in the pasture."

It was difficult for Raelynn to comprehend wild animals since she and Hailey lived in the city. "Is John okay?"

"Oh yeah," He smiled and kissed her quickly, "he just took the gun back to where we lock them in the barn."

Another thing, Raelynn didn't know much about, guns. Maybe she should learn, if she was going to be on the ranch it wouldn't hurt her to be prepared. She mentally berated herself, there is no reason to assume she would be here continually.

Seth noticed Raelynn thinking about something but he didn't want their night to be ruined by some jackass who decided to lurk around unwelcomed. He clapped his hands together, "Hailey, let's get your mom into a game in the living room."

The three went into the great room and found some board games in the closet. Hailey set up the board on the coffee table and everyone sat down to a rousing game of monopoly. They laughed and played and teased one another.

Seth took the time to watch mother and daughter interact. He could see they loved one another because he felt the same way about his own parents. He wondered how Hailey felt not ever knowing her dad. Already he was protective of her, any father figure would be. Did she see him as a possible candidate? The question had him wondering a good many things. He stopped woolgathering when he noticed two sets of eyes on him.

"Uh yes," he said.

Hailey looked at him questioningly, "It's your turn."

He was embarrassed by being caught off guard, "Sorry," he mumbled and rolled the dice.

After the game Seth asked Hailey if she wanted to go with him out to the barn to check on the horses. She jumped up quickly, not even giving Raelynn a second glance and practically danced out the door. Raelynn would have felt abandoned if she wasn't in awe of how much Hailey seemed to like Seth. Guilt over not giving her daughter a father loomed in the back of her mind.

When the game was picked up and put away, Raelynn wandered around the house. She poked into rooms, just wanting to be familiar with Seth's home. She entered his office and sat down behind his desk.

Awareness ran through her body when her skin touched the leather chair he sat in. She felt a connection to him here. She reached over and touched a pen, straightened a pile of papers, and closed a drawer he left partially open. A picture was sticking out of the top of it so she pulled it out.

The picture was of Seth holding a smiling blond woman. Was this the Nicole person he mentioned? They looked happy, her in his arms in much the same way he held Raelynn. The similarity provoked a cold shiver down her spine. Why did he still have a picture of someone he was over? Why did he hold her the same way he used to hold this Nicole woman? Her heart beating fast, Raelynn put the picture in the drawer and left the room.

She was shaking and unsure of what she should do. It was like betrayal, he said he was over his ex but the picture made things seem unclear in Raelynn's mind. She herself understood not being completely free of the past as Anthony still crossed her mind but Anthony was gone and couldn't come back. This woman most certainly could.

Seth came back into the house with a laughing Hailey. She was somewhat disappointed none of the mares were in labor yet, he told her, "They'll come in their own time, usually when it's most inconvenient for John and I."

They entered the great room to Raelynn standing with her purse near the door, she looked shaken.

"Oh good you're back, Hailey we need to get going." Raelynn said quietly, a forced smile on her face.

Hailey didn't understand, she thought they were staying overnight at Seth's house, "But," she got out when her mother interrupted.

Raelynn put her hand up in a sign of motherly control, "We're going."

Seth was uneasy, something wasn't right. Did he ask in front of Hailey? He didn't think Raelynn would care for that. He already neglected to tell her about the lurking guy, what if she found out about that? He would ask John as soon as he had the chance.

Hailey looked at him apologetically, "Bye Seth." She got her purse and went to the front door to join her mom.

Seth started to walk them out, Hailey went down the front steps first, and then Raelynn turned to him, "Please don't." She said.

He didn't understand, what was going on? "Raelynn I," what was he going to say?

"It's okay, I'm just beat." She said but she knew that he knew she was lying.

Seth stood on the porch and watched their cars pull down the driveway. When they were out of sight, he headed straight for the barn. He didn't see John so he headed over to the foreman's house where John lived. He knocked quickly then entered.

John was seated in his favorite chair in front of the television, a beer in one hand and a bag of chips in the other. He appreciated his alone time and told Seth on more than one occasion that what he did on his off time was his own business.

Seth stood just inside the door, "Did you see Raelynn while Hailey and I were out checking on the horses?" He and John didn't beat around the bush.

"No, why?" John asked.

He looked at his boots then back up at his friend, "She just left and I have no idea why."

John put his beer down and stood up, "Then maybe you shouldn't be lying to her," he knew he was right when Seth's eyes looked away, "and I damn sure know you shouldn't be lying to me boy."

Seth knew John only called him boy when he was mad. There weren't that many years between them but enough that they both knew who was really in charge. "I just don't want to discuss it is all."

John was not prone to violence, he believed a man's fuse should be long so as not to get into scuffles too many times. But he wanted to whip this boy's hind end for not being up front with him. "What the hell is going on here? I live here too and I don't appreciate having some nosy hoodlum sneaking around here with a camera."

It was not often these days that Seth felt like a chagrined child but he certainly did now. He sat down on the old, but comfortable couch and started to tell John a story. The story was not a happy one and Seth didn't like the taste it left in his mouth. He believed the past was the past but sometimes it came back like a snake in the grass and bit you.

For the second Friday in a row, Raelynn surprised Melissa by showing up to work when she was scheduled to be out. She thought about staying home but work was the excuse she gave Hailey for going home last night. It hurt to know her daughter was disappointed but Raelynn needed time to figure out what to make of what she saw at Seth's house. It was only a picture, maybe it was left over from something and he never looked in that drawer?

But that picture represented something Raelynn was not quite ready to accept yet, that there was another woman in Seth's life. She knew it was ridiculous but her feelings were such that she didn't want to compete for his attention with someone who wasn't there. Is that how he felt about Anthony? She wouldn't blame him if he did, she still slept with her late husband's picture beside her bed.

When he first died, Raelynn would lay in bed and just look at it for hours. Then when she found out she was pregnant, she talked to the picture about everything. To her, it was like having him there to listen to her. Her logical side told her it was not healthy but her heart demanded that she do it, to help her heal. She thought for many years that she did a good job of it but now she wasn't so sure. Well, it was what it was and there was no use in dwelling on something she would not figure out in a day so she went to work to drown it all out.

Raelynn was proud of herself on Monday morning for not going crazy over the weekend. She managed to avoid Seth but in a way that made it seem like she wasn't avoiding him. If he called, she let the voicemail pick up and then sent him a text saying she was working all weekend. The lie left a bitter taste but for her heart, it was a necessary one. She was no closer to figuring it all out when Melissa came into the office in a flurry of excitement.

"That man!" She said when she came into Raelynn's office.

Raelynn smiled, "Dare I ask to which man are you referring?"

Melissa sighed, "Mr. Wesley, who else." She pulled papers out of her briefcase and handed them to Raelynn. "He's crazy, I double-checked all the numbers and these are correct."

Raelynn remembered scanning them last week as well and was unable to see the so-called mistake he mentioned. "What time is our meeting with him?"

"Oh two o'clock this afternoon," Melissa replied. "Can we get drunk before we go? Please say yes!"

It was funny to see Melissa beg her like a child, but they had to be professionals so she gave her friend the best "mom" look she could and shook her head no.

Melissa got up and slumped her shoulders dramatically, "Fine." She left Raelynn's office.

The morning flew by and, at lunch, Raelynn looked at her phone to see a text from Seth on it. *I miss you, please call me so I can see you.*

She wanted to call him, but it was too much right now. These feelings were all jumbled and if she was with him, he would make her forget her insecurities and the challenges they faced. Not to mention Hailey, she already adored Seth. What if it didn't work out? Would Hailey hate her for it? It was a risk she wasn't sure she wanted to take now.

Fifteen minutes before their meeting, she and Melissa got into her car and drove over to Wesley's office. It was a welcomed distraction for Raelynn this time, she didn't have to worry about her problems for a while; she could focus on this.

They were shown into the conference room and, surprisingly, Mr. Wesley was already there. He smiled and stood holding the back of their chairs. She and Melissa exchanged puzzled looks as they sat down to the table. He sat across from them.

"Ladies, it seems I owe you an apology," He started, "I had my in-house accountant go over the paper and he was the one who made the error."

This was news, they weren't even aware he had an in-house accountant. Melissa recovered first, "If you have someone on staff Mr. Wesley, why did you hire us?"

Wesley smiled, looking uncomfortable, "My Corporation is getting too large for one person and his assistant to handle and I'm trying to figure out if I should retain someone here or contract out."

Raelynn nodded, "You could've told us that in the first place." She tried to sound non-judgmental but wasn't sure she pulled it off.

"I realize that and I apologize," He stood and walked around the table, hiking his hip up and half-sitting on the edge looking at both of them, "I wanted to see how well you would do because I want to acquire your company and have you work for me."

No one said anything, both she and Melissa just sat there staring at this man who wanted to buy their business.

Mr. Wesley smiled, "I'm sure this has been a little bit of a shock to you both, please think about it, I'll courier over the details tomorrow."

Raelynn was numb but managed to stand and take her briefcase. This was turning out to be a very confusing day for sure.

As they were leaving Wesley, called after her, "Raelynn could you stay a moment?"

Melissa gave her a 'do you want me to stay?' look but she discreetly shook her head and turned back to him.

"Yes sir," She said looking at him. He was a handsome man, if a little too arrogant for his own good.

He walked over to her, stopping a foot away, "Let's dispense with the formality, I would like to see you socially." He took her hand in his, "Maybe we can discuss the possible merger of our businesses."

Raelynn had the distinct feeling he was not really talking about business. She managed a smile, and, for some reason said, "That would be nice, thank you."

He was surprised but recovered quickly. "Okay then, I'll have my assistant call with some times."

She nodded and smiled weakly before turning to go. A few minutes later, she caught up with Melissa outside.

Melissa looked concerned as she stood by the car, "What happened?"

"He asked me out and I said yes," Even saying it out loud made her wonder about her own sanity.

Melissa looked shocked, "What? Why?"

They got in Raelynn's car, "I don't know, because I'm not sure about Seth I suppose and this is all too much." The tears started and she put her forehead against the steering wheel.

"Hey," Melissa murmured, "our afternoon is freed up because we didn't know how long this would take, what do you say we go and get a drink?"

Raelynn nodded and wiped her eyes. She pulled the car out of the lot and headed for a restaurant a few blocks over. It was a local place that had a nice bar. Since it was still too early for the dinner crowd, it wouldn't be too busy.

They went in and were able to get a table in the back. Each of them ordered a drink, Melissa asking the young waitress to keep them coming. She gave Raelynn a "what" look when she didn't look happy.

Neither spoke until their drinks arrived and they each took a big sip. Raelynn appreciated a good drink now and then but with her mind and heart in this kind of turmoil, she wanted to numb it. Melissa spoke first.

"Okay spill," She demanded, looking pointedly at Raelynn.

Sighing, Raelynn started with telling her about the day at Seth's when he rode out and yelled at John about her. Then she explained the night she and Seth were in her bed and she noticed the picture of Anthony. She jumped to being at Seth's house and finding the picture of a woman in his desk.

301

Melissa listened closely, she did not envy her friend's situation, "Do you know if this woman was Nicole?" She asked when Raelynn finished.

That was something she didn't really consider, she assumed it was. "No, so I don't know for sure."

Shaking her head, Melissa couldn't believe it, "This isn't like you; you're the level-headed one about things like this."

"I know right," She said, exasperated with herself. "I honestly don't understand what's going on with me."

"You're in love Raelynn," Melissa said flatly. She was a victim of the feeling herself a time or two and, unfortunately, she did not have a happy ending.

Raelynn nodded again, "I was suspecting as much the other night and then I was thinking about being at his house all the time, and then I was so scared."

Melissa's heart ached for her friend's obvious confusion, "I know sweetie, it's been a long time and you have Hailey to consider now."

She tipped her glass back and finished it in one gulp then motioned to the waitress for a refill before answering, "Yes, I don't know if I can do this and now I'm going out with Mr. Mark Wesley." She snickered, "I'm screwed."

It wasn't funny but they were both laughing about it with the help of their drinks. "Yes you are," Melissa lifted her glass and finished her round as well.

An hour and four drinks later, they decided they would not be able to drive. Melissa called a cab and they went back to her place because it was in Lake Jackson. Raelynn sent Hailey a text letting her know she was staying at Melissa's for the night. They got into pajamas, ordered a pizza, and continued to drink until almost midnight. Raelynn was not thinking about Seth or Mark or Anthony or anything for a while.

In the morning, Raelynn realized why she didn't drink often, her eyes were blood shot and her mouth was as dry as a desert. At least she didn't have a head ache. Since she and Melissa were close in size, she borrowed clothes to go to work in and they got a ride from a friend to the restaurant where they left the car so they could go to work.

At the office, Raelynn finally took the time to check her phone. There were several missed calls from Seth and one from Hailey. She called her daughter to make sure everything was okay.

Hailey answered on the second ring, "Hey mom."

"Hey yourself, did you eat? Are you on your way to class?" She couldn't help but worry.

Laughing, Hailey answered, "Yes and yes."

She smiled, "Have a great day baby girl."

"You too," Hailey paused, "Mom?"

Raelynn had a bad feeling but replied, "Yes?"

Hailey just wanted to know what was going on, "What happened between you and Seth?"

There it was. "I'm just unsure sweetie, he didn't do anything wrong, I just need some time to figure it out."

This was not what Hailey wanted to hear, "Is it because of dad?"

"A little bit," Raelynn said, "you know I have to think things through."

Sighing, Hailey looked out the window of her room, "Mom don't wait too long, he's a good man and somebody else will snatch him up."

That was what Raelynn already feared had happened but she would not admit it to Hailey. "I will, thank you." She did appreciate Hailey's concern even if she was blindly optimistic about their situation.

"Bye," Hailey said and hung up.

Raelynn sat at her desk and thought about her daughter. She should have known it would be easy for Hailey to have an attachment to Seth, he was a good man. The problem was, was he the right one for her?

Seth sat atop his mount looking out over the pasture at the horses grazing in the distance. The cool breeze of morning felt good on his skin but it was his heart that was in trouble. He heard the sound of an approaching horse and looked over to see John come up on his side.

"Mornin," Seth grumbled.

John nodded his head, "Are you going to chew on this much longer? We're not gettin any younger you know."

It was hard not to smile at John's straight forward logic. "I'm working on it John."

He didn't want to talk about this anymore, he wanted to ride. He prodded Lex and they took off across the paddock.

Maybe if he rode hard enough and fast enough, he could outrun the heartache he felt chasing him down.

The day was busy but productive. Raelynn and Melissa had lunch in the break room and laughed about their drinking excursion the previous evening. It was nice to be silly and not have to think too much about what was going on. She was at her desk when a call came through the office line.

"Hello, this is Raelynn Woodsen," Was her standard greeting.

A voice cleared, "Ms. Woodsen, this is Karen, Mr. Wesley's assistant. He has asked me to call you with his availability this week so that you may set up your dinner."

Raelynn felt the chill from the woman's voice, "Oh yes, one moment," She got out her calendar and picked the phone back up, "go ahead."

They discussed dates and decided on the next evening. After she hung up, Raelynn took a deep breath. These split-second decisions were going to get her into trouble. She went back to work and tucked the impending dinner date in the back of her mind.

After five, Melissa came into her office, looking tired. "I'm beat, are you ready to go?"

Raelynn nodded, "Hold on," she finished up the tax form she was filling out for a client and put it in the folder. "Okay, ready."

They got their bags and made sure everything was secure. When they were locking the door, Melissa turned to her, "Did you want to stay over tonight?"

She appreciated what Melissa was trying to do, buy her some more time before leaving her alone with her thoughts. That's why they were best friends. "I would love to but it's time to go home."

Melissa nodded, gave her a hug, and headed for her own car. They pulled out and waived as they turned in different directions.

The night was mild and Raelynn left the windows open as she traveled down Hwy 288 North. The wind through the car drowned out her rampaging thoughts. She actually considered pulling off at the exit that led to Seth's place but decided she shouldn't see him until she was certain of what she was going to do. Plus there were things to be done at home and she wanted to see Hailey. If she saw him, she would let it all go out the window.

When she arrived home, she checked her phone and found a voicemail from Hailey letting her know she was studying with friends. Oh great, now she had to be home alone. Not only that but she had to be home alone with her thoughts. She had the feeling it was going to be a long night.

After shedding her work clothes and putting on sweats, she threw her laundry in the washer, made a sandwich to eat for dinner, and cleaned up some dishes.

What was she going to do? Without dwelling, she went over to the coffee table and pulled a box out of the bottom of it. She sat on the floor, her knees pulled to her chest and looked through the box. It contained pictures of Anthony from his childhood throughout his life. She got as many as she could from his family after he passed away so that she could provide Hailey with her dad's history. She even made a note of describing the picture and its circumstances on the back so she wouldn't get it wrong. It was important to be accurate for Hailey's sake.

She slowly looked through pictures, running her finger over his face as if she could feel him. He was a good man who loved her so much but he wasn't without flaws. She remembered a few arguments they had before he went out to the platform. She was mad about some silly thing he did, she couldn't even remember what it was anymore, and yelled. He was surprised by her anger and tried to coax her into forgiving him. She eventually cracked and laughed. She missed him even now but she wondered if it was the idea of him she missed more than anything.

She laid her head back against the sofa and wondered how she got so churned up with all of this. Only a month ago she knew what she was doing and her life was calm. Staring at the ceiling, she admitted it was just safe. And once she met Seth, that safety went right out the window and she was forced to open up again.

Anthony would say, "go for it," and he would laugh in his jovial way. He would be cheering her on all the way. So why did she feel so unsure about it?

This was not going to be sorted out tonight, she went into the bathroom and got ready for bed. She turned down the bed and looked around her room. It didn't feel the same anymore. Nothing did. She was about to get in when her phone went off. It was probably Hailey so she grabbed it. Her feelings sunk when she noticed it was from Seth. Oh Lord, she didn't want to deal with this, but she read his text:

Hey there. I've been thinking about you and hope you're ok. I miss you.

She didn't want to cry, she knew she was hurting him by not responding so she typed quickly, *I've been so busy, I'm sorry. Can I talk to you tomorrow, I'm exhausted.*

Seth read the text, his hopes plummeting. He typed his response, not being able to keep the hurt out of it, *I won't bother you. Just know that we can't avoid each other forever, we need to talk at some point.* He hit send.

Raelynn read it and knew he was right. She was too afraid and wasn't sure she would get over that. Not to mention the questions about his feelings. She didn't even respond to his text, she took the phone into her room only because she was afraid that she would miss a call from Hailey if she didn't.

The next day Raelynn came into work and did everything that she normally did. Years of practice at being regimented could allow you to do it. This was the only time she could remember being glad about not having to think about it.

She worked through lunch and avoided all calls, letting her voicemail pick them up. She finally looked up at four-thirty and realized she needed to wrap it up so she could get ready for her dinner date with Mark Wesley.

Why did she agree to it? She would rather go have a root canal done by her dentist. She did as expected though, having left Hailey a note about her plans this morning. She mis-worded her dinner date, calling it a meeting to ensure Hailey wouldn't call her about it. She didn't need her daughter's attitude added to the mix of confusing thoughts spinning around in her head.

At five-thirty she came out of the restroom satisfied with her appearance. She wore a black dress, form fitting but not suggestive, and some wine colored pumps. She freshened her make-up and hair. Melissa stood in her office doorway, an eyebrow arched, not saying anything.

"I know," Raelynn said, "this shouldn't be happening."

Melissa shook her head, "It's not that, you can see whomever you like," she moved closer, "it's that you look like you're about to face a firing squad."

Forcing a smile, Raelynn nodded, "I'll figure this out and I'll sincerely try to be polite and a good dinner companion."

"We really didn't discuss his offer, what if he asks you about it?" Melissa just thought of it.

Raelynn shrugged, "I'll just tell him we're still considering it." She checked her hair once more in the mirror and turned to grab her bag off of a nearby table, "Did you look at the paperwork he sent over?"

Melissa looked over her shoulder into her office, "Nope, it's still on my desk in the envelope, I wanted us to review it together."

She put her lipstick in her small clutch, "Why don't we do that tomorrow then."

"Ok," Melissa looked out the front door, "looks like your ride is here." She gave Raelynn a quick hug, "Have a good time."

Raelynn hugged her back, "I'll try." She went down the hall to the front door, dutifully locking it behind her and put her best smile on as she neared Mark's car.

Mark got out and met her halfway up the walk. He smiled appreciatively, "You look lovely."

She nodded, "Thank you, you do too."

He guided her to the passenger side of his Mercedes and tucked her inside. He was rounding the sedan when he noticed a man standing on the sidewalk, "Good evening," he said and got into the car.

The car went down the road and Seth stood on the sidewalk, flowers in his hand, watching the woman he loved leave with another man. A rich man by the looks of things. He threw the flowers on the ground and walked back to his truck. The petals from the arrangement blowing every which way across the grass, like the pieces of his heart as they shattered.

Chapter 15

The morning was bright and sunny when Raelynn entered the office. It was Thursday and the week was dragging on for some reason. She knew she would be called in to regale Melissa with the events of her dinner date with Mark the night before. He insisted she call him that since they were in a social setting but it still felt slightly uncomfortable.

They had a lovely dinner and he was actually quite a pleasant dinner companion. His conversational skills were excellent, covering a vast variety of topics. They found they shared some common interests. It occurred to Raelynn that she could have been very interested in him if she never met Seth. But she did meet Seth and she found herself comparing the men at every turn. It was clear that Mark simply did not make her "feel" as Seth did.

She was listening to her voicemails when one of her assistants knocked on the door. "Are you busy?"

Raelynn paused the voicemail and motioned him to sit, she liked him, his name was Kyle and he was a hard worker. "Can I help you with something?"

Kyle shifted in the chair, "No, I just wanted to say thank you but I've been offered another internship that would be more lucrative for me."

She nodded, "That's fine Kyle, we understand." She got out a pen and paper, "Would you like a letter of reference?"

"No thank you," Kyle said shyly. "I'll get my things and go now."

Raelynn was puzzled, "Oh, okay." What else could she say? After he left she got up and went to Melissa's office. Melissa was on the phone so she waited.

She jumped right in, "Did you know Kyle was leaving?"

Melissa looked confused, "No," she rummaged through some papers on her desk. "Some of my files are missing, I just spoke to Mr. Sanchez and he was supposed to come in today to sign his papers and I can't find them anywhere."

That was odd, Raelynn thought, they were very meticulous about the paperwork. Any good CPA would be. She helped Melissa look for a few minutes longer then went back to her own office to check the papers in case they were misfiled. An hour later, she was getting very frustrated when her phone rang.

"Raelynn Woodsen," She answered absently.

"What is this I hear about you going bankrupt?" Mr. Reynolds asked, his voice tense.

Raelynn frowned, "Mr. Reynolds we are not going bankrupt; where did you hear that?" This was conversation was very strange.

He cleared his throat, "It's in the paper."

"What!" Raelynn shouted. She shook her head when Melissa ran to her office. "Mr. Reynolds, can I call you back? I'm sure it's a misprint." She managed to hang up with him and looked at Melissa. "Do you have today's paper?"

Melissa nodded and went to the break room. She handed it to Raelynn, "What up?"

The feeling of impending doom was speeding up Raelynn's spine, "Mr. Reynolds called and said he read in the paper that we are going bankrupt."

Her partner repeated her earlier, "What?" in a loud voice.

They found the story and read it together. Sure enough, it was an investigative piece basically accusing their firm of impropriety. By the time they finished, they weren't sure who they were going to kill, but somebody's head would roll. The phone was ringing off the hook so they asked their remaining intern to just take messages and if it became too much, to just unplug the phone and lock the door. They got their purses and arrived at the newspaper office within a few minutes.

Melissa led the way, because she was calmer than Raelynn, and they went to the editor's office to speak to him. His name was Carl Bergman and they knew him for years. He came out of his office, looking very worried. Raelynn thought he should, he would be lucky if she didn't sue him for slander.

"Carl?" Melissa asked. The one word held a lot of meaning.

He stepped aside and gestured for them to enter his office. He closed the door securely behind them and sat across from them. "I'm sorry, I don't know what happened."

"What do you mean?" Raelynn asked, appalled.

He pulled something up on his computer, "It means, no one on my staff wrote the piece. We noticed it this morning after the papers were delivered. I've checked with all of the department heads here and NO ONE authorized this piece to be written."

Melissa stood and paced, "So let me get this straight, a newspaper article just magically ends up in your paper?"

"I'm telling you both, we did not write this, I've checked the templates and this was not on them. " He said sorrowfully.

Raelynn sat forward and put her fist on his desk, "You'd better send the retraction out NOW Carl!"

He nodded, "It's being written as we speak."

"But that doesn't help our clients who may believe this crap does it?" Melissa pointed at him. "Expect to hear from our attorney." She shook her head in disgust and left the office.

Raelynn tried to calm herself, "Call us when you figure this out."

Carl nodded.

They left the newspaper office and prepared to call all of their clients to explain. It was going to be a very rough day. They walked into the office to a frantic intern and started answering the phone.

Hailey called Raelynn in the afternoon on her cell phone, "Mom, what is going on?" One of her classmates asked her about her mom's company after class and she didn't know what the girl was talking about.

"Baby, can I explain when I get home?" She felt sorry that Hailey had to be touched by any of this.

Hailey sighed, "Okay, I'll be home right after my last class."

Raelynn tried to smile, "I'll meet you there."

She hung up the phone and laid her head in her hands. If she thought her mind was oatmeal the night before; that was nothing compared to this. Her world was literally unravelling right before her eyes.

They finally called it a day at a little past seven that evening. Both she and Melissa left everything work-related at the office and just left. It was the first time she could remember feeling so hopeless over the future of their business.

Raelynn drove straight home and managed a shower before she heard Hailey come in. She sat on the sofa and waited for her daughter. Her heart broke when she saw the worried look in Hailey's eyes. They never had this kind of upheaval before. She held her arms open and was relieved when Hailey sat down and hugged her. They held each other for a while then Raelynn moved so they were facing one another. She explained the events and apologized to Hailey.

"Mom," Hailey was outraged, "it's not true. They can't believe it."

She would've liked to assure her daughter that was what was going to happen but they lost almost half of their clients in one day. People didn't always have the faith. She knew they would get through this, it would just be rocky for a while.

They sat up for a few more minutes, Raelynn trying to assure Hailey that it was going to be fine in the end. It was tough because she wasn't at all sure of it herself.

She called Melissa to check on her before going to bed. They shored each other up emotionally and Raelynn was so thankful for her friend. When she finally got to bed, she laid on her side and cried. She wished Seth was there to hold her and, for the first time in nineteen years, she took Anthony's picture and placed it in the drawer of her nightstand.

Friday was spent fielding more phone calls and trying to get lost clients back. The paper came out with the retraction which helped them recoup some of the lost confidence the community had in them.

The weekend was spent at work, both she and Melissa going over every last file in the fifteen years of their business. Double-checking everything. Looking for some clue as to who would want to ruin their business reputation. They didn't come up with anyone who they could logically think would do such a thing.

A detective from the police department came by and got statements from them. Since there was website hacking involved, it was a cyber-crime so there was going to be an investigation. They said they would cooperate in any way they could but both were skeptical of the culprit being caught.

For the first time, they decided to close on Monday; posting a sign on the door that assured anyone who came that they were still in business, just needed to take a personal day. Melissa changed the answering machine message to say the same thing.

Raelynn was still in bed at ten o'clock on Monday morning when Hailey came in and sat on the end of her bed, "Are you okay mom?" Her daughter asked.

It was hard, but she smiled, "Yes baby, I'm fine, just emotionally and physically exhausted."

Hailey nodded and looked around everywhere but at her mom, "Um Mom?"

"Yes," Raelynn answered. She could see Hailey was chewing on something. She did the same thing herself.

"I don't mean to upset you with everything weird going on at work," She took a deep breath, "but what happened with Seth?" She placed her hand on her mom's leg, "I would've thought he would be here for you through this."

Oh goodness, Raelynn prayed for strength, "Hailey, I've not spoken to Seth since we were last there, we've both been busy."

A tear wound its way down Hailey's cheek, "But you said you loved him."

Seeing her daughter so hurt, broke Raelynn's heart, "I did say that yes, but sometimes it doesn't work out sweetie."

"That's a cop out, you lied!" Hailey shouted and left her mother's room, slamming the door.

Raelynn closed her eyes and took a couple of cleansing breaths. She wasn't sure if she would make it through all of this. She threw back the covers and went into the bathroom to shower and figure out what the hell to do with her life.

Seth read the paper, his temper flaring immediately. He only subscribed to the Houston papers so he didn't know about the article in the Lake Jackson paper until it made the news up north. Some jackass hacked the paper and slandered Raelynn's business.

As if that wasn't bad enough, she didn't call him and tell him herself. That was what really rotted his gut. She professed love then went out with some rich bastard and her company is threatened and he didn't even rate a phone call. John came into the kitchen through the back door while he was finishing the article.

"I see you've seen that garbage," John said as he poured himself a cup of coffee and sat down across from Seth at the table. "Your lady is in trouble."

Seth scowled, "She's not my lady."

"Dammit boy!" John slammed down his fist on the table, causing coffee to splash out of both of their mugs. "What is wrong with you?"

Seth did not understand, "John, I," he started.

"No!" John yelled again, "your lady is in trouble and here you sit, wallowing in your damn self-pity." He tried to calm himself, "She ain't like that crazy one, Nicole, she is a damn fine woman and you're just giving her cause to kick your carcass out."

It annoyed him that John was right on all counts. His pride was a factor here though, if he went to her and she sent him away, he'd be lost. So he sat there, staring into his coffee. He heard the door slam behind John a few minutes later.

The rest of the week was spent fielding phone calls from everyone who thought they would put their two cents in about the situation. Most of their clients spoke to them after the retraction and they were able to hold things together.

On Wednesday, Raelynn called Hailey to say that she was going to stay down in Lake Jackson with Melissa until they had a better handle on it all. That way she wasn't commuting late in the evening or early in the morning. Hailey assured her that she would be fine. Their relationship was strained since the talk on Monday and Raelynn couldn't figure out how to fix it.

Friday evening, they wrapped up around eight and both of them sat in Melissa's office just staring into space. Neither was willing to say this fiasco was officially over, because there was no progress on finding out who did it in the first place. Finally Melissa stretched and stood.

"We need to get out of here," She announced to Raelynn.

Nodding, Raelynn stood, "Okay."

Melissa led the way out to the car, they carpooled since Raelynn was staying at her place. "Hey," She stopped at the car door and looked over the hood to Raelynn, "let's go out."

"What?" Raelynn asked, astounded by Melissa's statement.

Melissa got in behind the wheel, "Yes, let's go out and have some fun."

Raelynn shook her head, "I'm not really in the mood to have fun Melissa."

"And that," Melissa started up her car, "is exactly why we should. I'm fed up with the doom and gloom."

She could definitely relate to that, she was just afraid her sour mood would make the evening horrible for them both. But she owed it to Melissa to at least try. "Okay, fine." She mumbled.

They went back to Melissa's place and changed. Melissa wore some form-fitting jeans, a white silk tank, a blinged out belt, and some cowboy boots. She encouraged Raelynn to go out of her comfort zone so she chose a light cotton dress and a pair of brown boots. They helped each other with their hair and makeup and finally were ready to go and try to have a good time.

Raelynn drove, since she decided to be the designated driver for the evening, and went out to a local honky tonk fifteen minutes outside of Lake Jackson. It was a popular spot on the weekends, with loud music and dancing. It was just the distraction they were looking for.

An hour later, Raelynn wasn't so sure this was such a wise move. Melissa danced a lot with the guys and was having a ball but Raelynn chose to sit in the corner and watch the other regulars. A couple of gentlemen asked her to dance but she politely declined. She got up to get a refill on her soda and wound her way through the thickening crowd.

She ordered a diet soda and was bumped by a man in a large cowboy hat, "Sorry ma'am," he slurred as he brushed by her.

She watched him walk away, pitying whoever had to get him home later, and turned to get her soda. She paid the bartender and took her soda back to their table. After a few minutes, she took a sip of her drink, needing to quench her thirst.

Melissa came back to the table and they chatted for only a little bit before another cowboy came up and asked her to dance. Raelynn smiled at her friend, it was good for her to find some fun. She took another drink of her soda and watched the dancers.

Fifteen minutes later, she was feeling funny. She was pretty sure she ordered a soda but maybe the bartender added some alcohol. It felt kind of good to be off kilter and she smiled. Someone asked her to dance and she nodded absently.

There was a slow country song playing, making her head spin, the man she was dancing with was tall and lean and expertly spun her around the dance floor, increasing the unbalanced feeling coursing through her brain. She smiled benignly and allowed him to lead her.

By the time the song ended, she was almost hanging on her dance partner. It was difficult to stand for some reason. He was kind enough to escort her back to her seat and set her down gently. Luckily she was next to the wall so she could lean against it. Melissa came up to her and was asking her questions but it was hard to answer. Her mind was fuzzy, she wanted to just lay down and sleep. She heard people talking around her, she thought it was Melissa and a man but she was unsure.

Melissa was trying to get Raelynn to focus on her when she felt someone behind her. When she turned she saw Seth standing there, her stomach sank. He looked tormented at first but then he looked from her to Raelynn and back again and looked mad. She didn't have time to worry about his emotions right now, she was worried about Raelynn.

"Don't!" She said sternly, "She hasn't been drinking at all."

Seth picked up Raelynn's glass and sniffed, he didn't smell any alcohol. "Did she get her own drinks?" He asked.

Melissa was frustrated by his accusing tone, "I don't know Seth; I wasn't babysitting her."

His lips pursed, he tried to control his anger, "Let's get her out of here."

Melissa nodded and stood up. Seth bent down and lifted Raelynn into his arms. They walked out of the bar, a few people staring after them curiously. Seth put Raelynn in the cab of his truck first, then helped Melissa get in and went around to the driver's side.

"What happened?" He asked when they were on the highway going toward Lake Jackson.

Melissa looked shaken, "I don't know, she was the designated driver and she was only drinking soda, I swear Seth."

He shook his head, "That's not what I meant." His tone was tense with trying to hold back his raging emotions.

She looked out the window, "I don't know that either." She did know some of it but she wasn't going to get into details with him.

He drove silently until they were in the city and then he asked where Melissa's place was. She gave him the address and directions but that was the extent of their conversation. He pulled up in front of her small house and got out. He opened her door and helped her out.

"If you'll help me get her inside, I'd appreciate it." She turned to reach in for Raelynn when he put his hand on her shoulder to stop her.

He was seething and didn't know exactly why, "She's coming home with me." It was not a question.

Melissa nodded, if Raelynn would have given her any indication that Seth would hurt her, she would have fought him, but Raelynn never said anything of the kind. She said a quiet, "Thank you," and went inside.

Seth drove directly to his ranch, barely maintaining the speed limit. On the way he made a phone call to his cousin, who was a doctor in a nearby town, and asked him to meet them at the house. When he pulled in, he saw that his cousin, Will, was getting out of his car.

"Thanks," He said as he rounded the truck to get Raelynn.

She was slumped over and non-responsive. He checked her pulse more than once on during the trip to make sure she was still okay. Her pulse was strong and she roused when he picked her up into his arms.

"Seth?" She slurred.

He smiled for the first time in days, "Yes Baby, I'm here." He kissed her forehead and took her into the house while Will got his bag out of the car.

Sunlight.....bright.....hurt eyes. Raelynn was trying to shield herself from the brightness. She felt awful, nauseous even. As soon as the thought formed she sat up and covered her mouth. Hands came around her and held a bowl in front of her. She was sick, throwing up everything inside her. It caused her head to turn. After she was done, she was exhausted and fell back on the bed. The sweet oblivion of sleep claimed her.

She opened her eyes and didn't know where she was. The room was not familiar to her, she sat up out of fear and realized her mistake when her head spun. She put her hand up to it to try and stop it. She opened her eyes and saw Hailey sitting on the bed beside her, looking tired.

"What...." Was the only word she could get out.

Hailey cried tears of relief, "It's okay mom. We're here." She got up and went to gently coax her mom to lay back down.

As soon as Raelynn was asleep again, she walked out of the room.

Seth watched Hailey leave and was torn on whether he should go or stay with Raelynn. He glanced at the bed and saw her breathing deep so he chanced leaving to make sure Hailey was okay. He found her down the hall, in the bathroom, splashing water on her face. He waited for her to finish, leaning up against the door jamb.

"Are you okay?" He asked. His heart ached for her.

323

She nodded, "I'm okay, I'm just pissed Seth!" She hadn't meant to yell. "Why is all of this happening?" She started to cry again.

Seth pulled her to him, wrapping his arms around her. "It's okay sweetie, she's going to be fine."

Raelynn got up, not knowing where she was. She walked out into the hall to see Seth holding Hailey in his arms and kissing her head.

Her stomach sank to her feet and she felt a rage as never before, "You get your hands off of her!" She screamed and moved toward them.

Raelynn's words startled Hailey and Seth, causing them to break apart quickly. Hailey started toward her mother, being more scared for the terror she saw in her mom's eyes.

"Mom, it's okay." Hailey tried to say.

It was hard to focus but she was not going to let him hurt her daughter. She grabbed Hailey as soon as she was close enough and pulled her back away from Seth. What the hell was going on? She couldn't think straight and she was having trouble walking. They had to get out of here, she felt desperation course through her. The adrenalin surge was holding her together. She found the stairs and dragged Hailey with her.

Seth didn't know what to do, at first, he just stood there but as soon as he figured out Raelynn planned to leave, he knew he couldn't let her. He slowly followed them until they hit the landing at the bottom of the stairs.

He was calm, "Raelynn, it's okay."

"You," She screamed, "don't touch her!" No one would hurt her baby.

John came into the room wondering what all the ruckus was about and was shocked at the sight of Raelynn holding Hailey like a rag doll and Seth on the stairs. He made a sound and stopped when she turned to him, her eyes looking wide and scared. She looked like a wild horse, ready to bolt at a moment's notice. He looked up at Seth, who silently conveyed the seriousness of the situation.

Seth moved down another step, John had Raelynn's attention for the moment so he took advantage of it by quietly getting closer. Hailey was petrified and didn't understand what was wrong with her mother.

"Hello there missy," John said nonchalantly.

Raelynn couldn't focus, she thought she was going to faint, but she had to get out of there. They were going to hurt her baby and she couldn't let that happen. She knew the door was around here somewhere. If they could get out, they could run away. Hailey was shaking, she was scared of them. She finally focused on the door and moved toward it.

John moved closer to the women, he was trying to be calm and talked to Raelynn like he would one of the horses he broke. It was about the tone, if they didn't feel threatened they wouldn't run.

She felt the door and turned the knob, they were almost okay, she thought. The door opened and she moved through it with Hailey against her side. She backed up and stumbled down the stairs, taking Hailey with her. They fell into a pile at the bottom of the stairs, Raelynn crying out in pain.

John and Seth were there in an instant. John was able to get Hailey away from Raelynn and took her around the side of the house, out of sight.

Seth grabbed Raelynn and held her to him. She was screaming like an animal, reaching out.

"NOOOOOOO," She just kept crying out.

He was crying as he got her back into the house and to the couch. He held her down until John came in and helped him while Hailey called his cousin. Will instructed him to give her a shot of something in the leg to calm her. He did as he was told and gave her the shot, knowing he was going to hell when this was all said and done.

She hurt, Raelynn thought. Her body ached everywhere. She opened her eyes tentatively and saw Seth. He was sitting in a chair next to the bed, sleeping. He looked very uncomfortable but she didn't want to disturb him so she just laid there and watched him.

He woke with a start, worried about Raelynn. Once he focused on her, he saw she was awake. Relief washed over him. "Hey," He said softly.

"Hey," She answered, her throat hurting.

He got her a glass of water and helped her sit up so she could drink a little bit. Once she was done, she laid back down out of sheer exhaustion.

She looked around the room and back to Seth, "Why am I here?"

He didn't know whether to be relieved that she didn't remember what happened or not. He didn't know what to say.

"I'll be right back," He whispered, squeezing her hand gently. He went out into the hall and called Melissa.

When he came back in, something about his demeanor scared her, "Is Hailey okay?" She was on full alert.

He sat down on the bed and absently rubbed her arm with his hand. "Yes, she's coming over with Melissa."

She looked around, embarrassed, "Seth, I need to use the bathroom."

"Okay," He helped her get up and guided her into the bathroom. Once she was inside, he stepped outside to give her some privacy and wait for her to finish.

She held on to Seth tightly, she was so weak, until she was back in the bed. "Are you going to tell me what's going on?"

"Nope," Melissa said from the doorway, "but I will." She looked at Seth, "Out so we can get her in the shower and dressed."

He didn't have to be told twice and exited the room.

Hailey, John, and Seth waited downstairs for a while. They decided that Melissa would relate the details of the last two days to Raelynn. It was too bizarre to be believable from anyone but her. They were in the kitchen fixing lunch when a wobbly, but better Raelynn came in.

Seth looked at her and thought she was the most beautiful creature on earth. He smiled when her eyes found Hailey and she opened her arms. John cleared his throat as the women embraced. Seth was having a difficult time dealing but he loved her so he would.

She looked at him over her daughter's head and mouthed thank you. The tears started then and she swiped at them.

"Okay, let's sit down," Melissa said.

Everyone sat down at the table not sure what to say.

Raelynn looked at each of them, "I am monumentally sorry for my behavior toward all of you."

The tears were streaming down, she thought she shed them all upstairs when Melissa told her what she did. How were any of them going to forgive her? How would she forgive herself?

Surprisingly, John answered first, "No need Lynn, we knew it wasn't you actin like a crazed coyot."

Everyone laughed at his description and at his name for her.

She reached across and squeezed John's hand, "Thank you."

Hailey and Melissa stood up and got some sandwiches and drinks for everyone. Raelynn ate slowly, not sure how her stomach would take the food. The men discussed ranch business to take the focus off of Raelynn. She was grateful for the distraction.

When lunch was finished, John asked Hailey and Melissa to help him with some of the barn chores. Melissa looked terrified which caused Hailey to laugh and tease her as they left out the back door. Raelynn stayed where she was at the table. Seth sat across from her.

"Do you hate me?" She asked.

Her torment broke him, "Baby," he got up and went over to her, kneeling in front of her chair. "Didn't Melissa explain that you were drugged?"

She nodded but couldn't look at him, "Yes but why would I act that way?"

He took her hands in his and kissed them, "Will said it was some designer hallucinogen probably and the best thing was to let you sleep it out of your system. You woke up when I was hugging Hailey and you thought I was hurting her. No one can blame you for that."

"I can," She said through the tears.

He took his thumb and wiped the tears from her eyes, "No," he smiled, "you just get better and we'll figure it all out."

She shook her head, "Why are you being so nice to me?"

He was confused, "Why wouldn't I be?"

She stood slowly and walked out of the kitchen. Her head was still a little fuzzy but her balance was back so she moved easily. She heard his footsteps behind her and went directly into the office to the drawer. She opened it and pulled out the picture and handed it to him.

"I found this the last time Hailey and I were here," She looked at him, questions in her eyes.

He looked at the picture and then back at her. He wasn't sure what this meant.

She took the picture and sat down in his chair, staring at it, "Is this Nicole?"

A feeling of dread settled in the pit of his stomach, "Yes it is."

Raelynn nodded, "You held her like you hold me."

"Okay," He wasn't sure what the correlation was.

She sighed, "No Seth, it's not okay."

He wasn't trying to be dense here but really didn't understand what she was getting at. "I'm sorry?" He asked.

She tried to keep herself from falling apart, "I'm not her."

Seth frowned, "Yes, I know that."

Frustration filled her, "I am not her! I cannot be her! I will not be her!"

The dread was filling him up, "I know that Raelynn, just like I'm not the guy in the Mercedes who picked you up for a date outside your office. What's your point?" He yelled.

Raelynn's insides collapsed. They would not be able to get past this and the pain was crippling. She heard a noise and looked over to see Melissa, John, and a crying Hailey at the doorway to the office.

"Hailey," Melissa said softly, "you go out to the car," she looked behind her, "John can you help her out please?" Her tone was extremely calm.

Once Hailey and John went out the front door she turned back to the couple of idiots in the office. "What the devil is wrong with you two?" She demanded.

Without waiting for their answer, she marched over and helped Raelynn stand. "That poor girl out there has had enough craziness," She poked at Seth, "no more!"

Seth stood there and watched Melissa help Raelynn out. The front door clicked behind them with a finality. He sat at his desk and wondered what happened.

Chapter 16

A month after leaving Seth's house, Raelynn was still not quite herself. She couldn't understand the events of that week and a half and was frustrated with trying to. She and Hailey went to a counselor for a couple of weeks to make sure Hailey was okay with what she went through. The counselor commented at their last session that Hailey was well adjusted but he felt Raelynn should continue as it seemed she had some issues to resolve. She thanked him and left, knowing he was right but wanting to get their life back to normal.

Work was almost back to stable, they declined the offer Mark Wesley made them and were surprised by how well he took it. They explained the newspaper article and he seemed appeased with the explanation.

Raelynn wondered briefly if he was the one behind the act in the first place since he was a competitive person and he had motive but she refused to say it out loud even to Melissa. They might never know. She would need to reconcile that fact at some point.

She hadn't heard from Seth since she left his house either. She assumed he came to the same conclusion she did, they just weren't meant to be. Knowing that in her mind did nothing to alleviate the physical ache her body experienced for missing him. Every time she went into a room, she was bombarded by memories of him. He invaded her dreams at night, refusing to leave her be. She seesawed between despair and anger at him.

The good thing was that she and Hailey seemed to be on an even keel. She was busy this week taking finals and appeared to be doing well. They would find out when grades were posted. She promised Hailey they would take some time after school let out. Lord knew they both could use the break.

She was on her way to work in early May, enjoying the fresh air when she looked behind her to see a car going fast. She was in the left lane so she turned on her directional to move over for the vehicle. When she looked up into her rearview mirror again, she saw the vehicle moved into the right lane behind her but was still coming up fast. What was the problem with this driver? She motioned with her arm for him to go around her. Dread filled her heart when the vehicle filled her mirror, all she could see was the grill of it.

The moment the vehicles made contact, Raelynn screamed. Her little car was no match for the big SUV and started skidding off the road. She took her foot off the gas and let the car go, she saw on some show to allow the car to find its own footing, don't force it. But once the wheels his the shoulder with loose gravel, she thought she was going to die. Her vehicle flipped once and landed on its side in some tall grass.

Shaking, Raelynn could only sit there and thank God she was still alive. A few minutes later, another driver ran up. He looked in the vehicle and asked if she was okay. He was relaying information into his cell phone to the authorities.

Sitting at the police station, Raelynn was in shock. She could no longer answer the questions for the detective assigned to the accident. Witnesses said the driver of the other vehicle aimed for her car. It was frightening to think someone would want to harm her.

Seth arrived at the county sheriff's office and ran inside. A friend of his, a fellow skydiver, knew he and Raelynn dated so he called Seth as soon as he heard about the accident. Seth didn't dispute that they were together, instead he told John what happened and went to see Raelynn.

When he saw her, he couldn't believe the difference in her. She looked so thin, like a waif, and almost as white as a sheet. She was shaking and looked confused. He went over to her and knelt down.

"Hey there," He said softly. He smiled when her eyes finally focused on him. They looked haunted.

She whispered his name, "Seth," and took a deep breath. She knew he would make it alright. "I'm glad you're here."

God he loved her, "I am too baby." He gently helped her stand, "let's get you home."

She looked around, "Melissa is coming."

Melissa was walking in the door as Raelynn said her name. She stopped when she saw Seth with Raelynn. He pleaded with his eyes for her to allow him time with Raelynn and was relieved when she smiled and left without saying anything.

Seth escorted her outside to his truck. He got her in and jumped in the driver's side. He turned around and headed out of town and toward the ranch. He looked over at Raelynn, "Do you need anything."

She looked at him, "Just you," and started sobbing. She unbuckled her seatbelt, moved over on the bench seat and rebuckled the center seatbelt so she could touch him.

Seth kissed the top of her head and wrapped his arm around her to hold her to his side. The feeling of being whole again took him over, making his body breathe a sigh of contentment. This was where she needed to be; beside him, and where he needed her to be.

Raelynn woke up when the truck stopped, she didn't even realize she was sleeping. The exhaustion of the past couple of months caught up with her. She looked at Seth, her body humming with awareness from him being so close. He reached across and unbuckled her seatbelt, and helped her out of the truck. They walked up to the house, arms around one another. Once inside, he led her upstairs to his bedroom.

"You lay down and take a nap," He said softly.

Raelynn felt panic rise up, "Where are you going?"

He smiled, "I've got to go out and let John know you're okay and let him know we'll be in for a while."

She loved the wicked gleam in his eye, her body recognizing it as an unspoken promise to hers. "Okay," she said breathlessly and crawled onto his bed. Even after being separated and put through the ringer, her body still responded to his.

He left, quietly closing the door behind him. She waited until she heard his footsteps on the stairs then got up off the bed. She wanted to give him a surprise when he returned. She felt hope for the possibility of them together. Smiling, she started poking through drawers.

Seth walked out to the barn, a dopey grin on his face. He found John in the corral working with a colt they got last year. John looked up and saw him so he handed the hand the reins and came over to where Seth stood.

"How is she?" John asked, his concern written on his face.

It amazed Seth how attached his friend was to Raelynn. It shouldn't be surprising really because of how Raelynn made him feel. "She's good, she's resting. The seatbelt did its job."

John took off his hat and hit it against his thigh, "Seth, this is all happening for a reason you know."

The thought crossed his mind too, he contacted friends in the local police department but everyone came up empty. It was all too coincidental. He nodded, "Yes, we'll just have to figure it out."

The colt was getting antsy and started snorting so John nodded to Seth and turned to go back to him, "Oh, tell Lynn I'm sure glad she's here and if she wants to ride fences with me tomorrow, I'd be pleased to have her along."

High praise indeed from John, Seth laughed and replied, "I will."

He went back to the house, the smile still on his face.

Raelynn felt all of her efforts were well worth it. She closed the drapes and blinds in the room, making it really dark. She found some candles under the sink in the bathroom when she was here last so she pulled them out and placed one on each of the nightstands. The light from them cast a lovely glow into the room.

It felt cozy and private. She found a t-shirt of Seth's in a drawer and put that on after she stripped off her clothes. She used his brush on her hair until it shone. Looking in the mirror, she still looked wiped out but she hoped he would overlook that fact.

Seth opened the door to his room and stopped. There were lit candles beside the bed and Raelynn laying in the middle of it, in one of his t-shirts. "Well, what have we here?" He asked in a husky voice.

Raelynn smiled and sat up on her knees on the bed, "I am hoping to seduce you Seth, so shut up and get over here so I can get started."

Oh, "How do you plan to do it?" His voice raspy with need.

She patted the bed beside her, "You take off your shoes, shirt, pants, and come here by me."

He was always good at following directions so he obediently did as she asked.

Her breath caught when Seth took off his shirt, his muscles rippled with the motion and she was quivering low in her belly. The immediate response was a welcomed respite from the loneliness she'd been feeling.

Seth crawled onto the mattress and mirrored her position of kneeling on the bed. He smiled, "Now what?"

Raelynn reached behind her and grabbed a bottle of lotion. She poured a little bit on her palm and rubbed her hands together, making a wet sound that reverberated through her. She licked her lips and put her hands on Seth's shoulders, working the lotion into his skin.

She was touching him and he wanted to beg her for more. His hardness strained against the fabric of his underwear but he didn't care, she was with him. The way she looked at him, like he was the only lover in the world for her, caused his love to open up like a spring flower when it first finds the sun.

Her hands moved over his chest, one dipping lower, pulling his sex from his underwear and gently stroking the length of him. Her body pulsing in response to the hitch in his breathing.

"Baby, I've missed you so damn much," He ground out, then kissed her.

Oh, she was home now. His lips on hers, their tongues mating and swirling. Pulses of pleasure shot through her; making her thighs quiver. When his hand softly traveled over her thighs and found her hot, wet core, she bucked against him, her body knew exactly what it needed.

"Yes," She groaned against his lips.

He pulled her down in one movement, tucking her body beneath his. He rid himself of the scrap of clothing he had on and pushed the t-shirt up so he could look at her beautiful breasts; their peeks hard and begging for him to love them. He leaned down and took one nipple into his mouth and suckled.

Raelynn held his head against her breast, the exquisite desire she felt cover her like a blanket made her bold. She reached between them with her other hand and grabbed a handful of chest hair and yanked.

Pain shot through him followed closely by wild impulses. He needed to bury himself deep inside of her. With his leg, he parted her thighs and pushed his hard sex into her until they were hip to hip.

She was complete, that was her only thought. Seth filling her like this made her complete. "Oh God, yes!" She yelled out.

Her voice only drove him further into the fury of desire. He wasn't sure how much he could take or how much she could take but he was going to use them both up until they were no use to anyone else.

Seth started to drive into her, the sensations skyrocketing up her body, she parted her hips farther so he could go deeper into her; she needed him so deep!

It was never like this before, this primal, this all-absorbing need to be one with another person. His love was flowing over him, making him feel torn in half by this stunning woman. Her eyes were like fire, daring him to love her. Damn it he would!

337

"Yeeess," Raelynn hissed, her orgasm was coming quickly, but she wanted him to topple over with her, "Seth come now!"

Her plea was the only incentive he needed, he drove into her one last time, feeling them both explode with the impact of a million fireworks. He was above her, holding her to him, feeling her body convulse with the aftershocks of her climax. Tears were streaming down her cheeks, he looked down and noticed he was crying too. Crying for them both.

"Baby," He murmured, and put his forehead against hers. He didn't want to crush her with his weight.

Raelynn was transported to some other level of consciousness in the moment they came together. "I love you," She said between sobs. "I love you so much Seth."

His heart was healing with her words. It didn't matter what they went through, what mattered was that they were together now, "I love you too baby," he whispered.

They cuddled up on the bed, Seth pulled the comforter over them for warmth, and they fell asleep wrapped up in each other's arms.

Raelynn was driving in her car down the road and she was looking for something. It was dark and she was wondering where Seth was when a car came up behind her fast, she felt fear and heard the crash of metal when she called out. "No!"

Seth came out of the bathroom at the sound of Raelynn's voice. "Baby, baby," he murmured to her when she sat up. "It's okay, it's just a nightmare."

She looked at him, her eyes focusing. She was safe here with Seth. "Okay, I'm sorry."

He shook his head, "No need to be."

She put her arms around him, letting him rock her into relaxing. When she was calm again, she pulled back so she could look at him. "What time is it?"

Seth looked around her to his bedside clock, "Almost two in the afternoon." He looked around for her phone, "do you need to call Hailey?"

Hailey, Oh Lord, how could she forget? "Yes, I should."

They looked around and found her phone. Seth sat beside her on the bed while she called Hailey and reassured her she was okay.

"Mom, where are you?" Hailey asked.

She never lied to Hailey, "I'm at Seth's."

"Oh," Hailey said, shocked. "Really?" She was afraid to hope that her mom and Seth would make up.

Raelynn smiled, "Yes really." She winked at Seth.

Hailey shot her fist into the air, silently saying YES! "Cool."

Seth motioned to Raelynn, asking her to let him speak to Hailey. She handed him the phone and he put it to his ear, "Hey kiddo." He said.

"Seth," Hailey said, "are you guys okay?"

She was asking a loaded question but Seth felt like they were. "I'm pretty sure we are."

Hailey nodded, it was about time. "Ok, take care of mom."

"I will," He answered and gave the phone back to Raelynn.

He walked into the bathroom, fighting back the emotions he didn't know he was feeling until he spoke to Hailey. It wasn't just Raelynn he wanted in his family, it was Hailey too. Now, he just had to convince them it was right. Lord knew he didn't deserve the love Raelynn gave him but he wanted it more than anything else in his life.

Raelynn hung up the phone and wondered where Seth went. Her daughter was happy that she and Seth were together and so was she. It was just the unknown that scared her, why was all of this happening? And who was behind it?

Seth composed himself and went back into the bedroom, a smile on his face. "Hey, are you hungry?" He asked brightly.

Raelynn watched him and wondered if he was as confused as she was. He was probably just better at hiding it. "Yes," She answered and scooted off the bed. Surprisingly she was steady on her feet and walked with him downstairs.

They ate a lunch of leftovers, talking about the ranch mostly. After eating, Raelynn insisted he let her help him load the dishwasher. As they were finishing up, she looked out the window, "I'd like to go for a walk if that's okay?"

He was pleasantly surprised, "Sure, we can do that."

They finished dressing and went out through the back door. Clouds loomed in the horizon, the sun peeking through them here and there. They looked tumultuous to Raelynn and reflected her heart. She tried not to focus on that, only being with Seth and relaxing. When she saw John coming toward them, she smiled and picked up her pace.

John saw Seth and Lynn walking toward the barn and sighed in relief, the filly looked well enough to him. It was a damn shame she went through what she did in the last month. He smiled at her and lifted her up into a big bear hug.

"Lynn," he looked over her shoulder to Seth, "you're a sight for this cowboy's sore eyes."

How could she not love the man, he was adorable. She stepped back when he released her and looked at him closely, "You look good too John." She winked, "Has Seth been taking care of you."

"More like the other way around if you ask me," John dodged the look of thunder in Seth's eyes.

Raelynn laughed, "I believe you." She put her arm around his and they started walking toward the barn.

Seth stood there and wonder how he was thrown over for a cowboy. Wonders never ceased. He would probably be jealous if it were any other man besides John.

He was about to start for the barn when he heard a noise behind him. He turned around and didn't see anything. The back door was ajar and he was pretty sure he closed it behind them. The hairs on his nape stood up as he neared the door, something didn't feel right but he couldn't put his finger on it. He reached up to shut the door and felt a sharp pain in his arm. 'What the hell?' was his last thought before darkness consumed him.

Raelynn and John walked through the barn, taking time to stop for all the horses. She wondered where Seth ran off to but didn't worry too much, one of the ranch guys probably needed him for something. They stood outside the barn at the fence of the corral and watched a young hand work a colt in the ring. Raelynn was fascinated by the animal. Even at such a young age, you could see the animal's grace. His sinewy muscles glistening in the sunlight.

"Are you going to stay put now?" John asked, his eyes straight ahead.

She was startled by the question but he deserved to know. "I'm thinking about it." She replied.

John looked over at the girl, her eyes were full of worry. Lord knew he noticed the same look in Seth's enough times in the last month and he didn't care one bit for it. "Do you love the boy?" He asked.

The number one question, "Yes I do," She said with certainty.

He looked away for a moment, not feeling very comfortable with talk of feelings, "But?"

She turned around and leaned her back against the fence. "I'm scared John." She fought the tears that wanted to come, "it's not just me here, it's Hailey too."

John nodded, "I've met the little girl, she's strong Lynn." He only spoke the truth, there was nothing more to say but that, "and I can see the shine she's taken to Seth and him to her."

It really wasn't something Raelynn wanted to delve into right now. If she did then she'd have to admit that she might have to share Seth. It was not like her to be selfish but she couldn't help it. Not to mention that building up Anthony's memory over the years, she thought Hailey would only see him as her father. If Seth was there, would she forget Anthony? Did it matter? She never met him, and Raelynn firmly believed he loved her. Hailey believed it too. And if her daughter was willing to risk loving, then why couldn't she?

She looked over at John, "Did anyone ever tell you that you are a brilliant man?"

He shook his head, "Can't rightly say I've ever heard that particular saying about me."

"Well you are," She laughed and hugged him.

They watched the horse learning the steps and Raelynn could relate. Sometimes it was hard to learn new things, especially when you were going against your basic feelings. Most people did that. Lord knew she did. Eighteen years of trying to play it safe made her fearful. But now Seth opened her up, in every way, to the possibilities life held. She should be holding him tight instead of pushing him away. No more of being scared! She pushed away from the fence.

"Where you goin Lynn?" John called after her.

She turned and smiled, "To find my man!" She hollered back.

John just smiled, thinking he was a fine matchmaker.

Raelynn looked for Seth in the barn. When she didn't see him, she went into the other buildings in the yard but couldn't find him. How strange, she thought. It wasn't like Seth to disappear. Thinking maybe he was in his office in the house, she turned back that way.

John was watching the horse, yelling out instructions to the hand when he saw a rider approach. When the man was close enough, John could see he was a hand named Charlie. The kid was good on a horse but was riding way too fast for John's comfort. He was prepared to give the boy a piece of his mind when he jumped off the horse and ran to John. The boy's eyes looked wild.

"What's wrong?" John asked.

343

Charlie bent over, trying to catch his breath, "I was out," he panted, "in the west pasture when I saw a truck I didn't recognize." Another breath, "I followed it, wondering if it was somebody lost and they went round the back part of the property."

John was getting a very uncomfortable feeling come up his spine, "Spit it out boy!" He said.

What he heard next made his blood run cold. Lynn? He took off in search of her.

Raelynn walked into the house through the back door and slipped on something wet on the floor. She caught herself before she fell onto the ground by gripping the wall. Wondering what was on the floor, she turned on the light and looked down. Her face contorted in confusion, what was that? She knelt down and touched it with her finger. The smell was unmistakable, it was blood. Seth? Had something happened?

She stepped out of the mud room and kicked off her shoes, not wanting to track it through the house. "Seth?" She called out but received no answer.

The house was dark, the encroaching clouds depleted the natural light and someone closed all the curtains. Odd, she didn't remember them being closed when they came downstairs earlier. She was about to leave the kitchen when she heard a noise behind her. As she turned around her eyes flew open, all she saw was a fist coming toward her face and was not fast enough to avoid it. She saw stars as the punch landed on her cheek, pain shooting through her head.

344

She groaned and was about to go down when she felt hands on her sides. A voice came through the fog of pain. "Take her in with Seth." An unfamiliar female said.

Raelynn was trying to clear the haze of pain in her head. She was being half carried, half dragged through the house. After a few minutes she felt herself being put on a chair in the office. When she was able to open her eyes, she looked up to find Seth in another chair, his eyes on hers. She looked around and saw a woman leaning on his desk, her arms crossed over her chest and a disgusted look on her face.

"So, you're the bitch who's trying to take Seth from me!" The woman yelled.

If she wasn't already thoroughly confused about what was going on, this would have tipped her over the edge. Raelynn narrowed her eyes to focus and recognized the woman; she was the one in the picture in Seth's desk drawer. Oh God!

The woman looked from her to Seth, "Well sweetie, it seems your little whore here isn't as stupid as I thought."

Seth was feeling a rage he could not describe, it took over every fiber of his being. "Sam, don't do this." He said very slowly, emphasizing each word.

Sam? Raelynn was not understanding, she was sure Seth said her name was Nicole.

The woman walked over to Raelynn, the heels of her boots clicking on the hardwood floor. She crouched down in front of Raelynn and slapped her across the face. "He didn't even have the guts to tell you about me did he?"

Now her face was on fire and throbbing, she looked at Seth, tears creeping out the corners of her eyes. He was fighting against whatever they had him tied up with. Raelynn realized her hands were bound behind her too. It felt like rope and was rubbing harshly against her skin.

Sam stood up and walked back to the desk. If she was too close to the sorry excuse for a woman, she'd kill her for sure. She doubted Seth would still love her if she did that. Although the temptation was pretty big. Instead she walked over to him and bent down, grabbing his chin with her gloved hand, and kissed him.

Raelynn squeezed her eyes shut, this was a bad dream and she just needed to wake up. Her eyes shot open when the woman yelled, "You open your eyes and watch you slut!"

"Enough Sam!" Seth screamed. He'd be damned to hell for allowing this to happen.

Sam caressed his cheek with her gloved hand, "Oh no Seth, it's not near enough."

Something about the tone of her voice, made fear shiver up Raelynn's spine. This woman was going to kill her, she knew it as well as she knew her own name. Now Hailey would have no parents and be alone. NO! She yelled at herself, she needed to get out of this. She slouched forward, pretending to be passed out.

"Not very tough is she?" Sam asked with a sneer.

Seth was not above begging when it came to Raelynn, "Please Sam, don't hurt her, I'll go with you, whatever you want, just leave her alone."

Sam laughed, "Right, you don't think I don't know what's been going on around here. I have the pictures" She picked up a pile and threw them on the floor at his feet.

The pages spread out and Seth saw that they were of him and Raelynn here at the house, at Raelynn's house, at the restaurant. Oh dear Lord. She was crazy!

"I've been keeping a very close eye on you and your little tart Seth." She paced in front of him. "I knew the moment you put your cock in her," She spit at Raelynn.

He wanted to be sick, he was so irate. "Sam, you left."

She shook her head hard, "You put me away; you said there was something wrong with me!" She screamed at him.

Provoking her would not do him any good, he saw two guys bring Raelynn into the room so he figured even if he could overpower Sam, he might have a difficult time taking them out and getting Raelynn out of the house safely. He looked at Raelynn, her shape slouched over. He prayed she was okay.

"No," Sam said, "you look at me." She wanted his attention. "I was the one who hired a hacker to print that lovely little article about this whore and her friend. It was easy to bribe her little intern to misplace some files." She smiled, "It was funny to see them run like little mice, trying to figure it out."

Seth looked over and saw Raelynn's hands moving behind her, she wasn't asleep and she was working the ropes loose. Good girl, he thought. He looked back to Sam. "Did you drug her Sam?" He wanted to keep her focused on him.

"No," She ran her hand over her hair, "but an old boyfriend did me a favor and spiked her soda." She walked over and kicked Raelynn in the foot to see if she would move, "She can't hold her drugs very well can she?"

He wanted to vomit, this was because of him that it all happened. "Sam, why don't we get out of here and go somewhere, just you and I."

Sam wanted to believe him but he sent her away before. "Oh Seth," She purred, "if only you really meant it, I'd be willing to spare her." She paced again. "You see," She reached behind her and pulled a knife out of her back pocket. "I'm going to slice her up real good and then you won't even look at her."

Dear Lord, Seth thought, "Sam, I won't look at her ever again." He swallowed his fear, "I see you and I don't give her a second thought." He needed to make it good, "She doesn't compare to you, especially in bed."

Walking over to him, she rubbed her hand up his thigh, "Oh we sure could screw couldn't we?"

"Yes," He said, "let's go right now."

Her mind wondered if it was possible for them to be together. They could move to some beach and make love all day. She could give him babies and he would be hers.

Seth could see her internal war, she was walking closer to him.

Raelynn's hands were loose. The rope started to fall and she grabbed it with her fingers. Now, she just had to wait until this lunatic was not expecting it and she could get out of this.

Sam rummaged through the desk drawers and found the gun she remembered Seth kept there, "I have a better idea Seth." She checked the chamber and saw there was a round inside. "I will put a bullet in her head and then neither of us will ever have to think of her again."

No, no, no, Seth kept thinking. He could do nothing to stop her if she wanted to kill Raelynn. For that, he would never forgive himself. Lord help him. "Sam, you don't want to do that, they'll think I did it and arrest me." He was trying to think of something quickly.

That held an appealing possibility for Sam, "Oooohhh, that's good Seth, then you'll be locked up and won't look at any other women."

Oh shit, Seth thought, his plan backfired. Cold fear caused sweat to break out on his forehead as Sam came back around the desk and moved toward Raelynn.

"Sam please," He begged.

She tilted her head, "Oh Seth, you are so dumb for loving this piece of trash when you could've had me." She felt pity for him.

Her moment was there so Raelynn took it, "NO," she stood up, "he found someone better you bitch!" She kicked Sam in the shin as hard as she could. The woman teetered off balance, yelling in pain.

Raelynn pushed her and watched her fall down, the gun flying across the floor. She jumped on Sam's chest, pinning her body to the floor. "You," She punched Sam in the face, "will not hurt anyone," another punch to the gut, "you crazy psycho!"

Seth was in shock, Raelynn was pummeling Sam on the floor and he was trying to get the gun. He heard noises outside the room and was fearful that the two goons with Sam were coming in. He sighed in relief when John, Charlie, and a few other of the ranch hands came in, shotguns in hand.

They stood in the doorway and gawked at Raelynn beating the crap out of the woman on the floor. John was impressed, he knew Lynn was a keeper. Better get this all settled down; he could hear sirens in the distance.

He walked over to Seth and pulled his binds loose, "Lynn," he said loudly to get her attention.

John's voice permeated the haze of fury coursing through Raelynn but she couldn't stop hitting Sam. A hand caught her fist as it was raised to deliver another blow. She looked up to see Seth. The love in his eyes dissipated all the anger she was letting out. Tears started and she let him help her up.

Charlie walked over and held the shotgun at the ready over the lady, she lay on the floor like a bloody rag doll. Boy, Miss Raelynn had his respect for sure.

Seth held Raelynn to him and wouldn't let her go. He held her while the Sheriff's deputies came in a blur of activity and hauled out Sam and her two thugs.

Finally, he walked her out of the office and into the great room. They sat on the couch and waited to be questioned. John came in a few minutes later with a blanket to put around Raelynn's shoulders and mugs of coffee for both of them.

Raelynn was shivering, her body trying to absorb all it was put through. She looked absently out the window while the Sheriff was talking to Seth and John. When Seth's hand squeezed her shoulder, she turned to see a half circle of men looking at her.

"Ms. Woodsen, can you give us a statement?" The deputy said softly.

Why did men think women were so fragile? "Yes," She said stronger than she actually felt and started to relay the story from when she came into the house.

Seth's jaw clenched when Raelynn described how Sam struck her. He wanted to kill Sam! He caught a glimpse of John, whose eyes said, calm down, she's fine.

Raelynn told as much as she could, as calmly as she could. She was pretty sure she'd have to repeat it again at some point. That woman was going to jail at the very least. When she was done, she took a sip of the coffee, its warmth easing some of her anxiety.

The deputy nodded, "The detective assigned to your car accident, called us. Someone reported seeing a vehicle matching its description nearby. Then when Charlie told John he saw the SUV on your property, John called us."

Raelynn looked to John and smiled, his returning wink made her fill with thankfulness.

John sat down, "Poor Charlie described Nicole to me and I knew something was up."

"Wait a minute," Raelynn interjected, "you keep saying Nicole but Seth called her Sam. I don't understand."

Seth squeezed her hand, "Her name is Samantha Nicole but she hated Samantha so went by her middle name of Nicole, she always thought it was more her style." He said coldly, "I was the only one allowed to call her Sam."

Raelynn wasn't sure if she was relieved or more frightened. The woman was obviously unhinged in many ways. If this was who Seth was going to marry, why didn't he tell her about Sam and what really happened? She was positive that the version he gave her weeks ago was not the whole story.

Seth knew he was in some serious trouble with Raelynn. He wasn't honest about Sam and nearly lost her because of it. His pride and stupidity almost got her killed!

The deputies took everyone's statements and finally left. It was dark outside and Raelynn hadn't moved from the couch in hours. Seth, John, and the guys were in the kitchen talking. She looked around and realized she needed to call Melissa and Hailey, she had no vehicle so they would need to pick her up and take her home. She got up, dropping the blanket on the sofa, and walked back into the office.

On her way to the desk, Raelynn saw the blood on the chair and floor where she and Sam got into their fight. That had to be cleaned up, she thought, and went to the phone. She reached Melissa first, giving her a rundown of the situation and asked her to come over with Hailey to get her. She was sure there were a thousand questions but she was too numb to answer them right now. After she hung up, she found some tissues on the edge of Seth's desk and grabbed them to clean up the blood in the room. Hailey couldn't show up here and see this.

Seth found her on her hands and knees with tissues, trying to wipe up the floor. "Raelynn, what are you doing?"

She didn't stop, just said, "I wanted to clean this up before Hailey got here." She grabbed another tissue off of the desk, "She's been through enough."

He walked into the room and crouched down beside her, "Baby we can close the door so Hailey won't see, come on now, let's get you cleaned up." He gently put his hand on her arm.

She shook his hand free from her arm, "I'll do this now."

Was this the shock talking? He didn't know what to do. John was in the doorway now and Seth pleaded with his eyes for his friend to help.

"Lynn sweetie," John said softly, 'why don't you and Seth go upstairs and clean up so Hailey doesn't see you lookin like this?"

Raelynn didn't think about how she looked, "Do I look that bad?" Raelynn asked him, looking up from scrubbing.

John smiled, "Sweetie, I've seen bronc riders look better than you after they've been thrown a few times."

"C'mon baby," Seth whispered and helped her stand.

She wanted to look decent when Hailey came so she went with Seth upstairs. "John, can you clean up that blood please?" She asked over her shoulders.

John nodded, "Yes ma'am."

Chapter 17

The next few days passed in a flurry. There were interviews with the police and detectives from several counties. The authorities managed to put the pieces together and it was not a very pretty picture.

Seth's ex-fiancé did leave him, but Seth neglected to say it was because she suffered from some psychological disorders. No one knew except John and that was only because Seth told him the night at his house. It was easier to just let everyone think she left him because he didn't have enough money. She found out through some mutual friends that Seth was seeing Raelynn and that caused her to go off her medication.

The private investigator was one she hired, she knew Mark Wesley through a friend and convinced him to pursue Raelynn in order to take her away from Seth. She had a friend of hers hack the newspaper to put in the article and was stalking Raelynn for weeks. It seemed that whenever she saw Raelynn and Seth together, her disorder would go into some manic mode. The final straw was when she tried to run Raelynn off the road with her brother's SUV. The guys with her said she intended to kill Raelynn.

When Raelynn heard that, she was shocked. It was incomprehensible to her that anyone could have those thoughts about another person. She almost felt sorry for the woman; almost.

The group sat around Seth's kitchen table and discussed it all. John, Melissa, Seth, Raelynn, and Hailey all stared at their mugs, trying to sort it all out. Finally Hailey spoke up.

"Mom," She looked at Raelynn, "how did you get free?"

Raelynn swallowed, "I remembered that self-defense course you and I took when I was on that kick before you went to college," she took a sip of her coffee, "they said something about 'playing dead' and I figured she would leave me be long enough to get the ropes around my wrists off.

Seth piped up, "I saw what she was doing and tried to distract Sam."

"Thank God," Melissa said.

John reached over and squeezed her hand, "Amen."

Raelynn watched her friend and John closely. Over the last couple of days, she was sure she saw something between them but maybe it was her imagination. They both looked happy and that was all that mattered.

"Did mom really beat that woman up?" Hailey asked. It did not seem like something her mom would do.

"Hell yeah," John said loudly, "I thought me and Charlie were going to have to go in and point the shotguns at Nicole but there was your mom, beatin the tar out of her like nobody's business." He stopped quickly when Melissa laid her hand on his arm. "Oh," he said and looked down.

They all made a deal that Hailey would be spared from as much of it as possible. She did not need to know it all.

Seth smiled, he always thought he would be the one to save Raelynn and it turned out to be the other way around. He looked at her through different eyes. She was stronger than he gave her credit for.

Hailey would not be deterred, "Don't sugar coat it guys, I can handle it."

"Well," Raelynn said, "I just thought that if she hurt me, you'd be left here with no one and I sure as Hell wasn't going to let her take me away from you or hurt the man I love."

The announcement caused the other four sets of eyes to stare at her. She wasn't sure what the problem was, "What?" She asked.

Melissa spoke up first, "About time," she said and raised her coffee cup up like a toast.

Everyone laughed. It was just what they needed, to find the joy in the situation rather than focusing on the chaos. They talked a while longer, moving on to what they should make for dinner when Hailey jumped up.

"I have a great idea!" Hailey said, she looked around the table at the four people she loved the most in the world, "We should all go skydiving!"

John snorted, "Don't count me in on that craziness, that's his department," He pointed at Seth accusingly.

"It's a great idea," Seth said, he looked at Raelynn, "Are you up for it?"

She smiled, "I think after what we've gone through, we could use a little bit of excitement."

Melissa laughed, "Oh yeah, she says that now." She looked at John, warmth in her eyes, "I'll go if you do."

Women! John thought. They got into your mind and heart and just made you do some crazy stuff. "Fine," He mumbled.

Raelynn laughed, "Let's do it!" She exclaimed.

A week later they were all at Skydive Spaceland getting ready for their group jump.

Seth was right at home, confidently getting his gear on and smiling at her like a mischievous child. She looked at him and wondered if he was up to something. Melissa and John were standing next to one another, the look of terror on John's face making Melissa tease him. Their friends were most definitely involved and both Raelynn and Seth were happy for them.

Hailey stood by Chris, asking him what everything was as he was helping her into her harness. The man was patient, had to be to deal with the barrage of questions Hailey was bombarding him with. It made her smile that her little girl was going to experience this with her.

She was worried when the dust settled, that they would all be too traumatized to get past it. Luckily the love they all shared brought them together and made it easier to deal with the adversity. She remembered Seth taking her upstairs to wash up when Hailey was coming over and talking to her softly. He helped her get into the shower, holding her like a child and comforting her. Maybe it was just the whole life threatening thing but she wanted him. She kissed him as they stood under the spray of hot water, telling him with her body how much she loved him. He was worried and pulled back to look into her eyes. He must've been reassured by the look in her eyes because he went back to kissing her like there was no tomorrow.

They made love in his bed, softly touching and whispering their love to one another. The climax was slow and lasted so long that Raelynn thought she would melt into a puddle on the bed. He roused her when Hailey arrived, kissed her forehead, and told her he loved her so much. The words and the act of his love was all she needed to help her. It was like a salve on the hurt in her heart. Nothing seemed impossible, nothing seemed wrong, they had their love and that was enough.

Seth walked over to Raelynn, a smile on his face, "What are you thinking about with such dreaminess?" He asked.

She looked at him and put her arms around his neck, "What do you think I'm thinking about?"

"Well," Seth said, a kiss on her lips first, "if you're thinking what I'm thinking, then we really shouldn't be jumping right now."

He was so adorable. "I think we can pull it together enough for this." She leaned close and whispered into his ear, "But I have to warn you, I'm going to come up with something good for later."

Oh his body buzzed with love for this woman, "I'm counting on it," He whispered back and went back over to where the others stood.

She watched in awe, the man could make her body sing in response to his in a millisecond. She desperately hoped that never changed.

"Raelynn," She heard behind her and turned around to see a tall, lean gentleman with dark hair behind her.

She smiled, "Yes?"

The man held out his hand to shake hers, "I'm Jason and I'm the manager here."

"Nice to meet you Jason," She shook his hand.

He was impressed, she was as nice as Seth described her, "I'm going to be your tandem instructor today."

"Oh, okay," Raelynn said. She was wondering who would jump with her since Chris was going up with Hailey.

They walked over to where the equipment was and he helped her get into her jumpsuit and harness. He was self-assured and very sweet. She asked him about his experience and was impressed, he had more jumps than Seth did. They chatted about things until it was time to go up.

Hailey was all but hopping around, the excitement in her bubbling up. Seth strapped on his helmet camera and was talking to Melissa and John about the jumps; their tandem instructors joking with them to ease their nervousness.

The group made their way to the plane and got in. The remembered thrill bubbled up through Raelynn. She was trying to absorb it all so they could remember it. Seth had the camera on and was asking Melissa and Hailey questions. John looked like he was going to throw up which made Raelynn laugh.

Jason leaned close when they were almost at their jump elevation, "Are you ready Raelynn?"

She nodded, "Yep, I sure am Jason," She yelled.

Seth opened the door on the side of the plane. He turned back to her, "I love you baby, I'll see you on the ground." He kissed her quickly, "Have fun."

She smiled, "I will, I love you too."

He left the plane, followed closely by Melissa, John was next, then Hailey, and finally Raelynn and Jason went out.

The wind made her feel like she was flying. Oh my, this was THE BEST! She tried to see the others, but it was difficult with the speed they were going. Jason tapped her shoulder and pointed to her altimeter. She nodded and reached up to pull the chord. The chute opened and they were pulled upward. As they drifted, she could see the others below them and hoped they experienced the same thrill that she did while skydiving. Like making love with Seth, she hoped she would feel this thrill every time.

They were coming down and Jason instructed her to pull up her legs so they could land. Just as with Chris, they floated down and landed softly. It was amazing!

Hailey ran up to her mom, "Oh Hell Yeah!" She yelled.

Raelynn laughed, she'd let the word go this time because she knew exactly how Hailey felt. As soon as Jason released her harness from his, she hugged Hailey. "Did you have fun baby girl?"

"Yes!" Hailey screamed and jumped up, her arms wide above her.

Seth was laughing as he came over to the two women, "Good?"

Raelynn nodded, "It was perfect!"

His love for her overwhelmed him, how could he ever doubt it? She was the other part of him, in every way. She understood him, the good and not so good parts; she accepted all he had to give and gave him all of her.

"I love you." He said.

She was going to answer but Melissa and John walked over to them. Melissa laughing, delight shone in her eyes, "That was fantastic!"

"Yeah, great," John said. He was very happy to be back on the ground. Put him back on a horse, this was a one-time deal for him.

The group of them moved toward the hangar, wanting to give the next group of skydivers a clear landing zone. Everyone was laughing and talking.

Seth pulled over his helmet and pulled Hailey aside, "Can I talk to you real quick?"

"Sure," Hailey said and held back from the others. They spoke for a couple of minutes then Seth excused himself to go in and get their jump video downloaded and edited.

Raelynn was looking for Hailey when she spotted her coming into the seating area of the hangar, "Where did you and Seth go?" She asked.

Hailey shrugged, "Seth went in to do our video and I was just taking a breather." She answered.

Jason walked into the video office and saw Seth at the control panel, viewing his video. He looked way to serious in Jason's opinion. "You okay?" He asked.

Seth looked at his friend and boss, "Yeah, I'm good." He messed with some of the knobs and added some text into the video.

Jason watched the screen and smiled, "I'll leave you to it then." He stood and walked out of the room.

Melissa was sitting down on a chair, John beside her, and laughing with their tandem instructors. Hailey was talking to her mom and Chris, trying to convince Raelynn that she should jump again now so she would be able to remember everything.

Seth walked out of the office and headed for them.

Raelynn smiled and held her hand out to him, "Is it good?"

He assumed she was talking about the video, "Yep, it should be up pretty quickly."

They all went over and sat down to see the video when it came up.

The video started, introducing their names first. Everyone hooted and hollered. They watched as snippets of their jumps were put together. It was funny and Hailey was the best of the bunch. Raelynn would have to speak to Seth about getting her into the sport on a regular basis. Her personality fit it perfectly.

The credits started to roll and Raelynn was about to stand up and walk to the office when she felt Seth's hand on her arm, he looked at her, "Keep watching."

Something in his voice made her turn her head to the screen. The credits finished when some more came up, she gasped as she read the screen.

Raelynn:

I love you

You are everything I ever dreamed of

in a friend, lover, companion,

Be with me,

every day,

For the rest of our lives.

I'll help you finish the list

And make you happy

Marry Me!

Love Seth,

P.S. Hailey said it was okay

They all just sat there, no one saying anything, and everyone looking at Raelynn. She was shocked and looked at Seth. Finally, Hailey jostled her out of her trance.

"Mom if you don't say yes," Hailey came up behind her, "I'm never speaking to you again."

Raelynn looked down then back up at Seth, "I can't very well disappoint my daughter now can I?"

She was trying to be cute here and he was dying inside, "Marry me…." He whispered.

"Yes!" She said and leaned over to kiss him.

Everyone in the hangar started yelling. They broke apart and were congratulated by all of Seth's friends and co-workers. Hailey was talking wedding plans with Melissa while John was trying to keep from going nuts from the girly talk.

So this was how her life was going to be now, full of excitement, thrills, a little craziness, and a lot of love. Who could ask for anything more?

Watch for the release of Book Two in the

Love As Big As Texas Series:

Grace in Texas

October, 2013